"Need a ride?"

Nick knew that if she was any kind of a lady, she wouldn't take it. He told himself he should never have asked.

Lucky smiled. "I need a lot of things, mister," she drawled, aware that her mode of speech had instantly labeled her as Southern and chose to ignore the slow grin that spread across the man's face when she spoke.

She hated herself for her surge of interest in him. From the corner of her eye she watched his face light up, and when he took his hands from his pockets she had the distinct impression that he was itching to put them somewhere on her instead.

"I'm picking someone else up. If you're willing to wait, I'd be happy to give you a lift to wherever you're going."

"Look, mister," Lucky drawled again, "I know I look like I just got off the bus, which in fact I did. And I may look young and green to you, which I am. But I'm not stupid. I get my own rides, under my own steam, and I don't need any worthless man to help me do it."

"I didn't mean . . ."

Lucky stopped hi̲̅m̲̅ ̲̅ ̲̅ ̲̅ ̲̅ "Like hell you didn't," she said softly.

Other Books by
Sharon Sala

DIAMOND
FINDERS KEEPERS
QUEEN
SECOND CHANCES

SHARON SALA

Lucky

AVON BOOKS
An Imprint of HarperCollinsPublishers

This is a work of fiction. Names, characters, places, and incidents are products of the author's imagination or are used fictitiously and are not to be construed as real. Any resemblance to actual events, locales, organizations, or persons, living or dead, is entirely coincidental.

AVON BOOKS
An Imprint of HarperCollins*Publishers*
10 East 53rd Street
New York, New York 10022-5299

Copyright © 1995 by Sharon Sala
ISBN: 0-06-108198-1
www.avonromance.com

First Avon Books paperback printing: July 2002
First HarperCollins paperback printing: May 1995

Avon Trademark Reg. U.S. Pat. Off. and in Other Countries, Marca Registrada, Hecho en U.S.A.
HarperCollins® is a registered trademark of HarperCollins Publishers Inc.

Printed in the U.S.A.

10 9 8 7 6 5 4 3 2

Dedication

Anyone who is willing to gamble, whether it be on life or on money, is a breed apart. Many of us go through our lives on a narrow, structured path, unwilling to take the chance that might throw us off of that track forever, while others waste their lives in a constant search for Lady Luck, in hopes she will bring them happiness forever.

This book is dedicated to those who are "lucky" enough to find the path in between.

Acknowledgments

Once upon a time I visited Never-Never Land. I didn't know it had another name—Las Vegas.

My undying gratitude to several people must be acknowledged before I can put The Gambler's Daughters Trilogy to rest. *Lucky* was, for me, the most difficult book to write. And it was entirely because I did not know the world in which Lucky found herself after arriving Las Vegas.

Like Lucky, who found friends who helped her find her way, I met people—busy people—who took time out of their hectic lives to make a stranger feel at home. I must give them credit for my understanding of the world of casinos and gamblers, for it is they who showed me that gambling is not the real soul of Las Vegas; it is the people within the industry who keep it alive.

To Barbara Abrams, who took me into her home and shared several days of her life and work, as well as her friends, I say thank you, thank you, thank you!

To Pat Fallon, a lady in every sense of the word, who fed me, laughed with me, and taught me that "real" people do exist within the City That Never Sleeps. Another thanks!

To Curtis Jacks at Railroad Pass, I kneel at your feet in awe of the world in which you live and flourish. What is frightening and strange to some is the very breath of life to others. A very big thanks to a gentleman ... and a gambler.

To Henry Gonzales at Prima Donna, who took time out of a busy day to answer questions and share a meal. Another thanks.

Many others, including Carol Bennett-Whaley and Mike Ulmer, took time to answer my questions. I'm sure they've long since forgotten the writer who ventured into their lives. They may have forgotten. I have not.

1

Ashes to ashes, dust to dust.

Lucky Houston shifted restlessly in the nest she'd made of her bus seat, moaning softly as the dream carried her through the ride with no end.

Don't let 'em do it, Lucky girl. Don't let 'em bury me. It's all a mistake. I'm not really dead.

A tear seeped from beneath her sooty lashes and hung on the high curve of her cheekbone as the nightmare continued. She was unaware of the solicitous glances from fellow passengers across the aisle as she struggled with the horror in her mind.

Queenie! Something's happened to Di! I can't find her. Lucky shuddered softly as the dream played on. *Queenie! Queenie! I can't find you either! What's happened to my family? What's happened to my world?*

The Greyhound bus had been her home for the better part of four days. Lucky Houston walked up the steps and plopped into a seat with her head full of dreams, but now that she was about to arrive at her destination another kind of dream had superseded the first.

Her bones vibrated with every catch and jerk of the leather seat at her back while a thin film of sweat beaded across her skin. The nightmare danced behind her eyes as her head rocked with the motion of the bus's maneuvers through city streets.

After days of despair, after countless hours of fear alternating with hope, the inevitable was at hand, and she was sleeping through it.

Clods of dirt hit the top of the white pine casket with a dull thump, splattering upon impact. Queenie's fingers felt warm. And Johnny was so cold. Don't put too much dirt on top of him! He won't be able to breathe!

Lucky's cry for help went unheeded. Someone had to stop them! They had to uncover Johnny before it was too late. Instinctively, her hand flew up; in her mind she could see the shovelful of dirt falling toward her. But it wasn't dirt that she felt. It was the seat in front of her.

She woke with a start, then sat up, her eyes wild, her lips trembling. It was then that she realized that Cradle Creek and Johnny Houston's grave were countless miles and too many days behind her to worry about it now. And with the squealing of brakes, reality came calling.

Amid blinding heat and a pall of diesel fumes, the Greyhound on which she was riding turned off of the busy thoroughfare of downtown Las Vegas and into the bus terminal with bulky finesse. Lucky leaned back in her seat, shaking from the leftover nightmare, as well as the realization that she was in Las Vegas, the land of her father's dreams.

Weak from the onslaught of emotions the dream had left her with, she felt her legs shaking as she struggled to get out of her seat.

"Good lord," she mumbled, as she pulled damp, hot denim from the backs of her legs where it had stuck. "I haven't even gotten off the bus yet, and I feel as used up and worn out as that prostitute looks who lived across the street from our old house. Oh, Queenie, I think I'm going to need backup and you're nowhere in sight. What do I do now?"

No sooner had she admitted her misgivings than Lucky imagined she could hear the ghost of her father, Johnny Houston, whispering in her ear. *Just go for it, girl.*

Without giving herself time to panic at the thought of being alone in a city of this size and reputation, Lucky grabbed her carry-on bag from the empty seat beside her and slung it over her shoulder as she wound her way down the aisle behind other anxious bodies trying to disembark. Her quest for a new life was about to begin.

Nicholas Chenault was cursing. Silently and constantly, while the motley assortment of people who traveled by bus, as well as the hodgepodge who accumulated at the stations, kept coming too close to the shining chrome and mirrored glass of his champagne-colored Jaguar.

At thirty-six, and as a son of the privileged class of what Las Vegas residents called the City That Never Sleeps, Nicholas had never before had the dubious pleasure of visiting the bus station. And if it weren't for Cubby

Torbett's imminent arrival, he would have abandoned his post hours ago.

But his father, Paul Chenault, needed Cubby in more ways than could be counted. Bound to a wheelchair by the aftermath of a stroke, the once vital, elder Chenault's activities had been drastically limited. Were it not for Cubby Torbett's presence in their household, Nick would not be able to carry on the family business in such a close, hands-on fashion.

For the fifth time in as many minutes, Nick stuffed his hands in the pockets of his gray linen slacks and scrunched his shoulders, feeling the sanded silk fabric of his blue shirt slide and then stick to his back from the blast of heat and air swirling around the building. He didn't know what was worse: what he'd been forced to deal with here, or what was waiting for him to cope with back home.

If Charlie Sams, chauffeur for the Chenault family, hadn't been arrested yesterday, he would have been here picking up Paul Chenault's valet/nurse. As it was, Nick was still trying to explain to the authorities that he had no idea a man in their employ had been buying and selling drugs, or that he'd been doing it while on duty, and without their approval, from a limousine belonging to the Chenaults. All Nick knew was that he'd trusted Charlie, and it had been a mistake. Something Nick rarely made.

A drunk staggered against his car and Nick swore beneath his breath as he watched the man shakily right himself and stare glassy-eyed and dumbfounded at the car, as if it had sprung out of nowhere.

"Careful, buddy," Nick said, gently moving the man aside, rerouting his staggers to a different location.

If only he or his father had been able to talk to Cubby personally, then they would have had an idea of which bus he would be on. But Charlie Sams had been the one to take the call and, unfortunately for all concerned, Charlie wasn't talking to anybody except his court-appointed lawyer.

Nick sighed and ran a hand through his hair, tousling the already windblown length. But he didn't care. He was too busy trying to assess the latest batch of passengers to disembark from the incoming bus, hoping against hope that Cubby Torbett would be on it.

And then he saw her getting off the bus, and in that moment, forgot why he was here.

Beautiful women were as commonplace in Las Vegas as poker chips ... and as plentiful. He shouldn't have even noticed her. But he had. And now couldn't seem to take his eyes off of her.

She was tall, but saved from appearing too boyish or slender by the generous curve of breast he saw pushing defiantly against her faded red shirt. Her features were a remarkable assembly of what would have been ordinary on another woman. But on her, the high, Slavic cheek-bones, fine slim nose just the least bit upturned, and wide slash of mouth, did things to her face that Nick knew could cause men to make fools of themselves.

A wash of heat came with the wind gust that tunneled through the breezeway, but Nick didn't feel it, or the crush of people around him. He was too lost in watching the way that her long, black rope of hair swung back and forth against her shoulder blades like a pendulum, now and then bouncing against the bag she'd slung over her shoulder for balance.

As owner and manager of Club 52, one of Las Vegas's oldest and more lucrative nightclubs, Nick Chenault had seen more nude bodies and bare skin than an entire army on leave. He should have been immune to the now-and-then glimpses he was getting of her brown skin through the tears at the hips and on the knees of her jeans. He found, to his surprise, that he wasn't. He found himself wondering if her skin was as silky soft as it looked, and if she was that brown all over. He also decided that he must have passed boredom and had been in the heat too long when he began fantasizing about a total stranger dressed in tatters who had just walked off a bus.

He watched her from afar as she wandered around the station, calmly picking up free brochures of businesses and clubs in the area, as well as furtively claiming a discarded newspaper someone had left on a bench. In spite of his own connection to the world of gambling and all it entailed, he found himself watching intently as she saw the slot machines.

He recognized the look on her face. Or so he thought, until he saw her bend down and pick up a quarter lying on the floor beside one of the machines. He fully expected her to drop it in a slot and then stare glassy-eyed at the rolling fruits until the game had run its course.

But when she slipped it into the pocket of her jeans instead, he nearly dropped in his tracks. In all his thirty-six years of living in Las Vegas, he'd never seen that happen. She'd put the damned thing in her pocket, not the machine.

"Well, well, well," Nick muttered, "there must be a lot more to you than meets the eye."

Casually, he scanned the crowd around her and found himself resenting the man across the way who was also staring at the woman as intently as he had been. She should have been fair game to whatever male chose to look and he knew it. Instead, he found himself fighting the urge to enfold and protect her. He had to convince himself that it was because he needed a woman. Not that particular one.

She disappeared from his sight while he was lost in thought. And the panic that settled in the pit of his stomach seemed out of place when he realized she was gone. Before he could do something so foolish as to walk away from his car to go in search of her whereabouts, she walked through a crowd of people milling in the doorway and then stopped and looked around with caution. The feeling of relief that surged through his system made him angry with himself.

Quietly, almost regally, she surveyed the scene before her. And while he watched, still fascinated by her behavior, she seemed to make some sort of decision and unexpectedly turned in his direction.

His heart surged with an odd sort of joy, and he almost lifted his arm in greeting and then remembered. He'd come for Cubby Torbett, not this ragtag lovely with stars in her eyes. Nick took a slow breath and held his ground.

As she came forward and then drew abreast, every promise he'd made with himself died on the spot. He heard himself whistle softly beneath his breath and then forgot what he'd meant to say as she turned and glared.

He shuddered instinctively. Her eyes—a bright, vivid green—were the coldest eyes he'd ever seen on a woman. Her lips were smiling, but her heart damn sure wasn't. It made him wonder why. It also made him do something he hadn't done in years. He tried to pick her up.

"Just get into town?" he asked, and was rewarded by a slow, stunned blink from those same green eyes before she answered.

"Obviously."

Lucky's answer had been a reflex. Her pulse was pounding nervously as she quickly turned away and tried to wave down a cab. She thought of that cashier's check for five thousand dollars that she'd stuffed in her bra this morning and resisted the urge to feel and see if it was still there.

All of her life she'd always known that if worse came to worst, she had her sisters . . . and a part-time father— full-time gambler, who'd come to her aid if need be. But now there was no one left to call on should Lucky get in trouble. Last week, they'd buried Johnny Houston. And by now, her sister, Diamond, was somewhere in Nashville with a man who'd promised to make her a star. Her older sister, Queen, was on a bus to somewhere else, destination unknown. Lucky couldn't bear considering the fact that their paths might never cross again.

She took another deep breath, and as she did, relished the roughness of the cashier's check poking against her skin. She had to take care of that money. It was the only backup she had left.

She heard the scrape of the man's shoes against the pavement behind her, and she bit her lower lip as she continued to search the traffic for an empty cab to flag down, remembering all too vividly the diamond ring on his finger and the Rolex on his wrist. If Queenie was here right now she'd be having a fit. This was just the type of man Queenie had warned her about. He was probably a drug dealer . . . or a pimp. Where Lucky came from, no man was this good-looking, wore these kinds of clothes, and came by that kind of car honestly.

Don't panic. There are hundreds of people around us. There's nothing he can do to me in front of that many witnesses.

"Need a ride?" Nick asked, telling himself all the while that if she was any kind of lady, she wouldn't take it. *If she was smart, she would run like hell from a total stranger*, he told himself. He should never have asked. This scenario could only get worse. It quickly did.

Lucky smiled. Her lips carved a sardonic path across her face that years of living in humiliation and poverty in Cradle Creek had perfected.

"I need a lot of things, mister," Lucky drawled, aware that her mode of speech had instantly labeled her as Southern and chose to ignore the slow grin that spread across the man's face when she spoke.

She hated herself for her surge of interest in him. From the corner of her eye, she watched his face light up, and when he took his hands from his pockets, she had the distinct impression that he was itching to put them somewhere on her instead.

"Cabs are expensive," Nick said, eyeing once again the

tears in her jeans, wondering if they were there for effect or from wear. Nowadays it was hard to tell chic from Salvation Army. "I'm picking someone else up. If you're willing to wait, I'd be happy to give you a lift to wherever you're going," he added.

"Look, mister," Lucky drawled again. "I know I look like I just got off the bus, which in fact I did. And I may look young and green to you, which I am. But I'm not stupid. I get my own rides, under my own steam, and I don't need any worthless man to help me do it."

"I didn't mean . . ."

Lucky stopped him with a look. She blinked once more while the smile slid off her face and her features froze into a cool mask.

"Like hell you didn't," she said softly.

She walked away, leaving Nick with his ego in shreds, his libido giving off warning signals, and that faint, enticing glimpse of her bare backside showing once again through the tears in her jeans. Nick Chenault had just experienced a first: he'd been turned down. Not once, not twice, but three times by the same woman in less than a minute. It had to be a record.

Moments later he realized she couldn't have been wearing anything under those jeans but herself. Not if she had skin showing in the places it had been. He groaned and then grinned. Hell of a woman. And he didn't even know her name.

"Hey, Nick! I'm surprised to see you here! Where's Charlie? I expected him to pick me up."

Nick sighed with relief as his father's valet thumped him on the shoulder. "Thank God. I didn't think you'd ever come. Get in, Cubby. I'll tell you about it on the way home."

The big man with the lumbering stride and gentle smile slid uncomfortably into the small front seat and tried to make himself as compact as possible, thankful that the ride to the Chenault estate was not going to be as long as his bus ride from Ohio.

"It's good to be home, Nick," Cubby said.

Nick's right eyebrow arched wickedly. "I wish to hell you would get over that damned fear of flying. You have no idea what I've been through waiting for you to arrive in this place."

Cubby's laugh rang loud and long as they drove away. And because he was looking the other way, Nick missed seeing the long-legged beauty climbing into a cab near the curb.

"Where to, miss?" the cabdriver asked, as Lucky slid into the backseat, relieved to have escaped that handsome pimp's unwanted attentions.

Lucky felt her adrenaline go flat. Where to? She had no idea. But from the way the sun was dropping toward the western horizon, dark was inevitable. And the last thing she wanted was to be on the streets at night in a strange city without a room.

"A motel, I guess. One that's cheap . . . but safe," she added.

The cabdriver rolled his eyes. Another newcomer thinking to make it big.

"Just get into town?" he asked.

Lucky sighed, rejecting the urge to rail at the man for stating the obvious. He was only doing his job. Driving a cab had to be monotonous. Small talk was a part of the game.

"Yes," she said.

He nodded. They drove for a bit and then he asked another question that was equally impossible to answer.

"Planning to stay?"

Lucky considered her answer before she spoke. And what she didn't say was more telling than what she did.

"I have no other place to go."

The cabby looked up in his rearview mirror and resisted the notion of telling her to go back home. He wondered if he would recognize her six months from now or if she'd even still be alive. Las Vegas, for all its splendor, was a fast-paced, dangerous town in which to live alone.

"Here we are," he said, and pulled into the parking lot of an Econo-Lodge motel. "Not too pricey, not too dicey."

Lucky handed him her fare and got herself and her bag out of the cab. She didn't even notice when he drove away. She was too busy absorbing her surroundings. There were still mountains visible, just like back home. But she'd gone from the rich, green mountains of Tennessee to harsh, unforgiving mountains surrounded by near-desert. It made everything seem that much more lonely, that much more frightening.

Less than half an hour later, Lucky took off her last item of clothing and walked into a hot, steamy shower, letting the water take away what was left of her blues. There was no time for sadness or last-minute regrets. Tomorrow was time enough for the places she had to go and the things she needed to see.

*   *   *

Sunrise in the valley came without warning. What had been a faint but colorful glow on the eastern horizon was suddenly a burst of white, cloudless light and a gradual warming that would, as the day progressed, turn into a blast furnace. And yet the locals claimed, because of the lack of humidity, one wouldn't really feel the heat.

Later, as she walked the streets, Lucky grimaced while sweat beaded across her upper lip. She not only felt the heat, she could see it. Dancing above the pavement, waving seductively down the ribbon of highway, blowing about in the basin that was Las Vegas's home. And as she looked around in total confusion, she wondered if she'd traded one sort of hell for another. One Whitelaw's Bar for a thousand casinos.

For Lucky, the previous night had been a sort of reckoning. She'd had to restrain herself from dashing out into the streets and gawking at all of the garish displays of lights she could see in the distance. Caution had made her wait. She had the rest of her life to explore this city. Losing her chance and her life on the first day here didn't make sense. First she had to know the rules. Then she could play the game.

Lucky might be a gambler's daughter, but she took no chances herself. Life had made a careful, thinking woman of Johnny Houston's baby girl.

Just when Lucky thought she was going to have to stop and ask directions again, the address she'd been looking for was suddenly right before her eyes. With little regard for traffic or lights, Lucky bolted through a break in the line of cars and sprinted across the street toward the realtor she'd read about in the paper.

Within the hour, she was seated and buckled in a company car, on her way to view apartments. The pad of temporary checks she carried in her bag was visible proof of her newly opened checking account. Several hours later, Lucky was still riding, her jaw set, her eyes glacial. The initial friendliness of the realtor, Tammy, had faded to blatant discontent.

Lucky's refusal to sign a lease, as well as her lack of furniture, had done nothing to aid their search for an apartment Lucky could afford.

"Look, honey," Tammy said. "In this town, if you want to get ahead, you need to live and work in the right places."

"I don't see why," Lucky said. "How can you save a penny if you're spending everything you make just trying to show off?"

Tammy sighed. In essence, this odd, but beautiful country girl made sense. But she just didn't get it. Appearances were everything. And then she remembered.

"Ooh, honey. I just had an idea. Since you're not too picky on the part of town you live in, I know of a place that might have a vacancy. It's on our listing, but I haven't taken anyone out there in months."

Lucky leaned back in the seat and said a silent prayer. *Please let this be the place.*

And it was.

Once the pink Victorian house had been magnificent. Now the white gingerbread decoration was peeling from every imaginable gable and corner. Three stories tall, it drooped along with the curtains Lucky saw hanging at the windows on the ground floor. Sometime during the last few years, a steep, angled staircase had been added to the south side of the outer wall, leading up to a single landing on the third floor. It figured.

"It isn't much," Tammy said, as she turned the lock and used her shoulder and hip to push the door inward. "The door sticks a little too, I see. But it's furnished, as you requested, and the price is well within your range."

Lucky stepped past the woman and walked inside. The simple relief of getting out of the wind and heat and away from the sun was enough to sell her on the spot. And as for style, it put her home in Cradle Creek to shame. Lucky grinned, thinking that Tammy should have seen Whitelaw's Bar and their house next door. In Lucky's mind, *that* was not much.

She made a quick but thorough inspection of the three rooms. The ceilings were high and the rooms felt drafty, but in this heat, who could care? The living room furnishings were straight out of the thirties, as was the old, four-poster bed and the claw-foot bathtub in the tiled bathroom. The only things faintly modern were the kitchen appliances. The stove was electric. The refrigerator made ice. The air-conditioning, window-unit style, worked. In Lucky's world, those were luxuries.

"I'll take it," she said.

"The rent is due by the first of each month. First and last month's rent payable now. If you want to come back to the office with me, we'll fill out the paperwork and you can pick up your key."

Lucky nodded. As they walked outside, she paused on the landing and stared off into the distance, absorbing the immensity of the city. She suddenly realized how far she would be from downtown Las Vegas and the places that she wanted to work.

Before she could voice her concern, Tammy spoke, removing the last trace of Lucky's doubt.

"You mentioned you don't have a car," she said, pointing toward the end of the street where a small convenience store set catercorner across the lot. "That's a bus stop. The local transit authority isn't perfect, but it's better than nothing."

Lucky nodded as they proceeded down the stairs, making a mental note to pick up a bus schedule.

"I'm going job hunting tomorrow," Lucky said. "It's good to know that."

Tammy paused and turned, looking back up the stairs toward Lucky, as if gauging for the first time exactly what sort of work someone like her might do. She pursed her lips and decided it was none of her business, and then heard herself asking anyway.

"What sort of work are you looking for?" Tammy asked.

Lucky's answer was so swift that Tammy could tell it had been long thought out.

"I'm going to work in one of the casinos. It's all I know how to do."

Tammy shrugged. "You're certainly pretty enough," she said, eyeing Lucky's long legs, shapely body, and striking face. "You should make a bundle in tips hustling drinks."

"I'm not a waitress. I deal."

Out here, the word deal had two connotations: cards or

drugs. Tammy hoped the woman had meant the former and not the latter.

"Deal?" Tammy asked, as she took the rest of the steps down two at a time.

"Cards. You might say it's my . . . legacy."

Relief that she was not renting to a drug dealer made Tammy miss the sardonic smile that slipped across Lucky's face. Even if she had seen it, she wouldn't have understood. She would have had to be raised a gambler's daughter to appreciate the irony of it all.

Here Lucky was, in a city that fostered and took pride in everything that had been the ruination of Johnny Houston. But the fire and desperation that had driven Johnny Houston to play one more game and make one more bet did not burn in his youngest child. He'd given her the skill and the knowledge, but not the passion.

Lucky would play the game . . . but from the other side of a deck of cards. She'd play for the house, or not at all.

"Where are you going to work?" Tammy asked, as they started back to the office on the other side of the city.

Lucky shrugged. "Somewhere . . . anywhere."

"I guess you've already got all your cards then."

Lucky grew still. She had a suspicion that the realtor didn't mean a deck of playing cards.

"Cards?"

"You know," Tammy added, "sheriff's cards. Health cards. There are all kinds. I hear it's sort of like being bonded. It's proof that you don't have any warrants against you, or that you've never been arrested. If you handle food, it's proof that you're disease free. Stuff like that."

Lucky shook her head. Where she came from, if you wanted to work, you sat down at a table and dealt the cards. You didn't have to pass any tests save that of skill to get a job. She sighed. She should have known it wouldn't be easy.

"Where do I get these cards?" Lucky asked.

"Beats me," Tammy said. "Call City Hall. They can probably tell you."

Lucky made her second mental note to herself. Call City Hall. She just hoped it didn't take a long time to get approved. This wasn't something she'd planned on. Living on her nest egg without adding to it would be scary. She didn't want to consider it, but taking a temporary job in another direction might be something she'd have to face.

2

The spring in Lucky's step was not accidental. Among other things, she now had a brand-new sheriff's card in her bag and money in the bank. Just thinking about the serious-faced man who'd taken her application and then run a wants and warrants on her name and driver's license made her smile. She could have saved them time if they'd just believed what she told them.

She had no arrest record—not even a ticket for speeding—because her father had never owned a car long enough for her to get in trouble with it. She'd barely learned to drive Johnny's last pickup truck before he'd lost it in a poker game across the border in Kentucky. But that part of her life was behind her. Lucky patted the bag she held tight beneath her arm, knowing that it held the key to her future.

A young man with a slick smile and too-bright eyes stood beside her at the traffic light, carefully gauging her threadbare jeans, faded shirt, and boots with the worn-down heels. He fidgeted with his collar, then slid his hands into his pockets to hide a nervous twitch as he sidled up to her, whispering beneath his breath.

"Hey, baby . . . you new in town?"

Lucky rolled her eyes. This must be the standard come-on in Las Vegas. It was the third time she'd heard it, and every time a man had been the one to ask.

"Get lost," Lucky said.

"Come on now, you look like you need a job . . . maybe a place to stay. And I know a place where you can make more money in one night than most people make in a month."

Lucky's lips firmed and one eyebrow arched as she turned and gave the man the once-over, then snorted softly before showing him a second view of her backside. He persisted with the grace of a Mack truck.

"Come on, honey. Ever hear of the Chicken Ranch? You'd be a natural for the lifestyle. It's the chance of a lifetime. God gave you a beautiful face . . . and a beautiful body. You oughta show it off while you've still got it. Besides, I know men who'd give a thousand dollars for an hour with you."

Lucky's mouth dropped. This man didn't waste time beating around the bush about his intentions, that was for sure. And as far as knowing what went on at the Chicken Ranch, she hadn't lived across the street from Cradle Creek's only prostitute for nothing. She might not have approved of the lifestyle, but she'd certainly had an eyeful of it, ever since the day Johnny Houston had moved himself and his three little girls into the run-down shack next to Whitelaw's Bar. She'd seen more men make fools of themselves for a jolt of fleeting pleasure than she could count.

"If that place and the people who work there are so special, why would they need someone like you doing their recruiting for them?" Lucky asked, unable to resist a dig.

"Now . . . I didn't actually say I worked for them. What I said was . . . you'd be a natural for that line of work. Not that you'd work there in that line. You'd actually be in partnership . . . with me. Know what I mean?"

"Get lost, pimp," Lucky muttered.

His slow smile made her sick to her stomach. She turned away again. Without taking her eyes from the light waiting to change, Lucky hitched the shoulder bag closer across her stomach and tried to ignore him. Then the traffic signal finally flashed walk and relief sent her flying across the street.

But the man obviously wasn't giving up this easily. Not on a woman who had what he considered "potential." He bolted across the street right behind Lucky, appreciatively eyeing the way her slender hips swayed in those soft, faded jeans. Just as she gained the curb on the other side, he put his hand on her shoulder. His intent was to turn her around.

Before he knew what had happened, he was flat on his back, with the silhouette of an angry woman blatantly visible between him and the bright sky above.

"You been in this line of work long?" Lucky asked, firmly ignoring the stares and smirks of the passersby.

He blinked, trying not to think of how the two teeth farthest back in his jaw were starting to throb. He'd just about decided that it must have been reflex that made him bite down too hard when he landed, then wondered how he'd gotten down here to begin with. Surely she hadn't decked him with one punch. He ran his tongue across the crowns of his teeth, praying that everything was still intact.

"Exactly what line of work are you referring to?" He started to crawl to his feet when she put a dusty boot in the middle of his chest, impeding his progress.

"Not just yet," she warned, putting a little more of her weight against his rib cage as a reminder that she was still in control.

He quietly complied, hoping against hope that no one he knew saw him in this state of humiliation.

"You bitch," he said softly, and let his gaze roam over her body.

"I asked you a question. Do you solicit girls for prostitution or are you just hard up and stupid?" Lucky asked.

His eyes narrowed and he refused to answer. The heel of her boot mashed against the soft part of his belly as she waited for some sort of response. He finally shrugged, then winced when the movement of his shoulders against pavement burned the skin on his back.

"Well, I think you do," Lucky drawled. "And . . . I suggest you think about how much you like lying on *your* back for money. Because the next time you tempt some stupid little girl by promising her the moon, remember that this is how she'll earn it. Beneath someone else's dirt."

To make her point, she ground the toe of her boot just enough into the front of his white silk shirt to make an imprint, then pivoted and stalked away, disappearing into the crowd with her head held high.

"Holy shit," the young man groaned and slowly crawled to his feet. "Someone needs to put a warning sign on her."

Two passing women giggled and then looked away, while a car in the street next to him honked in jest. He waved them away and then stomped off, ignoring the fact that he'd been bested. She was only one woman. There were thousands more just like her who would be a lot more willing.

Lucky made herself walk when she needed to run. She imagined his hands at her neck, squeezing then snapping it for her insolence. But her reaction had been instinctive. For Lucky Houston, ignoring him would have been impossible. She'd been raised to survive, not submit. And then she had a flashback of the look on his face when he'd landed, and grinned. Queenie would have been proud.

As she passed a store window, a shadowy image of her own reflection stared back. She stopped in the midst of the people on the street and looked in disbelief. She stood a head above most of the women and eyeball-to-eyeball with most of the men.

Her clothes made her look like a beggar. A beggar would not be hired in any of the casinos that she'd seen. They were brilliant and gaudy on the outside, and God only knew what they looked like on the inside. The ragamuffin woman in the window's reflection would never work there. Not in a city where sequins adorned women's shoulders twenty-four hours a day.

Lucky pivoted, scanning the crowds, hoping to see at least some people who were as casually dressed. In the same instant, she knew that knowledge wouldn't help. These people had come to spend money. The casinos didn't care what the spenders looked like. But they would care about the appearance of their employees.

A surge of impatience overwhelmed her. She'd come all this way to work in the casinos, but looking like this would just get her ignored. She needed style. She needed clothes.

"I need help," Lucky muttered.

A sudden burst of determination sent her down the street with purpose in her step. When she found a store that suited her purposes, she went in with full intentions of coming out a different woman. One who would blend in and not stand out like a sunflower in a roomful of orchids.

"Welcome to the Downstairs Closet," the saleswoman said, as the bell over the door signaled Lucky's arrival.

Lucky smiled. "Thanks," she said. "That's the first real welcome I've had since I got in this city."

The woman smiled, instantly liking this tall young thing, in spite of her ragged appearance. "What can I do for you?" she asked.

"Make me over," Lucky said.

The saleswoman clapped her hands in delight at the request. "With you, honey, it'll be a breeze."

Moments later, the two were head-to-head, deep in discussion as they shuffled through racks of well cared for, but secondhand clothing that had been tastefully displayed around the floor.

* * *

Nick Chenault had some renovating of his own to do. But it was on the family reputation, not his appearance.

"Sonofabitch!" he swore softly, as he went through the morning paper. All night he'd slept in fits and starts, dreaming about a woman with legs that went all the way to heaven, a mouth that could take a man to hell, and green eyes that had cut him in two without speaking his name. Now this insult had been added. And in the city-wide paper, no less.

"Good morning to you too, son," Paul Chenault said, as Cubby wheeled him to the table and scooted his chair before the place setting bearing his favorite dish of tropical fruits.

Nick flushed and then managed a cocky grin, aware that he'd been caught expressing his opinion of the article regarding their chauffeur's arrest in a less than proper manner.

"Sorry, Dad," Nick said, and then tossed the paper in his father's lap. "But this article made me so damn mad that I couldn't help myself. You read it and then tell me I'm wrong."

Giving his bowl of fruit a regretful glance, Paul righted the paper and quickly scanned the page Nick had indicated until he came to the article in question.

Nick watched the frown lines on his father's forehead deepen as he read, and the tug of worry lowered the smile on his aging face to one of somber repose. When Paul ran a shaky hand through his thick white hair, agitating the carefully combed style, even Cubby began to fidget.

The last thing either of them wanted was for Paul Chenault to fret unnecessarily. His recovery from the stroke he'd suffered two years ago had been long and painful. And although his mind and the upper half of his body had recovered, he would never walk again. Yet keeping him in the dark about something this public would have been impossible.

"I don't get it," Paul said, when he had finished the article. "Why hasn't Charlie Sams been charged? Why are they holding him indefinitely without giving a reason? The way this article reads, it makes it sound like we're the force behind the drugs he was selling, and that he's trying to cut a deal in order to implicate us and lessen his charges."

"Don't worry, Dad," Nick said. "I have an appointment with the detective in charge of the case this morning. I'll get some answers before the day is out or know the reason why."

Paul slumped back in his wheelchair, absently watching Cubby's hands. The meaty fists that could smash a man's head with little effort were delicately parting and then buttering a biscuit to put on the plate next to his fruit.

"I hate this," Paul said quietly, clinking the tines of his fork absently against the crystal dish, while he stared at his coffee cup.

Nick knew what his father hated. It wasn't this latest scandal. In their business, there was always the danger of making enemies that wanted retaliation. What Paul Chenault hated was not being able to do anything about it. He had to sit on the sidelines, crippled in body, but not in mind, and let his son bear the burden of it all.

"You trained me well, Dad," Nick reminded him. "There's nothing I can't handle. But if I get myself up a creek, I'll come for advice. Deal?"

Paul grinned. He couldn't ever remember his son asking for help. But they played this game with each other, knowing that it was a small consolation for their inability to voice the depth of their feelings for each other.

Lauria, Paul's wife, had died nearly thirteen years ago. She'd been the affectionate one in the family, coaxing the hugs, begging the kisses, flirting shamelessly with both of the loves of her life, her husband and her son.

With her death, Paul had never been able to get the words past the pain. And Nick had not known how to close the gap his mother's death had left in their lives. And so they'd existed, using Club 52 as their emotional link, trying to maintain it in the elegant and honest manner in which it had been founded, though it was nearly impossible these days. And this latest faux pas of their chauffeur didn't help matters a damned bit.

"Eat your fruit, boss," Cubby urged. "It's got all your favorites. Kiwi. Mangoes. Papaya."

Paul grinned at the big man. "So sit down and eat with me," Paul said. "Nick looks ready to bolt and I hate to eat alone."

Cubby ducked his head, sending thin blond hair falling across his forehead and shadowing his pale blue eyes. "It don't seem right," he said softly. "I work for you and all."

"You have to do everything for me, right down to washing my ass, dammit," Paul said. "I think we've gotten past the employer/employee relationship. At least I know I damn well have."

Cubby sat. Put that way, he had no other choice. And it was true. He held more than high regard for the two Chenaults. They were almost like family.

The maid came in, took one look at Cubby in residence at the table, and went for another place setting as well as a double order of food. At six feet, seven inches and three hundred twenty pounds, it took a lot of food to feed Cubby Torbett.

"I'll call you from the club," Nick said, patting his father's shoulder as his passed. "Don't let this worry you. We'll get to the bottom of Charlie Sams, or else."

Paul grinned. He'd heard Nick use that tone of voice before. And it usually got results.

"In that case," he said, "Cubby, pass the jam. I feel an appetite coming on."

Nick left with the two men arguing amiably with each other, like brothers. But he knew that the Chenault family was simply a state of mind, not an actual fact. In fewer years than he cared to count, he would be alone. His father couldn't live forever. And Nick had no wife. No children. Nothing but Club 52.

He shrugged, masking the empty place in his heart with a casualness he did not feel. In his line of work, people either married and divorced with ritualistic regularity, kept mistresses who were easier to dispose of, or simply faced the fact of the job and lived alone and lonely with a casual liaison for release.

Nick's path had been chosen for him long ago when he'd witnessed his own parents' love for each other. If he couldn't have a marriage like that, he didn't want one at all.

He left the house and was on his way to the police station before he realized he would be two hours early for his appointment with Detective Will Arnold, Narcotics Division, Las Vegas Metro.

"Look who just came in the door."

Will Arnold stared over the rim of his coffee cup, taking care not to swallow too much of the scalding brew as he watched the Chenault heir enter Las Vegas Metro with purpose in his step.

"I knew he was coming," Will told his partner, and then he sauntered back toward his desk, leaving Nick Chenault to find his own way there.

When Charley Sams had been arrested for dealing, the detective's first instinct had been to suspect the employer, namely Chenault Incorporated. But after yesterday's seven-hour interrogation with Sams, he had a completely different opinion of the situation. In fact, if what he suspected was true, Nick Chenault was in trouble all right. But not from the law. From old enemies.

"Detective Arnold?"

Will turned and waved his coffee cup toward the empty chair beside his desk. "Have a seat, Mr. Chenault. You're early."

Nick didn't apologize or offer an explanation as to why. He went straight to the point.

"Have you read the morning paper?"

Will Arnold shrugged. "Parts of it. UNLV won the quarterfinals last night. Hell of a game. Wished I'd seen it. But I was on duty."

The reference to the University of Las Vegas's college basketball team was just as deceptive as the man's rumpled exterior. Nick found himself staring into a pair of cool, hazel eyes. Will Arnold was no one's fool. He liked that. Suddenly, Nick felt comfortable with this interview, even though he'd spent the previous night stewing about it.

"Why haven't you charged Charlie Sams for dealing narcotics? Who leaked that crap to the paper about Chenault Inc. being the money behind the man? If you suspect us, then why haven't we been arrested? Did Charlie say . . . ?"

"Mr. Chenault, would you care for a cup of coffee?"

Nick took a deep breath, skidding on his next set of thoughts as he heard the warning behind the request.

"No. But thanks," he added. "What I would care for are some answers. My father isn't well. This stuff is making him crazy. I don't want to get a phone call in the middle of the day telling me he's had another stroke because of this stress."

Will nodded. "I understand. And I appreciate your concern for your father. I will admit that when we made the arrest, the connection between employer and employee did cross my mind."

He grinned at Nick's angry flush, suspecting that, under other circumstances, he and this gambling man could have been friends.

"So . . ." Nick prompted.

"So I've changed my mind, Mr. Chenault."

Nick leaned back in his chair and returned the grin. "Please . . . call me Nick."

Will Arnold laughed. It was unexpected, but so was the man at his desk.

"So what's the scoop about Sams?" Nick asked. "I'll do whatever it takes to clear our name."

Will frowned. It was past time to reveal his hunch. And while it wasn't normal protocol to relate the subject of a suspect's interrogation, in this instance, keeping it to himself could have serious consequences for the Chenault family.

"Who hates your family?"

Nick was so surprised by the question that for a moment, he couldn't speak. And then he shrugged.

"No one . . . anyone. I don't know. Hell, Detective, I run a casino. For the few that win big, hundreds more lose more than they can afford. Sometimes they blame me instead of themselves for not knowing when to quit."

Will shook his head. "No. It's bigger than that."

Nick sat upright in the chair as a chill moved across his skin. "What's bigger than that?"

"The plot to ruin you and your family."

Nick frowned. "I don't believe you."

Will shoved a typed copy of Charlie Sams's interrogation in front of Nick and leaned back in his chair.

"Read that. Then tell me you don't believe."

Nick picked up the stack, then began to read.

Five minutes later, he dropped the last page in place and looked up. The flush of anger that Will had watched come and go on Nick's face while he read was now replaced by a grayish cast.

"Oh, Jesus," Nick said softly. "Who? Who in hell hates this much? Who would want to plant a spy like Charlie Sams in my family just so he could funnel out everything he learned about us? We have few secrets, Detective. And none of them earthshaking, I can assure you."

Will shrugged. "All I know is . . . Charlie Sams doesn't want to be released, because he swears he'll be killed for getting greedy and peddling drugs on the side. He was supposed to be a watchdog for some nameless entity who wants what you have. He says if he's bailed out, he'll never live to see his court date."

Nick's fingers curled around the arms of the chair as he considered the contents of the interrogation transcript. "I don't get it. If he's told you all of this, then why didn't he name the man who hired him and be done with it?"

"According to Sams, he doesn't know the man by name. Only by a voice over the phone. He got paid by direct deposit into a checking account, which by the way, does exist, as do the records of money being regularly transferred into it. He swears he doesn't know squat . . . except, of course, that your days are numbered."

Nick stood up. As far as he was concerned, the interview was over. He'd learned much more than what he'd come to learn.

"What are you going to do?" Will asked.

Nick looked down at his watch. "Go to the casino and do about five miles on my Nordic Track while I still can. I want to be in good shape when I die."

Will laughed in spite of a premonition that the statement might be more truth than jest.

"Just be careful of who you trust," he warned.

Nick's sardonic smile disappeared. "I'm *always* careful. That's why I'm still alive and single."

"You like?"

Lucky almost shivered with delight at her own reflection.

"My God," she said, staring at herself in first one mirror and then the other. "Is that really me?"

The saleswoman grinned. "Honey . . . it's you in spades."

Lucky grinned. Considering her background and chosen career, the description was apropos.

"I don't think they'll turn me away at the casinos now," she said. The saleswoman hovered with pride, looking more and more like a fairy godmother with every passing second.

"Oh, they'll let you inside, honey. But they may never let you go. You are, as my grandson would say, one hot babe."

Lucky's smile came from the inside out. If only the people in Cradle Creek could see her now. And at the thought, a little bit of regret slipped into place alongside her joy. If only Diamond and Queen could see her like this.

Stop that! she told herself. She didn't have to see her sisters to know that she was still in their hearts. Just as they were in hers. It was an accepted fact that Johnny Houston's girls were as thick as the thief the people of Cradle Creek had claimed him to be.

"How much do I owe you?" Lucky asked.

"You get changed while I total this up. All in all, honey,

you're one whale of a shopper. You've got four fabulous outfits for less than the price of what one of these cost new."

Lucky all but danced to the dressing room and into her clothes. She'd been wearing hand-me-downs for years, so this was nothing new. But they hadn't been designer originals.

Less than an hour later, she got off at the bus stop, holding her breath against lingering diesel fumes as the Metro transit pulled away. Lost in thought, she started walking the block and a half toward home.

Her head was full of fanciful visions of one day returning to Cradle Creek and, in a flagrantly foolish gesture, buying the whole town and renaming it something like Houston Holler. Just the thought made her giggle. Because of daydreams, she almost didn't hear the cries for help.

Lucky rounded the corner of the aging three-story building, aiming for the steep flight of stairs that would take her up to her apartment. Her foot was on the bottom step when she heard the cry, and at first, imagined it was just a cat mewling in distress.

She listened again. Then again. And when she broke out in a cold sweat of fear, she dropped her parcels and raced around the corner of the house, frantically searching for a window to see into, or a door that would open. The last time she'd listened, the call for help had been distinct.

"Help! Oh, help! Please . . . somebody help me."

Lucky pressed her ear against the side window, unable to see through the old, gauzy curtains.

"Oh no," she muttered, trying without success to push the window up. It was either locked or hadn't been opened in so long that it had grown to the sill.

Now that she knew that it hadn't been her imagination after all, she had to face the fact that the voice sounded feeble and weak. But it was definitely female. And she was either in pain or in danger. This only increased Lucky's agitation at being unable to gain entrance.

"I'm here," Lucky called aloud, rapping sharply on the window, hoping to get the woman's attention. "What happened? Are you hurt? Do you need an ambulance?"

"No, no! No ambulance," the woman groaned. "Just come help me up."

Lucky didn't hesitate. "How can I get in?" she asked.

"Thank the lord," the woman groaned, and this time when she shouted out, her voice was louder . . . stronger, simply because help was at hand. "The front door is locked, but if you come around to the kitchen, you can crawl in over the sink."

Lucky didn't wait for a second invitation. Her long legs quickly covered the distance around to the other side of the house. In no time, she spied the partially open window just above an untended oleander bush.

"Good grief."

The window was open all right, but the bush in front of it was a good six feet in diameter and halfway up the side of the house.

"Here goes my last pair of jeans," she said as she struggled through the bush to the window above.

Just as she'd feared, the bush did its part in impeding the rescue, but when she finally reached the window, the screen obligingly came off in Lucky's hands. With a grunt, she boosted herself through the small window and came face-to-face with a spitting black tomcat who arched his back and began dancing sideways across the cabinet for effect as Lucky slid across the sink. She threw out her arms in reflex just before she went head first onto the faded linoleum.

"Here! I'm in here!" the woman cried, giving Lucky no time for apologies to the cat who'd taken instant offense at her arrival.

Lucky closed the window behind her, giving the cat no chance of escape. It would be all she needed, to have to call 911 for the woman, and then be forced to chase her cat through an unfamiliar neighborhood.

Following the sound of the woman's voice, Lucky sprinted through the rooms, getting only brief, but vivid impressions of faded velvet, limp black fringe, and gilded wallpaper that dully reflected the half-lights burning in the shadowy rooms.

"Oh my!"

It was enough said. Lucky never missed a beat as she bent down and with a grunt, lifted a massive, overstuffed chair off of the elderly woman's prone body. She expected blood and broken bones. What she got was a fluff of molting feathers from the black boa wrapped around the upper half of the old woman's face, and a yellow satin dressing gown sporting several days worth of food spills. She knelt at the woman's side and cupped her head in her hands, while scanning the room for a phone to call for help.

"I fell."

Lucky smiled. She couldn't help it as the old woman began struggling to her feet under her own steam.

"You should let me help you," Lucky said, trying not to stare at the odd blend of peroxide and henna crowning a face of inestimable age and unbelievable paint.

"Then do it, girl, and be quick about it. I've been lying down here for four hours. If you hadn't come when you did, I would have peed in my pants. And I haven't done that since I was four years old. I'm old all right," she muttered. "But I haven't lost control of anything but my figure. That went to hell after the war."

Lucky didn't argue. Nor did she ask which war. She was too busy helping the faded floozy toddle toward a small bathroom down the hall. The woman disappeared inside, shutting the door firmly between herself and her rescuer, and did what nature had been telling her she needed to do for hours. Minutes later, she exited the bath with a smile that made her face look years younger.

"The pause that refreshes, don't you know," the woman said. And then peered at Lucky, as if seeing her for the first time.

"I know you. You're my new renter."

Lucky stared openmouthed. "You're my landlady? But I thought that—"

"Pooh! I list with that realtor because I don't want to mess with interviews. Had plenty of them in my day. Don't like to take them. Rather give them, if you know what I mean."

Lucky didn't, but had a feeling she should.

"My name is Lucille LaMont."

Lucky bit her lip and when the woman's fixed stare became a glare, started to fidget, suddenly certain that she'd been expected to recognize the name. Shamefaced, she had to stand, knowing that her silence was an admission of her ignorance.

The old woman shrugged, blaming the lack of respect on the young woman's age, and hobbled her way back into the living room to inspect the damage, if any, to her chair.

"My name is—"

"I know what you call yourself. But no one is named Lucky. What's your real name, girl?"

Lucky grew still. Suddenly, childhood shame and cruel taunts came out of hiding and stuck to her belly with sick persistence.

"It *is* my name," she said quietly.

Lucille LaMont hadn't lived to be eighty-four without knowing when she'd put her foot in it. But because she *was* that old, she didn't figure she owed anyone much of an explanation.

"Sorry. Age makes asses of us all. Sit, girl. I haven't thanked you for saving me yet. So, thanks."

Lucky grinned. "I didn't exactly save you. You almost saved yourself." And then Lucky thought of something she should have asked sooner. "What made you fall? Were you dizzy? Did you get sick? Maybe we should call a—"

"It was that damned cat. He jumped up on my antimacassar. It's Belgian lace, you know. I've had it for years and that blasted Lucifer knows he's not supposed to be up there. He does it just to annoy me."

Lucky tried to follow the explanation but had gotten lost. "Antimewhat?"

The old woman rolled her eyes, making them seem twice as large as normal beneath the Cleopatra blue shadow.

"This," she said, and picked up a fragile, lace doily from the floor that she primly dropped on the arm of her chair. "It's to be placed on fine furnishings . . . behind one's head, you know. I swung at the cat and lost my balance. I caught the back of the chair instead of that damned cat and pulled it down on top of me."

Lucky nodded, trying not to laugh at the images the old woman's words created. "Are you sure you don't hurt anywhere?" she asked, worried by the length of time she'd been beneath the chair.

"Oh, lord. Of course I hurt, girl. I'm eighty-four, for God's sake. The day I quit hurting is the day I'm dead. Pain just tells me that I'm still ticking."

Her head lolled a bit against the old brocade covering the chair, while she sighed from the vent she'd made of her temper.

"You can call me Fluffy. Everyone does," Lucille said, and absently patted the wild mop of hair Lucky had desperately tried to ignore.

Lucky grinned again. "Fluffy?"

Lucille's eyes opened and her chin lifted just the least little bit. Suddenly, Lucky saw past the years into the face of the woman Lucille had been and was stunned by the life and vitality she saw dancing in those dark gray eyes.

"It was my stage name. When I stripped, it was all I

wore. Tiny bits of yellow chiffon that looked like the down of a chick. That's what I took off. That's where I got my name."

"Stripped? Wore?"

Lucille rolled her eyes again, giving Lucky another look at the underside of her eyelids.

"Good lord, girl! Where are you from, the sticks?"

"Yes, ma'am, I believe I am," Lucky said quietly.

"Fluffy," Lucille corrected.

"Fluffy."

"How far in the sticks?" Fluffy asked.

"Um . . . Cradle Creek, Tennessee."

"Have mercy!" Fluffy muttered. "Why on earth would you come out here? A young thing like you has no business in a city like this. Not alone."

"I came because Johnny couldn't," Lucky said, unable to hide a quick spurt of tears.

"Johnny?"

"My father. Johnny Houston. He was a gambler. He died last week."

"Sorry, honey," Fluffy said. "But it's an end we all have to face."

"Yes, ma'am . . . I mean, Fluffy. I know."

"Okay. You're here. What can you do?"

"I deal cards."

This wasn't the answer Fluffy expected. This young girl child was beautiful. She'd expected to hear her say she wanted to be a dancer. She wouldn't even have been surprised to hear cocktail waitress as a prospective job opportunity. But she hadn't planned on this.

"Do you know how?" she asked, unable to keep doubt from her voice.

"It's about all I *do* know."

Fluffy nodded. "Then that settles it. But you need to get in with one of the older casinos. Maybe one down on the old strip."

"Why? I thought that I should try the MGM Grand . . . or maybe the Luxor. Even Caesar's Palace has to have a turnover."

"Oh hell, honey. They all have turnovers. This is a wide-open town. Way too many of the workers are either stoned or drunk. So many of them are in debt up to their eyeballs from making bets they can't cover that it isn't even funny. Why I know men who've simply walked away, without packing or bothering to declare bankruptcy. They simply gave up and got out. This is a place of delight and a city of sin all at the same time. Do you understand what I mean?"

Lucky nodded, remembering the pimp earlier in the day who'd accosted her right on the streets in broad daylight. A small shiver of fear slid up her spine at the thought of being alone in a place like this. It wasn't exactly the way she'd imagined.

In Cradle Creek she'd known whom she could turn her back on and who might do her harm. Here everyone and everything were unknown. And then she looked up into Fluffy's stern face and started to relax. But she wasn't alone. Not entirely. Not anymore.

"So why should I try for work in the older part of the strip?"

Fluffy made a face. "Because the new places are like an adult Disneyland. Nothing like the old days when Bugsy came and went with an entourage you wouldn't believe. And Hollywood and all its stars came down here to shine a little brighter. And . . ." she added, "because I know my way around down there. I'll give you names of people you can trust. You make your own choices. How's that sound?"

"Like a deal," Lucky said, and then grinned at her own wit.

Fluffy's pencil-painted eyebrows rose sharply. And then she grinned. A wicked cackle slid out the corner of her mouth as she fluttered her hand across her bosom in delight.

"Girl, you and I are going to be friends. I can tell."

Lucky smiled. "I hope so, Fluffy. My daddy said that was something you never had too many of."

"Your daddy was a smart man."

Lucky considered the statement. "Not really. But he had his moments. He surely did."

Fluffy laughed. "Just like a man, honey. Just like a man."

3

Nick stood on the mezzanine above the gaming tables of Club 52 and watched the action below with a practiced eye. Although their old-fashioned security system had been replaced with new, high-tech cameras that filmed each dealer and table with the precision of a laser beam, he still liked the personal touch of firsthand observation. The "eye-in-the-sky" method was state of the art and highly trustworthy, but his instincts were even better. He could tell, simply by watching the crowd around a table, whether all was going as it should.

"Hey, boss. Aren't you going to call it a night? It's almost midnight."

Nick turned. His right-hand man, Manny Sosa, was bearing down on him with a carton of new tapes for the security cameras in one hand, and the shift totals in the other.

"No. Just put the stuff on my desk," Nick said. "I can't sleep. I may as well be working."

Manny stopped to gauge the tension behind his boss's words. He'd been in this business too long not to recognize the fact that trouble must be brewing.

For Manny, middle age was almost gone, but one could never tell by his behavior or appearance. Long after his body had given up the pretense, he'd vainly maintained his Latin good looks by dyeing his white hair black to match the small, pencil-thin mustache he sported above his upper lip. His dark eyes sparkled constantly with the verve of a man who loved life and all that it encompassed, including women. At the age of fifty-nine, Manny considered himself irreplaceable to Club 52 and to the ladies. He'd known Nicholas Chenault since the day he was born, and now he could tell something was wrong. He could feel it.

"You can't sleep? Maybe you just need a woman, Nicky. You spend too much time alone, that's what."

Nick grinned. "You, my friend, have a one-track mind."

"No, no! Never one-track. Always, the man should run on many tracks. And then he will have many friends."

Nick shook his head. "Not everyone wants to be my friend. Someone wants me dead."

Manny frowned, dumped the armload of stuff he'd been carrying onto Nick's desk, and pulled him into the office without giving him time to argue. "You aren't being serious . . . are you?"

Nick's expression was cold. "I want a name, Manny. Give me a name. Who from our past would hate that much?"

"That is something you must ask your father. But you

must tell me now, Nicky. What makes you think such an evil thing?"

Nick gave Manny a slow, thoughtful look. "Charlie Sams was a plant in the organization. Did you know?"

"*Basta!*" Manny cursed and then crossed himself to negate what he'd said. "Why would I know of such a thing and not speak of it to you? Of course not! But how do you know? Maybe you're wrong."

"I'm not. But I wish I was. I don't know how much to tell Dad and how much to protect him. If I don't tell him anything, he might get careless, and that could cost him his life. If I tell him too much, it still might cost him his life."

He circled the desk in frustration and then tunneled angry fingers through his hair.

"You know, Manny, for the first time in as long as I can remember, this business is no longer enough for me. It's crap like this . . . and the newspaper articles . . . and the federal regulations . . . and . . ." He picked up an appointment book and threw it across the room with a vicious snap. "Sorry. It's been a hell of a day."

Manny loved and respected this man like the son he never had. He'd do anything for the Chenaults. But he didn't know how to fix this. He walked across the room, picked up the book, and replaced it on the desk.

"*De nada.* It is nothing. Go home, Nicky. Rest. Make love to a beautiful woman. Live before life makes an old man out of you."

"As soon as I go over the totals," Nick said.

Manny shrugged and left. In his world, a man must do what a man must do.

Nick stared down at the papers and tried to concentrate. But all he could see was the memory of that transcript and the terror that it promised for his family. He closed his eyes, expecting almost anything to surface but the face of the woman from the bus stop.

"What the hell," he muttered, and rubbed his burning eyes with the heels of his palms. "Am I now being haunted by a stranger?"

And as he waited, in his mind's eye, her features became clearer and clearer. When his pulse accelerated, he opened his eyes, halfway hoping she'd be there. He exhaled slowly when he saw he was alone.

"Why? Why in hell is it you I keep remembering when I don't even know your name?"

He had no answers, except that maybe Manny was right. Maybe he did need a woman. But not just any woman—one with green eyes. He sighed and settled back to work.

Just after two A.M., Nick got in his car and drove away from Club 52 with the bright lights of Las Vegas reflecting off his windshield and into his eyes. Waiting at a traffic light, he realized that there were as many people on the streets right now as there were in the middle of the day. But it was a different crowd of people who came out after sundown, compared to the people on the streets at sunup.

A tall young woman in white sequins and three-inch heels paraded across the crosswalk in front of him, full breasts bouncing with every step she took. Long blonde hair blew away from a face of great beauty. The short, tight skirt of her dress emphasized the perfection of long tan legs. And when she absently glanced toward his car, the emptiness and desperation behind her pasted-on smile made him shudder. Noting his interest, she paused.

Nick shook his head. Theirs was a silent conversation that needed no words. She'd asked if he was interested, and he'd rejected her.

She blew him a kiss and then disappeared into the crowds of people going into, and coming out of, the casinos lining the strip.

She was beautiful, but definitely not his type. The last time Nick had paid for sex, he'd been nineteen years old. Just about the age of the woman who'd just offered herself to him with a single look. And at the same moment, he remembered the one at the bus station who'd turned him down just as abruptly as he'd rejected the blonde.

"What the hell is it with me?" he muttered. "I don't have enough grief on my mind without mooning over a passing stranger?"

He stared through the glare of oncoming traffic, certain that he'd just about lost his mind, when the car behind him honked. The light had changed. It was time to move on. Nick accelerated through the intersection, for the time being leaving his job and its worries behind.

Lucky sat cross-legged in her bed, admiring her four new outfits hanging in the closet, mentally planning which one she should wear tomorrow when she went to search for work.

Twice she almost called aloud for Diamond to come help her decide what to wear, and earlier in the evening, she'd been in the middle of preparing her supper and actually shouted Queenie's name, intent on asking about ingredients that went into Johnny's catchall stew.

"Will I ever get used to being without you two?" she groaned aloud and fell backward onto the bed, gazing up at the ceiling as she tried to ignore the heartsick pain pricking her chest and the tears burning behind her eyelids.

Then she remembered Fluffy LaMont and smiled. She'd made one friend. Something told her that this one would be a keeper. *One day, one friend—it was enough to start on,* she thought.

She reached over to turn off the light and smiled as the faded fringe from the lampshade tickled the back of her hands. Just like Fluffy, this place was old, but everything still seemed to work. What more could a woman ask?

Lucky rolled over onto her side, cuddling her extra pillow beneath her chin in lieu of the sister who usually slept beside her. And soon, the slow, deep regularity of her breathing was a sign of the end to an exhausting day.

Hours later, her long legs had scissored across the mattress, wadding the sheet and riding her T-shirt above her waist. But she was unaware. She was lost in dreamsleep, held in the arms of a man with hair and eyes the color of bourbon, while he whispered words of love that kept turning to lies every time she looked away.

Manny Sosa was on duty. As shift manager, he was in charge of all the department managers during his eight-hour shift. But Manny often stayed long past time. As Nick Chenault's right-hand man, he felt a proprietary need to make certain that all phases of Club 52 went as smooth as clockwork.

The dark, rich wine-and-gray interior of the casino was reflected back from one side of the room to the other by immense, floor-to-ceiling mirrors. And the crystal chandeliers that were suspended from the second-floor ceiling gave the room the appearance of being starlit.

The sleek tuxedoed dealers and the minuscule black-and-white French maid's uniforms that the waitresses wore gave a European elegance to the club.

No volcanoes spewed here. No children ran crying after their parents. No live birds or exotic fish were on display for passersby. No clowns paraded or lions roared. Here they came to wager . . . and sometimes win. The faint of heart did not belong here. Only the risk-takers. The gamblers.

And they came, as they had for the past forty years since Nick's father had built the club. The rich . . . and the poor . . . and the ones who never left. The ones who won, only to lose it back and more besides, trying to regain that surge of power they'd felt when the lights had flashed, and the bells had rung. And like Nick, it was all that Manny knew. He was satisfied with his life.

Then Lucky Houston entered his world.

When Manny finally noticed her, he realized that she'd been circling the floor for several hours, because he distinctly remembered the chic, virgin-white suit she was wearing, and her long, tan legs visible beneath the short, slim skirt.

But that had been three hours ago. And to his knowledge, the woman hadn't bought or spent a chip the whole time. His dark eyes narrowed as she disappeared again into the crowd upon the floor, certain that she was up to no good. The thought of a heist and a possible accomplice sent him scanning the crowds for someone else who didn't belong. But everyone else he saw seemed to be absorbed in the games around them.

Just when he told himself he'd imagined it, she suddenly reappeared near one of the blackjack tables. And as before, she stood at the edge of the crowd around it, watching, listening, ignoring the appreciative stares of men and the subtle but jealous glances of other women. She seemed to care for nothing but the games.

Manny was just considering calling for security when she moved away from the tables and seemed to do a little crowd searching of her own. For the space of several seconds, the people between them parted, and they stared straight into each other's eyes. Manny's expression was one of shock. Hers one of determination. And then they were face-to-face, and Manny found himself looking at one of the most stunning women he'd ever seen in his life.

Black hair crowned a face of unusual features. Her wide, full mouth was a slash of ginger against a complexion only shades lighter than his own. But it was her eyes that commanded attention. Almond in shape, their true, spring green color was framed in sooty lashes that looked too long to be real, and yet Manny knew instinctively that there was little artifice about this one. If her take-it-or-leave-it attitude could have been bottled, she would have made a fortune.

And then she spoke, and Manny forgot not to grin. She might look like she'd stepped off the pages of a magazine, but her fashionable image faded with the slow, country drawl that wrapped around his senses.

"Are you the manager?"

Manny smiled and nodded. "And you, I believe, must be lost." Her confusion was obvious as he continued. "I know that I've seen you circle this floor at least seven times in the last three hours. What, my dear woman, are you doing? Casing the joint?"

"Yes, I guess I was," Lucky said, a little pleased with herself when she saw that she'd scored a point of her own. Manny was now the one wearing a confused expression.

"So, *are* you the manager?"

Manny sighed. He recognized persistence when he heard it. "*Sí, chica,* I am the shift manager. How may I be of assistance?"

Lucky waved her hand in an airy gesture of dismissal and shifted her small envelope purse to her other hand. "It's not me who needs help. It's you. And I want a job."

Manny frowned. "We do not have a floor show here, miss. And I don't hire the waitresses. You need to see—"

"I don't dance, and I don't sing. And I *don't* sling drinks."

"Then what, may I ask, *do* you do?"

"I'm a dealer. A good one."

Manny shook his head. "We have no need for a dealer at this time. But you can apply. We keep applications on file for a couple of months. Maybe by then we'll—"

"Oh, but you do need a dealer. Actually, you need three. You have one on duty that's stoned out of his mind.

You have one who's palming chips like peanuts, and another who's so busy getting customer's room numbers, he can't deal the shoe."

Manny's mouth dropped, and his black eyes flashed. This impudent stranger had just waltzed into his inner sanctum and accused him of running a shoddy shift. He wasn't having it. Not any of it.

"You don't come in and walk all over a man's business and his pride and then expect him to drink from your cup, *chica*," he said, unable to mask his displeasure. "I want to know the real reason why you're here. How do I know you're not a decoy while an accomplice is busy elsewhere robbing us blind?"

Lucky frowned. "I'm here because Fluffy LaMont sent me. She recommended this casino as a good place to work. I'm beginning to think she doesn't know what she's talking about."

With that, Lucky turned away, intent on leaving, when the little man's hand closed around her arm.

"Please don't," she said, and quietly shrugged off his grasp.

Manny frowned. A woman who didn't like to be touched? Again this didn't fit the mold.

"Fluffy? Fluffy LaMont really sent you?" He'd lived in Las Vegas all of his fifty-nine years and had known as a young boy of Fluffy LaMont's legendary status in the old Vegas. He hadn't even known she was still alive.

Lucky nodded.

"Come with me," Manny said. Remembering her warnings, he gave the floor one last regretful glance before motioning for the slot manager to take over until he returned.

Before Lucky could rethink her strategy, she was inside a small office just off the main gaming room. When the door closed behind them, she was amazed at the contrast between the constant dull roar and the instant silence.

He slid into the chair behind his desk. If he was going to look up at a woman, at least he could be sitting when he did it. "So . . . why do you want a job here?" he asked.

Lucky folded her hands before her like a child about to recite, then smiled.

"Because it's more like the places Johnny used to talk about. Because here there's less flash and more class. And because I need to work and you need a dealer."

Manny frowned. "So you said." He stared, waiting for her to fidget or look away. She did neither. "Who's Johnny?" he finally asked.

"My father."

"So . . . he's been here before and recommended the place to you?"

Lucky sighed. "No. I told you. Fluffy recommended Club 52. Johnny just talked about the shiny places, like Vegas and Reno. As a child, I always promised him that one day I would come for him."

Manny sensed there was more behind this simple answer, but he wasn't into family histories. And ordinarily he would have brushed off a woman with an approach like this. Yet something stilled the impulse. He handed her a deck of cards.

"Show me," he said, and then leaned forward, openmouthed, when Lucky's fingers began to fly. Cards slid between each other without a sound. She spread them, then cut, fanned, and shuffled again, yet this time, with only one hand.

He handed her a stack of chips and played twelve hands of blackjack with her, watching as she skillfully and quickly calculated his winnings and losses in her head.

"Where have you worked?" he asked.

"Nowhere. Before, it was just play."

"*Madre de Dios!* Then where did you learn to handle cards like that?"

"My father was a gambler."

Manny sat back in his chair with a thump. The tension in her voice was now unmistakable.

"And you . . . you have this fever too?"

Lucky's voice was full of anger when she answered. "Never. But he gave me the skill. It's all I know. I'll play, but only for the house. I never gamble with anything that belongs to me. Do you understand?"

Manny understood much more than that, but he let it pass.

"Do you have a sheriff's card?"

She displayed all of her permits proudly, thankful that the realtor who'd rented her the apartment had let the necessity slip.

Manny nodded and then smiled. "They are exactly . . . twenty-four hours old. So, you're new in town."

Lucky laughed. Aloud. Without reserve.

"I've been waiting for that," she said, swallowing a last chuckle.

Manny didn't understand her remark, but it didn't

matter. He'd been on her side since the moment her lips
had parted in a smile. And when she'd laughed, he'd been
sold.

"When can you start?" he asked.

"Tomorrow."

Manny nodded. "Go by the office and pick up an application. For now, you'll be on the three to eleven shift.
Come early. I'll get you outfitted with a uniform and show
you where you'll work."

"What do you pay?"

Manny grinned. "I wondered if you were going to ask."

"First things first," Lucky said. "Didn't matter if I didn't
get the job now, did it?"

"We're a cut above the average on wages in town, and
you can ask anyone to verify."

When she nodded her approval, he grinned.

"As usual, the woman has the last word. Welcome to
Club 52."

"Thank you, sir."

"Manny. Call me Manny."

Lucky nodded. "And you can call me Lucky."

The little mustache above his lips fairly danced with
amusement. "You're name is beautiful . . . just as you are,
chica, but you'll have to put your legal name on your application."

"That is my name," Lucky said quietly. "I told you . . .
my father was a gambler. My oldest sister's name is
Queen. The middle one is Diamond."

Manny frowned at the defiant way in which she'd explained, and something told him that her youth had not
been all doll babies and bubble gum.

"Then Lucky it is," he said. "I will see you tomorrow."

She was almost out the door when Manny remembered to ask.

"Lucky!"

She stopped and turned toward him.

"You say I have three dealers who are screwed. Which ones are they?"

She frowned. "You hired me to deal cards, not snitch. You're the manager. You find them. I only work here, remember?"

Manny grinned. She certainly was a fiery one. But it was good. Manny liked things peppery and hot. Especially the women.

It was midafternoon as Nick stared absently down at the crowd from the floor above, wondering where Manny had gone, when a woman walked into his line of vision, sauntering through the crowd with a slow, sexy sway.

Nick's gaze caught and then held on her figure, and he frowned and wondered why. There were hundreds of women below. Again, why did he keep singling one out from all the rest?

Minus the heels that she wore, this one, he could see, would still be tall. But all he could see was the top of her head, and then the back of her suit as she walked away. From the crystal reflection of the room around her, that black crown of hair almost looked blue. An enticing length of tanned leg was exposed from beneath the miniskirt of her suit, and she clutched a small purse as if it were a shield.

He had an inexplicable urge to follow her. Just as impulse had him heading for the stairs, he saw Manny walk out onto the floor and squashed the notion before it became deed. He needed to forget monkey business and concentrate on the business at hand.

Manny looked up, and when he did, Nick motioned for him to come. As Manny started up the stairs, Nick headed for his office.

Inside his office, away from the teeming crowd below him, Nick still felt the urge to watch her. He found himself strolling toward a window . . . just for a glimpse . . . just to assure himself she was no one special.

There she was—on the street—then climbing into a cab. His belly rolled as the door swung shut and the cab moved away. He would have sworn he'd seen those legs and that slender backside before on a ragtag lovely in a downtown bus station. And then the moment he thought it, called himself twelve kinds of a fool.

"You wanted to see me, Nicky?" Manny asked, as he entered the office.

Nick spun away from the window. "Who was that woman?"

There'd been several hundred women down on the floor at the same time Lucky had been there. And yet Manny instinctively knew who Nick meant.

"A new dealer. I just hired her."

Nick frowned. "We don't need any dealers."

Manny shrugged. "If I believe my instincts, we're about to need two more besides her. I'm on my way to Security. I want to take the Eye on a table-to-table visit. *Comprende?*"

Nick read between the lines. For some reason, Manny

suspected dirty dealers. The camera system they had in place was so sophisticated that it could zoom into any specific table and see everything up close and personal . . . even a single hair on their dealer's arm. Only Manny and Nick weren't splitting hairs; they were on a witchhunt.

"I'll come with you," Nick said. "Four eyes are better than two."

To Manny's dismay, the woman had been right. It was with great pleasure that he promptly fired two of the dealers and had the other one charged with theft.

By the time the turmoil was over, Manny had gone off shift, and Nick realized that he hadn't even asked Manny the woman's name.

"Oh hell," he told himself. "It doesn't matter. She's just another woman with a pretty face. They're all alike."

Fluffy LaMont sat at her front window, watching the street in front of her house, waiting to spring her surprise. It would have shocked her oldest acquaintances to know that Fluffy LaMont had developed such an interest in Lucky Houston. She'd lived long enough in this world to learn that there were few she could trust.

But something had clicked between Lucille and Lucky. They'd both sensed it. And wasting time was not a luxury Lucille could afford. She had no family and who knew how many years left.

She'd puttered for hours, dusting things that hadn't been touched in months, and cooking tidbits of her favorite foods while maligning the cat's constant presence beneath her feet. But now the preparations were over. The time of waiting was at hand. Lucifer lay curled in her lap, purring in sleep while Fluffy's arthritic hands absently stroked his silky black fur. For the time, their antagonism was at a cease-fire as the late afternoon sun made layabouts of them both.

And then Fluffy saw Lucky coming up the street, her long legs making short work of the block and a half to home. Fluffy smiled. She could tell by the length of her stride and the set of her jaw that she'd gotten a job.

"But where, my pretty?" she muttered to herself, and promptly stood, dumping Lucifer unceremoniously on the floor and anxiously smoothing the front of her dress as she hobbled to the door.

Lucky was walking on air. Three days in Las Vegas and she had a home, a friend, and a job. It was more than she'd ever dreamed possible when she'd hugged Queenie good-bye and crawled on that bus, leaving Cradle Creek behind and Johnny in his grave.

"Lucky! Lucky Houston. I've been waiting for you."

Her eccentric landlady was waving at her from the front door. With a spurt of joy, she started to run.

"Fluffy! You won't guess!"

"You have a job, of course. Now come in. Come in. Tell me all about it."

Lucky took the steps two at a time, glad to have someone with whom she could share her news.

Lucifer darted between her feet as he made for the back of the house, hissing and spitting with every leap.

"He doesn't like me much," she said. "I scared him yesterday when I came headfirst through your window."

"Pooh," Fluffy muttered. "He doesn't like me much either. Pay him no mind."

Lucky grinned and then looked around, suddenly seeing all that had been done in her absence.

"You've been, ah . . . fixing up the place, haven't you? It looks wonderful." As did Fluffy. She was cleaner and much more presentable than she'd been when first they'd met.

Fluffy smoothed the front of her magenta gown and readjusted the brooch she had pinned at her breast to replace a missing button. She patted her hair and walked across the room with an arthritic sway reminiscent of her runway walk.

"It needed it," Fluffy said. Hesitation coupled with loneliness entered her voice. "I cooked. If you like, you could have dinner with me."

Lucky smiled and then impulsively hugged her. "It would be my pleasure."

"I don't cook ordinary food. I cook what I like to eat," she warned. "At my age, diets are a joke. Going without fat or cholesterol is not going to prolong my life. I've already outlived every friend I have, you know."

Lucky's eyes misted. Fluffy would hate to know that while her words were defiantly funny, her watery gray eyes gave her away. She was lonely. And Lucky could easily identify with the feeling. Save for her sisters and Johnny, she had never in her life had anyone close to her.

"We make a pair, don't we, Fluffy?" Lucky said, kicking off her shoes and wiggling her toes.

"Why don't you go change into something comfortable, then come back when you're ready. I boiled shrimp. It's chilled and just waiting to be eaten. I made macaroni and cheese too. It's one of my favorites . . . oh, and I bought a chocolate fudge pie."

The combination of foods Fluffy ticked off on her fingers threatened to stagger Lucky's constitution, but she wouldn't have missed this meal for a million dollars.

"Give me five minutes. I'll be back barefoot and hungry."

Fluffy patted her pocket and then removed a key, handing it to Lucky in a casual, offhand manner, when in fact it was a gesture of such trust that it brought tears to Lucky's eyes.

"Here," she said. "It's the key to the front door. It's an extra so you might as well keep it." She shrugged and turned away, unwilling for Lucky to see the emotion on her face. "You never know when I'll need rescuing again, and I don't want you to have to crawl through any more windows and scare my damn cat."

Lucky took the key and put it with her own door key. "Thank you, Fluffy. I'll take good care of it."

"I know that," Fluffy said shortly, "or else I would never have given it to you. Now hurry! I'm starving."

Lucky bolted toward the door.

"Oh, by the way," Fluffy asked. "Where did you find work?"

"Club 52," Lucky said. "I think I'm going to like it there."

Fluffy's eyes narrowed. She pursed her mispainted lips in concentration as she watched the beautiful young woman bounce out of her home with the enthusiasm of a young deer.

"Hmmm, so it's to be the Chenaults." And then she smiled, making her look younger than her true age for a moment. "That Nick Chenault is one fine man, my dear. You will know that soon enough on your own. Maybe this is fate. Maybe this is fate."

But Lucky was gone. She didn't hear Fluffy's remarks, and if she had, would have pooh-poohed them as nonsense. The Houston women didn't have much use for men.

But the die had been cast. Fate had already set events in motion that none of the players in this game could have predicted.

4

"Nick! I can't remember the last time you came home for dinner." Paul's elation was evident as Cubby wheeled him out onto the patio. "Cubby, tell Shari to bring another glass. Nick can join me for an aperitif."

"I've already got a drink, Dad," Nick said, lifting a soda and lime. "I don't want anything stronger. I may go back to the club later and it would only make me sleepy if I indulge now."

Paul grinned. "You sound like an old man. What you need is a change of pace. Walter Warner's daughter is home from Europe. Celebrating her third divorce, I think. She's lethal but pretty. You should give her a call. She could be someone to pass time with."

Nick didn't answer. Paul gauged the extent of his son's absent gaze across the manicured lawns of the estate, then frowned. Something else was bothering him. He could tell.

"You want to talk, Nicky?"

Nick sighed. A spurt of longing for the good old days came swiftly. Days when Paul Chenault had dealt with the problems and all Nick had to worry about was which car he could drive and how much he had to study for exams.

But those days were long gone. He'd been in charge of the family businesses far longer than he cared to remember. Yes, he wanted to talk. But how much good was it going to do? Sharing the information wasn't going to make the problem go away.

Nick slowly turned and faced his father. It had been years since Paul had called him by his childhood nickname. But it was somehow endearing to know that sometimes his father must still think of him in those terms.

He set down his glass, and then pulled up a chair to face his father's wheelchair.

"We do have to talk, Dad."

"I'll just wait in the——" Cubby began.

"Wait, Cubby. This concerns all of us," Nick said. "You grab a chair too. We've got a problem on our hands."

Paul's expression turned serious. All thoughts of matchmaking were forgotten.

Nick leaned forward, his elbows on his knees, and looked his father in the face. Then realizing how harsh the question was going to sound, gave his father's thigh a comforting pat before he began.

"When I went down to Las Vegas Metro, the detective in charge let me read Charlie Sams's confession."

Paul's eyebrows rose. "Isn't that a little unorthodox?"

Nick nodded.

"Then why?"

Nick inhaled slowly. This was where things would get sticky. How much to tell . . . and how much to hold back? And as he watched the expressions changing on his father's face, knew that holding back was impossible. Both of their lives might depend upon his honesty now.

"Because . . . according to Charlie Sams, he was a plant in Chenault Incorporated. Everything, and I mean everything, that Charlie learned about our business, he funneled back to his boss."

"Who was his boss?" Paul asked.

"The detective says that Charlie didn't know. He was contacted by phone and paid by direct bank deposit. He never had a face or a name."

Paul waved a hand in disgust. "That's ridiculous! We're no high-tech corporation with secrets to sell. And we don't have any underworld ties to be held over our heads. What the hell is the point?"

"Maybe hate . . . or revenge?"

Paul's face turned ashen. When Nick gently squeezed his knee as a reminder to temper his emotions, he sighed and leaned back in his chair. After taking a deep breath he sipped the wine Cubby offered.

"Sorry," Paul said. "It was just a shock."

"That's not all," Nick said. "According to Charlie Sams, someone doesn't want to just ruin us. Someone wants me dead. Who, Dad? Who do you know that could hold a grudge like that?"

Paul Chenault blanched again. Only this time, the

wineglass he was holding slipped from his fingers and shattered on the flagstone, scattering the wine like red tears.

"My God! You can't be serious!"

Nick grimaced. A shaft of panic centered in his belly as he watched his father pale.

"Dad . . . calm down. It's okay. We've been warned. We can stop this. But I can't do this alone. I need you to think. I need you to remember. Is there someone . . . anyone from the past who would hold a grudge like that?"

At first Paul shook his head vehemently. And then Nick saw the indecision sweep over his father's face as memories surfaced. When Paul buried his face in his hands, Nick knew he would have an answer. Finally the man got control of his emotions enough to speak.

"In my lifetime, I only knew one man who would hate on that level. But I thought he was dead." He shuddered, and a firmness seared his lips. "No! I'm sure he's dead. It can't be him. Besides, if he'd wanted revenge, he would have done it years ago when we had the falling out. Not now. Not when I'm too old to care whether I live or—"

"It's not you he wants dead, Dad. It's me. Would this man hate you enough to want to kill me?"

"When he was young, he killed a man. I know that for a fact. That he could hate me enough to kill someone I loved . . ." His chin quivered. "Oh, yes."

"Then I want a name."

Paul looked away, unwilling for some reason to impart that information.

Cubby scurried to pick up the broken wineglass while

Shari, their maid, came bustling out with a pan of soapy water and a cloth.

Nick took his father's chair and wheeled him back into the house. "Look, Dad, whatever happens will never be your fault. Together we can lick this, but I need you to be strong. Don't panic. Plan."

Paul closed his eyes and swallowed a lump of fear. Nick was right. They needed a plan.

"His name was . . . Dieter. Dieter Marx. Once, he was one of my best friends."

An angry string of Spanish oaths drifted from the open door of the hacienda on the outskirts of *Ciudad Rio.* Servants crossed themselves and scurried away, their heads ducked, as they fled from their master's wrath. Someone, somewhere, had angered *El Gato.* They didn't want to be in his path and be made to pay.

Palm trees nodded in the market-day breeze of the old Colombian town as coffee merchants argued on the warehouse docks while their merchandise was being loaded onto trucks. The going price for coffee beans was down and they didn't like it. Their loud voices rang out, determined that someone, other than they, should suffer the loss.

Back in the hacienda, *El Gato* had suffered a loss of his own. A plan that he'd spent months putting in motion had just gone awry. He'd just learned that his inside man was now in jail, awaiting arraignment. It would take weeks of plotting to reorganize and resurrect what he'd wanted to do.

"*Señor, cómo está*—"

The servant's question never saw daylight as a bourbon bottle whizzed past his head and broke against the red tile wall at his back.

"Get out! Get out!" *El Gato* roared, forgetting in his anger to speak in the Spanish tongue.

After all these years, he still thought in English and had to translate to Spanish in his head before speaking. When he was frustrated or angry, his native tongue always took precedence.

As the servant scurried from the room, the man tried to channel his emotional rage into planning.

It would have been impossible to guess his age. He was simply a weathered survivor of life. With no spare flesh on his body and no hair on his head, his skin had the look of leather about it, and his pale blue eyes stood out from their sockets. On his left cheek he had a trio of parallel scars that he'd gotten when he'd first gone over the border.

Young and alone, certain that he'd been betrayed by those he trusted best, he'd been lost in the South American jungle for exactly four days, weak and hungry, nearly eaten up from the insects bites when it had happened.

To this day, he had only a vague memory of leaning over a riverbank to get a drink and then seeing, along with his own reflection, the jaguar poised on a limb above and behind him. He remembered jumping to his feet and then throwing up an arm to ward off the animal's attack. Days later, he woke up in a village with some local's daughter crooning over him like a baby.

When he left, he took the woman with him. She soon abandoned him, but the scar remained. A lasting reminder that survival of the fittest still held true. It hadn't taken the superstitious natives long to attribute this man's strength of purpose to the mark the cat had left on his face. Thus, *El Gato*, The Cat, was born.

And yet, alone in the opulence of his home and wealth, *El Gato* was still the same young man at heart who'd bolted across the border with the syndicate, as well as the law, right at his heels. He'd escaped with his life and little else. It had taken him years to recoup what he'd left behind, but no amount of years could ever account for the thing that burned deep in his bitter soul: revenge! *El Gato* wanted . . . needed revenge. Only then could he go to his grave a happy man.

Lucky had been on the job at Club 52 exactly three minutes when someone overheard Manny Sosa call her by her name. The whispers had flown like wildfire among the players at the tables. There was a new dealer named Lucky. The fact that she was a young and beautiful woman hardly entered into the scenario. Many dealers were women. For the serious players, it was the game and the winning that counted, not who dealt the cards. But if they were superstitious enough to want a real live Lady Luck actually dealing their cards, so be it.

She stepped behind the green felt with a surge of elation. If only Johnny could see her now. And as she thought it, she knew that if he were here, he'd be on the other side of the table, waiting to place a bet.

Four players watched with jaundiced eyes as the manager oversaw the switch in dealers while the pit boss looked on from a short distance away. Lucky smiled casually at the players, then, as if she'd done it all her life, took the cards from the shoe, the box that held the four decks of cards that each dealer used, and began to shuffle.

Precisely. Competently. With no show of the magician-like skill that she'd given Manny Sosa the day before. The hours that she'd spent observing yesterday also stood her in good stead. She'd made a mental note of every casino rule regarding dealer behavior. Both hands in plain view at all times. No casual brushes of hands toward pockets or hair. Tips from happy customers went in a special slot on the table, while cash went in another, and so on, and so on. She hadn't missed a thing.

When the shoe of cards had been shuffled, she pushed it toward the man to her right and handed him a large, colorful, plastic card. He took it, inserted it about halfway up the cards in the shuffled shoe, thereby proclaiming that the cards had been "cut." As she was about to begin, her concentration was broken by a player's question.

"Hey, babe. Did I hear the man call you Lucky?"

"Yes, sir."

"Is that really your name?"

Lucky sighed. How many times in this city would she hear that question?

"Yes. It's really my name."

He grinned like the Cheshire cat, deciding that he'd just fallen down a rabbit hole of immense proportions, and shoved five one-hundred-dollar bills toward her.

"Change, please," he barked. "All quarters, honey. I suddenly feel lucky."

Lucky calmly counted out the twenty-five-dollar chips that he'd requested, then announced:

"Players . . . place your bets."

And so it began. Manny Sosa stood a distance away, assessing the calmness of the woman. Her instant skill at mental calculation of the three-two payoff that the tables made was unusually adept, as was her cool, professional attitude in dealing with the customers who tried to get too friendly. At this point, Manny knew that he'd found himself a jewel. Part of his dealer shortage had been dealt with.

But another, more serious situation remained. Someone wanted Nicky dead, and Manny wouldn't have it. Even if it meant losing sleep for the next six months, he was ready to bed down at Club 52 just to assure himself that Nick Chenault made no deadly mistakes.

Lucky was unaware of the turmoil surrounding her place of employment, or the owner she had yet to meet. She was too absorbed in the play and the players.

Yet in every ointment, there is a fly. And a croupier named Steve Lucas would be Lucky's. He was milling about in the break room when Manny came through with the tall, black-haired beauty on his arm, giving her the new-employee tour. He'd watched with the intensity of the predator that he was, and when Lucky's back was turned, he mentally stripped her of every garment she was wearing. From the classy blue slacks and jacket to the plain black flats.

When Manny took her away to be outfitted in a dealer's black tux, Steve knew that his day had just gone from suck, to so fine. He went through the motions of croupier, while patiently waiting for the golden opportunity to make his move on Lucky. By the time his dinner break came, he realized it would coincide with hers. It was just as well. He'd worked himself up to hot and hard in anticipation of the successful swath he intended to cut through her path.

Lucky didn't see him coming. If she had, their first impressions of each other might have been different, and the rest of their lives might never have been altered. As it was, Lucas, in all his six-foot, body-builder perfection, assumed that an introduction was a flat waste of time. He waited until Lucky had a sandwich and soft drink in hand, and then made his move.

"Hey, little Lucky, I feel like getting lucky myself tonight. What do you say?"

Lucky froze. The hand squeezing the right side of her waist and the low, masculine whisper in her ear were an invasion of her space that she did not allow. Without spilling a drop, she pivoted.

"Excuse me," she said quietly. "But I don't like to be touched."

Steve grinned at the cool flash of her green eyes. He assumed she was playing coy and accepted the challenge. He liked them hard to get. He took a step back, raising his hands in a gesture of playful arrest, and gave her his best Vegas smile. It always worked before.

Lucky carefully eyed the tall, sandy-haired man, assessing his thick, muscular build as dangerous, the cut of his chin as weak, and the smile on his face as deceptive. It was a total and instant dislike of the first employee of Club 52 who'd made an overture of friendliness.

"Sor-ry," he said, and smoothed the front of his fly, assuming that the motion would draw her attention to the bulge behind it. When Lucky's eyes never left his face, but only turned a shade cooler, and the polite smile on her lips went a shade straighter, he shifted into second gear and tried the ingenuous approach.

"I thought since it was your first night that you'd like a little company while you ate. That's all I meant. Nothing pushy. Just a little employee association . . . if you know what I mean."

Lucky looked down at the chicken salad sandwich in her hands and felt the condensation from her soft drink running down the side of the cup.

How do I get out of this without making an enemy of him? She could hardly flip this man on his back as she had the pimp on the street who'd accosted her.

"Maybe another time," Lucky said, and turned away.

It was the seductive sway of her slender hips beneath the form-fitting black pants of the dealer's tuxedo that made him lose his train of thought. She was gone before he had time to try another line. He shrugged and walked away. She was new, and there was always tomorrow.

Lucky didn't taste a bite of her food. Every time she tried to swallow she imagined she could feel his hands on her body and his hot breath down her neck all over again, and it literally made her sick to her stomach. It was an odd but definite fact. The Houston girls didn't take to being handled, not without an invitation. And Lucky was no exception.

When the pit boss strolled through the break room and announced a return to the tables was nearly at hand, she gave up all pretense of eating, thankful to be going back into the comfort of a crowd.

Then, finally, the night was over. With her first day of work behind her and nearly one hundred dollars in tips in her purse, Lucky was walking on air. All her life she'd hated her name, and now in a city where gambling was a way of life, it seemed as if it was going to be her meal ticket to financial security.

Every player seemed to want a piece of the action at Lucky Houston's table. If they won, they tipped big, telling themselves that it was Lucky who'd brought them luck. If they lost, they tipped even more, as if in some odd, gambler's superstition that they were appeasing their goddess, Lady Luck.

Lucky hugged her joy close, wishing she had someone at home with whom she could share the news. But it was nearly midnight. Fluffy would long ago have gone to bed. Tomorrow would be time enough to talk.

While she waited for the city bus on the street outside the club, the high wire her emotions had been on began to stretch. All at once, the day's stress fell in on her with a thump.

By the time the bus arrived and she took a seat, it was all she could do to keep her eyes open until it reached her stop. Determined to stay alert, she sat up straight and stared out a window.

As the bus rumbled through the residential areas of the city, it suddenly dawned on Lucky that parts of Las Vegas really did sleep. In spite of the streetlights, the alleys and shadows beneath the trees and between the houses took on an entirely different appearance. The assumption that she could handle anything began to weaken along with her strength.

Her resolve was gone by the time the bus pulled to her stop. She got off, certain that her blue jacket and slacks would be a beacon for doers of bad deeds, and could hardly walk for searching out every shadow between herself and home. The dark had become a strange and sinister being with which she must contend.

Every sound she heard was an attacker about to pounce. Every rustle in the bushes along the block seemed to be an indication that she was in constant and dire danger. Despite the lights on the streets and the ordinary night sounds of an occasional barking dog or a squalling cat, Lucky felt as if she'd stepped into a nightmare. When the sound of squealing brakes shattered the night air, Lucky bolted into an all-out sprint.

Suddenly, Fluffy's three-story Victorian appeared like a pink and peeling island of refuge. There in the downstairs window, in plain sight of the path that she took, was a lamp burning bright and yellow, welcoming her home.

Lucky's eyes blurred with tears, certain that Fluffy had lit it for her. Her dash decreased to a trot as a stitch in her side reminded her that she'd been a frightened fool for nothing. With shaky steps, she climbed the steep staircase to her apartment, then unlocked the door.

Inside, the light she'd left on in the hall was a warm yellow welcome of silence. Sighing at her undue worry and shaky with relief, she locked and chained the door. Safe behind four walls. For tonight, it was enough.

Moments later she'd shed her clothes and crawled into the tub, moaning in relief as water ran hard and hot upon her tired, aching toes. Her tummy growled, but her eyes burned worse. She was too tired to consider a late-night snack. All she wanted was to go to sleep.

Nick stood at the window of his office overlooking the downtown strip where the Golden Spur, the Nugget, the Lucky Lady, and all the rest burned bright with lights against the velvet darkness of the Las Vegas night sky. White lights, yellow lights. All colors of the rainbow lights. Neon "glory holes" with riches beyond belief, there, just waiting for the lucky man or woman to come along. And as he looked, wondered what quirk of fate had judged his birth should be here, in a make-believe world of impossible dreams.

Here, in every casino, by the hundreds of thousands, people came and crowded around the tables or the machines, waiting for that magical dollar to hit the slot and spill a lifetime worth of winnings onto the floor at their feet.

The city lay in wait for the dreamers, the players who replaced the miners of yesteryear. The ones who left their marks in the hearts of the mountains beyond the city. The believers who were certain that the next shovel of dirt they dug out would unearth the vein that would make them rich.

These were the spirits of many who came to Las Vegas. And if the strike wasn't obviously imminent, they didn't quit. They just moved on . . . to the next table, or the next machine, certain that their luck was about to change.

Nick sighed and rested his head against the window. He hated himself for this doubt that had crept into his soul. He'd loved this frenetic world and the lifestyle that accompanied it, or so he'd thought, until he'd been told someone wanted him dead. It was then that he began to wonder if it was all worth it. If the luxury of his surroundings and the family wealth was enough to compensate for the fact that someone coveted it, and hated him and his father enough to want to kill.

He'd given Will Arnold the name of Dieter Marx as a possible suspect with the promise that if the detective came up with some information, he would share it with him. Although Paul Chenault still insisted that Dieter Marx was surely dead, Nick wouldn't . . . couldn't dismiss the man's existence out of hand until he was given proof. He waited impatiently for answers that didn't come.

"Dammit, Dad. Who is Dieter Marx? What happened between you two that could have fostered such hate?"

"Talking to yourself, Nicky?" Manny asked as he entered the office with the assurance of a trusted friend.

"May as well. At least that way I get the answers I want."

Manny grinned.

"How did it go tonight?" Nick asked.

Manny threw up his hands in a Latin gesture of amazement and started to talk.

"Fantastic! The new dealer . . . she is a jewel. I tell you the truth. . . ."

Nick listened without really hearing. He was too busy wondering if Cubby had set the security system before going to bed, and wondering if his father had eaten his evening meal or if he was still brooding about secrets he didn't seem willing to share.

". . . and came away with tips out the ass."

Nick looked up as the last bit of Manny's monologue caught his attention. "Whose ass?"

Manny grinned. "A beautiful woman's, 'mano. But you weren't listening, were you?" When Nick started to apologize, Manny repeated part of his praise for the woman all over again.

"You should have seen her. She handled the pros and the neophytes with the same calm demeanor. Explaining the plays to greenhorns didn't seem to faze her any more than the constant and increasing bets at her tables. Everyone wanted a piece of Lady Luck."

Nick shook his head. "I know there's a connection in there somewhere, Manny, but I'm not getting it. Why would the players want to play at her table rather than one of the others? She's not nearly the only female dealer we have. In fact, I'd say the majority of our dealers are women . . . aren't they?"

"Maybe so, Nicky. But she's the only one with the given name of Lucky."

Nick's eyebrows shot upward as a smooth smile slipped into place. "That can't be real."

"Oh, but it is. I saw her identification. Even her sheriff's card has the name Lucky Houston."

"Well! I'll be damned," Nick said softly. "So Lady Luck has come to work for us?"

Manny laughed. "So it would seem."

Nick's smile died. "Good. I can use all the luck I can get."

"Still no news about the man who hired Charlie Sams?"

Nick shook his head. "Not so far. And the damnedest

thing . . . Dad has almost clammed up. He gave me a name and then seemed to withdraw. I can't figure it out."

"What was the name, Nicky? If you don't mind me asking?"

"Hell no. I should have told you sooner. Dad said his old friend's name was Dieter Marx. Ever hear of him?"

Manny frowned. "No. I'm sorry, I don't think so. But you have to remember that fourteen years separate our ages. When your father opened Club 52, I was only ten or twelve years old and you weren't even born. You were just starting to school when I started working for your father. I knew nothing of the times before."

"It's okay. I didn't really expect that you would. Go home, Manny. Get some rest. Take tomorrow off if you want. I don't think you've had a day off in weeks."

Manny shook his head. "No. Not until this is over. Not until I see a smile in your eyes again." With that, he left, quietly shutting Nick in and the noise out.

5

Except for Steve Lucas's presence, the first four days on the job had gone smoothly for Lucky. Things about Club 52 that had astounded her at first, she now ignored. No longer did she notice the players glued to their seats at the slot machines, with plastic buckets of quarters clutched between their legs and glazed expressions on their faces. She'd even quit staring at those players whose faces often bore streaks of dirt caused by their handling so much grimy coin. Now, when someone in the casino let out a screech, she no longer looked up to see if it was out of delight or despair. She was too busy concentrating on her own job.

With little more than an accelerated heartbeat, she'd received and refused a marriage proposal from an Arab prince. Then afterward she had wondered if her heart raced out of fear, or from the shock of his offer, and the pleasures that he had promised.

But at the end of the week, her life went on a sudden roller coaster and all because of a man she didn't know.

Undetected because of the two potted palms at the hall entrance, she bent over her untied shoelace, and found herself suddenly frozen with fear as she listened to the thick, raspy voice of the man at the pay phone.

He was clearly plotting someone's death.

"Look! I told you, it's in the bag." Woody mopped the fat furrows on the back of his neck with a handkerchief that looked like it had gone about a week past laundry date. "His routine rarely varies. He'll eat his breakfast with his old man, just like he does every morning. He'll make a few calls from home and then dress for work. But when he goes outside and starts the engine of that Jag, he and his breakfast will blow sky high and there will be one less Chenault on the face of the earth. You can trust me. They don't call me Woody the Wire for nothin' you know."

Oh, my God! was all Lucky could think as she ducked out of sight.

While she was debating about going back to work, she heard a sharp click and knew that she'd waited too long. The man had hung up the phone.

Before she gave herself time to reconsider, Lucky knew that she had to see his face. She had to know, because she was going to tell. She took a deep breath and sauntered into the hallway as if she'd just arrived.

The man was short, and his girth seemed to be twice his height. He actually seemed to roll when he walked, like a cannonball on wheels. The Pillsbury Doughboy in pin-stripe. That was how Lucky saw him.

When he saw her, Lucky knew a moment of fear. The

look in his eyes was that of a fat, trapped rat. In a spurt of genius, she gave him a wide, flashy smile and winked as they passed, hoping that her flirtatious attitude would distract him from wondering if he'd been overheard. It worked like a charm.

Woody the Wire had known that using the phone here would be risky. But his check-in time with the boss had come before he'd realized. If he left Club 52 to make the call, then he couldn't play keno. And Woody the Wire loved keno almost more than he loved food.

But when the lady dealer sauntered past the palms like she owned the place and looked him in the eye, he figured he'd been made and was actually considering the best way to kill her . . . when she smiled.

Then he completely forgot that he'd been in the act of confirming a man's murder or thinking of hers. Unabashed by the fact that she towered above him in height, he even considered making a date when he remembered what he'd been about to do.

Cursing beneath his breath about the interference of fate in his love life, he waddled past her and out into the main gaming room and disappeared quickly within the constantly moving crowd.

Lucky slipped into the ladies' room and leaned against the door in shaky panic as she tried to regain her equilibrium.

"Oh, God! Oh, God! Now what?" she muttered. Shock and nerves kicked in as she realized the risk that she'd taken by letting him see her face.

A woman came out of a stall while Lucky was talking to herself in near hysterics, and she realized she had to get out before she made a fool of herself and the fat man somehow learned that she'd overheard.

Manny! He'd become her mentor. His awareness of Steve Lucas's unwanted attentions toward her had prevented more than one brawl. He would often step into the break room at a crucial time and prevent the harassment from escalating. Lucky knew it was only a matter of time before something ugly happened between them. But one ugly thing at a time. Right now, she had to tell a man about a murder and hope that it would never take place. She bolted out of the bathroom, anxiety lending speed to her steps.

Manny saw her coming across the floor and saw the look of panic on her face. He went rushing to meet her.

"What is it?" Manny caught her in full stride and pulled her toward the hallway near his office.

Before Lucky had a chance to catch her breath, he began peppering her with questions.

"Is it Lucas? Has he overstepped your boundaries, *chica?* Did he—"

"Manny! We need to talk!"

Her voice was shaking as hard as her body. Her eyes were wide, the pupils dilated to twice their size from the adrenaline racing through her system. And had he not been the macho Latino that he was, the grip she had on his arm could have sent him to his knees.

"Come inside my office. We talk there." He motioned to one of the managers that he was leaving the floor and taking Lucky with him.

Moments later the door shut behind them and the utter silence of the room made Lucky's legs go weak.

"Manny . . . I just heard someone who called himself Woody the Wire talking on the pay phone in the hallway next to the bathrooms. He said that tomorrow a man was going to be murdered."

Manny reacted as if he'd been shot. He slumped against the back of his chair as he absorbed what she'd just told him, and then he thought of the danger she'd inadvertently put herself in.

"*Dios mío!* Did he see you? Did he know that you overheard?"

That Manny didn't doubt her story said a lot for the things that went on within the multi-billion-dollar world of Las Vegas.

"No, I don't think so. But to be on the safe side, when he did see me, I acted like an airhead and actually flirted a little as we passed."

Manny worried his little mustache with the tips of his fingers as he considered their course of action.

"Good! That is good. But the first thing we should do is call the—"

"Wait! That isn't all," Lucky said. She dropped down into the nearest chair to keep from falling and clasped her hands together in her lap as she tried to control her breathing. "The man said that tomorrow . . . there would be one less Chenault on the face of the earth. I haven't met him . . . but isn't that my boss's name?"

A slow, steady stream of Spanish invectives matched the stride of his march as Manny came across the room toward her like a bullet. Lucky actually considered ducking when the little man jerked her from her seat and almost dragged her from the room.

"Where are we going?" she asked. In spite of Manny's short legs, she had to hurry to keep up with his pace.

"To see the boss!" he said. "You have to tell him exactly what you told me. It is imperative that he know of this now . . . while there is still time to prevent a disaster."

Lucky's stomach did a flip-flop as Manny dragged her up the stairs, toward what she'd learned days earlier was the inner sanctum of "The Man."

Among the employees, Nick Chenault was a name that was said in whispers. Not in fear, but in awe. Proclaimed to be a handsome, unattached man of great wealth and power, he was held in high esteem by the people who worked for him. But at the same time, many remained wary of him too. That much power was always frightening to someone who did not have it.

Manny didn't bother to knock. So when they burst into his office, to say Nick Chenault was surprised was an understatement. And when he saw the woman that Manny had in tow, he couldn't believe his eyes. It was the one from the bus station. Only this time, she wasn't dressed in ragged, hand-me-down clothing. She was wearing one of the tuxedos reserved for the dealers at Club 52.

"You!"

Nick's and Lucky's accusations were simultaneous. Manny stared at them as if they'd suddenly grown warts.

"What are you doing here?" they both asked again, and then Lucky shook her head and was the first to stop the farce from being carried any further.

"Good lord, it's the pimp."

Nick continued to stare. He couldn't get past the fact that the waifish woman who'd come off that bus had turned into an elegant, classy-looking female who now seemed to be in his employ.

Manny was stunned by her words. A pimp? His boss? It was obvious that these two knew each other, but how? Where and when could they have possibly met? He knew for a fact that Lucky hadn't been in town long enough to run in the same circles as the Chenaults. And although they recognized each other's faces, it seemed that neither had been aware of the other's identity.

"You work here?" Nick couldn't believe she was wearing a dealer's uniform and he hadn't even noticed her on the floor.

"Nearly a week," Manny said, answering for Lucky who seemed to have gone mute.

Nick's dark eyes narrowed as he looked back at the woman in black. "This isn't the new dealer." He stated it with such unequivocal assurance that it made Manny laugh.

At this, Nick flushed. Obviously, it was. While he was trying to get past the embarrassment and shock, he remembered the story Manny had told him yesterday about their new dealer's latest dilemma on the floor. "She's not the one the Arab prince tried to buy . . . is she?"

"Nicholas . . . I would like for you to meet Miss Lucky Houston, late of Tennessee, now a resident of our fine city. And . . . your newest dealer."

"He didn't want to buy me. He offered to marry me," Lucky said, slightly insulted by the tone of his voice. And then, as soon as she said it, she was afraid that it had sounded rude.

In spite of the urgency of the moment, Manny couldn't

resist another grin. Something was going on between these two that he'd waited years to witness. If he didn't miss his guess, Nick Chenault was slightly smitten. He glanced at Lucky, unable to tell how she felt. She looked as if she could either faint or throw up. She was pale around the mouth and shaking like a leaf.

Nick couldn't quit staring. The long, ropy braid that he remembered hanging down her back was now wound into an abundant crown on top of her head. He had the strongest urge to thrust his fingers into the mass, search out the pins holding it up, and then stand back and watch it spill around her face and shoulders like so much black silk.

The tuxedo she was wearing made her look even taller than he remembered, but he noticed that she still wore no makeup or jewelry. She had none of the artifice he'd come to associate with members of the opposite sex. But the expression on her face hadn't changed. She was still glaring at him with a mixture of disgust and disdain.

He couldn't believe his eyes. Ever since their meeting at the bus station, she'd haunted his dreams and sneaked into his thoughts at the oddest times. Now, here she was, right before him, and he couldn't think of a thing to say.

Fortunately, Manny could.

"Boss, Lucky has something to tell you."

Lucky jerked almost as if she'd been slapped. Whatever she'd been thinking died on the vine when she remembered why Manny had hauled her up the stairs like a limp doll. Her expression went from nervous to near panic as she realized this was the man Woody the Wire had been talking about! This was the man who would die!

"You! It would have been you!"

He saw her sway. In seconds, both he and Manny had an arm around her as they led her to the sofa near the window.

"Sit down before you fall down," Nick said sharply, angry with himself for the feelings bubbling inside his belly. He didn't want to want this woman. He didn't even know her. Men his age didn't *want* total strangers. That went with youth and carelessness that he'd left behind long ago.

Or so he thought, until Lucky Houston turned those wide green eyes his way and cast a witch's spell he couldn't resist.

"Now," he said, "what is it you have to tell me . . . other than what you've already said?"

Lucky flushed, remembering the way she'd cut him down at the bus station with little more than a glance, assuming that he'd been out to use or harm her to suit his fancy.

"You shouldn't have tried to pick me up," she said.

Manny had to stop himself from laughing. In spite of where this would all lead, it seemed only to be getting better and better.

Nick nodded. The accusation in her voice held a strong ring of truth. He smiled slightly and sank down onto a seat two cushions over from where she was sitting.

"You're right, lady. You're right. I shouldn't have done . . . or said what I did. Especially to someone who'd just gotten into town."

Then he smiled.

And Lucky forgot that she'd heard someone threaten

to kill him. She forgot that only days earlier she'd been invited to join a harem. She forgot that she was long overdue on returning to her table. All she could see, all she could think of, was that when Nick Chenault smiled, his eyes lit from within. For a heartbeat, she imagined she could see straight into his soul. And as she did, she thought that she saw a loneliness in him that matched the kind she felt.

"They're going to kill you."

His smile died. First in his eyes. Then on his lips. The skin on his face seemed to grow taut and turn ashen. He inhaled sharply. Without making a sound, he leaned toward her as she sat, pinning her with a hand on either side of the sofa behind her head until their faces were separated by the space of their breaths.

"Who the hell are you? How did you know that? Who sent you? Are you the next plant in Chenault Incorporated? What happened, woman? Did you lose your nerve and decide to switch sides?"

Manny grabbed at Nick's arm, but not in time to prevent the damage from being done. "No! No! Nicky, you don't understand. It isn't like that at all."

Nick straightened, then spun toward Manny as the fury in his voice echoed within the room.

"Like how, Manny? Tell me. Explain how someone this beautiful and this seductive suddenly shows up at my club, in the middle of this goddamned mess, with a warning, no less? How stupid does this sonofabitch who wants me dead think I am?"

The stricken look on Lucky's face was spreading.

Manny had all but dragged her here to tell what she knew and this was the way she was being treated? She doubted if she'd ever speak to him . . . or Nick again.

"Pretty stupid, as men go," Manny said quietly. "She didn't just announce this. She overheard a phone conversation in the hall when she was on break and had enough decency to come tell me, so that a man she didn't even know could be warned."

Nick flushed and turned to her. "Is this true?"

Lucky stood. She'd had just about enough of men and their selfishness to last her a lifetime. This one might be dressed in Armani suits and wear hundred-dollar cologne, but he still had the mentality of one of the patrons at Whitelaw's Bar back in Cradle Creek.

"What the hell does it matter what I say?" Lucky said. "I told you the truth once and you accused me of being some kind of spy. I don't know what's going on in your world, and after the way you've behaved, I'm not sure I care. But Manny seems to think you deserve to know, so here goes. I truly believe that if you get in your car tomorrow morning, you—and as Woody the Wire said, your breakfast—will blow sky-high."

"Well, hell," Nick said quietly, and walked to the window overlooking the Las Vegas skyline, staring blankly through the glass and out into the darkness.

"If you two will excuse me, I need to get back to my table," Lucky said as she headed for the door without waiting to be excused. "And the next time I overhear some sinister plot in this godforsaken city, I'll ignore it like everyone else who doesn't want to get involved. Then when it happens, I can read about it with my toast and coffee and feel nothing except the jelly dripping on my fingers."

The door didn't slam. But it was the firmest thump either man had ever heard.

"Nicky . . . Nicky. I think you messed up."

Nick glared. "Thank you so much for pointing that out," he said as he went for the phone.

"Who are you calling?" Manny asked.

"First Cubby, to make damn sure that neither he nor Dad get in any of the cars, then I'm calling Detective Arnold. He'll know what to do. After that . . . who knows. Maybe I'll have some crow before going to bed. It's been years since I've felt the need."

Manny sighed and shook his head as he started out the door.

"Manny."

He turned at the doorway, waiting for Nick to continue.

"Thank her for me."

"Thank her yourself, Nicky. Maybe she knows how to cook this crow you feel you should eat."

Nick rolled his eyes, and then picked up the telephone receiver and punched in the numbers to his home as Manny left, leaving him alone to consider what he'd done. He'd dreamed of this woman and had actually considered looking for her. Then Manny handed her to him on a silver platter and he attacked her with the viciousness of a lunatic.

He dropped into his chair as he waited for someone to answer the phone. So many things to do. And if Lucky Houston was to be believed, so little time.

* * *

"Your lady was right on the money," Will Arnold said. "Plastic explosives too. There wouldn't have been enough left of you to pick up and bury, boy."

Nick blanched. The bomb squad was pulling out of the gate to the estate with the explosive device still intact. And thanks to Lucky Houston, who was everything *but* his lady, Nick was intact to watch it happen.

"It was a professional job, that's for sure," the detective said. "Gives credibility to Miss Houston's statement about the man calling himself Woody the Wire. Even her description fits. I just didn't know the little bastard was back in town. Last I heard, he'd gone south . . . way south."

"As in out of the country?" Nick asked, wondering if his father could possibly be connected to South America.

Will Arnold nodded. "Yeah. Jumped bail outrunning some indictment or other out of New York State."

Nick's shock grew. "New York? I'd swear my dad has no New York connections of any kind."

"Oh, that's not how case clues usually work," the detective said. "Just because he was last working in New York doesn't mean that your father had anything going up there. Little worms like that get around. They just squiggle down deep in the dirt and disappear until the next time they're needed. Obviously someone wanted something bad to talk Woody into coming stateside."

"Obviously," Nick drawled, and turned away, unwilling to let Arnold see how rattled he'd become.

Moments later, the police were gone, leaving Nick to face the aftermath alone. He shuddered, then stuffed his hands in the pockets of his gray slacks as he walked back into the house. Although it was a warm eighty-five degrees and he was wearing a jacket over his shirt and tie, he suddenly felt cold, as if someone had walked over his grave. Which in fact, they almost had.

"Nick, are you all right?"

Paul Chenault's question was asked an octave above his normal voice level. His hands gave away the rest of his tension as he gripped the arms of his wheelchair as if it might take flight and waited for Nick to answer.

"Yes, no thanks to Woody the Wire," he finally said.

Paul blanched. He recognized that look on Nick's face. It was the same look he'd worn the day they'd buried his mother. Somewhere between disbelief and fury.

"I want to know everything about the old days."

"Why?" Paul asked, his voice just below a shout. "Do you actually believe that I'd keep secrets from you and risk endangering your life . . . and mine? Tell me you don't. For God's sake, Nicky . . . tell me you don't!"

Nick's eyes narrowed. His gaze went from off-center to meeting his father's eyes straight on.

"Of course not," he said. "But you're in here. I'm out there. I can't go into this blind. Talk to me, Daddy. It may save us both."

Paul's mouth worked. The childhood name had come out of Nick's mouth without thought. It was proof of how deeply disturbed he'd been by the events of the past twenty-four hours.

"Come have some breakfast with me. Cubby should be bringing it soon. We'll talk then," Paul promised.

"No, Dad. You talk. I'll listen."

Nick grabbed the handles of his father's chair and wheeled him toward the morning room, unable to appreciate the warm yellow glow spilling in through the stained-glass window over the table, or the bowl of red and yellow tulips Shari had put there this morning as a centerpiece. He needed answers, not ambiance.

But Cubby was slow in arriving, so they settled for coffee. They were on their second cup when Paul started to talk.

"We were kids. Stupid kids. Just out of our teens. But it was the forties. The war was just over. Everything was wide open and fair game. There was money . . . big money to be made for the ones willing to take the risks."

"Who's we, Dad?"

Paul blinked, startled to be called back from his muse. "Oh, yes. Right. There were the three of us. We laughingly called ourselves the Three Musketeers. But Dieter was the one willing to take the risks. He was the real gambler among us all. J. J. and I went along for the rides."

Paul's voice droned. Nick found himself going in and out of focus, only picking up the thread of a story just long enough to know that it would have little bearing on the situation facing them today.

And then Paul's voice changed, and his mannerisms began to indicate the nervous tension he was feeling. Nick tuned in just as his father's voice cracked from emotion.

"I just couldn't do it," Paul said, and looked to his son for understanding. "It was a scam. A dangerous, foolhardy scam. I'd already met your mother. I didn't want to ruin what chances I had with her. You understand, don't you?"

"What, Dad? Exactly what was it that Dieter Marx was into?"

"He was going to rip off the mob."

"Good lord," Nick muttered. "That's a hell of a friend."

"I told you. We were young and foolish."

"How was this heist supposed to work?" Nick asked.

"Dieter knew lots of people in Vegas. He found out that one of the councilmen was on the take, big time. He learned that there was a land deal going down, and that the councilman had given the mob some inside information that gave them the upper hand in obtaining it. They needed land to expand their operations here in Vegas. The councilman was willing to help them get what they wanted for a price. A big price."

Nick's lips thinned. This was getting worse by the minute.

"Go on," he urged his father. "Get to the point. How big a price, and why should Dieter Marx hate you because of a crooked politician?"

Paul sighed. "Because it was a quarter-million-dollar payoff and because when it all went down, Dieter wound up with the money, but had accidentally killed the councilman in the process. I knew he was going to rob him, but J. J. and I refused to help. He was all alone. He had no one covering his back. If he had, the councilman might not have died, and Dieter wouldn't have had to run."

"That's bull," Nick said shortly. "Dieter Marx sounds like a petty thief. A man who would rather steal than work for what he wants. I have no sympathy for someone like that."

Paul blanched. "Then you should know that I fall somewhere between Dieter and the mob in guilt," he said quietly. "Because after it was over, Dieter came to J. J. and me. He wanted us to hide him. We refused. He was furious. We fought, and then all of a sudden in the middle of the fight, we heard sirens. Dieter panicked and ran. Without the money. So then he was wanted for murder by the police, and for robbery by the mob, and he had nothing to show for it but the blood on his hands. He was running, but for all intents and purposes, he was already dead. If one of them didn't get him, the other was bound to."

Nick realized that his father had left out one very important detail regarding the story. And he could tell by the way Paul kept avoiding his look that there was definitely more to tell.

"What happened next?" he urged.

"We heard that Dieter was headed for South America. And then we heard later that he'd been killed. That's the last time anyone ever mentioned his name."

"But a fight between friends isn't enough for a man to want to destroy you . . . is it?"

Paul didn't answer.

"Dad, what happened to the money?"

Paul looked up. There were tears in his eyes as he answered.

"I kept it. It was what I used to get Club 52 off the ground."

"Sonofabitch!"

Nick bolted from his chair, unable to face his father's agonized expression.

"But I paid it back later . . . with interest. It was done anonymously. As far as the mob was concerned, Dieter Marx had just paid off a debt. But I couldn't fix the other thing, Nicky. I couldn't bring the man back to life that

Dieter killed. As far as I know, dead or alive, there's still a warrant out for Dieter's arrest."

"So you and this J. J. made out like bandits while your buddy was dodging bullets and bad guys. It would make a hell of a movie, Dad."

Paul grimaced. "No. Actually, the presence of the money actually finished breaking up the Three Musketeers for good. J. J. took to drinking and gambling. I bought off so many of his bad debts that I began to feel like his father. Finally, one day we'd both had one too many and wound up punching each other in the nose and calling it quits. To this day, I haven't seen or heard from him, either."

"So you got rich and lost every friend you had in the process." Nick rubbed his hands over his face. "Now, for the rest of my life, every time I walk into the club, I'm going to remember that it cost you more than money to build it."

Paul looked away. He couldn't argue with his son's estimation of his dirty past. It was no more than what he'd told himself for the last forty-something years.

"Hell, at least one thing's for sure," Nick drawled. "If Dieter Marx is alive, I'll bet my next dollar that he's the one pulling the plugs on Chenault Incorporated. I'd say, right or wrong, he probably thinks he has reason to hate you."

Cubby came into the room carrying a tray of food. "Anyone hungry?"

"I'm going to the club," Nick said. "Cubby, take care of Dad. This thing's a long shot from being over."

Nick left without saying anything more. And as the

door slammed behind him, Cubby saw his employer wilt in his chair. Paul's shoulders slumped as the lines in his face deepened drastically.

"What's wrong?" Cubby asked. "Are you sick? Do you want me to call Nick back?"

"No. For God's sake, let him go. I'll be lucky if he ever comes back." Then Paul buried his face in his hands. "Oh, Cubby. Have you ever wished you could live your life over again?"

Cubby sighed. His huge hands gently shifted Paul Chenault to a straighter position in his chair and then he wheeled him toward the table and the food waiting to be eaten.

"Of course not," Cubby said. "Because we are who we are, we'd just make the same mistakes all over again. I don't want to experience my youthful stupidity more than once, thank you."

Paul managed a weak laugh. "You're probably right. But I hope to God that my youthful stupidity doesn't get my son killed."

"Nick can take care of himself . . . and you, boss. Eat. You need to keep up your strength."

Paul had no option but to obey. He wasn't going anywhere.

6

"There. What do you think?"

Lucky held up the mirror so that Fluffy could see, smiling at the old woman's joy as she saw herself in a different light. The new hair color Fluffy had coerced Lucky into applying had done wonders for her appearance. It was no longer streaked and spotted like a molting retriever. Now she was one color all over. Audacious red. Somehow it suited her.

"Ooh, honey, if I squint just right, I can almost make myself believe I look good at eighty-four."

Lucky laughed and impulsively hugged the old woman's stooped shoulders. "You look fantastic," she said. "What next?"

Fluffy grinned. "I think we need to go out for lunch. Show off my new look, don't you?"

Lucky frowned. "We'd have to take a cab. I don't think you'd like riding the bus."

"Pooh!" Fluffy said. "I've got a car. I'll drive."

Lucky knew she was staring, but she couldn't seem to stop. The shock of Fluffy's announcement didn't bear consideration.

"How long has it been since you drove?" she asked, thinking of the hectic traffic on the city streets.

"Not so long," Fluffy muttered, as she began hobbling toward her bedroom to change. "It was just after the inauguration. We had a hell of a party. I danced all night. Come help me pick out something to wear."

Lucky complied. Arguing with the woman was futile. She'd been alone too long and too set in her ways to accept anything but her own ideas.

With each passing day, their friendship was growing from casual to something deeper.

"The party was held at the Flamingo, you know." Fluffy continued her story as Lucky followed her into the room. "All the pretty boys from Hollywood came. And the women. There were three women to every man. Just the way they liked it."

Lucky nodded, watching with a nervous eye as Fluffy sorted through dress after dress, costume after costume, praying that she chose one without feathers. And then something Fluffy said made her think to ask.

"Fluffy!"

"Hmmm?" the old woman said, as she held a black satin dress beneath her chin, squinting her eyes once more to get the full effect of her new red hair against the sensuous fabric.

"Exactly which president was it who was being inaugurated?"

"Oh! Eisenhower, of course. But it wasn't his real inauguration, you know. It was a mock one to coincide with the one he was having in D.C. I just love men in uniform, don't you?"

Lucky took the dress from Fluffy's hands. "Are you telling me that your car hasn't been driven since Eisenhower took office?"

Fluffy pursed her lips. The astonishment on Lucky's face was beginning to be aggravating.

"That's what I said. That's what I meant. Now come along. Do let's hurry. I'm starving."

"I just had a brainstorm," Lucky said. "Why don't we take a cab? Then we can talk instead of worrying about traffic and stoplights."

Fluffy considered the idea, and then nodded, realizing that it had more merit than her own plan.

"And after we're through, you can show me where you work," Fluffy said. It would be like the good old days. Hitting the clubs with her friends. She smiled at Lucky and patted her on the cheek. It was good to have friends.

Lucky looked down and pretended to pick a dust bunny off of the shoes Fluffy tossed behind her. Fluffy was old, however, not blind. She sensed the change in the young girl's behavior.

"What's wrong, dear?" she asked.

"It's nothing," Lucky said. "I just don't think it's such a good idea to go to Club 52. I might not be working there much longer."

Fluffy's eyes glittered with indignation. She dropped the dress she was holding onto the back of a chair.

"Why on earth not? And don't tell me you're about to

be fired because you can't do the job. I've seen what you can do with a deck of cards, remember?"

Lucky shrugged, remembering their weekend card game. She also remembered that Fluffy cheated outrageously.

"Sit, girl. Now talk. It helps, believe me."

Lucky sank down on the bed with a dejected sigh. The slump of her shoulders matched the droop of her mouth. Fluffy frowned and sat down beside her, patting her hand as she urged her to continue.

"It's all a mess there," Lucky said. "Someone seems to have a grudge against the owner and I had the bad luck to get myself involved. After today and the confrontation we had, I don't know whether I've got a job tomorrow or not."

Fluffy sighed. Some things never changed. "Maybe it's not as bad as you think."

Lucky rolled her eyes. "No, actually it's worse. I'm just an optimist."

Fluffy laughed. Audacious red curls bobbed against the back of her neck as she slapped her knee in delight.

"Honey, whatever happens, something tells me you'll do all right." And when Lucky would have argued, Fluffy cut her off. "No, hear me out! I'm always right. It's a prerequisite of old age."

This time, Lucky was the one to chuckle. "All right, so get yourself dressed. I'll change too, and when I come back down to call the cab, we'll decide where we're going to eat."

Worrying about what Fluffy LaMont wore in public

was no longer an issue. She could wear feathers and diamonds for all Lucky cared. It was the woman's friendship
that she treasured.

"I feel like Italian," Fluffy muttered, as Lucky started
out the door. "So . . . if we're going to eat pasta, I need to
dress accordingly. Hmmm . . . I wonder what I did with
my gondolier's hat? It would look fabulous with my green
silk pajamas. Maybe it's upstairs."

Lucky remembered the tour Fluffy had given her of the
floor between her apartment and the ground floor where
Fluffy now lived. It was a veritable museum of clothing
from another era. Lucille LaMont clearly didn't believe in
throwing anything away.

As the old woman headed for the stairs to unearth her
treasures, Lucky grinned. She wouldn't miss this lunch for
the world.

On his way up to Nick's office, Manny saw the mis-
matched females enter Club 52. Between the fashion
statement that Fluffy LaMont had chosen to make, and
Lucky Houston's height and beauty, they were an impossible pair to miss. He grinned, and then took the rest of
the stairs up two at a time.

He opened the door and shouted, "Nicky! Come
quick," then disappeared without waiting to see if Nick
even heard.

He had. And after the events of the past few days, he
felt obligated to hurry. He was ready for anything except
the two women he saw cutting a swath through the
crowded floor.

"Isn't that Lucky?" he asked, and felt the same familiar jolt of interest he always got when she was around. Her sexy saunter and that black crown of hair were unmistakable. And then he leaned a little farther over the mezzanine for a better look. "But who on earth is that with her?"

Manny grinned. "Hell of a hat, isn't it, boss?"

Nick returned the smile. "I think I saw Errol Flynn wear one like it in an old pirate movie once. Who is she?"

"That, my young friend, is the one and only Lucille LaMont. Fluffy, to her fans. In the old days she was one of the hottest exotic dancers on the strip."

Nick shook his head. "I thought she was dead."

"Doesn't look much like it," Manny said. "Look! She's giving some of your patrons a little teaser from her old routine."

Nick chuckled as the aging lady flirtatiously slid the sleeve of her green silk jacket off her shoulder and then managed a small bump and grind just to prove that she could. A round of clapping accompanied her stunt, and Nick knew that it was probably time to make an appearance before someone taunted her to "take it all off" and she did.

Lucky tried not to blush, but it was impossible not to be affected by Fluffy's outrageous behavior. Before she had time to regain her composure, she saw her boss coming down the stairs. And as he walked in their direction, she felt an odd sense of being cornered, although the room was full of people.

The urge to run was strong. She just wasn't certain if it came from disdain for his way of life, or fear that she might actually grow to like the man. Whichever it was, she hated to admit, even to herself, that he caused any kind of reaction within her at all. She rolled her eyes and muttered to Fluffy beneath her breath, "Here comes my boss."

Fluffy abandoned her intrigued audience and spun, not disguising her interest in the dashing young man who was headed their way.

"Lucky, you little miser! You didn't tell me you worked for such a dreamboat. No wonder you've been keeping him to yourself." She batted her eyes at Nick in a way that said everything about her past, and offered her hand in a flirtatious gesture.

Nick winked and then smiled, looking at the blue veins and swollen knuckles as if they were the most appealing sight he'd had all day. With a dignitary's aplomb, he lowered his head and pressed a gentle kiss just between her wrist and the two-karat diamond on her finger.

"Welcome, ladies."

Lucky was in shock. Other than the bus station, she'd had only one other meeting with this man, and at neither time had he shown this side of his character. "The Pimp" had a twinkle in his eye she would do well to ignore.

Fluffy batted her eyelashes and then elbowed Lucky. "Honey . . . aren't you going to introduce us?"

Lucky took a deep breath. There was nothing to do but get this over with . . . and fast.

"Lucille . . . this is my boss, Nick Chenault. Mr. Chenault, my landlady and friend, Lucille LaMont. We've just finished lunch. She asked to see where I worked."

It all came out in a rush. Only after she'd finished did

she think to catch her breath, and then told herself it was what she'd said, and not who she was with, that had taken her breath away.

Lucille preened. "Please, call me Fluffy. Everyone does, you know."

"Fluffy . . . it's an honor to meet you."

Fluffy couldn't help but notice that although Nick was talking to her, he kept looking at Lucky. This was getting better by the minute.

Lucky started to fidget beneath Nick's interest. "I guess we'd better—"

"Oh, no. At least . . . not yet," Fluffy begged. "I want to play a little roulette, honey. It's been years since I got out to do this. Come join me. I'll bank us."

An odd expression slid across Lucky's face. "No. I don't gamble. You go ahead, Fluffy. I won't be far."

Nick couldn't help but be intrigued by his prettiest dealer's remark. She worked in a casino, and yet she stood there claiming she didn't gamble?

Then he instinctively realized what she meant. Where Lucky Houston worked, the house's money was at stake, not hers. *How odd*, he thought, and wondered what had made her so cautious and bitter.

Fluffy hobbled toward the roulette wheel, masking the limp from her aching knee by adding a little more sway to her walk. When Lucky would have followed, Nick caught her by the arm, and then quickly dropped his hold when he saw the expression in her eyes turn cooler than usual.

So . . . my Lucky Lady, you have more secrets. You don't gamble, and you don't like to be touched. He gave her the space she seemed to need and pretended to ignore what she'd done.

"Quite a friend you have there," Nick said quietly.

"Yes, she is," Lucky answered, pretending interest in the jacket buttons on her blue pantsuit.

"Lucky."

Her name seemed to vibrate on his tongue. She shivered and looked over his shoulder rather than at his face when she answered.

"Yes, sir?"

"Yesterday the bomb squad removed enough plastic explosives from my car to level a city block."

She turned pale. Her voice shook as she stared at the intensity on his face. "Oh, no! Then it *was* true!"

"You saved my life. I owe you more than you'll ever know."

A couple passing behind her, boisterous from a recent win, bumped into Lucky and sent her careening into Nick's arms. His chest was solid but warm, and when she realized that she could hear the steady thump of his heartbeat, she jerked away as if she'd been shot.

"You don't owe me anything but the wages that I earn."

The words trembled on her lips as she tried to think of an excuse to escape. If she stayed, she would have to admit, at least to herself, that he'd held her a little too long before turning her loose.

"I wish I could take back everything I've ever said to you," he said quietly.

Lucky shrugged. "It doesn't matter, Mr. Chenault."

Nick frowned. "It matters. And dammit . . . don't call me Mr. Chenault!"

There was a look in his eyes she wasn't sure she recognized. It was almost . . . if she didn't know better . . . she could swear that he . . . *No way!* she told herself. *He's not interested . . . not in me . . . not like that.*

"So, what do I call you?"

"I'd prefer darling," he said with a mischievous grin. "But I'll settle for Nick."

Lucky blushed and looked away, thrown off balance by the shift in their conversation. In the space of minutes, they'd gone from antagonists, to employer/employee, to something she wasn't ready to consider.

"I'd better go check on Fluffy," she said. "I don't want her to break the bank."

Nick looked toward the roulette wheel. From here he could see the sweep of that white feather in the woman's hat rising above the heads of the crowd.

"She seems all right. Besides, from the size of the crowd around the table, it looks as if she's good for business. While she's playing, would you join me for a glass of wine?"

Oh, no! He *was* interested. But to what extent? Lucky knew nothing about his personal life. He could be the world's most dangerous playboy. The last thing she wanted or needed was to fall for a man like that. He was too rich and too available, and she was too lonely and too vulnerable.

"No way," she said. "Not even if it means my job."

"Why not?" Nick was more than a little stunned by her constant refusals.

"Because if I'm seen with you, then everybody will think I'm fair game." Her voice shook, but the surge of emotion could not stop the power of what she said. "Someday I'll be somebody's special girl, but I don't want to be everybody's girl first. Thanks, but no thanks."

With that, she walked away, leaving him alone in the huge crowd of people, with the truth of her words ringing in his ears.

"And she says she doesn't gamble," he muttered. "Finding someone special is the biggest risk of all." He watched her progress until she'd reached the roulette wheel, and then he walked away, hating himself for not being able to take that wistful expression off of her face.

As Lucky struggled to push her way through the crowd around Fluffy, another man approached her from behind. Only he lacked the charm of Nick Chenault, and the finesse to ask for what he so obviously wanted.

When she felt a hand slide beneath her jacket and then fingers cupping the curve of her hips before giving an uninvited squeeze, shock gave way to fury. She pivoted and came face-to-face with Steve Lucas. He wore a smirk he should have been hiding.

"How dare you!" Then she lowered the strident tone of her voice and cast nervous glances around her to see if she'd been heard. In Lucky's experience, being stared at came right before gossip. She didn't need any more trouble in her life.

Steve grinned. He'd known that the crowd would hide his behavior and had easily dared.

"Don't play innocent with me, honey. I saw you flirting with the boss. Forget him, baby. I'm better in bed . . . believe me."

Lucky was so furious she couldn't even answer. Her

anger was instantaneous and so intense that she had doubled her fists and was actually considering throwing a punch when she remembered where she was.

Steve thought he was on smooth ground. That she'd taken his gesture as the invitation he'd meant it to be. So when she answered, his first mistake was in believing that the soft tone of her voice indicated interest, and not the overwhelming fury that it actually was.

"I don't flirt," she said. "And I don't care where I am or what I'm doing, if you ever touch me like that again, you'll be sorry."

He sneered. "Honey, you're the one who's gonna be sorry. Besides, you can't do anything to hurt me."

She took a step forward. Her breath hissed hot against his face as she whispered softly, "Oh, yes I can, Steve Lucas. I can, and I will hurt you. In places you don't want to consider."

Steve's eyes widened. The threat was unexpected, but unmistakable. "You teasing bitch," he said, and tried a smile to mask his shock. It never got past a grimace.

Lucky didn't move, nor bother to answer. She simply stared, her green eyes blazing, until Steve started to wonder if she was as deadly as her expression supposed. When the color of her eyes turned to a glitter so cold they looked black, he began to sweat. Unwilling to admit that she'd rattled him, he managed a shrug, then walked away.

The moment he was gone, she began to shake. Her stomach tilted, and her legs went weak. Steve Lucas's constant harassment was just more of the same from her life in Cradle Creek. Something she'd hoped to leave behind.

But this last stunt had brought back every memory of every bad incident she had ever endured. Only this time, she had no sisters waiting at home to back her up. She's never felt as alone in her life.

Without giving Fluffy a second thought, she bolted for the ladies' room, hoping for some solitude in which to recover her sanity. Her space had just been raped by a man who acted as if he would have liked to continue the act for real.

Just inside the lounge, Nick was talking to one of his father's old friends, when a flash of blue caught his eye.

Lucky! And the way she was moving told him something was wrong. Instinctively, he followed, unwilling to give up on a woman who seemed to have given up on men.

"Lucky!"

The last thing she needed now was to hear her boss's voice. Compelled by the command in his tone, she stopped, and then stared down at the pattern in the carpet beneath her feet as if she couldn't get enough of the design.

"What's wrong?" he asked.

She shrugged and stared more intently, unwilling for him to see her upset.

"Someday you're going to have to trust someone. I wish it could be me," he said softly.

It was the shock of what he said that made her look up. Trust a man? Not likely. Not after growing up within the debacle Johnny Houston had made of their lives as well as his own.

"I can take care of myself."

He instantly took her statement to mean that something or someone had hurt her. Maybe not physically, but the invasion was written all over her face.

"What the hell happened to you?"

The urge to tell was overwhelming. To lay Steve Lucas's harassment at the feet of Nick Chenault would be the height of luxury. But the years and the people in Cradle Creek had done a number on Johnny Houston's daughters. Trust would not come easily.

"Nothing," she finally said.

"You're lying."

Lucky drew back as if she'd been slapped.

"It's none of your business," she said shortly. "You're my boss, not my keeper."

"Then I am applying for the job," he said, as anger deepened his voice. "Someone needs to look out for you. It may as well be me."

Lucky couldn't believe her ears. "You're crazy. I don't need looking after. Especially by a man who picks up his women at bus stations."

Nick flushed. Her taunt hit home. He would never be able to live that stunt down.

"Believe it or not, I was waiting for my father's valet. I'd been there nearly four hours. I was hot. I was bored. I opened my big mouth in a moment of weakness and I don't seem to be able to put it behind me."

Lucky's eyes flashed wild and green. Steve Lucas was forgotten in the heat of new anger.

"Well my lord but you're a sweet-talkin' man," she drawled. "So you got so bored that you decided to hit on

the hicks who crawled off the buses? Do you do that often . . . or was it a one-time experience?"

Nick groaned. This was getting worse by the moment.
"That's not what I meant and you know it," he said, not
realizing that his own voice was getting louder and louder
with each word.

She glared. He stared. And Fluffy came hobbling into
the hall and capped off the moment by announcing: "I
heard shouts. May I join in, or is this a private fight?"

Lucky rolled her eyes and stomped past both of them.

"I'm going to call a cab. I'll wait for you out front," she
told Fluffy.

Nick shoved his hands in his pockets and tried not to
throttle her on her way past.

Fluffy grinned. "It was a pleasure to meet you, Nick."

All he could do was nod.

Then Fluffy LaMont did something unusual: she med-
dled. "I don't know why," she said softly, patting Nick's
arm in a motherly manner, "but she doesn't trust people
easily. And she doesn't trust men at all. If you're interested,
you're going to need more than an attraction to keep it
alive. You're going to need a jackpot full of patience."

Nick slumped against the wall and combed his hands
through his hair. He should have been embarrassed by his
lack of composure, but he was too far gone in the moment to care.

"I don't know how I feel, other than the constant need
to dodge," he said.

"Do sparks fly like that every time you two are together?" Fluffy asked.

He shrugged. "So far."

She smiled. "Sparks start fires, you know," she said. Then she patted his arm. "I've got a friend and a cab to catch."

Despair stole the light from his eyes. He could use a friend right now. Someone wanted him dead, and the first woman who had piqued his interest in years kept telling him to get lost.

Fluffy paused at the doorway and then turned. A mischievous smile lit her eyes as she put a hand on her hip and let the green silk jacket to her lounge pajamas droop just the least little bit.

"Oh, Nicky." When she was certain she had his full attention, she finished with a bad rendition of an old Mae West line. "Come up and see us sometime. We're in the book."

With a dash of feathered plumes and green silk, she left Nick standing in the hall with a silly grin on his face. For now, the secondhand invitation was enough to get him by.

He remembered that he still hadn't learned what—or who—had sent Lucky running from the floor in fear.

Hours later, Lucky was still pacing her apartment, mortified by the fact that she'd shouted at her boss, and had been near to an actual brawl with Steve Lucas.

"My God. I have the job I've always wanted, and I'm afraid to go to work. It can't get any worse."

"And now . . . the news at ten," said the voice on the television set. Her one and only purchase of the day: a nineteen-inch portable color television. It was new, and it was all hers.

She sighed with frustration and absently eyed it as the announcer's voice caught her attention. She stretched her bare feet and legs out on the sofa, picked up the remote control to adjust the volume, and straightened the hem of the T-shirt she was wearing. It was old and faded from pink to near white, and suited her mood to a T.

With the sound low enough to cushion her headache, she picked up her hairbrush and began to pull it through the thick length of her hair, hoping that the repetitive massage against her scalp would do what hours of pacing had not been able to do: give her some relief.

Events of the program came and went without note until a man's face was suddenly pictured across the screen. The reporter began to speak, but Lucky didn't need to hear an identification of the man. They'd already met. In the hallway of Club 52. Right after he'd plotted Nick's murder.

"Today the body of Woodrow Mosconi, better known as Woody the Wire, was found floating in the pool of the motel where he'd been staying. Though he had registered under an alias, the police were able to quickly identify the man due to his lengthy record. Believed to have been involved, both directly as well as indirectly, in more than twenty bombings over the last fifteen years, the hit man will go to his grave with the secrets of his accomplices' names.

"Because of the large roll of thousand-dollar bills found shoved in the back of Mosconi's throat, the police are speculating that Mosconi had either double-crossed someone or fouled-up on a job he'd been hired to do. In the old days, symbolic gestures such as this were intended as a warning to the next man who tried to cross the mob. In other words, people who talked too much paid a high price for the luxury."

The hairbrush fell from Lucky's hands as her heart hammered against her chest. He'd talked. And she'd told. And now the man was dead!

"Oh, God! Oh, God! It's him. It's him."

The knock on her door coincided with a commercial for building materials. So for several seconds, Lucky thought that the hammering on her door was the carpenter on TV. It was when she heard someone call her name that she hit the mute button on the remote and then jumped from the sofa and turned out the lights. Her first thought followed the train of what she'd just learned. *He told before he died and they've already found me!*

It only stood to reason that she might be right, because she knew that Fluffy wouldn't climb these stairs in the dark, and there was no one in Las Vegas who should come calling on her. A spurt of fear accompanied her racing heart as she stood in the corner in the dark and listened . . . waiting for the sound of receding footsteps that never came.

But her efforts at concealment had been too little, too late. The lights had been on when Nick had walked up the three flights of stairs. He had knocked until his knuckles hurt and then he watched in amazement as the lights suddenly went out. And all during this time he'd heard not a peep out of her. Suddenly the anger and frustration that had been building up all day got to him.

"Dammit, Lucky, it's just me. It's Nick . . . your boss. Open the door, for God's sake. I need to talk to you."

Lucky's bare feet danced in a little circle in the darkness as she tried not to panic. Oh, God! Not Nick Chenault!

What on earth was he doing here? She couldn't face him. Not now. Not dressed like this.

"Lucky . . . please. I stopped downstairs and spoke to Fluffy first. She knows I'm here, so you're safe. I'm not going to hurt you."

It was the horror of the newscast and fear of being alone, accompanied by the fact that Fluffy knew he was here, that sent her to the door.

Nick was almost at the point of giving up when he heard the slide of a dead-bolt. He held his breath and waited as the door opened, an inch at a time. She was a darker silhouette against the room's shadows, highlighted only from the intermittent flash of the light on the television screen behind her.

"He's dead, Nick. The man who was going to kill you. He's dead. I just heard it on the news. What if he told someone about seeing me before he died?"

"Sonofabitch." The curse was an apologetic ramification of his anger. Regret overwhelmed him. The reason for his arrival was moot. She already knew.

Without thinking, he took two steps forward and pulled her into his arms. She was mute and shaking, and from what he could tell, near the point of collapse as she pressed herself against him like a leaf trembling in a gale wind.

He kicked the door shut with his heel and felt her sigh, as if she'd given up a fight he knew nothing about. And when he knew that she wasn't going to rage at him for coming too close, he began to let himself feel the woman he was holding.

Hair. It was his first and strongest impression. It fell across his hands and down her back in a thick, satin veil. Unable to resist the temptation, he tested its depths with the flat of his hands, and groaned silently to himself. He'd known it would be as sensuous as the woman to whom it belonged. And then his hands raked over the surface of her arms and he had to stifle a groan. *Good God! Her skin is even softer.*

Lucky's good sense returned when his hands started roaming her body. Every warning signal in her head went off. She had to put some distance between them, for more reasons than she cared to consider.

"Why did you come?" she asked, and pushed him away.

Her question shocked him. He'd lived with her image for so long, even before he'd known her name, that she'd long ago ceased to be a stranger to him. Regretfully, he acknowledged that she could not feel the same.

"I wanted to be the one to tell you about Mosconi," he said, and tried not to care when she stepped out of his arms.

"Oh." And then she remembered the way that she'd thrown herself into his arms and wanted to die of embarrassment. She moved quickly to turn on a light. "I'm sorry. I didn't mean to do that."

The light revealed more of Lucky Houston than he'd been prepared to see. In that moment, with the jut of her breasts an impudent match to the thrust of her chin, and more long bare legs than he'd ever seen in his life, he wanted. He needed. He could almost say desired, but this feeling she evoked in him was too new. Too scary. Too final to consider.

"Do what?" he asked, and then cleared his throat. He'd never been this ill at ease around a female in his life and resented her for making him feel that way.

"Go all weepy and helpless. I'm not normally like that. I always take care of myself."

"So you've told me before," he said, and smiled to soften the rebuke.

But he remembered the way she'd flown into his arms, and knew by that action alone that she had been badly shaken by the news of Mosconi's death. After the constant rejections he'd suffered from this woman, he suspected she had to have been terrified to have let him this close.

Nick waited for her to make the next move. He found himself lost in the aura of the woman before him.

Good lord, Lucky thought, as she suddenly remembered her skimpy attire too late for concealment, and almost crossed her arms across her chest in a futile effort to hide what he was already seeing.

The urge to lock herself into another room was overwhelming. While her T-shirt went almost to her knees, she wore little else and saw that he knew it. Bikini panties seemed a flimsy barrier between this dark prince and the desire that he chose not to hide.

"I think you'd better leave," she said.

He wasn't prepared for the rudeness of her request.

"It would be my pleasure," he growled. "And don't bother to see me to the door. I can find my own way out."

Lucky sighed. "I didn't mean to be rude," she said. "It's just that . . . I don't need any complications in my life."

Nick frowned. "Lady . . . you don't know the meaning of the word." And when she glared at him, he got mad.

The whole day had been a bust, and when he'd tried to do a good deed, it had only served to make things worse. "For two cents I'd show you—"

"Don't you dare," Lucky warned, and doubled her fists.

He grinned. She looked less like a fighter than anyone he'd ever seen. "Never dare a gambler," he whispered, and pulled her into his arms.

He hadn't meant to do anything but shake her. Just a little. And just once. But her head fell back, and her lips were too close to ignore. The contact came unexpectedly, and it would have been difficult to say who was the most shocked. Nick for having crossed a line she'd asked him not to cross, or Lucky for letting him cross it.

What started out as exploration ended in a breathless gasp and shaking hands.

Nick was the first to stop. Lucky was the first to pull back. His feet refused to move, but hers couldn't take her far away fast enough. When she was on the other side of the room, crossing her arms around her waist to keep herself from coming apart at the seams, he found his voice.

"Don't make me apologize," he warned, eyeing the defensive look she was wearing once more. An apology for what just happened would be a lie. He wasn't one bit sorry. "Will you be all right, Lucky?"

She didn't know whether he was referring to the news about Woody the Wire, or the kiss that they'd shared. But either way, the answer still fit.

"No. I doubt if I'll ever be all right again. Get out, Nick. Thank you for coming. Thank you for caring. Now get the hell out."

Nick grinned. "This thing between us scares the hell out

of me too," he said, and left before she could refute the inference he'd made about the change in their relationship.

When she heard his car start up, she bolted for the door and turned every lock with a firm twist. But it was too late to lock out the damage that had already been done.

His kiss had been like the prince's kiss that had awakened Sleeping Beauty, and Lucky was aching in places she'd never known existed. But this was no fairy tale. It was a nightmare. She couldn't fall for a man like Nick Chenault. He was no prince. He was a gambler, just like Johnny.

One gambler had almost ruined the beginning of her life. She couldn't let another ruin what was left.

7

Lucky fought the covers of her bed while struggling with a nightmare. The bad dream she was having was an old, ugly memory from her past that kept her hanging in the twilight between fantasy and reality while she cried along with the pain.

You can't make me cry. You'll never make me cry.

Long black braids had whipped across Lucky's baby cheeks, stinging her lips and sending tears to her eyes as she bent down and angrily hurled a handful of rocks at the boys who had followed her home from school.

As a first-grader, trying to adjust to her second school in a single year had taught her much. Being a gambler's daughter in a poverty-stricken town like Cradle Creek was something of which to be ashamed. Every day was a fight for survival.

Your daddy is a joker. Your daddy is a joker.

The old, childhood taunt unconsciously puddled real

tears beneath her eyelids as she slept. Crying was a thing her conscious self would never have allowed. But the boys' foolish rhymes had coincided with her shame and her father's passion—a deck of cards and a wager yet to be made. At seven years of age, Lucky had been no match for their wit.

Restlessly, she tossed upon the bed, trying to escape the memories in the dream, just as she'd tried to escape the boys all those years ago. The sheet covering her body tightened another hitch around her legs, holding her firmer in its clutch, and drawing her deeper and deeper into the nightmare that had taken her back to her youth, to the time in Cradle Creek when every day was a test of endurance.

As the dream continued to play out, Lucky jerked, an unconscious reaction to the pain of a rock peppering the back of her leg that one of the boys had thrown. And just as if it were happening all over again, she felt the pain of her bare toe as it caught on the tip of a rock in the road and sent her sprawling in the dust, only feet from her front door.

Lucky's arms flew outward, but it was too late now, as it had been that day, to catch herself from falling. Moments later, blood began oozing from her bruised toe and scraped knees as the boys taunts continued to fall.

If you was so lucky then how come you hurt yourself?

Lucky moaned and rolled over on her stomach, burying her face beneath the pillow, much in the same way that she'd hidden her face in her hands that day long ago.

Lucky Houston ain't got no luck at all. All's you got is a no-count daddy who cheats at cards.

My daddy doesn't cheat! My daddy doesn't cheat!

But her shrieks of rage went unheeded as the boys continued their vicious chant.

And then out of nowhere, like a setting hen after the fox who'd gotten into her nest, came a long-legged girl with her red hair flying. It was her older sister, Queen, a twelve-year-old child who already had the fearless heart of a woman twice her age.

Git! Git! Go home where you belong, you little cowards. Look at the lot of you! Picking on one little girl like a pack of dogs. You ought to be ashamed!

Lucky thrashed atop the bed as she watched in her dream while the boys ran away. She could almost feel Queenie's breath on her cheeks . . . see the look of concern on her face as she wiped at the blood on her baby sister's knees. It was so vivid . . . much too vivid to be borne.

Lucky kicked restlessly, and the sheet slid to the end of the bed. She sighed and almost smiled, waiting for the weightless feeling that would come from being carried in her big sister's arms. The dream was so real that she imagined that she actually felt Queenie's hands sliding beneath her knees and around her shoulders. While she lay waiting for the gentle whispers of remorse, her dream went black, like a television screen that just lost its power.

Queenie!

Lucky sat up in bed as tears continued to streak her cheeks. She looked around the room in sleepy confusion for Queenie, but the sister who'd come to her rescue was gone, along with the nightmare.

"Good grief. Where did that come from?" Lucky groaned and rolled out of bed.

Her bare feet made no noise as the aging Persian carpet in her bedroom muffled her steps. Her T-shirt was damp and sticking to her body with rude persistence. Without thinking, she yanked if off and dropped it on the back of a chair as she entered the kitchen.

Now, wearing nothing but bikini panties and a waist-length cloak of hair that she wadded into a loose rope and pulled over her shoulder, she took a can of soda from the refrigerator and popped the top. The spritz of carbonation that fizzed out the opening tickled her nose when she lifted the can to drink. As the cold, sweet liquid was sliding down her throat, Lucky absently ran the frosty aluminum against her heated body, letting it glide over her forehead, her cheeks, and then down to the valley between her breasts.

A glance at the clock told her that dawn was little more than a thought away. But after that nightmare, returning to bed was unthinkable. She plopped into a chair beside the living room window, set the can of soft drink on the windowsill, and then rested her chin in her hands as she pulled the curtains aside and stared moodily out into the burgeoning light of daybreak.

"Damn you, Johnny. You sure did a number on us."

Then she grimaced. Blaming her father was futile. He was dead and buried. He'd blamed his lifetime of bad fortune on losing the "Houston Luck," when all it had really amounted to was a gambling addiction.

She'd heard his story all of her life. How, as a young

man, he'd lost a family heirloom—his grandfather's gold pocket watch—in a crooked poker game. He'd blamed everyone, including his best friend, for the loss.

Lucky sighed and took another drink of her soda, then made a face when she realized it was getting warm. Unable to shake the dream, her mind returned to the past as quickly as the soft drink went down her throat. The memory was so fresh that she could almost hear herself, as a child, making promises impossible to keep.

I'll find our "luck," Johnny. One day when I'm all grown up, I'll find that watch and bring it home. Then we won't have to be hungry anymore.

Tears burned the back of her throat and nose. She could almost hear her father's laughter.

"Dammit!" Lucky bolted from the chair. She didn't have time to sit there and feel sorry for herself about things that couldn't be changed. She had enough to worry about without stewing on old problems that would never be resolved. Someone was trying to murder her boss. And while he was dodging hit men and bullets, she was finding herself forced to dodge his attentions.

She stomped into the kitchen with the lukewarm soda still in her hand. "If we're not careful, neither of us will survive," she mumbled to herself.

Refusing to consider that what she'd just said was an admission of growing feelings for a man she didn't trust, she dumped her half-empty can of soda in the sink, picked up her T-shirt as she walked past, and headed for the bath. Figuratively speaking, if she couldn't forget the past, she could at least wash it away.

Reluctant to turn on a light and let reality into the room, Lucky readied for her bath in the dark. She wound the length of her hair upon her head, fastening it with a handful of pins while her bathwater ran. When the tub was full, she stepped out of her panties and into the water, letting it touch her in a way that no man had ever done.

She lowered herself slowly, careful not to slosh over the sides. And when she was completely submerged, with only her head above the water, she let go of the anger and the pain and was finally able to relax. Minutes later, she was in a state of complete and silent satisfaction.

Then, with her guard down, the memory of Nick Chenault's embrace came calling. She groaned and pressed her legs tightly together in reflex to the surge of desire that feathered through her belly. But desire didn't stop her from remembering how his broad chest and strong arms had felt against her breasts. Or how his manhood had thrust against her, pressing her T-shirt to her panties, refusing to be ignored. And how devastating and frightening the kiss that they'd shared had been compared to the gentleness of his hands upon her body.

A different kind of warmth began to assert itself into Lucky's senses. She was a woman, with a woman's needs. But using Nick Chenault to assuage them seemed, to Lucky, the epitome of danger.

Disgusted with herself, she rose from the tub, letting the water drain out as she stepped on the mat to dry. But her inner heat couldn't drain away as easily as her bath. And every swipe of the towel's nubby texture across her sensitive skin made it worse, not better.

"What's wrong with me?" she groaned, and dropped the towel where she stood. "I don't even like that man. Am I so frustrated that I let a near-stranger get that close?"

She turned to stare at herself in the mirror above the sink. A shadowy face reflected back in the steamy glass. Even though the surface had fogged and there was little left to see, she knew that she had changed. Somewhere between Nick's kiss and her nightmare, she'd become aware of him as a man. A man who, she suspected, wanted her in a way she couldn't allow.

It would be difficult to face him again, but impossible to go back to where they'd been before the kiss. And if Lucky were honest with herself, she wasn't certain whether she wanted to go back. She was just afraid to go forward.

"I'm sorry, Mr. Chenault, but that's all we know about Dieter Marx. He was last seen in Venezuela, South America, around 1950. Rumors of his death came back from several different sources, but no body was ever found."

Nick frowned and hung up the phone before he remembered he hadn't thanked the police detective for the information. Detective Arnold had been honest with him, and more helpful than he had needed to be. There were plenty of crimes more serious than his that were being committed on a daily basis. He was just thankful that Will Arnold hadn't told him to hire his own detectives and leave Las Vegas Metro alone, because all of that would delay whatever information he might get.

And the worst of it was, this latest bit of news told him exactly nothing. Granted, Dieter Marx might have hated his father with a passion. But that still didn't prove that he was the one trying to ruin them. All the news had done was to leave Nick with nothing but a lapful of problems with no solutions.

Their only option was to be wary. Someone wanted to destroy the Chenaults in any way possible, even if it took murder to do it. The attempted bombing was proof enough that they were willing to go all the way.

"Nick, who was on the phone?" Paul asked, as Cubby wheeled him into the library.

Nick considered lying. At this point, upsetting his father again seemed useless. He'd told all he knew and it had still not garnered them enough information to get a handle on the invader hovering outside their midst. But the trusting expression in his father's eyes made him change his mind. If the situation were reversed, he would want to know too.

"That was Detective Arnold. He had no firm news about Dieter Marx. The last thing they have on record was that he'd been sighted in Venezuela in 1950 and then later was reported to have died."

"Then who?" Paul asked, his voice trembling and weak.

Nick shook his head. "At this point, your guess is as good as mine." He patted his father's shoulder and then gave Cubby a straight look that the valet could not mistake. "Take good care of Dad while I'm gone. If you need me, I'll be at the club."

Cubby's massive shoulders went taut, and his beefy hands gripped the handles of the wheelchair as his lips thinned in firm resolve.

"You can count on me, Nick."

Nick nodded and managed a smile. "I already knew that, Cubby. I'll see you two in the morning."

Paul watched his son leave and then cursed the infirmities of age that had set him in this chair for the rest of his life, while Cubby pretended not to hear his master's rage.

But Paul was not the only one suffering from bitter frustration. *El Gato* strode from his hacienda, his pale blue eyes glazed with the fury under which he was suffering. Again, his plans had gone awry. He'd paid dearly for the second man who'd been sent on a mission of revenge, and all it had netted him was a botched job from a hit man who couldn't keep his mouth shut. *El Gato* sneered. Woodrow Mosconi's mouth was shut now, permanently.

The sun was hot. Dust boiled beneath his shoes as he marched through the marketplace wearing a fierce expression as an accessory to the white linen suit and the wide-brimmed Panama hat that shaded his eyes.

As he passed through the area, the loud chatter of buyers and sellers blended with the intermittent shrieks of children playing in the alleys. At the end of the street, a group of men pushed and shoved to get the best view of a pair of game cocks that were fighting. Bets flew as fast as feathers.

As he drew closer, now and then he could actually see one of the feathers as it would float up above the men's heads, a sure sign that the cockfight was nearing an end. The rancid smell of men's sweat accompanied the stirring dust from shuffling feet as well as the sickly sweet smell of blood.

A loud roar went up. It would seem that one fight was already over. A limp, lifeless carcass of one of the cocks was dropped against the wall.

El Gato's nostrils flared as the men's crude ways and unwashed bodies assailed his sensitive senses. When he would have circled the mob rather than mingle, fate stepped in and reestablished his seniority, as well as his menace, in the small mountain village.

"Rojo es muy macho! Rojo es el rey!"

But the red rooster was not destined to be king for long. Just as *El Gato* passed, *Rojo's* spur unexpectedly struck an early blow on the next cock that had just been set in place. The wounded fowl's death squawk was accompanied by a set of loud groans. The men began exchanging *pesos* as they stepped back, away from the dying rooster.

In a final flurry of bloody feathers and dirt, the rooster's last flop was onto the pristine white shoes Dieter Marx was wearing. To add insult to injury, blood from the slashed artery in the game cock's neck then spurted an arterial spray of crimson up the legs of his white linen pants.

The men inhaled as one, and then held their breaths in collective fear as they watched *El Gato's* eyes go from blue to white with rage.

Dieter's cheeks paled, then suffused with red. Without missing a beat, he lifted a small handgun from his pocket and took absent aim at the winning rooster. As they watched, the bullet hit the target and the feathers spewed, and *Rojo* dropped at his owner's feet with little ado. Each man there said a silent prayer of thanksgiving that it was the bird, and not them, that lay dead in the dirt.

"Filthy game," Dieter said softly, and then pocketed the gun as he walked away.

Seconds later, there was nothing left to tell the story of what had transpired but two dark puddles of blood being absorbed in the dust.

Lucky made a dash through Club 52 with one eye on the clock and the other on the dressing room where she still had to change. Her bus had been caught in traffic, making her late for work. Her shift was about to start, and she had yet to dress.

Taking none of her usual care with her hair, Lucky tore off one set of clothes and jumped into another, all the while praying that buttons stayed on and zippers didn't get stuck.

"Hi, Lucky," Maizie said.

"Hi," she said, and kept on dressing.

Maizie was a cocktail waitress whom Lucky barely knew, and was always going off shift when she was coming on. She wished just once that they could work the same shift. Given half a chance, she thought that they could have been friends. But Maizie had young children, and needed off at three o'clock in the afternoon when Lucky's day was just beginning.

"You'd better hurry," Maizie warned. "I saw two of your regulars out there, watching the clock."

Lucky rolled her eyes. "Why me?" she moaned, and knew exactly who Maizie meant.

Of the thousands of gamblers who came through Club 52 on a daily basis, two of the more persistent ones had attached themselves to her. They were convinced that because of her name, she was their lucky charm, and they refused, on a daily basis, to wager a cent until she came on duty.

Finally the last button was in place and her tie neatly beneath her chin. Her face was composed, her expression solemn, but there was nothing she could do about her hair. She had no time to put it up in its usual thick crown. Today, it would have to hang. Tying it back with a thin, black ribbon was the best that she could do. She bolted for the door.

Unaware of the attention her beauty drew, as always, she made her way across the floor to her table with mere seconds to spare.

Manny saw her flight through the crowd and grinned to himself. The panic on her face was unnecessary. In the weeks since she'd started work, she was the most reliable employee he had. Then he saw that silky swath of black hair swaying from side to side as she walked.

Madre de Dios, he groaned. *She is too young . . . but I am not too old to appreciate . . . just too old for her.*

He saw her roll her eyes and mask disgust at the two veteran gamblers who'd already claimed their regular seats at her table, waiting while she went through the process of setting up shop. *It is odd*, he thought, *that she has such disdain for people who like to wager, when she works in a casino.*

He shrugged and turned his attention to more pressing things. Lucky Houston was *bella*. Beautiful women were allowed their idiosyncrasies.

Her voice was quiet and controlled as she entered the world of chance. "Gentlemen, place your bets."

She deftly traded the players' cash for "checks," another name for the colored chips used to play the games, and then one by one, dealt the cards. With a covert peek at her own pair, she was ready to play. She lifted her head and waited for the players to make their moves.

The first player scratched the felt with the tip of his card, an indication that he wanted a hit. Lucky dealt the man his third card and then calmly raked in his lost bet while he threw in his hand in disgust and stomped off to another table. He'd gone bust, gambling that the third card would not take him over the count of twenty-one. He'd lost the bet with himself and the house had won.

The second man stayed pat, and the third grinned and quickly turned both cards up when he realized that he'd hit twenty-one on the first deal.

With slow but sure movements, Lucky paid out the win, and waited for the last man to make a move. Twice she saw him look at his hole card and then up at her, trying to gauge her expression, trying to outguess the dealer as to what hand she held.

"Sir?" she asked, indicating for him to make a decision.

He shook his head. He too would stay pat. He wanted no more cards.

And when the cards were revealed, once again the house had won, and Lucky's long, slender fingers quickly stacked the chips into the dealer's pot, readying for the next round of bets.

As the evening grew old, and the players continued to come and go, Lucky's tips grew. By the end of the shift, she figured that she'd collected more than seventy-five dollars. It was free money in the bank.

Nick leaned over the mezzanine and watched the action below, trying not to focus his entire attention on the blackjack tables. But it was no use and it was all Lucky's fault.

For some reason, she'd left that damned hair of hers hanging loose, and it was all he could do not to drag her off that floor and into his arms. Memories of holding her half-dressed body and feeling that hair tangling in his hands still left him weak. He'd had dreams of stripping her naked, laying her on a bed of white with her hair fanned out beneath her like devil's wings, and then driving himself into her body until he was used up and weak, and she was clinging to him in quiet satisfaction.

Below a familiar swarming began to emerge, and Nick realized that it was after eleven P.M. and that the last shift was taking place. Suddenly Lucky was no longer in sight and Nick had a moment's regret that he hadn't seen her leave the floor.

"What's the matter with you, Chenault?" he asked himself. "You've got feet. Go down and say hello . . . or goodbye. Whichever she'll accept."

Before he gave himself time to reconsider, he was on his way down the stairs with a lilt to his step he hadn't had in weeks.

Steve Lucas was off duty. He should have been somewhere else, minding his own business and staying out of Lucky's. But he was still fuming over her rejection . . . and her threats. Steve Lucas was a man with a need for revenge. He'd show her she couldn't talk to him like that and get away with it.

Lucky put on her street clothes a lot more slowly than she'd taken them off, and as a result was the last woman to leave the dressing room. The jeans she was wearing were new and stretched from stem to stern along the long, slender length of her legs. Her brown leather half-boots added inches to her height that she didn't need, but they matched the braided belt at her waist that kept her white, long-sleeved shirt in place.

She could have passed for a model. Yet style was the last thing on her mind. The last two hours of her shift had moved with the speed of a dirge, and Lucky could think of nothing but a good soak in the tub and at least nine solid hours of sleep.

It was with relief that she stepped out of the women's dressing room. Because she was so weary, she was caught off guard by Steve's attack.

Before she could scream, he had her held fast, slapping one hand over her mouth and the other under her breasts. While she struggled futilely, he yanked her into the storage area one door down.

The room was dark and smelled of cleaning solvents and collected dust. His knee was between her legs as he pushed her roughly against the wall. He hadn't spoken a word, but Lucky knew, as surely as she knew her name, that it was Steve Lucas who'd crossed the line of decency.

Well aware that she'd scream bloody murder given half a chance, he kept one hand clapped roughly across her mouth, while he used his greater weight to pin her between him and the wall, leaving his other hand free to roam her reluctant body at will.

Lucky fought and scratched, and once or twice thought

she'd connected with enough flesh to cause serious pain. But he wouldn't let go and she couldn't get loose. As he began to fumble with her belt and jeans, terror replaced the fury that had been her first reaction. If something didn't stop him, Lucky was in serious danger of being raped, and she knew it.

And then fate and an empty bucket changed the course of Steve Lucas's life.

It was when he staggered sideways to dodge the constant but restricted swing of her knees toward his turgid manhood that he stepped into the bucket. Instinctively, he released Lucky to keep from falling. It was all the chance she needed.

She pushed at him with every ounce of strength that she had, and then started to run. Realizing that she was about to escape, Steve lashed out in desperation. His fist caught the side of her mouth, and Lucky swallowed a cry as pain shot up the side of her face. But years of learning how to survive had taught her never to give up, and so she kept moving toward the faint light showing at the edges of the door.

Just as the knob turned beneath her fingers, his hands closed around the back of her neck, then slipped and tangled in her hair instead.

So certain was he that he'd regained the upper hand that he cursed with shock as he realized that he only had hold of her hair instead. He was nowhere near her mouth, and he feared what she might do. She proved him right.

Lucky screamed. The echo inside the small, dark room was startling. Steve was so desperate to silence her that he let go of her hair with full intention of shutting her mouth instead . . . maybe permanently if the situation warranted.

She sensed rather than felt her freedom, and pivoted, kicking upward with deadly force. The pointed toe of her boot did the most damage. Halfway up his body, it hit soft flesh. His agonized groan and the thump he made when he hit the floor told her that she'd finally hurt something that mattered. In seconds she was out the door and running down the hall.

Steve Lucas rolled on the floor in agony with his hands between his legs, praying that if he was ever able to get up that his dick didn't fall off in his hands.

The woman's screams ripped above the noise level on the floor with the power of jet wash. And it was an eerie silence that followed as shock gripped the crowd and everyone stopped to look around, searching for the woman who had cried out in terror.

Nick forgot to breathe. He had already begun to wonder why Lucky was taking so long to emerge from the dressing room when he heard the scream. Seconds later he was running through the crowd with a host of managers at his heels.

He caught her as she burst out of the hallway and onto the crowded floor. Blinding rage came swiftly as he absorbed the condition of her face and her clothes. Someone had hurt her!

Half the buttons on her shirt were missing, and the swell of her breasts was blatantly obvious through the gap in the front. But it was the dark, spreading bruise next to her chin and the drops of blood seeping from the cut on her lip that made him almost lose control.

Instinctively, he turned her away from the curious crowd on the floor and guided her back into the hallway where she'd come from. Security arrived and swiftly moved the curious onlookers back.

Manny was only seconds behind Nick, and when he saw Lucky's battered face, and the condition of her clothing, the first words out of his mouth nearly sent Nick to his knees.

"Where is he, *querida?*" Manny asked.

"He who? Are you telling me you know who the hell did this to her?" Nick asked.

Manny frowned. Nick's question was barely above a whisper, an indication of terrible rage.

"Oh, God, Oh, God," Lucky groaned, and tried to cover herself with her hands. "Manny . . . Manny . . . I didn't see him coming."

"Jesus Christ!" Nick yelled. "If someone doesn't start talking, I'm going to—"

The door to the storage room opened. The last thing Steve Lucas expected to see was an audience. And when he realized that Lucky Houston was in the boss's arms, he started to talk.

"She asked for it," Steve said. "Hell, she was even enjoying it until—"

Nick's fist caught him halfway between ear and chin. He heard, rather than felt, the snap as his jawbone broke. What he felt was relief as security guards led him away. He'd rather be in jail than alone with "The Man."

"Get an ambulance," Nick ordered, fearing for injuries that Lucky had yet to reveal. She cringed at the order and turned away in shame, unable to face the onlookers' sympathy.

"I'm not hurt," she said, and started to shake. "He just scared me."

But before Nick could argue, she went limp in his arms. He looked down. She hadn't fainted, but was so near unconscious that it mattered little.

"Help me get her to my office," Nick ordered.

Minutes later, Lucky was stretched out on the couch in Nick's office while one waitress was sent for ice, and another for a first-aid kit.

And then finally they were alone. Nick didn't know where to start. Desperate to hold her, he still restrained the urge, fearing that after what she'd just endured, she would run screaming from his office as well. So he knelt instead, and when they were eye-to-eye, gently swept the hair from her face and watched for signs of subsiding shock.

A little embarrassed and in misery, Lucky started to turn away, when pain stopped the action.

"Oooh . . . ouch," she mumbled, and carefully felt along the side of her jaw and then traced the path of blood to her lips. Her eyes widened with surprise when her fingers came away red-stained and shaking.

"I will kill him with my bare hands," Nick said softly, and wished with all his heart he could take away the look of horror in her eyes.

She covered her face with shaking fingers, unable to look at what she was sure would be condemnation on his face.

"I'm sorry," she mumbled. "I didn't lead him on . . . I swear it," she mumbled and waited for him to say the words that would terminate her job.

"God almighty, sweetheart, do you think I didn't know that?"

Sweetheart! Lucky's breathing stilled momentarily. That wasn't what she'd expected to hear.

The gentleness of his touch softened the anger in his voice, and when she realized that his rage was not directed at her, she went limp with relief. Slowly, he removed her hands from her face until there were no barriers between them but the truth.

Lucky stared, searching his eyes for something she didn't really believe existed.

"Did he actually, uh . . . are you . . . ?"

Nick couldn't get out the words he needed to say.

Lucky blushed. "No. I'm still as intact as I was the day I was born, no thanks to that sorry sonofabitch."

Nick rocked back on his heels in shock, but it wasn't from hearing her curse. It was what she'd said before that had him at a loss for words. If she was to be believed then no man had ever . . .

"Are you telling me that you're a virgin?"

A second sweep of red went across her cheeks. "I guess I did, didn't I?" she muttered. "Believe me, it slipped out. It's not something I advertise on a daily basis."

Nick didn't know how he felt, but it was somewhere between pure joy and ungovernable fear. He'd already faced the fact that he more than wanted her. He desired, even yearned, to make love to this woman on a daily basis. But now, this bit of news added to the mess he'd already made of trying to establish a relationship. If they ever made love, it would mean that he would be the first. His stomach rolled as he realized that it also meant he had to make another decision. Was he was also going to be the last man who loved her? Did he want that kind of commitment and complication in his life?

The waitress burst back into the office with a bucket of ice and a handful of clean white napkins from the restaurant. Another woman wasn't far behind with a first-aid kit that security had provided.

Lucky sat up and made way for the cleanup crew to descend. She might have refused an ambulance, but the collage of makeshift paramedics her fellow employees had become would have put the doctors of *M*A*S*H* to shame.

When it was over, she was left with a bandage on her forehead, safety pins in place of buttons to hold her shirt in place, and a small ice pack for her bruises in her lap.

"Come with me, honey. It's time to go," Nick said.

"Where?"

"I'm taking you home," he said.

Lucky didn't argue. She desperately needed a refuge, and her home above Fluffy's abode was all that she had.

They were nearly at their destination before Nick realized that he'd called her sweetheart and honey, and that she hadn't refuted his slip of tongue. It was that little bit of knowledge that kept him silent all the way up the stairs. And when she unlocked the door and turned on the lights, he was right behind her.

"Thanks for bringing me home," Lucky said. "Tonight, having to ride the bus would have been the last straw." She tried to laugh and only succeeded in making herself wince from the pain.

But Nick didn't answer, and didn't seem ready to leave.

"I'm all right," she said. "You don't need to—"

"Why don't you take off your clothes," Nick suggested.

Lucky gasped. *Not again*, she thought.

"And take that damned look off your face," he growled. "I'm not leaving until I know for certain that you can manage on your own. Where's your bedroom?"

Lucky shuddered. "I'm not getting into bed until I've washed Steve Lucas off my body."

Nick went pale. What she'd gone through must have been devastating to her.

"I'm sorry," he said softly. "I didn't think."

And then before he could reconsider the wisdom of the notion, he knew he had to hold her.

"Please . . . let me have this much. You may not need it, but I damned sure do," Nick said. Harshness deepened the tone of his voice as he held out his arms.

The shock on her face made him continue quickly, lest she misunderstand what he meant. "When I heard you scream, I thought I would die before I got to you. And then when I saw you, I was afraid to touch you for fear I'd injure something already hurt."

She shuddered at the thought of going into another man's arms and Nick saw it.

"Never mind," he said softly. "I think I understand. We'll save the hug for another day."

She wrapped her arms around her waist, well aware that his embrace might have been much more comforting, and smiled slightly, hoping it softened her rejection of his offer. "I seem to keep saying this, but . . . thank you."

He wanted to hold her—to take away Steve Lucas's touch from her body—but he settled for the smile that she gave him instead.

"It is of constant satisfaction to me that you will let me help you, girl. I just wish it were not always under such desperate circumstances . . . and I wish . . ." He frowned as his voice deepened slightly. "I wish I knew how to make you trust me."

The bitter twist of her lips said it all. "So do I, boss. So do I."

8

Lucky soaked in the bath Nick had drawn and tried not to think of how easy it would be to give in to his persuasive tactics. Using the rim of the ancient tub for a headrest, she stretched, letting the water's warmth ease her aches. It was daunting to know that she lay naked as the day she was born, with only a closed door between herself and Nick Chenault. His determination to stay with her was clearly stronger than her will to remain detached. At this moment she was so tired of being lonely . . . and so tired of being afraid.

And while the water felt good to her weary bones, by the time she crawled out of the tub, the muscles in her back and legs had started to knot, and a headache that seemed to have no intention of going away was throbbing at the base of her skull. Thanks to Steve Lucas, she was going to have a hell of a night.

Reminding herself to ignore the man who waited for

her, she emerged from the bathroom, wearing little more
than an oversize T-shirt and smelling of baby powder and
lilac, thanks to the bath salts Fluffy had given her days
ago. She walked into the living room a much calmer
woman.

Nick took one look at her wan expression and the dark
bruise on her chin, and he wanted to hit something,
preferably Steve Lucas's face. Unfortunately, he'd already
done that, and had to settle for a simmering rage instead.

"Are you hungry?" he asked.

Lucky shook her head. "I just want to lie down. I ache
all over."

And then she waited, expecting that he would take that
as his cue to leave. But Nick had other plans.

"Then go to bed, honey," he said softly.

"But aren't you . . . ?"

"Don't make me leave," he said. "I promise not to over-
step any bounds, but someone needs to be here for
you . . . please let it be me." And when he saw instant refusal, he felt compelled to add, lest she suspect him of ul-
terior motives, "I promise that you'll be safe."

His dark eyes begged further in a way he could not.
Lucky told herself this was probably a mistake, but she
had to admit that she was afraid to stay alone.

"My sofa is very small for someone your size."

"Get in bed before you fall on your face, and quit worrying about where I'll sleep."

She did as she was told.

Later, alone in the dark, she could still feel the imprint
of his hand as he'd cupped her cheek before tucking her

in. The way the pad of his thumb had gently grazed the place on her mouth where Steve Lucas had struck. The shadows of the room had prevented her from seeing his expression, but she had felt him tremble.

Weary beyond words, she rolled over on her side and closed her eyes. Seconds later she was asleep.

Which was more than Nick could claim. He paced from window to window in her apartment, looking through the curtains without seeing the brightly lit skyline of Las Vegas, or noticing the dark, constant shadows of the mountains that circled the city. All he could see was a replay of the terror on her face as she'd barreled into his outstretched arms at the club. He closed his eyes and still saw blood seeping from her lip, and that bruise . . . that purple, spreading stain beneath her skin that marked the beginning of pain.

Intermittent squeaks of bedsprings drifted up the hall and into the room where he was. Lucky seemed to be suffering some restlessness of her own.

Unable to find a comfort zone, Nick gave up and undressed, hoping that freeing his body from restrictive clothing would alleviate some of the tension he was feeling. It didn't help. He paced, wide-eyed and aching, quietly going crazy with worry.

A short time later, he gave up his solitary patrol and sat nursing a can of soda with the sounds of an aging house for company.

The occasional squeak a board would make as the old building shifted on its beams seemed oddly comforting, as did the sigh of the wind through windows loose on their frames. Even the countless lingering emotions of people long since gone seemed to hover in the air. The house was, in itself, a mirage of life.

Nick's gray suit coat was on the back of a chair, his shoes beneath. The silk, charcoal-colored tie he'd been wearing lay across the table, as out of place in this woman's world as he felt.

His eyes burned, his chest ached. But it was not from exhaustion. It was from a need he would not give name to. The room felt close, yet he decided not to open any windows, lest it would make Lucky feel unsafe. Instead, he shucked his shirt and took off his belt. The urge to undress completely was tempting, but stripping down to his natural state and getting caught by Lucky hours later was out of the question. After what she'd been through, he guessed it would scare the hell out of her.

Lying on the sofa proved to be as difficult and uncomfortable as she'd warned, but Nick Chenault had long ago refused to ever admit defeat. With his arm for a pillow, and his long legs hanging over the armrest at the other end, he closed his eyes and gave in to the weariness he was feeling.

Hours later, somewhere downstairs in Fluffy's part of the house, a clock chimed three times as Nick rolled off the sofa and onto the floor with a thump. He groaned as he crawled to his knees, cursing short furniture and long legs as a matter of course, then staggered into the kitchen and leaned over the sink, letting the water run swift. When it was as cold as the aging pipes would allow, he splashed it on his face and arms, letting the overflow run unheeded down his bare chest. The refreshing sensation was just what he needed to clear his head.

Water tunneled down the ridge between his ribs. He grabbed at a towel to stop its flow, then heard a sound that sent him running down the hall where Lucky was sleeping.

For a moment he stood silently outside her room . . . waiting . . . listening . . . unwilling to disturb her slumber if she was not in need. And then he heard it again. Heartbreak and despair were woven into the sound that drifted out from the crack beneath the door. A shudder rippled through him as he pushed it open, half expecting to be sent packing by her for the intrusion.

She was nothing more than a slight mound beneath the sheet, unmoving in her slumber. And then the sound came again, full force, with nothing between them but the truth. She was crying in her sleep.

"Ah God," Nick groaned. In seconds he was at her bedside.

"Lucky . . . honey . . . wake up." His hands traced the paths of her tears as he leaned down and touched her damp cheeks.

She moaned, muttering a name he couldn't decipher, and then sighed as the tears continued to fall. From the streetlight shining through the old lace curtains at her window, he saw her lower lip quiver.

"Dammit to hell," he growled. Seconds later he'd crawled into the bed beside her and had pulled her into his arms.

"Don't cry, baby," he whispered. "Don't cry. I've got

you. If you would let me, I'd never let you go." And it was at that moment that he faced the depth of his feelings for her.

Through the darkness of her dream, Lucky heard a voice. Its promise was sweet, its tone gentle and undemanding. She turned toward it with unerring accuracy and held out her arms. He caught her from falling into the ache of the past.

Cursing softly beneath his breath from a want he couldn't admit to, he waited while Lucky fit herself against him and then seemed to hold on for dear life. He gritted his teeth and closed his eyes, silently reminding himself that this could go no further than an embrace.

And oddly enough, sleep returned, even as daylight arrived. But neither Lucky nor Nick was aware of the sunshine streaming through the windows or of the garbage trucks on the streets below making their early morning rounds. They were lost in a place where loneliness did not exist. Asleep in each other's arms.

Lucky came to her senses slowly. In her entire life, she'd never awakened with her nose pressed against a man's bare chest. Her first thought, on realization, was why had it taken her so long to try it.

Warm, tan skin pillowed her cheek, and the hands that splayed across her back held her firmly and safely in place. The heartbeat against her ear was rock-steady and soothing. She knew she should have been wondering why Nick Chenault was in her bed, and why she was in his arms. But for the life of her, she couldn't bring herself to care. She felt too good to move.

Nick knew she was awake. He felt the change in her

breathing, as well as the tickle of her eyelashes against the bare skin on his chest when she blinked. The first thing he'd expected her to do was rail at him for invading her territory. But she proved him wrong. If anything, she snuggled just the least bit closer. Reluctant to move, unwilling to talk, he settled for savoring the moment, knowing all too soon it would have to end.

Lucky sighed. He was awake. She'd known it the instant his hands had gently lifted the hair from her cheek so that he could look at the damage to her face. His body tensed and his breathing changed in evidence of how he moved by what he saw.

"Why the hell are you in my bed?" she asked quietly.

"Good morning, honey," he whispered, and gave her shoulder a gentle pat before raising himself on one elbow so that their conversation could continue face-to-face. "You were having bad dreams. I couldn't stand to see you cry."

Lucky grimaced and turned away. She didn't want him to know how deeply his tenderness affected her. But in her limited experience, trusting a man was one step shy of stupid.

"This morning may be good to some, but personally, if I look as bad as I feel, I don't think my customers are going to be able to keep their minds on the game."

She shrank from him now as quickly as she had turned to him last night. When she looked away, he knew it was time to put some distance between them before she completely resented him. He rolled to the side of the bed, giving her all the space she needed between them to feel safe.

"You aren't going to work until you feel up to it," he said. "With no reduction in pay, I might add. You were injured on the job, remember?"

"I would like to forget the whole thing happened," she said. "But somehow, I feel like I should have seen that one coming. Steve Lucas has been stepping over the line almost from the first day."

"I wish I'd known," Nick said. "Maybe it could have been prevented."

Lucky shrugged. "I doubt it. Besides, Johnny always said . . . don't cry over spilt milk. It just makes a bigger mess."

Nick smiled and wanted to touch her, but wisely kept the action to himself. "I wish I'd known your Johnny. He sounds a lot like my dad."

Her laugh was short and her words filled with disbelief. "I seriously doubt it. There's an awfully big difference between Las Vegas and Cradle Creek. I can't imagine our fathers—or our lives—being anything alike."

Nick frowned at the way she'd reminded him of his wealth and her lack of it. He responded in sudden anger.

"We are born into this world with little choice, lady. It's what we do with our own shot at life that matters."

When he caught a glimmer of tears in her eyes, he sensed it was time to change the subject. "Thank you for letting me stay last night. You may not have needed it, but it made me feel better."

Lucky watched the way his lips moved around his words. She knew he was talking, but for the life of her, she couldn't seem to concentrate on what he was saying. All she could remember was that those lips had once been on hers, and for a heartbeat, he'd been in her blood.

Nick chuckled. "Just like a woman. You aren't listening to a word I say."

Lucky blinked, then allowed herself a grin. "I thought that was supposed to be the woman's line."

Nick laughed aloud, surprised by her jest, and then bent his head. He meant for the kiss to be friendly, and nowhere near her lips. But it didn't work. It seemed that every time they touched, the act became one of urgency.

When his mouth slid across her lips, marking their texture and shape with the touch of his own, she forgot to react. But when he moaned and wrapped her back in his arms, then took her with him as he rolled across her bed, she went as naturally as if they'd been attached at the heart.

Deeper needs triggered by the alignment of their bodies began to make themselves known. His burgeoning manhood tested the limits of metal zippers and expensive material, while her body warmed to a sweet honey flow. Their hands moved across bare skin with the skill of a sculptor, exploring a broad chest and generous breasts. Their breathing quickened along with their desire.

But when Nick's knee slid between Lucky's legs and pushed gently at the mound beneath the scrap of nylon across her hips, it was too close to what she'd endured yesterday at Steve Lucas's hands. The mood was broken and Nick sensed it immediately and cursed himself for going too far.

"All I can say is, I didn't mean to do that. You make me

lose control of everything I am," he said softly, brushing a tendril of curl away from her face. "I would never, never hurt you. Just don't be afraid of me. Please."

He held his breath and waited.

She stared at the flare of his nostrils and the need etched across his face, and then admitted something she should have kept to herself.

"You could very easily destroy me, you know," she said.

"Not in a million years, Lucky Lady," he said, and cupped her cheek.

She shook her head and caught his hand in her own before it strayed any farther south. "No. You don't understand. It would be too easy to fall in love with you, Nick."

He buried his nose against the curve of her neck, nuzzling beneath her earlobe in a gentle, teasing gesture.

"You make that sound like a bad thing," he said.

Her voice shook from warning . . . and from regret. "I can't fall in love with you. You're a gambler."

He wondered where that sound of distaste in her voice came from. Again, he realized how little he really knew of the woman he held in his arms.

"What's so bad about that?" he asked. "I rarely play, honey. I just furnish the place for others to enjoy themselves."

"Johnny gambled. It ruined our lives."

Nick sat up again. This was getting serious. He felt a wall going up between them that he didn't know how to climb.

"You work in the business. How can you just lie there and place a blanket judgment on everyone . . . including me?"

"I'm not judging you," Lucky said, and got out of bed, needing to put distance between them. "I simply don't intend to fall in love with a gambler."

Nick's heart began to pound as he searched for words that would find a way through her fear. "And maybe you're wrong. Maybe we could just agree to disagree and still have a relationship and see where it would go."

"I don't want to be just anybody's girl, remember? I want to be somebody's special girl. One man. One love. Forever."

"Hell, honey, you don't want much, do you?" Hurt put unintended anger in his voice.

The bed was a physical barrier between them. But it was the words that put the real distance back into their lives.

"Yes I do, Nick. I want a lot. I want to have—and I want to give—everything to the man I love."

Let it be me.

She saw it on his face. But because he didn't say it, she didn't have to find the strength to turn him down.

"I don't know why you hate this way of life so much, and you're obviously not ready to tell me. However, I think it's damned unfair of you to judge every man by the actions of one."

He walked out of her bedroom without giving her time for rebuttal. And even if he had, she would have been hard-pressed to come up with one. There was too much truth in his accusations.

"Where are you going?" she asked as she followed him to the door, suddenly unsure of what she'd done.

"Home to change. Home to check on my father. Home

to see if the police have turned up any new leads on the man who wants us dead. You name it, it's on my agenda. My father always said there is no rest for a wicked man. And I'd venture to say there's not a more wicked man in the world than a gambler like me."

Lucky heard more than anger in his answer. She had actually hurt him with her constant rejections. Only a man who cared could be hurt by a woman like her. It was a frightening and powerful knowledge.

"Nick. I'm sorry."

"So am I, Lucky. So the hell am I. Take care of yourself," he added, unable to stay angry at her for long. "Come back to work when you feel up to it."

She nodded and tried not to cry.

He was almost out the door. He would have made it, too, if he hadn't turned to look. When he did, he remembered that she'd cried in her sleep and he hadn't found out why. It was for that reason, and that reason only, that he retraced his steps for the good-bye kiss they both seemed to need.

Instinctively her lips turned up to meet the ones that were coming down. The floor moved. Or so Lucky thought. But it was only the touch of Nick's mouth upon hers that had set her world spinning.

"Damn your beautiful, hard head," Nick growled, inhaling sharply as he lifted his head to release their connection. "You're wrong, Lucky Houston. You're wrong about me. You're wrong about us. One day you'll be ready to admit it. When you do, you'll come knocking." His lips twisted sardonically. "And you know what? The most pathetic part is that I'll probably be waiting."

* * *

Fluffy LaMont pulled Lucky closer to the window for better light by which to see her young friend's healing face. She had been horribly shocked by what had happened to her, but had reminded her more than once during the passing week that she'd suffered a better end to the event than most.

"Yes. You're as good as new," she said, tilting Lucky's chin first one way, then the other, searching her flawless features for the remains of bruising. There was none.

"Outside, maybe. Inside I'm a mess," Lucky muttered.

Fluffy frowned. She'd known all week that there was more than shock from the attack putting lines in Lucky's face. "Don't do that," she warned, and traced her forefinger between Lucky's eyebrows. "It makes wrinkles, you know."

Lucky made a face. "Fluffy, my love, wrinkles are the least of my worries."

"Hmph! You say that now when you have none. Wait until you're my age. You'll be eating your words, young lady."

Lucky hugged her tight and then pulled at a curl dangling toward Fluffy's left eyebrow. Her red hair had given way to the new look of the week: Hot Honey. The color was somewhere between blonde and platinum.

"If I make it that far, I hope I have as much fun as you seem to be having," Lucky said, and poked the wayward curl in place.

Fluffy arched her eyebrows and pursed her lips. "You're only old if you believe it, girl."

Lucky slumped into a chair and stared at the floor. "I feel all . . . confused. Sometimes I feel ancient. Like I've lived forever in this skin. And at other times, I feel like a baby, unsure of my next step. What's wrong with me?"

Fluffy's hands were gentle, but her words were sharp. "You need a man, girl. You had one. What the hell have you done with him? He cares about you or he wouldn't have spent the night at your side after the attack. But he hasn't been back."

Lucky turned her head away, unwilling to let Fluffy see the truth of it all in her eyes.

Fluffy sighed. She'd suspected as much. A man like Nick Chenault didn't willingly walk away from a woman like this one. She patted Lucky's head, smoothing the loose strands of her braid back in place.

"Did you send him away?"

Lucky nodded but said nothing.

"Want to tell me why?"

"I can't have a relationship with a man like him."

"Like what? Employed? Rich? Tall, dark, and handsome? Are you mad, honey? The man looks like Tom Selleck."

Lucky's hands balled into fists in her lap. Fluffy's arguments were getting to her in a big way. She knew damn well and good how gorgeous he was. And how rich. And how sexy. And how dangerous. "Tom Selleck has a mustache," she finally said.

Fluffy rolled her eyes. "Details. Details. You're ignoring the obvious."

"He's a gambler."

"And you work in a casino!"

Then the truth came out. "I'm afraid to love him,"

Lucky said. "Johnny was a gambler and I loved him dearly. But he nearly destroyed us all."

Fluffy frowned. "I don't think you're afraid of him, personally, my girl. I think you're just afraid to love, period! You're afraid of getting hurt."

"So . . . you may be right. That still doesn't mean I trust this man."

"Honey. Thinking gets you nowhere. You have to act, do what's natural."

Lucky laughed through tears. "Where were you all my life?"

The catch in her voice made Fluffy sigh with regret as she pressed Lucky's head against her breast. "No, darling. In fact it's the opposite. Where have you been all of mine?"

Lucky shrugged and got to her feet. "I suppose I've put off the inevitable long enough. May I use your phone? I want to call Manny. To tell him I'll be at work tomorrow."

Fluffy waved her away. "Don't ask! Do! For Pete's sake, haven't I taught you at least that much?"

As Lucky went to the phone, Fluffy sighed and took the chair that the girl had just vacated. She suddenly felt every one of her eighty-four birthdays. It was hard being an adult, especially if you'd been trying as long as Fluffy La-Mont to get it right.

Manny put her on the day shift, and for that she was grateful. Getting back into the swing of work would be easier if she didn't have to face everyone who'd witnessed her attack. But getting to work by 7:00 A.M. required a difficult adjustment in her body clock. Her eyes were open and her feet were moving, but her brain hadn't kicked in gear.

Yet Lucky was to learn that she needn't have worried.

It was a different breed of gambler who was willing to play blackjack before most people had eaten breakfast.

Her legs shook as she walked into the club. Although she knew Steve Lucas could not possibly be hiding anywhere, the thought still gave her pause. Manny, who was rarely at work this early, met her at the door with a smile. She knew he'd come just for her benefit, and for that, she could have hugged him. She settled for a welcoming wave instead.

"*Querida*, are you sure you're ready for this?" he asked.

"As ready as I'll ever be," she said. "Thank you for changing my shift. It makes coming back easier."

"Just so you know," Manny added. "Steve Lucas made bail."

When Lucky paled, he added, "Don't worry. You will be safe here. Nick's security men would not allow him back on the premises."

Lucky shrugged. "I'm not afraid," she said. "And I won't be surprised like that again . . . by anyone."

Manny was stunned by her strength. He would have expected any woman to still be in a constant state of fear and tears having to return to the scene of such an attack. Had he known what it had taken just to survive being one of Johnny Houston's daughters, he wouldn't have been so surprised.

"But thanks for the warning," she added.

"It is nothing. Get changed and have a good day." He

winked, then watched as Lucky walked past the slot machines on her way toward the dressing rooms beyond the main floor.

"Lucky! Welcome aboard!"

Lucky turned at the sound. It was Maizie in full array, her hips giving sway to the minuscule net petticoat beneath abbreviated black velvet outfit she was wearing. The neck was low, the skirt high, with a lot of skin in between. A typical cocktail waitress's attire.

"Thanks," she said. "It feels good to be back."

Maizie frowned and shifted her empty tray to her hip as she slowly assessed Lucky's state of mind.

"You're a tough one, aren't you, girl?"

Lucky smiled. "Not as tough as I thought I was," she said. "But I'm doing all right."

"Thank God. When I heard what happened, it made me sick. I never liked that joker myself, you know." And then she grinned. "I also heard that the boss broke Steve's jaw with one punch. Sort of took your problem personally, didn't he?"

The flush on Lucky's cheeks told Maizie she'd scored on her hunch about Lucky's feelings toward Nick Chenault.

"Way to go, girl! He's been on the loose way too long as it is."

"Hey . . . there's nothing like that between us," Lucky said.

"Yeah, right! And I'm Marla Trump, with a capital T. I just do this for kicks." Then she rolled her eyes dramatically, and started down the narrow aisles between the slot machines. "Cocktails? Coffee? Cocktails, anyone?"

Lucky hurried to dress. Maizie had her thing and she had hers. And so the morning passed.

Nick felt empty. Everything he'd accepted as familiar now seemed false. He could hardly face going to work, knowing that the absence of one dark-haired female dealer was going to make his day long and empty.

And the pride he once felt in Club 52 was gone. One look at the crystal and velvet was all it took to remember his father's claim that mob money started it all. The fact that the mob hadn't known about the connection, or that Paul Chenault had anonymously paid it all back with interest, didn't seem to matter. Nick's world felt tainted, and he didn't know how to fix it.

Maybe Lucky Houston was right. Maybe a gambler's world was a dark and wicked thing in which to exist. Yet living any other way was beyond his comprehension. This was all he knew.

Breakfast this morning with his father had been strained. The tension of living from day to day with a death threat hanging over one's head didn't bode well for chitchat. The table had not even been cleared before Nick announced he was leaving for work a good two hours ahead of his usual time.

And for all those reasons, his steps were slow and his heart was heavy as he entered Club 52. He nodded and smiled as he passed the players at the slot machines at the front of the grand entrance, taking note of the ones who looked as if they'd been here all night. He could tell the repeats from the newcomers by their gloves. Old-timers knew from experience how filthy the coins could be, and often wore a tight-fitting white glove on their coin hand to protect themselves from the dirt on the money as they fed the machines.

The newcomers were all over the place. Fresh-faced, eyes shining, with all the excitement and wonder yet to be experienced. They ran from machine to machine, from table to table, always clutching handfuls of chips or small plastic tubs of coins, searching for the magic spot and the jackpot just waiting for their arrival.

Nick inhaled slowly, absorbing the world that was his, and started toward the stairs leading to his office. Right or wrong, Club 52 was his life.

Because he was deep in thought, he almost didn't notice the new dealer on shift. In fact, it was her voice and not her face that caught his attention.

"Sir . . . please place your bet."

He looked up just in time to see Lucky behind one of the twenty blackjack tables, dealing from the shoe to a single player who looked as if he'd spent the night on that very stool.

Shock spread through Nick, and he stopped only a few feet away. Then, without considering the consequences of his actions, he took a twenty-dollar bill from his pocket and scooted onto the empty stool next to Lucky's all-night player.

"Change, please." Nick laid the bill outside the betting square and waited for her to hand him his chips.

Lucky's hand stilled in the act of beginning a deal. The green expanse of the table in front of her narrowed until all she could see were the long, slender fingers of the new player patiently drumming the felt with an absentminded tattoo as he waited for change.

It was only seconds, but it felt like hours, before she gathered the nerve to look up. His warm brown eyes looked back at her from across the table, much in the same way that he'd stared at her from across her bed nearly a week ago.

"I need change," Nick repeated. "All reds . . . please."

Lucky's fingers shook a little as she quickly counted out four five-dollar chips.

Nick placed all of them on the table, betting the whole twenty dollars at once. It was a small but symbolic gesture that Lucky couldn't miss. He was an all-or-nothing kind of man.

Her eyes widened, but she remained mute as she began to deal, hoping that the other man at the table didn't know he was playing with the owner of Club 52.

The cards clicked as they came out of the shoe and then hit the felt with a firm slap before each player.

Nick couldn't quit staring at her face. The last time he'd seen her she'd been bruised and battered, with a pain in her eyes that no amount of comforting had been able to remove. But now, all the outer injuries seemed to be gone. She was healed and back where she belonged.

Then she looked up, and for a moment, he lost himself in deep green eyes.

She looked away, quickly breaking the spell, and as she did, Nick's sanity returned with a jolt. While part of her was healed, the old wariness that he'd seen before was still there.

"Hit me," the other man mumbled.

Only then did Nick remember there was a game in progress and absently looked down at his cards. A queen of hearts stared blandly up at him from the table. Before he touched it, he knew that his hole card was going to be good. He could feel it with the instinct of a man who knew the game.

He felt Lucky watching him, waiting for him to make his play. He lifted the bottom card and turned them both up without missing a beat.

"Blackjack," he said softly.

The other player snorted and tossed in his hand. "I'm busted," he said, and finally relinquished his seat. With a vacant stare, he watched the dealer counting out Nick's winnings and shrugged. "Oh, well, win some . . . lose some, I always say." Then he winked at Lucky. "Have a nice day, miss. Lady Luck just wasn't with me last night."

As he walked away, he tossed a couple of chips toward Lucky as tips. Ever careful of the "eye in the sky" security system, she slid them across the table and into the slot on the table reserved for that purpose.

"Thank you, sir," she said. But the man was already gone.

"Place your bet," she whispered, and waited for Nick to slide a stack of chips into place.

"I'm out," he said, picking up his chips as he stood. "This must be my lucky day. And I don't believe in pushing it."

Lucky couldn't believe what she was hearing. He was winning and he quit? Johnny would have already been glassy-eyed and counting money he hadn't even won.

Nick leaned forward and dropped every chip he'd just won into Lucky's hands.

"Welcome back, baby," he said softly. "Welcome back."

She watched him walk away through a shimmer of tears. It felt good to be wanted, even though it scared her to death to know that he cared.

9

Lunchtime came and went, taking Lucky's nerve with it. By two o'clock, she could hardly concentrate on the cards. When three o'clock rolled around and her shift was over, she was nearly sick from the tension of the day. After she cashed in her tips, she walked away knowing that a good portion of them had come from Nick's generosity.

All she wanted was to get out of this place before she made a complete fool of herself and burst into tears. And just when she thought she'd accomplished that feat, she found herself face-to-face with the man she'd been trying not to think about.

He was just outside the rear entrance, leaning against his sports car with his arms folded and an inscrutable expression on his face.

"Do you want a ride?" Nick asked.

Lucky was shaking from nerves and exhaustion after

her first day back on the job, and now this? It was so much like a repeat of their first meeting at the bus station on the day of her arrival that she was struck dumb. He was even leaning against the same black sports car.

"What do you think you're trying to prove?" she asked.

"I want to start over," he said. "I can't change the day we met, but if you are willing, we could start again."

Lucky tried not to smile. She didn't want to like this man. She did not want to trust him.

"And why should I believe that you are any more sincere than the first day we met?"

He grinned. "At least now you know I'm not a pimp."

She laughed, and then hated herself for giving in even that much.

Nick's expectations rose. One step at a time. For now, the smile he'd just put on her face was worth a lot.

"So . . . is it going to be me or the bus?"

Heat danced from the pavement between them as a hot gust of wind lifted her hair from her neck. Just thinking of the long, hot ride on a noisy bus made her ache.

"Just a ride? And only as far as my home?"

"Whatever you say, lady. Outside those walls, you're the boss."

She sighed. "I will probably hate myself later," she muttered, well aware that he could hear everything she said. "But I guess I choose you."

He chuckled. "Oh, hell, I can't stand the joy. I've never had to beg to compete with mass transportation before. You give a whole new meaning to the term 'hardheaded woman.'"

Lucky climbed into the passenger seat and tucked her

skirt beneath her legs. "You asked me if I wanted a ride. If you're expecting me to grovel at your feet, you're wasting your time. I need a ride, not a new set of problems from an unruly child."

Nick grinned again. She was prickly as hell and he found himself beginning to like it . . . even expect it.

He slid behind the wheel. "It's been a long time since anyone referred to me as a problem child."

Lucky bathed him in a slow, green stare. "That's just it, Nick. You're not a child . . . and neither am I. Playing games is beyond the both of us. And playing with someone's emotions can get a body hurt."

He started the car and tilted the vents, giving her full benefit of the air conditioner's frigid blast. "I only offered you a ride," he said softly. "One day we'll play, sweetheart, but I can promise it will be for keeps."

She snorted softly, refusing to acknowledge his prediction by anything other than silent disdain.

Nick sighed as he swung into traffic. He'd known when he started that this wouldn't be easy. But he'd never wanted a woman's trust in his life as badly as he wanted Lucky's.

The drive home was long, the conversation sparse. When they arrived, her hand was on the door before he killed the engine.

"Thank you for the ride," she said. She had one leg out of the door before he could think of something to say.

"I guess this means I'm not invited in."

She heard the wistfulness in his voice, but refused to let herself care. Just because he was being good to her now didn't mean it would last.

"One ride does not constitute capitulation on my part," she said.

Nick wanted to throttle her, but instead counted to ten before he spoke. "I don't remember asking for capitulation, Lucky. I only asked for a second chance."

She flushed. Her rudeness did not become her and she knew it.

"I know. But you have to understand things from my point of view. You gave me a ride. All I can give back is my thanks."

"In other words, don't push my luck?"

She nodded. "Or words to that effect."

"I know I said you're the boss, but don't let it go to your head," he grumbled.

She grinned and then slammed the door shut behind her.

Nick watched her long, angry stride as she started up the walk, noting the way the green fabric of her dress swung between those long legs. Then he looked away, unable to watch anything else touch her in a way he could not. When he started the car and drove away, he didn't notice her aging landlady in the window waving, or that Lucky hadn't climbed the stairs, but had headed toward Fluffy's instead.

Fluffy yanked Lucky inside, kicking at the cat who made a break for the opening in the same breath that she started her inquisition.

"Well now, didn't I see you get out of that fancy sports car?"

Lucky laughed at her landlady's lack of tact. "You know good and well what you saw."

Fluffy toyed with the black lace drape that served as a collar for a red organza dress that had seen better days.

"Well?" she prompted, giving Lucky a hard, inquisitive glare.

Lucky threw up her hands in disgust. "I've had a hard day, Fluffy. Don't give me a harder time now."

Fluffy relented and hugged her instead. "Come into the kitchen and have a snack with me while you tell me all about it. I've been cooking."

"Again?" Lucky asked, and tried not to groan.

"You inspire me, dear," she said. "You're going to love it . . . trust me."

The table was filled with platter upon platter of tiny finger foods. Most of them were the color of dirt. Lucky hoped that they tasted better than they looked.

"What's this one?" she asked, pointing to an assortment of little brown lumps crowned with green sprigs that she hoped was not the catnip Fluffy grew on the back porch.

"Liverwurst on cocktail rye with watercress."

"Ummm," she said, and hoped that the groan passed for interest. "And how about these?" She pointed to another platter where the lumps had been formed into squares rather than droplets and had bits of something red and slimy slathered across the entire surface.

"Oh! Those are my favorites. It's paté with pimento. I was out of diced pimento so I picked the middles out of a jar of green olives. Brilliant, right?"

Lucky laughed. Now she knew what it was that looked so slick. It was the olive oil. She tried not to shudder. Goose liver and olive-flavored pimento didn't appeal to her as much as it must to Fluffy.

"Maybe I'll try some of those first," she offered, pointing to the last platter on the table. "It looks like . . . they sort of remind me of . . ." She picked one up and sniffed, then grinned. "Are these peanut butter and jelly?"

Fluffy nodded, then frowned as she poked a fingertip into the top of one near the edge of the tray. "But I got too much grape jelly in the mix and made it turn gray when it should have swirled, instead. It tastes better than it looks, you know."

The anxious expression on her face was all it took for Lucky to choose some of everything. She told herself that if worse came to worst, she could feed what she couldn't eat to Lucifer. That cat would eat anything without leaving crumbs behind.

"I'm sure it all tastes wonderful," she said, and threw her arms around the aging woman's neck. "And you're a darling to ask me to share it. Pass me a plate."

The smile on Fluffy's well-painted face was all the impetus Lucky needed to stack her food high. To hell with the cat. She'd eat every bite of this if it killed her. And when she lifted a cracker square piled with pimento and paté too close to her nose, she knew that it very well might.

While Lucky basked in the glow of Fluffy's love and attention, Nick was left to face the daunting task of trying to find out who wanted him and his father dead, and at the same time find the way into Lucky Houston's trust.

He could tell she didn't like to be rushed, so he vowed he would not rush her. She seemed to be frightened when he tried to move their relationship past casual friendship, so he would be just a friend first if it killed him. Even though they had shared a kiss that rocked them both to their toes, he knew that for every step he'd taken toward her, she'd run two steps backward in return.

Hurrying into a relationship with this woman wasn't going to happen, because if he wasn't careful, there wouldn't even be one at all. And when he remembered that she'd inadvertently admitted to being a virgin, he realized that there was only one way in which to proceed that wouldn't drive her away.

For Nick, it was quite literally back to the playground. He wasn't going to pull her hair to show her he liked her, but making no more demands upon her than a boy might make upon his first love was as far as he dared to go. And so the campaign to win Lucky Houston's heart began.

"Time for your break," Manny told Lucky. "Today is Maizie's birthday. Nick had a cake delivered in her honor in the break room. She's back there squealing and blowing out candles like there is no *mañana*."

Luckily sighed with relief and stepped aside as another dealer moved into place. The fifteen-minute break she had coming would be more than welcome. She had a headache today that didn't want to go away.

She headed for her locker for some aspirin, only to come up with an empty bottle instead.

"Oh, great," she muttered. "Maybe someone has some I can borrow."

She exited the dressing rooms, only to bump into Nick who was passing through the hall just as she tossed the empty aspirin bottle in the trash.

He guessed where she was heading. "I saved you a piece of cake."

"I would settle for some aspirin instead," she said, and rubbed at a spot between her eyebrows that throbbed with rhythmic regularity.

Nick's manner changed instantly from teasing to solicitous. "Are you sick?"

She shook her head. "Just a really bad headache."

His hand grazed her sleeve. "After you greet the birthday girl, come up to the office. I've got half a pharmacy in my desk."

Come to your office?

The possible dangers of such an intimacy lasted in her mind only as long as it took the next pain to rip between her eyes.

"Well . . . I guess so," she finally said.

"Don't bother to knock," he said. "Just come on in."

He walked away before she could give herself time to reconsider his offer.

As she watched the way he moved through the crowd on the floor, she couldn't help admiring his long, confident stride. She told herself that he was just another man. His kindness was nothing more than what he'd offer any of his other employees.

After giving Maizie a hug and having a bit of birthday cake, she went to Nick's office. By that point she was about half an hour away from a real good cry.

"Here," he said, and handed her the tablets and a glass of water. "You've got a few more minutes left on your break, haven't you?"

She swallowed the medicine and then closed her eyes and nodded, praying for instant relief.

"Why don't you lie down on my couch? It's quiet up here. There's no smoke or noise and I've got the phone off the hook. Close your eyes and take advantage of the silence while I run down to security and check out some tapes. I won't let you go over your allotted break time . . . okay?"

Lucky didn't know what to say. He had her cornered, and all he'd done was offer a quiet place to rest. No pressure, no promises she couldn't accept.

"I guess it would be all right," she said.

"Hey . . . in here, I'm the boss, remember? If I say it's all right, then it's all right, Lucky Lady."

He walked out, closing the door quietly behind him. It took her exactly five seconds to consider the offer before she crawled onto the couch and rolled over on her stomach, using one arm for a pillow while trailing the other on the floor below.

She sighed and felt the tension sliding out of her body as she absorbed the solace of quiet darkness. Within minutes, she had fallen asleep.

Nick returned a short time later, wondering what he could find to talk about that wouldn't make her mad or get him in trouble. But he found, to his delight, that talking was the last thing on her mind. Though overwhelmed by the need he felt to lie down beside her, he knew that he had to put some distance between them or get in worse trouble than he already was with this woman.

And so he sat in the chair behind his desk, as far away

from her as he could be and still stay in the same room. While he sat there, he contemplated why fate had dealt him such a hand. Day by day, he was falling deeper and deeper in love with a woman he had barely even kissed. And with every day that passed, he felt less and less certain that he would succeed in breaking the emotional barriers she kept between them.

"How, sweet lady, do I make you understand that the last thing I would ever do to you is hurt you?"

And as soon as he said it, he felt despair. There was nothing Nick could do to change her mind. Lucky was the one who would have to change. She had to learn to trust, and he didn't know where to start.

He glanced down at his watch, then back up at the woman on his couch. It was time. He rose from behind his desk and started across the floor. A board squeaked beneath his feet and Lucky suddenly lifted up her head, her eyes wide with fright.

Shocked by her reaction to the sound, Nick stopped where he was and held up his hands.

"It's okay, Lucky. It's okay. It's only me. I was coming to wake you. It's time for you to go back on duty. Let me give you a hand."

She sat up and rubbed her eyes, then stretched her neck, expecting pain. "My headache is gone!" The relief in her voice was unmistakable. "Thank you, Nick. Thank you so much."

He extended his hand. Lucky hesitated only a moment before taking the help that he offered.

"It was my pleasure, sweetheart," he said softly, and eased a strand of hair away from the corner of her eye.

The low, even timbre of his voice rumbled against her nerves like a soothing balm. *His pleasure*. She shivered. She suspected Nick Chenault knew a lot about pleasure.

"I'd better get back to work," she said, almost expecting him to try to get her to stay.

But when he walked to the door and opened it, then stepped aside to let her exit, she was so surprised that she left without another word.

Nick's pasted-on smile lasted until he could no longer see her, then he sighed and shut the door with a none-too-gentle thump, cursing all the way back to his desk.

"Woman . . . you're trying every ounce of patience that I possess and then some," he muttered, as he gazed long and hard around the empty room.

In the days that followed, Nick's emotions went on red alert. He stayed one step ahead of his own lust, telling himself over and over, like a mantra, that she would be the one to make the call. But the more he saw her, and the quicker she broke into a smile upon his arrival, the more difficult it became each time he said good-bye. He'd never wanted a woman as much, or denied himself as constantly, as he did Lucky.

Lucky, on the other hand, was in limbo. Part of her felt as if she'd been uprooted and then stuffed back into the hole upside down. Everything she'd based her life upon was ceasing to matter. She went to work, going through the motions like a robot, coming alive only for the hours when she was in Nick Chenault's presence. She'd completely forgotten the warnings Queen had constantly given her as she was growing up. *Don't give a man more than he's willing to give back. Don't trust a man with a handsome face and a handful of money. Don't love a man who makes no promises.*

Everything she'd been taught was worthless against the constant and growing need she felt, that she had to belong, completely, totally, to Nick Chenault.

She watched him when he wasn't looking, gazing her fill of the way his features changed as his emotions ran the gamut. Imagining what it would be like to have nothing between them but the heat of their bodies, then trying to imagine what it would be like to lie naked in his arms.

And always, when she got to that part of her fantasy, she forgot what came next, because she didn't really know what came next. She just knew that she knew peace when she was with him, and ached when she was not. It was a vicious cycle of need that could only come to one swift and certain end.

But there was a nearly forgotten onlooker to their stalled romance who hated, and resented, and wanted revenge.

Steve Lucas walked the streets of Vegas, his broken jaw wired shut, jobless and penniless, blaming all his misfortunes on the woman behind the man.

In his estimation, Lucky Houston was a bitch. He told himself that she'd played him for a fool and then chosen the man with the money. He couldn't or wouldn't face the fact that Lucky Houston had never, not once since her first day on the job, even given him the time of day.

Steve Lucas wasn't a man who understood rejection. He was on a mission, and word on the street was that someone big wanted Nick Chenault to suffer. The number he'd been given was burning a hole in his pocket as he hurried to make the call. He knew how to make Chenault suffer. Hurt the woman . . . and you hurt the man.

"Lucky . . . this is for you," Manny said, and winked as he handed her a note while she and Maizie sat in the employee lounge on a break.

Maizie grinned and poked Lucky in the ribs as Lucky's face turned red. "So read it," Maizie urged. "I'll even turn my head if it'll make you feel better."

Lucky stuck out her tongue and then opened the note and scanned the sparse lines, unaware that with every word she read, her mouth was turning up at the corners, and her eyes got a dreamy expression that delighted Maizie no end.

Would you consider having dinner with me at the Hacienda, dancing at the Mirage, and making love in the backseat of my car for dessert?

Lucky laughed aloud. Nick's sports car didn't have a backseat. His request was so outrageous that she couldn't find it in herself to be offended and suspected that he knew it.

"What?" Maizie begged. "For Pete's sake, don't go all gooey-faced and dreamy on me and then leave me hanging. I've got to go home to an empty bed and two babies, remember?"

Lucky's sympathy for Maizie's situation was deep. The Houston girls had never known a parent who stuck by them. By the time Queen had turned two, her mother was dead, and her only parent was an untrustworthy father.

The woman who came after stayed only long enough to give birth to Diamond and Lucky, and then walked out one day and never came back. At the tender age of nine, Queen had been left with the responsibility of raising her baby sisters, as well as their father. The girls eventually grew up, but Johnny didn't.

"Your bed is empty because you keep ignoring that cute bartender, Mike Bernard, and we both know it," Lucky teased. "And you love your babies beyond words and can't wait to get home to them."

Maizie grinned. "So . . . that still doesn't mean I can't live vicariously through you."

"It's just an invitation to dinner that I may or may not accept," Lucky said, and stuffed the note in her pocket to keep Maizie from seeing the part about dessert.

"Damn funny invitation, if you ask me." Maizie pouted. Then she glanced at her watch. "Break's over. And thank goodness! That means only one more hour and I'm gone for the day. See you later."

"Yes, later," Lucky mumbled, as she felt for Nick's note in her pocket.

She thought about what she was going to do only as long as it took to get to the house phone and call Nick's office. He answered on the second ring.

"Hello?"

"I might consider the dinner . . . but I don't think I'm up for dessert."

His chuckle sent shivers up her spine. "One of these days, pretty lady, you're going to eat those words."

"I might, but tonight, I'll settle for a steak instead. Pick me up at the apartment at eight. I'll be ready."

Lucky hung up the phone with a breathless sigh that made Nick's gut knot.

"You're ready? Oh, hell, lady, you don't know the meaning of the word," he muttered, well aware that she couldn't hear a thing that he said, then dropped the phone into the cradle.

Ignoring his unquenched libido was becoming an everyday practice, just as the constant phone calls he made on his home to Cubby or his father. Even though nothing serious had happened since the bombing attempt, Nick still took precautions each time he moved from location to location, making sure that someone could reach him at a moment's notice. Tonight would be no exception. He made the call home and then watched the clock, counting down the minutes until he could hold his lady in his arms.

By the time night came and dinner was over, Nick was in want to the point of misery. He'd had his fill of food he couldn't taste, as well as the fleeting glimpses he had of the shape of her body beneath the wispy blue fabric of her dress. Her arms were bare, and her hair was pulled back and then up in some intricate knot he desperately wanted to untie. The skirt of her dress flared to a stop just above her knees. Glimpses of something lacy just below her top button kept teasing his senses until he thought he might burst.

After they left the restaurant, instead of driving toward the club Nick had mentioned, he turned in the opposite direction on another street.

"I thought we were going dancing," Lucky said.

"We are," Nick said, as he lowered his window and

changed lanes before accelerating. "But later. Buckle up, honey. I need to cool off before I'll be able to get out on a dance floor with you."

She eyed the elegant cut of his trademark silk suit and tie, the short wisps of his thick, dark hair blowing across his forehead, and casually remarked, "Maybe if you took off your coat, you'd be cooler."

There was recognizable sarcasm in his answer. "Honey, the only thing I want to take off are your clothes. And since that's not about to happen anytime soon . . ."

"Oh."

Even in the darkness, he could see her blush. He chuckled and grabbed her hand as he reached across the seat.

"I'm sorry, Lucky. I shouldn't have said that, but hell . . . you wanted honesty in a relationship. That's as honest as I can be. The last thing I'm ever going to deny is that I want to make love to you."

Lucky sighed and folded her hands in her lap like a schoolgirl, which is what she constantly felt like in Nick's company.

"Maybe I should be the one who's apologizing," she said. There was a firmness in her voice Nick had never heard. "Maybe I'm the one who's been teasing. Not intentionally, but nevertheless . . ."

"Hell no!" he said. "I'm thirty-six years old. Not some eighteen-year-old male who's overdosed on hormones. When you get older, you realize that some things are worth the wait. You, my love, are one of those things. I don't just want to take you to bed, you know. I like you, girl. A whole damned lot."

Lucky grinned as Nick's car took a corner on two

wheels and then fishtailed slightly before aiming down the freeway with the unerring speed of a bullet.

"Then what, my dear Nick, are we racing to see . . . if not my naked self?"

Nick laughed, then bared his teeth and growled at her playfully. "You keep putting ideas like that in my head and I'm going to lose my cool. Then, my sweet lady, you'll need more than your Lady Luck namesake to keep you out of my arms."

Lucky angled herself in the confines of the bucket seat until she was more or less facing Nick as he drove. Every day he was becoming more and more important in her world. *But do I let him all the way in? And if I do, will he stay?*

Lucky wondered what she was waiting for. What sign did she need to see to prove to her that he meant what he said? He was in her dreams, in her head, in her heart. There was only one place he hadn't been. She wondered if it wasn't past time she let him in there too.

"Where are we going?" she asked, wondering how to say what was in her heart.

"I want to show you what Las Vegas looks like at night from the foothills. All the lights look like precious jewels tossed on a bed of velvet. Every color . . . everywhere. It's a prettier view of my city than the view from across a black-jack table, believe me."

The casualness of her attitude did not prepare him for the question she asked. "Are we going to neck?"

Nick skidded around a dark, secluded section of one of the streets and braked to a sudden stop. His hands were gripping the steering wheel with the determination of a race car driver. His eyes had narrowed, and his lips were firming with every breath that he took.

"What the hell are you playing at?" he growled, pulling her so close that he could see the lights of the city below reflecting back at him through her eyes.

Lucky took a deep breath and made the final move alone. Their lips met. Their hearts raced. There was a moment of resistance in his response before Nick's mouth went soft, then opened, and the groan that slid from him to her was an indication of his need. Before Lucky had time to tell him what was on her mind, he'd unbuckled her seat belt and pulled her across his lap.

"Be still," he warned. "And don't tell me the goddamned steering wheel hurts your back, because it can't be anything to the pain I'm in."

As angry as he sounded, his touch was a lesson in opposites. One hand cupped the back of her neck and tilted her head in perfect alignment to his mouth. The other hand was somewhere down the side of her hip and traveling south across fragile blue fabric. Lucky moaned and then sighed.

"Nick, I'm afraid to tell you what I feel. I'm so afraid to get hurt."

"Ah God!" For a moment, their foreheads touched, and Nick closed his eyes and inhaled slowly, trying to calm his racing pulse. "You're the last thing on this earth that I could bear to see suffer. It isn't in me to do you harm. I swear it, lady."

"I can almost believe you."

"It's you that you don't trust, sweetheart. Not me. You need to learn how to take a chance."

"I don't gamble, Nick. You'd do well to remember that."

His nostrils flared and the short intake of breath told Lucky she'd struck more than a nerve. From the look on his face, there was a very good chance that she was about to see him come unglued.

"I don't know whose whipping I keep taking from you, but it's damned sure not mine. I don't deserve that, Lucky, and you know it."

Lucky wanted to cry. "I didn't mean . . . I never realized . . ." She turned away, looking out the window beside her, and refused to see herself in the reflection of the glass. It might be too revealing to ignore.

Nick sighed, and slid a hand beneath the heavy knot of hair at her neck.

"I'm the one who's sorry, sweetheart. I pushed when I should have stayed put. Forgive me?"

She nodded and the movement sent tears running down the middle of her cheeks.

"Are you ready for that dance?"

She sighed. At this point, being held in his arms might be more than she could handle. But she'd promised him. "Sure, why not?"

Nick frowned, then started the car and pulled back onto the street. It was because they were so involved in their own thoughts that they missed the persistent glare of lights from the car that had been behind them off and on ever since they'd left the Hacienda.

He was to wonder later if anything would have been different had he seen the car. But it was simply a "what if" thought. Unbeknownst to them, the hand had already been dealt. The play was in progress, and it was only a matter of time before somebody won . . . and somebody lost.

Minutes later, he wove through a knot of traffic, angling for the exit that would take them back to the strip and the Mirage. Accelerating, he turned off the highway and pulled into valet parking.

He skidded to a halt just inches from one of the uniformed attendants and handed the young man his keys. He waited for his parking stub while another attendant helped Lucky out of the car.

She stretched, observing the frenzy of guests coming and going inside the club, and then stepped up on the curb while she waited for Nick to finish. Looking up, she stared at the vastness of the western sky and thought how different the world had looked from the valley of coal surrounded by the Smoky Mountains where she'd grown up.

This too was a valley, with the same sky and stars, but it felt like another world. No pall of coal dust hovered in the air. No trees marred the view of the horizon or of the sky above them. This city was alive and thriving from the money that built it, while Cradle Creek was a town dying on coal.

Behind them, the screech of brakes being applied and the scent of burning rubber made everyone turn to look, expecting to witness an accident.

Lucky saw the car careening through the parked vehicles in the driveway, scattering people on foot in all directions.

"Good grief," Lucky muttered to herself and looked for Nick to make certain that he was safely out of harm's way. It was because she sought him out first that she did not see the man's face or the gun he aimed out the window toward her.

The sound of squealing tires was startling. And the first thing that shot through Nick's mind was the bomb that had been in his car, and Detective Will Arnold's warning about Charlie Sams. Instinctively, Nick spun and started to run. There was no earthly reason for him to assume anyone was in danger other than the driver who seemed to be out of control, yet the moment he'd heard the screech of brakes, a sense of doom hit him full force. His first instinct had been to get to Lucky.

He was halfway across the lane, only yards from the bumper of the speeding car, when he saw the gun aimed at her.

"No!" he shouted, "Lucky! Look out!"

He pointed. The car was now barely cruising by, obviously giving the shooter time for a clear shot. Fear lent momentum to his leap as his feet left the ground, clearing the curb and taking her down with him in a running tackle.

His warning was as frightening as the terror she saw on his face. From the corner of her eye, she saw the car slowing down and then the gun. The impact of Nick's body as he took her down with him upon the grass came before she had time to brace herself for the blow.

Shots rang out in rapid succession. Grass and dirt splattered in her face as she fell backward, screaming. Then the ground came up with shattering force, knocking the breath from her body, and momentarily blinding her to anything but the feel of Nick lying across her. So heavy. Too still.

Struggling with the melting blackness of unconsciousness, she pushed halfheartedly at Nick's shoulders and tried to move. But he didn't budge, and it was only then that she realized his shout of warning was the last word she'd heard him speak.

She had a vague impression of the taillights of a car as it sped from the site. Of hearing people's screams and shouts of fear. Of sirens wailing far off in the distance. But the reality of what had happened was not with her. All she knew was that Nick hadn't moved.

She held him, certain that any moment he'd raise his head and smile down at her with that go-to-hell grin and make it all right. But he didn't, and she couldn't roll him off of her body. People's faces began to appear above them in a blinding blur.

And when Lucky lifted her arms from around his neck and stared up at the palms of her hands, she started to scream. Over and over. In long, hair-raising shrieks of despair. Nick's blood was all over her . . . and all over him.

10

The room was dark, with no other light but the beeping monitors that were connected to Nick. Lucky sat at his bedside, her eyes wide and glazed with horror, living through a replay of the last few hours that kept running over and over within her mind. She stared without wavering at his face, ignoring the tubes and needles poking into his lifeless body, because to acknowledge they were there was to admit the tenuous hold Nick had on life.

And while she watched the face of the man who'd saved her life, she wondered why it had mattered so much to withhold from him the little she had to give.

"Please, Nick . . . be well. I promise you it will be different."

But the only one who heard was the nurse hovering on the other side of his bed, quietly checking his condition and making notes on his chart, while Lucky covered his fingers with the palm of her hand, needing the contact of his flesh to assure herself that he still lived.

Lucky kept telling herself that this wasn't real. That what had happened a few hours ago was nothing more than a bad dream from which she would wake just as soon as the alarm went off.

But when an alarm did sound, it wasn't a call to awaken. What was happening within Nick's room was all too real. She jerked in reflex to the noise, then jumped to her feet as the line on the monitor registering Nick's pulse went flat.

"Oh, God! Oh, no!" she said, as the nurse dropped her charts and frantically started searching for his pulse.

Before Lucky could think to move, a bevy of people in uniform came into the room pushing carts and machines. University Medical Center was on the job.

"You'll have to wait outside," someone said, and all but pushed Lucky from the room. Seconds later, doctors rushed past her. She watched as the door swung shut behind them, leaving her alone outside in the hall.

"No, Nick, No! Fight, damn you, fight!" Then her voice gave out and her legs went weak. She leaned her head against the wall and covered her face, her last plea little more than a whisper. "Please don't die! If you do, you'll never know that you were winning the game between us."

Her cry echoed down the hall. Manny heard it as he got out of the elevator. Fear spiked the adrenaline racing through his body as he ran toward the sound of her voice. When he touched her shoulder, she spun around, and he saw that all the life had gone out of her eyes. Seconds later she collapsed in his arms.

As fate would have it, Paul Chenault's first glimpse of the woman who'd stolen Nick's heart was in the arms of another man. Although he knew of her existence, their first meeting was not as he'd hoped or planned. Her beauty was as striking as Nick had alluded to, but he wasn't prepared for the sight of his son's blood on her dress, or the way she was clutching Manny.

His first thought was that he was too late. Cubby pushed the wheelchair as swiftly as good sense allowed, but it was not fast enough for Paul. As they came to a stop, it took everything he had just to ask.

"Manny! Tell me! Is Nick . . . ?"

Lucky lifted her head from Manny's shoulder and shuddered. The voice was so like Nick's that for a moment, she couldn't speak. And then she saw the silver-gray hair, and the man whose mobility had gone from feet to wheels, and knew that he must be Nick's father, Paul Chenault.

She had put off Nick's requests to meet his father because it seemed an affirmation of something between them that had yet to be acknowledged. And now that the meeting was here, everything she'd considered of importance faded in comparison to the fact that Nick might be dying. Shame overwhelmed her as she was forced to face the fact that this man's son was in danger because he'd taken a bullet meant for her.

Lucky turned away, hiding her face on Manny's chest, for the moment unable to face him.

"No . . . no, Mr. Chenault. We don't know anything. He just . . . they only went in a moment ago," Manny said.

Paul went weak with relief. Then frustration set in.

"Damn these legs. Damn these wheels." Paul hit his knees with doubled-up fists, but did himself no harm. He couldn't feel the blows he was raining upon his legs. "I should have been there. It should have been me."

Without thinking, Lucky went from Manny's arms to Paul's wheelchair at her knees. She grabbed the old man's hands and held his wrists, trying to focus his attention on something other than the fear that enveloped them all. She knew from hearing Nick talk that they lived to keep stress out of Paul Chenault's life. That any unexpected shock could finish him off.

"Mr. Chenault, you've got to stop. Please . . . you must listen. It's not your fault." Her voice broke. "They were aiming at me . . . not at him. I don't know why, but it was me they were trying to kill."

She choked on her words as she spoke. Despair came swiftly, and as it did, she lowered her head and buried her face against his knees. "It was me . . . it was me. They hurt him because of me."

Paul's hands uncurled. Slowly the anger drained out of him as her grief sank in. Her shoulders, too small for the weight of her guilt, shook from the depth of her sobs, while the men looked on helplessly.

Paul laid his hand upon her hair. At his touch, Lucky lifted her head, her cheeks damp with tears as Paul willed himself not to look at the blood on her dress. Gently, as he used to comfort Nick's pain long ago, he smoothed her hair from her eyes and wiped at her tears with his handkerchief. His words were a balm to Lucky's aching heart.

"It wasn't because of you, young lady. Whoever is behind this is trying to destroy me and all I hold dear. They know that I have little left to live for other than my son. That's the only way I can be hurt. And I'm afraid that if hurting him means destroying you . . . they'll do that too." His hands cupped her cheeks as his gaze pinned her to the spot. "I can't tell you how sorry I am that you've become involved in something this ugly . . . but I swear on my son's life that until he's well, you'll be under my protection, just as you were under Nick's. If he loves you enough to die for you, then I can do no less."

Lucky shuddered. It was the first time that she'd considered the implications of the attack other than the fact that Nick was near death because he'd taken a bullet meant for her. This wouldn't necessarily be the last time someone tried to take her life.

"Oh, my God," she groaned as Manny helped her to her feet. "Why? Why is this happening?"

Paul's words were filled with pain, and his age was never more evident than it was at this moment. "If I knew the answer to that, I could have stopped this before it got started," he whispered, and closed his eyes, unwilling to face the fear that held them hostage. Together, they waited, each in their own way making promises to a higher power in exchange for Nick Chenault's life.

Lucky's wait was as agonizing as it had been before, when the doctors went in, but no longer as lonely. She took the chair Manny offered, then clasped her hands in her lap as she leaned her head against the wall.

It had been years since she'd prayed. Years since Queenie had stopped taking them to the church just up the hill and two streets over from the cemetery where Johnny lay. Years since she'd thought to ask anyone other than her sisters for help. But this was different. Everything she cared about was on the line, and the results were out of her hands.

Either Nick lived, or he died. The doctors could only do so much. If praying would give them the edge that they needed, she was prepared to give her all.

Uncertain where or how to begin, she just closed her eyes and tried to empty her mind of everything but the thought of Nick's recovery. As she sat, assailed by the antiseptic smells and frightening sounds of clanking metal and frantic voices inside Nick's room, peace came. Slowly but surely, her fears settled. And as it did, the tears running down her cheeks receded, leaving her eyes a vivid, shimmering green in a face too pale for belief.

"Lucky . . . *querida?*"

She turned toward Manny's voice. His concern for her, as well as for Nick, was obvious.

"I'm fine," she said softly. "And Nick will be too. I don't know how to explain it . . . but I know that I'm right."

And when, minutes later, the doctor exited with news that backed up her claim, the men too sighed with relief. Lucky sat, silent and shaking, for she knew then that she loved Nick Chenault.

"Come," Manny said, eyeing her bloodstained clothes and weary face. "Let me take you home."

"No," she said. "I leave when Nick leaves, and not before. If you really want to help, send someone to tell my landlady, Lucille LaMont, what has happened. Tell her I need my things. She'll know what to do."

Paul was ashen. Only now, after the doctor's news, had the color started to return to his cheeks.

"I'll send one of my staff," Paul said. "They'll bring what you need now to the hospital, and the rest will be sent to our home."

Lucky opened her mouth to argue.

"Don't even start with me," Paul said, showing more of his former self than he had in months. "If anything else happened to you before Nick is well enough to cope, he'd have my hide . . . and everyone else's around him. It's settled."

She shrugged. Part of her didn't care. She only wanted Nick to be well. But another part of her started to panic. What if they never found the man who'd instigated all of this? What if she became a virtual prisoner in the Chenault home just to stay alive?

The men left, leaving her alone in the hall with a head full of worries that had nowhere to go.

Half a continent away, Dieter Marx flung his phone across the room and then roared with rage. Glass shattered as the telephone hit a bookcase, and books tumbled to the floor. Soon the rapid sounds of footsteps converging upon his study could be heard all over the house.

The servants were in terror. Whatever had happened could not have been good. *El Gato* was not a happy man.

"Why can't they get it right?" Dieter shouted. "I'm sending fools to do one simple thing. How can one man keep surviving beyond such odds? What the hell kind of luck does he have that keeps him alive?"

"*Señor . . . por favor . . .*"

"*Váyense!*" Dieter grabbed a vase from his desk and flung it after the servant who fled from the room in retreat. "Get out . . . Goddammit, just get out," he repeated, once again reverting to English as his voice and his rage were nearly all used up.

He stomped to the windows, and stared through the panes to the lush panorama before him. But he neither saw nor appreciated the beauty of all that was his. Leaves on banana trees swayed high up in the breeze, while a vivid palette of colors bloomed in the flowers that grew in mass profusion, climbing up walls, falling down trellises. Anywhere and everywhere Dieter looked, beauty was there for him to see.

But beauty was not the thing that he sought to obtain. He had beauty. It did not make him happy. He had money, more money than the entire village of people would see in a hundred lifetimes, and he was not complete. He had women at his beck and call who were young enough to be his daughters and granddaughters, and even they could not prolong his happiness enough to satisfy his blackened soul.

Dieter fought, breathed, and survived for revenge. He'd waited years for the right moment when it could be exacted. Planning, plotting, but always putting it off, waiting for the moment of ripeness, for the time when harvest of the ills he had planned would be at its peak.

But when he'd learned that Paul Chenault had nearly died from a stroke and was incapacitated to the point of immobility, he realized that he'd waited too long. What would be the point of revenge if the one it was intended for was not alive to suffer? It was that question that he'd asked himself that had shown him the path he must take.

With bitter joy, he'd set his plans in motion by installing Charlie Sams into the Chenault organization. But one after the other, Dieter's well-laid plans kept coming to unsatisfactory ends. He'd paid fortunes to men who kept screwing up.

"There is only one road left, my friend," Dieter muttered to himself, as he turned away from the window and strode across the room toward the stairs. "If you want a job done right . . . do it yourself."

Hours later, after night had claimed the day, Dieter lay naked upon his bed, absently watching the moonlight sweep its path across Amaleeya's body, while he made mental plans for his trip back into the States. She was his latest in a string of women who were in his pay for one reason and one reason only.

He had little concern that his sex lay flaccid upon his body. Nor did it concern him unduly that in spite of the enticement of her smooth brown skin and the sweetness hidden by the dark curls between her legs, his manhood had not responded. She was highly skilled and well paid in the art of giving pleasure.

Her body was young, but her soul was old. Forced into prostitution at the age of eleven, now, at twenty-two, Amaleeya was a full-blown beauty and skilled beyond the norm in ways to arouse an old man's libido.

Her tongue tasted and her body teased as her fingers traced the paths of unused nerves upon the man's sleeping sex. She smiled, and she coaxed with every skill that she'd learned, and when the absent glaze slipped from his face, and his eyes widened, his pupils becoming dilated and fixed upon the stroke of her hands along his slowly burgeoning manhood, she knew a moment's sigh of relief.

She would not suffer. There would be money in her pocket and no bruises upon her back tonight. At the moment, it was enough for which to be thankful.

As his breathing quickened, Dieter forgot about the bitter years of hatred that had consumed him. He forgot about the crippled man who lived a half a world away, and who waited in fear for the next blow to fall. All he could see, and all he could feel, was the spiraling wave of heat that boiled, flowing toward the center of his being and then erupting out and into her hands. His satisfied groan that accompanied the release was music to Amaleeya's ears.

But Amaleeya was not the only one who breathed a sigh of relief this night. Dieter Marx had performed like a man. It was proof enough for him that he could do what must be done.

Three and one half weeks after the incident, Nick was ready for a release of his own. Today he would be dismissed from the hospital, and he could hardly wait. He had lived with worry and anger for so long that it had eaten into his days and interrupted all his nights.

When Lucky was not at his side, he could not rest until he saw her face. Constant fear that the incident would be repeated and he would not be there to stop it, drove him crazy. He'd hired bodyguards, and pulled promises from her, as well as everyone around him, until they were all afraid to move without taking her with them and telling him first.

He had little memory of his first days in the hospital,

and from what he had learned, it was just as well. Remembering one's death and subsequent retrieval from heaven . . . or hell . . . wherever he'd been headed, was disconcerting to say the least.

All he could remember was the sound of Lucky's voice, and the touch of her hands, and the feel of her tears upon his face. Even now, when she was merely across the room, he had an overwhelming urge to call her back into his arms. Because the last thing he'd seen before his world went black was the gun aimed directly at her, and the shock upon her face.

He'd known then that if she'd died . . . if he'd been too late . . . he would not have wanted to go on. It scared him to death that she meant that much to him, and that he had no other claim upon her.

It was also proof of his full recovery that one constant ache he'd had before had never gone away. Nick now lived for the day when he would put his ring upon her finger and himself inside her. And not necessarily in that order.

Lucky was a shadow of her former self. Endless days and sleepless nights had taken more weight off her body than she'd had to spare. Her blue jeans hung from her hips, and the pink sweater she was wearing was loose and baggy in places it was not meant to be.

The wide green eyes that saw into Nick's soul on a daily basis were hollow and bore circles beneath them shades darker than her skin. Her hair hung loose down her back, and as she walked, it swung against her shoulders like a widow's veil. And Nick had never thought her more beautiful, or loved her more than he did on the day of his release. Even if the declaration of love that he longed to hear from her had yet to be said.

"Do you have everything?" Lucky asked, as she darted around the hospital room, poking in drawers, looking in cabinets. "We're about ready to leave."

"If I have you, I'm ready, baby. You're all that I need. You're all that I'll ever need."

Lucky stopped and turned. Once again, she looked at him as if she'd never get enough of the sight. He was paler than he had been, and a little thinner. But the fire was back in his eyes, and the passion in his voice. It was more than she'd ever thought to regain, and enough to last her the rest of her life.

"Oh, Nick," she whispered, and pressed her hands together to keep them from shaking. "You will never know how much you mean to me." She hesitated, but only for a moment, having learned the hard way that waiting might sometimes be the wrong thing to do. She'd waited once, and nearly lost the man she loved before she could tell him so. It was time to tell him the truth. Her eyes locked with his and her mouth barely trembled as she finally said what was in her heart. "I love you."

Shock suffused his body. He felt as if he had waited a lifetime to hear her say those words, and then they'd come when he could do nothing but hold her.

"Come here," he said, and held out his arms. Moments later she'd buried her face against his chest and wrapped her arms around his waist. He felt, rather than heard, her tears. "I love you too," he whispered, then his gut twisted. "Ah God, baby, don't cry . . . not again."

"I'm sorry," she sobbed. "But I nearly lost you. I'm afraid that when we leave here, something like this will happen again. If it does, next time we might not be so lucky."

Nick sighed and wrapped his hands in the length of her hair, wishing they were somewhere else . . . anywhere else but this damnable hospital room. No lock on the door. Nowhere to hide from the constant surge of busy nurses who lived out their lives on this floor and countless others like it.

"There will be no next time," Nick vowed. "And as long as I have my Lucky Lady in my arms, I don't need to worry."

She sighed. "How can you say that? I've brought you nothing but bad luck, Nick. Besides, don't you know that Lady Luck is fickle?"

Nick laughed and swooped down to catch her pouting lips, turning the moment from despair to desire with one kiss. "Damn you, woman." He groaned and flattened the palms of his hands across her hips, grinding himself into her with hopeless frustration.

"Maybe you need to stay in the hospital another day or two," Lucky said with a wink. "I think I feel something swollen. Maybe you're not all well."

"You've been around Fluffy LaMont too long," Nick growled, and then grinned when she swung out of his arms to finish his packing.

"She's been a godsend to me, Nick," Lucky said, as she zipped his suitcase shut.

"I know, baby. I was just teasing you. She's one in a million. By the way, what color is her hair this week?"

Lucky made a face at him, and then could not prevent an answering grin when she replied, "Buxom Brunette, I think. And don't laugh. At least now it's all one color. She goes out and has it done in a salon. When I first moved in, she was doing it herself."

"Hey, Nicky, we're ready to roll. Let's blow this pop-up stand," Cubby said, as he burst into the room without knocking.

"I think the phrase is Popsicle stand, buddy. But it doesn't matter. Hell yes, I'm ready. Lead the way."

"You have to ride down in a wheelchair, Nick," Lucky warned.

"Honey, I'd ride a damned camel if it took me out of here."

Moments later a nurse wheeled in a chair and they all left with light hearts and rapid steps.

Downtown, Detective Will Arnold was scratching his head as he read the report on Metro's latest John Doe identification. Fingerprints had been impossible to obtain from a body with no hands. And the damage done to John Doe's face was even worse. But the broken jaw that had been wired shut was the clue that triggered the ID.

Whatever Steve Lucas had been doing, it had pissed someone off big time. In the old days, cutting off a hand had been the underworld's way of dealing with a thief. But to his knowledge, Lucas wasn't a thief. Only an asshole. Why both hands had been removed was beyond him. What mattered most to Will Arnold was that people connected with Nick Chenault kept coming up dead. And always after a murder attempt. If he didn't know better, he'd think that Chenault was into a little payback of his own.

His eyes narrowed as he considered the ramifications of that thought. If his sources were right, Nick Chenault would be released from the hospital either today or tomorrow. It made the detective wonder if there was a connection between Lucas and the men who'd tried to kill Lucky Houston. In a way it made a wicked sort of sense, from a criminal's point of view.

Steve Lucas had gone to jail for an attack on Lucky Houston, and Lucky Houston was now, for all intents and purposes, Chenault's girl. Maybe the hit on Miss Houston wasn't connected to the threats to Nick Chenault. But the more he thought about it, the more he knew he was right. It was too coincidental to ignore. The clues were right in front of him. It was the connections that were still too vague to make.

"One thing at a time, Arnold. One thing at a time," he told himself.

The only one who was still alive to tell his story was Charlie Sams. Maybe another talk with him could net some useful information. Will Arnold whistled softly through his teeth as he continued to read the coroner's report on Steve Lucas. No wonder Charlie Sams had refused bail. Jail was probably the safest place he could be.

"I hate this," Nick growled, as the limousine turned into the Chenault estate.

He didn't have to look to know that the car following them, as well as the one in front of the car they were in, was there. He'd hired both of them himself. But it was the first time he'd gotten a dose of living behind armed guards. He didn't think he was going to like it one damned bit.

"I know," Lucky said. "Your father said I would get used to it." She tried to smile and didn't make it. "I've failed miserably. I keep forgetting that they are there. And then when I do realize someone's behind me, just for a moment I think it's the same people who . . ." Her chin quivered and she looked away, unable to finish the sentence.

Nick pulled her into his arms, cushioning her next to his chest as they came to a stop.

"It will be all right, honey. We've survived this far. Nothing can stop us now."

"Welcome home, Nicky! Welcome home." Paul Chenault sat in the doorway with a smile on his face that could have lit up the world.

"I'd rather be necking with you," Nick whispered in her ear, putting a blush on her cheeks that was still there after they'd entered the house and closed the door.

As Lucky had feared, Nick had overdone it. His endurance was not up to full strength, and his insistence upon sitting through dinner had finished him off. She'd seen him turn pale, watched nervously as he hid shaky hands in his lap, and knew it was time for someone with some brains to take control.

"I made chocolate mousse for dessert, sir," Shari said, waiting for a smile to appear on her boss's face. It was his favorite dessert.

"He's not having any," Lucky said, and laid her napkin

by her plate as she got to her feet. "He's going to bed, whether he likes it or not."

"Oh, hell," Nick muttered. "How long has she been like this?"

Paul grinned. "Since the day she put her shoes under your bed."

Lucky flushed, but would not be swayed. It hadn't taken her long to learn during the past three weeks that living in an all-male household was a far cry from the one she'd grown up in. She'd also learned to give as good as she got.

"My shoes are not under his bed, and you know it," Lucky muttered. "Please, Nick. Don't argue. You're exhausted. The last thing you need is a setback."

He leaned forward in his chair, forced to admit the wisdom of her words. "She's right, Dad. I think I'd better call it a night."

Lucky sighed with relief. At least he wasn't going to argue. He rose and then paused in the doorway to look over his shoulder at Lucky.

"Well . . . aren't you coming to make sure that I brush my teeth and wash behind my ears?"

Paul laughed aloud. "Here's where I make my own exit," he added. "Cubby, get me out of here before the dishes start flying." Moments later, the room was empty except for Nick and Lucky.

"Well, are you coming?" he asked.

She came toward him from across the room, her white palazzo pants and sleeveless blouse moving gently with the sway of her body as she walked. Tendrils of her hair had escaped their pins and hung seductively down the back of her neck. He could see bare toes peeking out from the gold straps of her open-toe sandals. It made him want her. But in the last few weeks he'd learned a hard lesson. He could not always have what he wanted.

She stopped at his side and looked up. Her eyes were shimmering with unshed tears. Her hands trembled as she slid them up the length of his arms to touch the back of his neck.

"Brush and wash what you will, my love. But when you sleep, I will hold you. It's the only way I can be sure you're all right."

Tears sprang unbidden to Nick's eyes, blinding him to the love upon her face. But he didn't need to see it to know that it was there. The evidence of her love was in every nuance of her voice and every look that she bestowed upon him. It was the first time that he'd considered how deeply Lucky had suffered through his ordeal as well.

"Ah, God, lady, you take my breath away," Nick whispered, and brushed his lips against hers before they turned toward the stairs.

"When you are well, we will talk."

"About what?" he teased, knowing full well what she was referring to.

"Things," she said, and pointed toward the stairs.

Nick rolled his eyes and tried not to groan. She was the damnedest woman he had ever had the fortune to love.

A short time later Nick walked out of his bathroom wearing nothing but a towel, his hair still damp and glistening from the shower that he'd taken. Almost simultaneously, Lucky walked into his room without knocking and closed the door behind her.

She stood silently within the confines of the room, a waif of a woman in a gown and robe that reminded him of translucent butter. The pale yellow fabric hid little. Vague but enticing images of her long, slender limbs and shapely hips, taut breasts, and the shadowy vee between her legs made him shake. But it was not from weakness; it was from want.

"Come here," he said. When her dressing gown parted, revealing even more of the woman beneath as she followed his command, his breath caught at the back of his throat.

Lucky walked into his arms and felt the wild hammering of his heart as it pounded beneath his chest. As badly as she wanted this to go further, she remembered all too well where he'd been only hours earlier.

With a reluctant sigh, she centered a kiss on his chest and then feathered her palms across his back, gazing with new horror at the pink, scarring tissue healing around the wound below his shoulder.

"Will you take me to bed, Nick Chenault? I want you to hold me and make promises you don't have to keep."

"My Lucky, lucky charm, you should know by now that I keep every promise that I make."

She sighed and tried to smile, but her own weariness was almost overwhelming her.

Nick shuddered at the thought of lying next to her and not being able to take their relationship that last step. And while he'd regained most of his strength simply by solitude and the relaxing warmth of the shower, Lucky looked ready to drop.

"I've always wanted to do this," he said, and dug his

hands through the thick ropes of hair she'd piled loosely upon her head. Seconds later, pins went flying as her hair fell down her back and covered his hands and arms like a sensuous veil. "God, Lucky," he whispered, and combed his fingers through it in fascination. "I love your hair. It feels like silk against my skin."

She slid onto one side of his bed and crawled beneath the covers, then pulled them a little farther back, giving him the room and an invitation to come in.

Nick stared long and hard at the sight that she made, lying still and waiting for him to join her. With a groan of defeat, he leaned over and turned out the light. Instantly the room was in darkness.

Lucky bit her lip and waited. And then she heard his towel hit the floor and felt the bed give as he crawled in beside her. Before she had time to consider the consequences, Nick was lying full-length beside her, and pulling her gently but firmly into his arms.

"Just so I can sleep," he promised. "Just so I can sleep. If you're in my arms, then I know that you're safe."

Tears squeezed out from beneath her eyelids as she pressed her face against his chest. It should have felt unfamiliar, even slightly uncomfortable, lying body-to-body against Nick's nudity. But somehow she felt as if they'd been doing this all their lives. He was safe, and strong, and well. She sighed and shifted once against his side.

In the dark, Nick felt her hand as it slid out and across the breadth of his chest. When it centered upon his heart, she paused and then stopped. He felt the tension in her body ease, and moments later, heard the soft, even breathing as she slept.

He shook, and tried not to cry. It was the most moving gesture he'd ever experienced. Only after she'd been able to feel life beating in his chest had she relaxed within his arms.

"Sweet baby," he whispered, and lifted her hair from her neck and spread it out across the pillow behind her. "My sweet, Lucky girl. Say a prayer for us both that we can live through this."

Beyond the walls of the Chenault estate, far below in the city streets, life went on at its normal, frantic pace. But for Nick and Lucky, it existed only within each other's arms.

11

Lucky's laughter echoed from her room and out into the upper hall, drawing Nick closer and closer into the web of enchantment in which he'd found himself caught since his release from the hospital.

Nearly a week had passed since he'd come home, and in that time he'd watched the shadows disappearing from Lucky's eyes, and seen her appetite, as well as her state of mind, returning to normal. It was only a matter of time before the living need to claim his woman got the best of him.

Lucky laughed again, and Nick wondered who, or what, had tickled her fancy to such a degree. He paused outside the door, thinking that an intrusion might not be welcome. And then he heard the unmistakable sounds of a baby, and he was so stunned that he walked into the open doorway in spite of good intentions to acknowledge her right to privacy.

"Pretty baby. Yes, you are," Lucky crooned, and laughed when the chubby little girl cooed and wrapped her fists in Lucky's hair, pulling the handful of hair closer and closer to her toothless little mouth.

"Oh, no you don't," Lucky warned, and laughed again as she unwrapped her hair from around the child's tiny fingers. "You can't eat my hair."

The baby gurgled, then kicked against Lucky's stomach as Lucky cradled her in her arms.

"Someday I'll have babies just like you," Lucky said, and brushed her fingertips through the wispy black strands of hair framing the fat little face. "Lots and lots of babies."

Lucky pressed a kiss against the petal-soft cheek and felt her heart tug as the baby began settling against her chest. Moments later, the girl poked her little thumb into her mouth and started to doze as Lucky's voice whispered against her ear.

"And you know what else, little angel? My babies will never be hungry . . . or afraid. They'll never wonder where their mother is, or why she didn't love them. Your mother loves you, yes she does. She'll be fine. You'll see. You'll see."

She chanted the promise and then started to rock, humming the tune to a lullaby she'd almost forgotten she knew. The baby fussed once or twice, old enough to recognize the unfamiliarity of the woman who was holding her. Yet not old enough to care that the comfort she needed was coming from someone else. Unable to resist the motion of the rocking chair, the baby's eyes shut. Finally, the only motion in her body was the occasional tug of her tongue against her thumb as Lucky's humming vibrated next to her ear.

Nick was motionless. Their hair was nearly of a color. The only difference was in the length of the curls. Touched beyond words at the sight of Lucky rocking a child that could have been her own—their own—moved him deeply. But the mystery of the baby's presence still remained. Unable to resist, he walked into the darkened room.

Lucky looked up and smiled. She pressed a finger to her lips in a plea for silence and then looked down with longing at the baby who'd fallen asleep against her breast.

"She's asleep," Lucky whispered. "But I hate to put her down. I've never held a baby this small before." And then her eyes filled. "Oh, Nick. Isn't she beautiful?"

His voice shook. It was all he could do not to kneel at her feet. "Beautiful is hardly the word."

Needing to be closer, yet afraid to disturb the peace of the moment, he settled for the edge of the bed instead of her arms. "But whose baby is she? And why on earth is she here?"

"Oh, Mr. Chenault!" Shari burst into the room, and then quickly lowered her voice when she saw that her grandchild had fallen asleep. "I'm sorry. It's just that I didn't know where else to turn, and Lucky offered to help."

"What happened?" Nick asked.

Shari Garcia had been with them since Nick was a child. She was part of his family. He couldn't imagine what had caused her such concern, or why she felt it necessary to apologize.

Lucky answered for her. "Shari's daughter-in-law, Angelina, had a car accident a short while ago." The tiny girl squirmed in her sleep, and instinctively Lucky patted her bottom in time to the rocker's motion, lulling her back into silence. "It wasn't serious, but she's in the emergency room getting a cast on her leg as we speak. This little thing was in the backseat and wasn't hurt a bit! Wasn't she lucky?"

Nick couldn't resist a caress of the baby curls that feathered across Lucky's hand as she cradled the child's head. The hair felt soft, almost weightless, yet at the touch, it curled around his finger as if it had a life of its own. An odd sort of pain settled around his heart as he watched the joy on Lucky's face.

"I'm glad she wasn't hurt," Nick said. "But I don't want to hear another word about apologies, Shari. After all, what are families for if they can't help out in an emergency now and then?"

"Thank you for being so understanding," Shari said. "I just came up to get her this moment. Her other grandmother, Angelina's mother, is downstairs ready to take her. Lucky dear, I can't thank you enough for helping." Shari gently removed the sleeping baby from Lucky's arms.

The maid's nervous explanation made Lucky's heart drop. She wasn't ready to give the baby up. And then Shari was gone, leaving Lucky with empty arms and a man who was waiting to fill them.

"Oh, Nick . . . she was the sweetest little . . ."

Nick took a deep breath, and when the words came out, they resonated from the passion he was feeling.

"I want to make love to you, Lucky. No more waiting. No more excuses. I would give you a dozen babies tomorrow if you wanted. Right now, I'll settle for a practice run on the real thing."

Within the space of a second, Lucky's heart felt like it had shot to the roof of her mouth and then dropped to the region of her stomach. The fire in Nick's eyes was impossible to mistake. But it was the longing in his voice that sold her. And after what they had endured, and while the love that she felt for this man had grown on a daily basis, she knew that waiting any longer would be ridiculous.

"Then lock the door. But I feel it only fair to warn you that I'm scared to death."

"Oh, hell," Nick groaned, as the lock turned beneath his hands. "Don't tell me things like that. It makes me feel guilty as sin."

"No! I'm not scared like that," Lucky said, and then blushed. "I know what you look like. I've slept with you naked in my arms, remember?"

He covered the distance between them in two steps. "Yes, honey. I remember vividly." He cupped her face and tilted her lips toward his, blending their breaths with a kiss of apology. "I'm sorry, but it'll probably be uncomfortable for you at first. I can't make that any better."

"You still don't get it," she said. "I don't know what to do." And then she shrugged and sighed. "I feel so stupid. I mean . . . yes, I know *what's* going to happen. It's just that I don't know *how* to make things good for you. That's what scares me."

Nick caught her hand and then pressed it to the center

of his chest, holding it in place with the pressure of his own. "This is what real fear feels like, baby. I love you. Beyond words. And no matter how much I try, what we do is going to cause you pain. I can hardly bear the thought." Their foreheads touched as his words settled around Lucky's soul.

"Then make love to me, Nick. Get me past this hurdle and I'll get you past the fear."

"I'll get some protection," Nick said, and started for the door.

"I'm on birth control pills," Lucky said. "Have been for weeks."

He groaned, thinking of how she'd prepared for this day to come and still feared it happening.

The room was in shadows. Outside the afternoon sun of late September was persistent and hot. Inside the house, a fire burned hotter as the last of their clothes went in a heap upon the floor.

Lucky stood at the side of her bed and watched as Nick came toward her. His body was long and lean and darkly tanned from years under the Nevada sun. His manhood surged out before him as he walked, jutting toward her with a sexual demand she could not miss. Deep in the center of her belly, heat coiled and writhed and left her shaking.

"Nick . . ."

Uncertainty was in her voice as she reached to his face. "Sssh." He caught her hand and coiled her fingers around his prominent sex, suspecting that it was the one thing she feared, and needed to confront.

He expected hesitancy, even rejection; instead she nearly sent him to his knees when, with both hands, she held, then encircled him, moving her fingers lightly upon the silken shaft in an exploratory manner as she marveled at the shift of skin against muscle.

"Oh, God." Nick gritted his teeth and closed his eyes against the need to thrust himself within the nest that she'd made of her hands. "Whatever you're doing, don't stop."

Lucky's pulse pounded. The feel of him within her hands was frightening, and yet intriguing. So big. So strong. Her lips went slack at the thought of taking all of this power inside of her.

His hands slid up her arms and then down, palming her breasts as his thumbs began circling the dark areola surrounding her nipples. Spiral after spiral, he increased the pressure in subtle increments so that when his thumbs finally found their targets and rubbed across the jutting pout of the nubs, she lost every skill she had, including balance. Nick caught her before she fell.

"Oh . . . I . . ."

The catch in her voice, and the grip she had on his arms, were all he needed to know. His teeth shown white through a fleeting smile before he resumed what he was doing. So she liked being touched like this. He would have bet everything he had in his pocket—if he had one—that his woman would not be a lady in bed. It was the best news he'd had all week.

"You like that, baby?"

She moaned in response to his question. It was the best and only answer she could manage.

His hands slid from her breasts to her back and then down to cradle her hips, pulling her gently but firmly against the thrust of his manhood, careful to center the tip of himself on that tender waiting bud between her legs.

One thrust. Slow, gentle. And only so far. Lucky arched against the surge of desire that ripped through her belly. She shivered as she heard herself moaning Nick's name aloud.

"More?" Nick asked, and rubbed the place where he'd been with the pads of his thumbs instead. Again, she would have gone to her knees had he not caught her.

"Oh . . . oh . . . I—"

"I'll take that as a yes," Nick growled, ignoring his own body's demand for relief.

Her hair fanned out behind her as she went from an upright to a prone position in nothing flat. Nerves jerked in every inch of her body while Nick's mouth and hands explored places she hadn't known existed. And it was not enough. Things hurt that wouldn't ease. Pressure built with no promise of release.

"Nick, what are you doing?" she gasped, as she watched the top of his head move south from her belly button. "Oh, my God!" she gasped, as it became patently clear. "I don't think . . . I can't do . . ." Then she arched, her legs parting instinctively to make way for the man who'd settled himself between.

"Oh, but yes, pretty baby, you can," Nick whispered, and found the tiny little nub that would trigger her explosion.

Blood thundered behind his eyelids as Nick's tongue snaked out, testing the territory around the fragile skin.

He needed to be inside her and it wasn't time. She had to be so far gone in need that when he thrust, she would not feel the pain. It was the only way he could fathom what had to be done.

Lucky moaned, and rocked upon the bed beneath the command of Nick's caress. His mouth and his tongue, and the sweep of his hands across her body, were driving her mad. It was an endless, driving throb that demanded release.

"I can't stand this," she groaned, and pushed helplessly at his shoulders, wanting him to stop or put this to an end. "It's too much. It's too much."

Nick's hand slid back into the curls at the juncture of her thighs, this time increasing the pressure to the point that he could actually feel the tremors of a climax beginning beneath his fingertips. Sweat broke out across his body as his own desire suddenly demanded completion.

Without warning, it came upon her. A blinding, mind-shattering burst of joy that rocked her senseless. As wave after wave of pleasure ebbed and flowed through her body, Nick lifted himself above her, poised at her threshold only long enough to aim and thrust.

It coincided with a wash of heat that ripped through her belly so perfectly that for a moment, Lucky didn't even know what had happened. But while the feelings of climax continued to ease, she slowly came to realize that she was full where she'd once been empty.

She opened her eyes and focused on the man who held himself suspended above her body with majestic grace, and lifted her arms to pull him down.

"Oh, Nick . . . Oh, Nick. It's over, and it was beautiful."

"No, baby, it's just beginning," he muttered, and started to move.

Lucky's eyes widened as she felt the returning surge within her body and realized in shock that Nick was already inside and she'd never felt him enter. Shocked by the size of him, she moaned with renewed delight as her own body adjusted to his presence, just as she'd known it could. Hard to the point of true pain, Nick felt a sweet relief as his slow but steady strokes inside of her increased with every thrust, knowing that it would soon be over. And then the feeling came, so strong it could not be denied, and he was too far gone to wait any longer.

"This time it's for me," he groaned, and lowered his head between her breasts, unable to stop the inevitable.

His hands slid beneath her hips, lifting her that much closer. But it was instinct that made Lucky lock him within a hold of her own.

Nick choked on a breath as her long legs coiled around his waist. It was a move he hadn't expected her to make. Her eyes were closed, her neck arched to the beat of a drum only she could hear.

He smiled, and then slowly gritted his teeth as release became impossible to deny. One push followed another, and with a final thrust of his sex, he came with a burst and spilled inside of her. Shudder upon shudder followed as his seed continued to flow.

She could not hold him close enough or tight enough to satisfy the urgency of her love. And it wasn't because she'd finally crossed a hurdle into complete womanhood. Nor was it from the complete and unbridled joy that Nick had given her.

It was because she'd felt him come apart in her arms. He'd let her know there was a way to destroy him. It was the ultimate gift of trust that knocked down the last rail in her defense. She could do no less than respond in kind.

"I love you, Lucky Lady . . . love you," Nick said over and over, pressing soft, gentle kisses upon her face and neck. "Tell me you're all right." He held her close, wanting to take away the pain.

"I'm not all right. I'm perfect," she said, and unwound her legs from his body, stretching beneath him like a waking cat, one arm, one leg, at a time.

Nick groaned and then chuckled softly as he stole one last kiss before levering himself away. Before she had time to complain, he slid his arms beneath her shoulders and rolled her toward him. Long silent moments passed while his hand stroked and gentled the racing pulse he felt beneath her skin.

"Did I hurt you?" he asked, hating to hear her answer, yet needing to know.

"I don't know," Lucky said with a sigh. "You made me too crazy to feel it."

"Thank God," he muttered. "Now, first things first. You should bathe. I'll go shower in my room."

"But why can't we—"

Nick leaned over and kissed the pout on her lips. "Because, honey. It was your first time. Whether you believe it or not, you're going to be sore. A warm bath will help, I promise."

"You're the expert," she said, and rolled out of bed and headed for the bath, as unconscious of her nudity as if they'd done this a thousand times before.

Nick rolled over on his back and stared at the ceiling above the bed as he listened to the water running in the next room.

"I thought I was," he muttered. "Something tells me I'm going to be outclassed in nothing flat." And then he laughed at himself as he gathered up his clothes and made for the door. "And I'm complaining? I must still be sick."

A few days later, Nick found her cross-legged in the middle of her bed, holding the phone to her ear with one hand while she absently flipped through a deck of cards with the other.

"But Fluffy, are you sure you're okay?" Lucky said.

"I'm fine, honey," Fluffy answered. "Just like I was for the first eighty-four years of my life before you came. And just because you've moved doesn't mean I can't manage."

"I haven't moved," Lucky argued. "Some of my things are still there, and I'm still paying rent. It's more like I'm here being housed for my own good."

Nick frowned. He hadn't realized that she might resent what had happened, or that she could possibly be bored. It gave him food for thought.

"I redid my hair," Fluffy crowed. "You're just going to die."

"What color is it now?" Lucky asked, glad Fluffy couldn't see the grin on her face.

"Miguel said it was black as a witch's heart. But the color is called Bad, Black, and Bouncy."

"Bad, Black, and Bouncy? You're kidding me."

"It's the truth, so help me God. It makes me look a little like Ann Miller. You remember her . . . that gorgeous long-legged dancer from Hollywood's glamour days?"

While waiting for Lucky to answer, Fluffy swung a fly swatter at her cat as he sauntered by. She missed, but out of respect for the thought, the cat hissed and danced sideways just to stay in practice and in doing so, knocked a vase off a table.

"What was that?" Lucky asked.

"That damned cat," Fluffy muttered. "Now I'm going to have to sweep up glass. Talk to you later. And bring that handsome hunk with you when you come," she said. "Gotta go."

The line went dead in Lucky's ear. Unaware of Nick's scrutiny, Lucky fell back onto the bed with a smile on her face and threw the cards up into the air, watching absently as they showered back down on her like a pasteboard snowstorm.

"Are you sorry you're here?"

Lucky jumped. "Good grief, Nick! You scared me half to death. I didn't know you had come in."

"Obviously, or you wouldn't have admitted you were here under duress."

She'd hurt his feelings. It was obvious by the way he was standing, and the fact that he'd shoved his hands in the pockets of his slacks. It was a gesture of his that she was learning to recognize as frustration.

"I was talking to Fluffy."

"I figured as much," Nick said. "Who else do we know who would put Bad, Black, and Bouncy on her hair?"

"She said it made her look like Ann Miller."

Nick grinned in spite of himself.

"Nick?"

"What, honey?" he asked, and scooted her across the bed, rolling them both onto the cards that she'd tossed.

"Who is Ann Miller?"

He laughed, then took another look at the puzzled expression on her face and laughed some more.

"I have an idea," he whispered, and started to trail kisses up one side of her neck and down the other.

Lucky smiled and wrapped her arms around his neck as she felt his manhood grow hard against her belly.

"You and your ideas," she teased, and slid a hand between them until she could feel him pulsing beneath her touch.

"I've got one of my own. You show me yours . . . I'll show you mine," she said, flashing Nick a wicked grin.

Less than a minute later, they were out of their clothes and back on the bed, making love on the cards that she'd tossed.

His mouth centered around her nipple as his tongue raked the point he'd made ache. Lucky moaned and shifted beneath him, urging him to come inside and ease her pain.

"Not yet, love," Nick whispered. "Let it burn a little while longer."

Lucky shuddered. From where she lay, she felt like she was already in ashes. Unaware of the cards she clutched in her hands, she wrapped her arms around his neck and arched beneath his caress.

And then it came, like a wildfire out of control, sweeping across her mind, taking everything in its path but the feel of Nick's hands and the imprint of his mouth upon her lips. Afterward, as she lay quietly replete within his embrace, she realized that she still held one of the cards that she'd tossed. She turned it faceup.

"Oh, my."

Nick shifted Lucky in his arms.

"What is it, honey?" he asked. "Am I hurting you?"

"Look, Nick. I didn't know it, but I was holding these when we made love."

He took the card and turned it over, then grinned. It was the king of hearts.

"That's me, all right. King of hearts. At your service day and night."

"Oh, shut up," Lucky said, and rolled off of the bed and stomped toward the bath, unaware that several of the cards still stuck to her naked backside.

Nick followed her into the room as she turned on the taps.

"What's so funny?" she asked. "I thought it was rather symbolic."

"Not half as symbolic as this joker stuck to your butt," he said, and peeled it, along with three others, off her back.

She grinned, then yanked the cards from his hands and gave them a halfhearted shuffle. "Wanna play a hand or two?"

"Jesus," he muttered. "What have I created?"

Lucky pulled him into the shower, ignoring the cards that scattered on the tiles beneath their feet, and wrapped her arms around his waist.

"I am not a what. I am a who. An insatiable who, but nevertheless . . . a who."

He grinned and shoved her into the shower spray, reveling in her look of shock before he followed. By the time they emerged, the cards had disintegrated into pulp, and were slowly but surely disappearing down the drain.

"I am going to go to work."

Nick threw a shoe across the room. "Dammit, Lucky. You can't. What if . . . ?"

"Tweedle Dee and Tweedle Dum will be right by my side."

Nick rolled his eyes and tried not to smile at the names she'd given to the bodyguards who now accompanied them everywhere.

"You went to work yesterday," she added. "Nothing happened. I can't sit here and watch Shari arrange any more flowers or cook any more chicken. I'm tired of letting your father beat me at five card draw, and he cheats at checkers."

Nick grinned again. "I know. How do you think I learned to play?"

"So? What do you say?" she persisted.

He sighed and threw up his hands in defeat. "You go on my time and come home when I do. It's either that or nothing at all."

"It's a deal," Lucky said, and stuck out her hand.

Nick's eyebrows rose perceptibly. In his opinion, she was taking this "deal" business a little too far.

"Either shake on it, or it doesn't mean a thing," she warned.

He grimaced and shook her hand, knowing he'd already lost another round with this woman/child who'd wrapped herself around his heart.

"Martin and Davis will be nearby. You have to put up with them or you don't go," he said, referring to the bodyguards in question.

"I've already said I'll endure them. I'll do anything to be able to get out of this house."

Suddenly the playing was over. Nick's expression turned solemn, and his eyes darkened. It wasn't the first time that she'd balked under the reins of their self-imposed security. He wondered if that was the only reason, or if she felt like their relationship had gone too far, too fast.

"Don't look like that," Lucky said, and threw her arms around his neck. "It's not what you're thinking. I love you, Nick Chenault. I believe you when you say you love me too. But we hadn't even gotten to the point of making love when fate confined us rather dramatically. It's not that I don't want to be here. It's just that the decision was made for us . . . not by us. Do you understand?"

He nuzzled her left earlobe and then pressed a swift hard kiss against the worry he'd put on her mouth.

"I know what you mean," he said. "It just doesn't mean that I like what you think. When I hear you say you wish you weren't here, I can't help but assume that means you wish you weren't with me."

"No, never. But I lost my freedom, Nick. When I was a child, I used to run and play in woods so thick that you had to turn sideways to get between the tree trunks. I could walk out of our house and down the road and never feel any kind of fear other than the fear of not being accepted. Even after I came to Vegas, I rode all over the city on the MTA without having to look over my shoulder.

Now I can't even go shopping. I can't go see Fluffy whenever I want. I can't even go to work. I'm living off of you."

"You are still drawing pay," Nick said, and when her expression darkened, he added, "It's only fair. I can't let your financial situation suffer just because I put you in danger."

"That's what I mean," Lucky said. "I'm taking your money for nothing except—"

"Goddammit! Don't say it! Don't you the hell say it!" he shouted, knowing where she was going. "I don't pay for sex. I don't buy love. I give it, lady, or it isn't there at all."

For a moment, the room was taut from the bitterness of the words that had been said. And then Lucky's shoulders slumped, and she dropped into a chair.

"I am a bitch."

Nick grinned in spite of the anger that had just overwhelmed him.

"Not really," he said, and offered her a hand up from the seat.

"Maybe it's PMS."

He laughed uproariously. As he did, Paul wheeled into the library and then rolled to a hesitant stop.

"If I'm interrupting something I can come back later," he said.

"Oh, hell, Dad. Of course you are," Nick said with a grin. "You heard us yelling clear down the hall and came in to make certain that we kiss and make up so that you are not denied any future heirs and you know it."

Lucky blushed and shifted nervously in her chair. It was weird how men talked to each other. Another adjustment of her life. Going from before, to now, was not always easy.

"I'm getting ready for work," she warned Nick.

Paul's eyebrows rose as Lucky left the room. He glanced at his son.

"Yes, she won the damned argument," Nick said. "She's a woman, isn't she?"

And then they both laughed, safe in the knowledge that without woman, man could not exist.

Lucky smiled to herself as she ran up the stairs. She could still hear the sounds of their laughter as she entered her room, but she didn't care. She'd made her point.

12

They got out of the limousine, and before Lucky could react, the breeze caught the skirt of her dress, lifting it several inches above her knees. She laughed and caught it before anything too embarrassing was revealed. But it was already too late for Nick's peace of mind. When a man walking by whistled, then winked, it was all Nick could do not to shove her back inside the car, order them to take her away, and deal with the consequences later.

"Suck it up, Nick," Lucky warned. "Your macho is showing."

He tried to frown, but the look on her face was too priceless to ignore. "Sorry." He grinned. "It's a man thing. Hey," Nick added as they entered the club. "If you can get away with that PMS excuse, I've got to have something to fall back on too."

Lucky laughed. He was impossible, and she loved him desperately.

"*Madre de Dios*, you have returned! Welcome, Lady Luck! Welcome!"

Manny's shout of delight echoed within the entryway, causing several people to turn and stare, curious to see the woman called Lady Luck. Instinctively, before the people could crowd around for a better look, the bodyguards slid into place.

"Oh, good lord," Lucky muttered, as Martin almost stepped on her toe. "How do you deal with this?"

Nick slipped his arm around her waist and gave her a comforting squeeze. "I do it because I don't want to die. I have too much to live for."

The seriousness in his voice stopped her complaints. It was enough said.

"Manny, I missed you." She returned the hug that the little man gave her. "I never had the opportunity to tell you how much it meant to me that you came to the hospital. Thank you. I really appreciate it, more than words can say."

Manny shrugged. "*De nada, querida.* It would have been impossible to do otherwise."

"Nevertheless . . ." Lucky leaned down and kissed him gently on the cheek.

"Don't I get a welcome back kiss too?" Nick asked.

"Nicky . . . you were here yesterday. You should have asked for it then, when I was so moved by the sight of your face." Manny shrugged, as if to say it was out of his hands, and then laughed at his own wit.

"I need to change," Lucky said. "I'll be right back."

Nick didn't even have to say it. As Lucky moved away,

Davis, the dark-haired member of the devilish-duo body-guards, was right beside her.

"She looks like herself again, Nicky," Manny said. "While you were sick . . . I thought for a time we might lose her too. I've never seen anyone so distraught."

Nick frowned. He'd had little sense of what Lucky's life had been like while he was fighting for his own. How frustrated she must have felt, knowing that everything in her world was out of her control. As he went toward the stairs, Martin, the other bodyguard, moved in unison with his steps, but always one jump ahead.

Lucky's pulse raced as she walked across the floor. A little part of her kept searching the faces of the people she passed, wondering if there was someone there who meant to do her harm.

And it felt strange to be back inside the club, as if she were seeing it again for the first time. A few of the players at the blackjack tables looked familiar. But most appeared to be visitors here for a short but good time.

The noise level was at its normal high. People crowded around tables, vied for chairs, and sat at the machines, staring in stuporlike silence to see what hand the computerized slot machine games dealt them. The piped-in music was barely over the hum of the crowd and the ever-present happy shrieks as money clanked against metal when a jackpot was hit in the slots.

"Cocktails? Cocktails anyone?"

Over the heads of the crowd, Lucky heard the familiar cries, and knew that somewhere in the bustle, Maizie and the dozens of other cocktail waitresses were hard at work, hustling drinks and smiling for the tips that kept them afloat.

A few moments later, Lucky reached the employee dressing room. Just as she was about to enter, Davis grabbed her arm and pulled her back.

"You will wait here, Miss Houston, while I check it out." He placed her firmly to the side of the door without giving her time to argue, and gave the dressing area a quick sweep. It was obvious, even to Lucky, that no one was inside.

"I'll wait here," he said, and pushed the door open, then stepped aside, waiting for her to enter.

"I won't be long," Lucky said, trying not to resent this change in her life. After all, it couldn't be forever.

"Lucky! I knew that was you. Oh, girl, it's great to have you back!"

Maizie ran down the hall dragging her tray, her tiny skirt bouncing in rhythm with her breasts, her arms outstretched. Lucky knew before it happened that the bodyguard was going to interfere. There was, however, little she could do to stop him. Maizie wasn't expecting the huge man who caught her in midflight and glared at her suspiciously while holding her suspended inches off the ground.

"She's my friend! It's okay. Please . . . put her down!" Lucky cried.

Davis shrugged and set the tiny woman back on her feet without apology.

"Sorry," Lucky said, as she pulled Maizie into the dressing room with her. "He's one of my bodyguards. Nick thought it best."

Maizie grinned and winked at the big man as she sauntered past. "No problem," she giggled. "He can sweep me off my feet anytime."

"If you want to talk, get in here," Lucky said. "I've got to get dressed. I can't wait to get back on the floor."

Maizie shook her head. "Girl . . . you need your head examined. You have it made. A drop-dead handsome man who loves you and wants you in his life, and you want to come back to work? I don't get it."

Lucky shuffled through her clothes as she hurried to change. "That's just the problem, Maizie. That dropdead man almost died in my arms. Until they catch the nut who's trying to hurt him, we're forced to hide behind walls. Or if we go out, we deal with men like him." She pointed to the door where the bodyguard waited on the other side. "I've got to put some order back into my life or go crazy."

Maizie hugged her. "Gosh! I didn't think of it like that. I'm so glad you weren't hurt and the boss is back and well."

"I'm here because Nick took the bullet meant for me." Lucky's voice shook as she buttoned the last of her buttons.

"No way!" Maizie gave Lucky a longer, more intent look. "Wow! He doesn't just love you, honey. If he's willing to die for you . . ."

"Miss Houston! Are you okay?"

"I'm coming," Lucky shouted. Obviously Davis had run out of patience.

Moments later, the three of them were back on the floor, each performing the duties for which they'd been hired: slinging drinks—dealing cards—protecting clients from people who wanted them dead.

Detective Arnold was also in the business of dealing with people who were in trouble. And from where he was sitting, Charlie Sams was up to his ears and sinking fast.

"Look, man," Sams muttered. "I swear to God, if I knew the name of the man who hired me, I would talk. Hell, no one wants him caught worse than me. I don't want to end up like Woody the Wire."

"Do you know a man named Steve Lucas?" Arnold tapped his pen on the edge of the table and watched the expressions changing on Charlie Sams's face. When he answered, Arnold would have sworn he was telling the truth.

"Sure. I worked for the Chenaults for nearly a year, remember? I seen him in Club 52 lots of times. He's a croupier, right?"

Arnold nodded. "What else do you know about him?"

Sams shrugged. "Nothin', man. He isn't in my league, if you know what I mean."

"He's dead," Arnold said. Charlie Sams paled as the detective went on. "What do you make of the fact that when his body was found, he was missing both hands?" he asked.

Sams started to shake. "Shit! You gotta be kiddin' me."

Arnold shook his head. "I don't make jokes about things like that. So what does that tell you?" he persisted.

Sams frowned. "I don't know. Maybe he took money for something that didn't pan out. Maybe he had alligators in his pockets. Who the hell knows?"

Arnold sighed. This was nothing more than a repeat of

all their other conversations, and it was getting him nowhere.

"Tell me again," Arnold said. "How were you contacted?"

"I got calls. I did what I was told. Money was sent to my bank."

Suddenly Will Arnold stood up. Something just occurred to him that he hadn't pursued.

"These calls that you got. You said they were long-distance, right?"

Sams nodded.

"Did you get them while you were on the job at the Chenaults, or after hours?"

"Always at my place. Once in a while he left a number on my machine and I called him back."

"That little house just off Main where you were arrested?"

"Yeah. My last old lady up and skipped with some trucker. It was all in her name, but I stayed on. Didn't make me no never mind where she went. One woman is as good as another."

Arnold decided against debating that subject with a man who had no conscience. He stuffed his pen into his pocket and headed for the door.

"Jailer . . . your prisoner is ready to go back to his cell," Arnold called. Moments later the door opened and an armed guard appeared.

"So, what does that mean?" Sams asked, as Arnold was walking away.

"I'm not sure, Charlie. But if I find out, you'll be the first to know."

Arnold had a request to file. Getting the phone company's records of all long-distance calls to a certain house just off of Main could prove very interesting. And after this last murder attempt toward the Chenaults, the case was heating up big. Old Man Chenault had been in this town a long time. He had a lot of pull, because Will Arnold had been told to assist the Chenaults in any way possible to make certain that their investigation, as well as Metro's, went unhampered. Arnold was good at doing what he was told.

Paul Chenault sat at the window facing the back of the estate and watched Nick and Lucky playing tennis on the court below. As he watched the way the young woman ran from side to side and back again, often laughing at her own lack of skill, the hair prickled at the back of his neck—as if someone had walked over his grave. She reminded him of someone . . . he just couldn't remember who.

"Damn," he muttered, and pounded the arm of his chair with his fist. "I hate it when this happens."

"Sir?" Cubby's quiet concern was evident, as was the gentle touch of his valet's hand upon his back. "Are you all right?"

"I'm fine, Cubby. Sorry." He stared out the window, continuing to watch the game in progress on the court. He smiled and pointed. "With every swat of that racket, Lucky's game smacks less and less of tennis, and more and more of a free-for-all."

Cubby looked out the window and smiled. "Yes, sir. She's quite a lady, isn't she, sir?"

"I'd say she's quite a woman, Cubby. Lady is the last thing I'd call Lucky Houston." He paused. "Does she remind you of anyone?" Paul asked.

Cubby thought, and then shook his head. "No, sir. I don't believe she does. Why? Does she to you?"

Paul nodded. "For days, every time she walks into a room, I can almost see someone else's face superimposed over hers. Do you know what I mean?"

Cubby nodded.

"And when she laughs . . . the sound gives me goose bumps. Like a ghost from the past. And then there's this thing she does with a deck of cards. It's so familiar I can almost feel it." Paul sighed and shook his head. "It's that damned stroke I had. I can't remember things like I used to."

Cubby patted him on the shoulder. "Memories are not all that important, sir. At least you're still here. In good health. Able to enjoy your life."

"More or less," Paul grumbled. "A few years ago, I'd have given Nick a run for his money on that court."

"That you could, sir. That you could. Would you like to go outside and join them?"

"Why not?" Paul muttered. "It's better than sitting in here driving myself crazy."

By the time Cubby pushed him outside, Paul had put away his bad humor and was in fine form, chiding Nick and Lucky for their lack of seriousness toward the game.

"You should lean into your swing," he suggested to Lucky as she served. "Put your weight into it. It'll give you more force."

"Damn, Dad. She doesn't need more force, just accuracy. She nearly took my head off a while ago."

Lucky sniffed lightly, pretending to be insulted by male criticism, and sauntered back to her spot on the court in preparation for her next serve.

"If you'd grown up like I did, worrying about the accuracy of fuzzy yellow balls would have been low on your list of priorities," she said, tilting her nose in the air just enough to make her point. "However . . ." She tossed the ball in the air and nailed it with a whapping sound as it came down. "Learning to duck is another thing altogether. Coal chunks hurt."

The ball sailed past Nick's ear as he dived toward the clay.

"I surrender," he mumbled, as he crawled to his feet and dusted off his clothes. "You win. I give up. If I had a white flag I'd fly it."

Lucky grinned. "Just what I love," she said, and leaned over the net, waiting for her congratulatory kiss. "A good loser."

Nick laughed, dropped his tennis racket onto the court, and pulled her across the net and into his arms without ceremony.

"You wench," he said with a grin, and kissed her firmly on the lips, in front of Cubby and his father, as well as a gardener who'd come out from hiding and was in the act of resuming his work. He too had suffered from Lucky's wild shots.

Her face was shining from exertion, her green eyes glowing from the kiss she'd just received. The smile on her mouth changed the shape of her face. And in the instant before she spoke, Paul Chenault almost had it. But then it was gone. As before, he'd lost the image hovering at the back of his mind.

"What is it, Dad?" Nick asked. He'd seen the look of confusion on his father's face.

"Her," Paul replied, pointing at Lucky, who was gathering up the stray balls. "She reminds me of someone. I just can't remember who."

Nick grinned, trying to gloss over his father's frequent memory lapses with a joke. "Lord help us. I hope there's not more than one of her. One is all I can handle."

Lucky hit him in the rear with the racket as she passed. "You cannot handle even one of me, Nicholas, and you know it," she drawled. "Come wash your face. You're glowing."

The men whooped with laughter. There was little else they could do. Lucky's facetious reference to sweat was impossible to ignore. And Nick knew good and well who'd put that word in her vocabulary. Fluffy LaMont.

"I'm going to wash up now," Nick said, and loped across the lawn after her.

Paul smiled and then stared at Lucky's back as the couple walked into the house.

"Even the way she walks . . ."

"Don't worry about it, sir," Cubby cautioned. "You know what the doctors say. When it's time, it'll come to you."

"To hell with the doctors," he growled. "Let's go inside. I'd love something cool to drink."

Upstairs, the joy of the moment had gone from play to passion beneath the steam of a shower. There was more soap on the walls than they'd gotten on themselves, but it didn't matter. Blood ran hot as the lovers continued to volley and serve. But in this game, there were no misses and no faults. Just a man and a woman who refused to let go of the life that had bound them in love. In spite of a madman. In spite of it all.

That night, dinner was almost jovial. A servant removed the last of their plates as Shari wheeled in a cart filled with dessert.

"Oh, my gosh," Lucky groaned, and pressed her hand to the flat of her stomach. "I can't possibly eat another bite."

Nick grinned at her, then eyed the array of chocolate. "I can," he said. "I'll have your share and mine."

"There's chocolate mousse, as well as fudge pie," Shari said.

Lucky took another look at the cart. "Well . . . maybe just a little piece of that pie. Did you say it was fudge?"

Paul smiled. Lucky still had weight she needed to gain back from what she'd lost during Nick's struggle for life. She could have eaten the entire array of desserts and suffered nothing but a bellyache for her indulgence.

"Just what I thought," Nick said. "If it says fudge, it's got your name on it, doesn't it, honey?"

Lucky tried not to grin, but the truth was too hard to deny.

"It's my favorite thing," she admitted. "Queenie always made it for my birthday."

Paul whooped with laughter. "You had fudge for your birthday instead of a cake? Why on earth would you do something like that?"

"Because welfare always gave us sugar and stuff like that. But we didn't often have the money to buy many eggs."

"Oh, Lucky, dear. I'm sorry I asked. Forgive me." Paul's soft remark was full of embarrassment and regret.

"No big deal," she said, poking her fork at the fudge pie Shari set at her place. "Nearly everyone in Cradle Creek got welfare. That's not what set us apart. My father's profession did that all by itself."

"Hell," Nick said, unable to take a bite of the mousse Shari set before him. Before Lucky's arrival into his life, he'd never realized how privileged his life had been.

Lucky rolled her eyes and then smiled in delight as she savored the bite she'd just taken. "Ummm . . . it's almost as good as sex." Then she looked up at Nick, who was turning redder by the minute. "Are you going to eat that?" she asked, pointing to his dessert.

He pushed it toward her plate and got another of his own.

"Here, baby," he said softly. "You can have it. There's more."

Unaware of the impact her simple admission of poverty had made upon them, Lucky ate with relish while Nick and his father only picked at their food.

Somewhere down the hall, a phone rang as they continued to eat. If it was important, someone would bring a phone to the table. If it could wait, the message would be on Nick's desk in the library. As fate would have it, Shari entered the dining room carrying the portable phone.

"Nick. It's a man who insists on speaking to you. He said it was urgent."

Nick shrugged. His appetite was gone anyway.

"Hello, this is Nick Chenault. What can I do for you?"

"For starters," the voice whispered, "you could die."

Unprepared for the impact of the words, Nick nearly dropped the phone. "Who the hell is this?"

Lucky went still. She'd never seen Nick this angry. His words were barely above a hiss. The first thought to enter her head was the threats on their lives.

To her dismay, she saw that her instincts about the caller were right when Nick covered the phone with the palm of his hand and mouthed to Cubby. *"Call the phone company. See if they can trace this call."*

Cubby ran without hesitation.

Satisfied that he'd done all he could from this end, Nick returned his attention to the man on the phone.

"You didn't answer my question," Nick said. "Who are you?"

"It doesn't matter who I am," the man growled. "Is your father there?"

"That's none of your goddamned business," Nick said, and inadvertently looked at his father's face. But in doing so, he gave away the question he'd been asked.

"I'm making it my business," the man whispered. "I'm making everything concerning you and yours my business. Did your pretty whore cry when you bled on her clothes? Next time I won't miss."

"You sonofabitch!" Nick stood abruptly. "You filthy coward. Don't threaten me with words when you haven't got the guts to show up and say them to my face."

"Nick!"

Paul's warning was loud and harsh. Without thinking,

he had shouted out of shock at hearing his son utter such a dangerous threat.

A slow, indrawn breath whistled in Nick's ear, then turned into an ugly chuckle as the caller rejoiced.

"I heard his voice. It hasn't changed much over the years. But he has . . . hasn't he, *chico*? He got old . . . and sick. It wouldn't take much to push him over the edge . . . would it?"

Nick frowned. The foreign word inserted into the conversation was impossible to miss.

But Dieter Marx was so high on revenge that he never heard himself say it. In all the years he'd spent in South America, he still thought in English. Yet, in the midst of this drama, without thinking, he'd used the Spanish word for *boy*.

"Where are you? Who are you?" Nick asked.

"In your head . . . behind your back. Right where you least expect."

And then the line went dead.

Nick groaned as, moments later, Cubby came back in the room with a defeated expression on his face.

"I couldn't get to the right people in time for them to start the trace, Nicky," he said.

"Don't worry about it," Nick said. "It was unexpected. But if it happens again, we'll be ready. I'm calling Detective Arnold. I want a tap on this phone."

Lucky hadn't moved or spoken since the incident began. Nick started out of the room, and in doing so, caught a look at her face. It was pale. Her eyes were wide and fixed. But it was the tears rolling unchecked upon her cheeks that sent him hurrying back.

"Lucky . . . baby . . . don't cry." He pulled her from the chair and into his arms.

Paul looked away, unable to face the devastation that this family was suffering, and all because of him. If only he knew why.

"He said he would hurt you again, didn't he?" she gasped, and wrapped her arms around his neck.

"What he said doesn't matter," Nick said, crushing her to his chest. "What does matter is that he gave himself away. Not much . . . but enough for me to know more than I did before he called."

"What do you mean?" Paul asked.

"He let a word slip that I don't think he meant to do."

"What? What was it?" Lucky asked.

"He called me 'boy.' "

"What's the big deal about that?" Paul asked.

"In Spanish, Dad. He said it in Spanish."

"*Chico?* He called you *chico?*" Lucky asked.

Nick was a little surprised that Lucky knew the word before he revealed it.

"I didn't know you spoke the language, honey."

"Lots of girls who cocktail at the club are either Latino, or married to one," Lucky said. "I guess I picked up more of the language than I realized."

Paul was quiet. Too quiet.

"Dad? Are you all right? Do you want me to call to your doctor?"

Paul's eyes were fixed and horror-filled. "The last place Dieter Marx was sighted was in South America, wasn't it, Nick? Oh, God . . . if it's him, we're doomed."

"Why? Because he holds a grudge longer than most? Because he's a hardheaded bastard who won't give up?"

Paul's voice softened. The light in his eyes seemed to fade as he stared back into the past.

"The first time we ever got drunk, we must have been, oh . . . maybe fourteen, fifteen years old. J. J. snuck a fifth of bourbon out of his daddy's house while Dieter and I waited in the bushes. J. J. and I got drunk first. So we got sick first. But Dieter . . . old Dieter . . . he was the master at everything, you know. He was still walking tall when we were on our asses."

Nick sensed that his father imagined a connection between that story and the drama unfolding now. He dropped back in his chair, taking Lucky with him, holding her tight upon his lap while she trembled and he listened. The tale continued to unwind.

"So three teenage boys got drunk. What's the point, Dad?"

"The point is, Nicky, drink made Dieter crazy. Sick in his head, crazy. While we were puking all over the place, Dieter was busy sawing off the feet of the neighbor's dog with a pocketknife for licking it up."

Lucky put her hands over her face to block out the horror of the words. But it was a pointless gesture. The image was already burned in her brain.

"Good God," Nick muttered. "He actually cut off the . . . ?" He froze as the memory surfaced. "I've got to talk to Detective Arnold."

Lucky jumped off his lap to keep from being dumped as Nick bolted toward the door.

"But I haven't finished," Paul said. "You've got to know how twisted and sick he can be when he's drunk."

Nick paused in the doorway. "That's just it. I think we already know. Remember when they found Steve Lucas's body?"

They nodded, unable to see the connection.

"There's something I didn't tell you. It was so grisly, I didn't see the need."

"What?" Paul urged.

"They had a difficult time making the identification on the body," Nick said. "Partly because he'd been dead a while before the discovery, and partly because they couldn't get any fingerprints."

Paul shrugged. "You just said he'd been dead some time. Surely the body had begun to . . ." He looked at Lucky, gauging her condition before adding, ". . . shall we say, deteriorate."

"They couldn't get any prints because he didn't have any hands."

"Oh, my God!" Lucky whispered, and felt the room start to spin.

"Oh, damn," Nick muttered, and caught her as she fell.

"I'm sorry," Paul said. "I shouldn't have said what I did in front of her."

"No, Dad. We have to know it all, or none of us will survive. She'll be all right." He lifted her into his arms, his face filled with concern as he started toward the stairs. "As soon as I get her to bed, I'm making that call. This is all too coincidental for my peace of mind."

And then Paul was left alone in the dining room with the remnants of their dessert staring him in the face. He covered his face with his hands and muttered, "I've come to believe that only in death does man achieve peace of mind."

But there was no one to hear his morbid thought. And less than an hour later, Will Arnold came calling with some news of his own.

13

The phone company readouts of the calls made from Charlie Sams's residence were strung out across the desk in the library. Nick and Detective Arnold were deep in conversation while another man worked silently nearby, setting up the phone tap that Nick had requested.

Lucky sat in a chair near the fireplace and stared at the blazing logs, absently watching the smoke spiral up into the chimney above. This whole fiasco was almost too theatrical to be believed. The urge to simply walk out on the play in action was overwhelming except for a few simple facts. The bomb that had been placed in Nick's car. The bullet scar high up on his chest. And the bodies of men that kept surfacing after each of these bungled attempts.

She hung her head in defeat. The web of death and deceit was woven too tightly for escape. She, as well as the Chenaults, were virtual prisoners until the man, whoever he was, was caught.

Nick knew she was frightened and depressed. It was a depressing situation. But because of the matter at hand, he couldn't let himself get bogged down in her fear.

The phone call tonight was their first solid clue since the terror began. It wasn't much, but along with the information Will Arnold had brought, it was an important link.

"See," Arnold said, as he ran his hand down the computer readouts. "Here ... and here. This date, and this one. All calls were made through an overseas operator."

"Can you tell the location?" Nick asked, making little headway in deciphering the log.

"Laws of disclosure, which control the right to acquire such information, vary from country to country. About all I know for sure at this point is that they were made from somewhere in South America."

As Lucky heard Arnold's words, the memory of Paul's childhood story, and the horror of what Dieter Marx had done, came back with startling clarity. She gasped and dropped the wineglass she'd been holding. It shattered on the flagstones in front of the fire with a brittle, tinkling sound. The web around them had suddenly grown tighter. A servant hastened to clean up the glass and the wine before any damage was done, but it was too late to stop the horror from spreading in Lucky's heart.

"I'm sorry," she said, unable to face the men who stared. "I've got to get out of here."

Before Nick could say anything of comfort, she was gone. He rubbed the back of his neck in a weary gesture as the detective began gathering up his reports.

"Coupled with what you told me about your call, this

adds up to enough reason to get some classified files res-urrected from inactive to active," Arnold said.

Nick frowned as he continued to press Arnold for an-swers the man clearly didn't want to divulge. "Classified? The old warrant that Las Vegas had on Dieter Marx was fairly open and shut, wasn't it? He committed a murder. He escaped. What was the big secret about that?"

"Yes and no," Arnold said. "There were rumors that af-ter Marx fled to South America, he got involved bigtime in gun running and financing wars and revolutions. More than one country had been after him when the story of his death surfaced."

"Oh, man," Nick said. "This keeps getting worse and worse. And the awful thing is, we still don't know if it's him. All of this is simply guesswork."

Arnold grimaced as he gathered up his men and his papers and headed for the door. "Everything the law is based on orbits around clues and facts, but a lot of a de-tective's luck comes from hunches. Never ignore your gut feelings, Chenault. It could get you killed."

"Thank you for that timely advice," Nick drawled. Giv-ing him advice on how to stay safe was, at this point in his life, a bit moot.

After Arnold was gone, the silence of Nick's home had never more been more eloquent, or more welcome. Nick started up the stairs. At the moment, getting to Lucky was the only thing on his mind.

Lucky stood at the window, clutching the parted curtains tightly in her hands as she watched the police drive away. If only they'd taken the danger with them, she thought.

"How much longer?" she muttered aloud. "How much longer will this last?"

"As long as it takes to keep us safe, baby," Nick said.

Lucky dropped the curtain and spun around as Nick entered the room, closing the door behind him. Moments later she was trembling in his arms and trying not to cry.

"I love you so much," Nick whispered. "Trust me to make this better."

The room whirled around her. Everything about the entire night seemed evil, and as hard as they had tried, the unknown assassin kept insinuating himself into their lives. It was suddenly all too much to endure.

"Then prove it," she begged. "Make me forget this is happening. Make me forget everything but you."

His eyes turned dark. A kick of emotion sent his pulse into overdrive as Lucky started to shed one item of clothing after the other. Desperation colored her intent as she began to tear at his clothes as well.

"Ssh," he whispered, and pulled her to him, cradling her head against his chest in an effort to calm her shaking. "Not so fast. Not so fast. Let me help."

She sighed and went limp within his arms as he began digging through the coils of her hair. One after another, the pins came out, and her hair fell over her shoulders and down her back. Black as the coal from the hills where she'd lived, what it covered of her body was just a tease for what lay beneath.

Motionless, she waited, absorbing the joy in Nick's gaze as he looked his fill. And then looking was not enough. His hands skated down the surface of her hair, testing the buoyancy of her breasts under the stray locks.

"Beautiful," he whispered, and then lifted her hair from her shoulders to make way for his mouth. His tongue raked across one nipple, while his teeth squeezed . . . just enough . . . not too much. One breast. Then the other. Back and forth until Lucky felt she would die from the pleasure.

She groaned as a wave of heat swept through her belly and beyond. With both hands, she clasped Nick's head to her breast and urged him closer, tighter. Inside, she felt the honey as it started to flow. She wanted . . . needed . . . that mind-altering drug of release that came only with the climax of Nick's lovemaking.

Nick grunted with surprise at the audacity of her movement and felt an answering nudge from his own body as it rose to the occasion, pushing against the confines of the clothes he had yet to remove. By the time he too was undressed, he was aching for her.

"Come to bed, lady," he whispered.

A storm of passion clouded his eyes and thickened his voice as he held out his hand for her to follow him down. She shuddered, rocking on her feet from the waves of excitement he'd unleashed in her. Nick caught her before she fell.

The bedcovers were smooth against her back, a cool contrast to the heat in her body. Her breasts rose as she took a deep breath. Moments later her eyelids opened, and she was staring back up at him, powerless to deny him anything he wished. Her world revolved around the man and his love.

Nick tried to smile. But the knowledge that he'd brought her to this point with so little foreplay was overwhelming. And in a strange way, also frightening. The responsibility of loving like this could be dangerous, for Lucky as well as for him. If he lost himself in this woman, he might lose sight of the danger that they were in. If that happened again, as it had on the night he'd been shot, next time neither of them might survive.

Lucky encircled her arms around his neck.

He shook as he succumbed to her plea, then lowered his head, feathering kisses across her lips and down and around the valley between her breasts.

She sighed as she shifted beneath his weight.

"I will die if you don't do something fast," she whispered, and slipped her hands between their bodies, then captured the hard, thrusting length of him within her fingers.

His eyes closed. His blood raced. All he could do was hold on and wait for the madness to begin.

After the shock of the phone call, oddly enough, the weeks passed with no further incidents. Slowly, the terror faded into a shadowy fear that never quite left. They worked, ate, made desperate love, and then drifted into sleep, only to repeat the routine again and again throughout the ensuing days.

Because of the onset of preparations for Paul Chenault's annual birthday bash, Lucky had begged a promise from Lucille LaMont that she would help her find something to wear. So they met for lunch in early October.

"Sorry about all the drama," Lucky said, eyeing the bodyguards as well as Fluffy's reaction to their presence when she slid into the circular booth at the restaurant and leaned over for her kiss.

Fluffy promptly returned the peck, then straightened the rather low-cut neck of her outfit to make certain that enough of her bosom still showed.

"Sweetheart, think nothing of it," she said. "I rather like it. It reminds me of the old days. Back then, anyone of any importance, whether good or bad, was accompanied by muscle, you know."

Lucky grinned. "I'm glad you could have lunch with me," she said. "I miss you. I miss hearing your stories. I miss picking cat hair off of my clothes, and helping you choose what to wear to the salon on Thursdays."

Lucky's innocent statement had the old woman close to tears. No one missed the company as badly as she did. But she would have cut out her tongue before admitting to the loneliness she'd felt when Lucky had been forced to move into the Chenault home for protection.

"One of these days this will all be over. And then you can look back on it and tell your grandchildren what exciting days you lived through," she said.

"If I live long enough to have any children to produce them," Lucky muttered.

"Hush! Enough of bad news," Fluffy pronounced. She changed the subject by patting her hair and arching her brows. "So . . . what do you think?"

Lucky grinned. "I think you wouldn't need headlights on a moonless night," she said. "What's this one called?"

The old woman chuckled at Lucky's apt description of her newest hair color. It did have a tendency to glow.

"It's called Power Platinum." She lifted her dinner

plate, using it as a mirror, and tilted it enough to catch the light. "Do you really like it?"

Lucky slid her hand across the tablecloth and tenderly clasped the old woman's hand. "Fluffy LaMont . . . it's just you!"

"It is, isn't it?" The plate went back in place as the waiter appeared and handed them menus.

"What are we having?" Lucky asked. She always let Fluffy choose. It gave her such pleasure to be in charge that it wasn't in Lucky to object when odd combinations of food arrived.

"Hmmm, how about lobster bisque, asparagus *en croute*, barbecued chicken wings, and for dessert . . . some Mississippi mud cake?"

Lucky hoped her expression didn't show the horror her stomach felt.

"Sounds like an experience, Lucille. Order away. I'm game if you are."

Fluffy's mouth pursed at the proper use of her name, and she imperiously waved to their waiter to summon his attention.

"Of course you are game," she said, as she waited for him to make his way across the room. "That's why we get along. You have guts, girl!" *And*, Fluffy thought, *you're so much like I was when I was young that it scares me.* "All or nothing," she muttered, unaware that she'd said that last bit aloud.

"All, of course," Lucky said, thinking she was referring to the food, "I'll have it all."

Fluffy smiled. "That's the only way to go." As soon as the waiter had taken their order and left, she added,

"Now. Tell me all about this party. When is Nick planning to hold it? And what on earth will you wear?"

"Next week. Sunday afternoon. Outdoors if weather permits. And I haven't the slightest clue. That's why I need you. You're the fashion expert. Oh, I almost forgot. You'll be getting an invitation in the mail. Nick said he'd send a car for you."

Fluffy clapped her hands. "Marvelous. Just like the old days when people knew how to party. Now . . ." She leaned forward, peering intently at Lucky's face, hair, and figure, assessing what she had to work with. "I think . . . something casual yet sexy. Maybe a soft, flowing pants and jacket ensemble. Possibly a lace or metallic knit camisole beneath. Something that covers just enough, but makes men want to snatch it right off."

Lucky leaned back in her chair, her eyes shining, her mouth split wide in a grin. "Fluffy . . . you never cease to amaze me."

"Why?" Fluffy said.

"Because no matter what you put on, you're always considering the best way to get it off."

Fluffy smiled. And as she did, Lucky had a flash of the fabulous female she once must have been. "But darling, of course. It was what I did. I took it off. All off. Remember?"

"Vividly," Lucky said. The waiter appeared with steaming dishes of food. "Oh, good. Soup and chicken wings. I suppose that means that the asparagus and cake come next."

"Don't be such a smart mouth," Fluffy remarked, waving her soup spoon at Lucky's nose. "Eat your food like a

good girl. When we're through, we'll go back to my place.
You can help me pick out something to wear. I wouldn't
want to shock the old dames of society who are certain to
be invited to Paulie's soirée."

Lucky frowned. "What did you call him?"

"Who? Paul? Oh, that. That's what he was called in the
old days. I didn't realize I'd used it. Don't repeat it or he'll
kill me. He absolutely hates it."

Lucky nodded and wondered why a chord of memory
had just been struck. But before she could pursue the notion, Fluffy's red satin jumpsuit caught the attention of
some old-timers passing their table. Their prompt recognition of the aging celebrity set the bodyguards in motion
as the people clamored for an autograph. By the time it
was all sorted out, Lucky had forgotten about the slip of
Paul Chenault's name. And when she heard it again, it was
already too late to prepare herself for the shock that
would come with recognition.

The day was perfect, just as Nick had predicted. But it was
only the weather that was cooperating with his father's
party. The rest of it was going to hell in a handbasket.

Nick's desk was cluttered with paper. He kept swiveling
his chair from one side of his desk to the other while he
made continuous notes. And every time impatience
struck, he shifted his phone to his other ear, just as he was
doing now.

"I want security at every gate as well as circulating on
the grounds . . . and at every possible exit. Do I make myself clear?"

Whoever it was he was talking to must have agreed rather promptly, because moments later, Nick hung up with a satisfied air.

Lucky's appearance in the library coincided with the latter part of his conversation. From the worry on his face and the shadows in his eyes, she knew he would be grateful when this day was over.

"Trouble?" she asked.

"Honey . . . is there ever anything else?" And then he sighed with satisfaction as she circled his desk. When she was close enough, he pulled her down into his lap, then began nuzzling the hollow at the base of her throat. "Oooh, lady. You smell good. What are you wearing?"

"Not much," she whispered, as a red flush swept across his cheeks. *The color of passion*, she thought as she noted his reaction, *is also the color of anger*. It was something she'd never considered before now.

"You will be the death of me," Nick whispered.

"Don't, Nick!" Lucky said, and threw her arms around his neck. "Don't ever say that. Not to me. Not even in jest. I already almost was."

The minute he'd said it, he knew it had been a mistake. But the phrase was so common, and so aptly fit the state his lust was in, that he'd forgotten the implications it had in their lives.

"Sorry, baby," he said, and feathered a kiss across her lips. "I wasn't thinking."

Lucky shivered and pressed her cheek against his shoulder. "I think, Nick. I think all the time. I think that I'm dreaming and one day I'll wake up and this will all be gone. I'm not a true gambler, and I've gambled everything I am on you. It makes me afraid."

"How so?" he said softly, hoping that once she'd spoken of her fears they could be put away.

"I'm superstitious about certain things. When I've had a run of good luck . . . which, may I say, in my life has been rare, I start waiting for the other shoe to drop. You know what I mean . . . the 'it won't be like this forever' feeling?"

"Nothing is going to happen to us, Lucky. I'm making sure of it. That's why I have thirty extra security guards on the payroll today, and why your two favorite men have orders to stick to your pretty little butt like glue."

Lucky rolled her eyes at the mention of the bodyguards. "Tell me you don't mean Batman and Robin?"

Nick laughed. "Ah, honey, you make my day. Every minute with you is like a shot in the arm."

At the word 'shot' Lucky bolted from his lap. "There you go again with the stupid clichés, mister. I'm leaving before you come up with one I can't forgive. Besides, guests should be arriving anytime. I promised Paul I'd help play hostess. I need to change."

"What are you wearing?" Nick asked, thankful that she'd changed the subject. The back of his neck had been prickling all day. He was starting to get a little paranoid himself.

Lucky waggled her finger. "It's a surprise," she said. "Fluffy helped me pick it out. You're going to love it."

"My God," Nick groaned. "That's what she always says right before she changes her hair."

Lucky grinned. "At least I don't intend to take off my clothes . . . except for you, of course."

"Thank God," Nick said, smiling as she walked out the door with a wiggle to her hips.

Soon he went to join his father, who was being installed in a place of honor out on the patio. A short time later, someone touched the back of his sleeve. He turned, expecting an old friend who was waiting to be greeted. It was Lucky.

"How do I look?"

She gave a graceful pirouette that sent the soft, fragile fabric of her white silk pants and jacket billowing and then clinging to the curves of her body like a jealous lover. The jacket hung open and loose, giving the viewer a more than generous view of wide expanses of a very bare top and totally bare tummy. A swath of gold lamé that just passed as a bra covered her womanly essentials.

"Lucky . . . sweetheart . . . you're   beautiful." Nick's voice shook with emotion. As he looked at the elegance of the woman before him, he couldn't help but remember the ragtag woman/child who had gotten off a bus in Las Vegas many months ago. She might look like a pro, but hesitancy was still fresh in her eyes. Lucky Houston still needed the assurance of having done something right.

"Your hair is magnificent, dear," Paul said, eyeing appreciatively the intricate loops and whorls she'd created from its thickness and length.

"I'm rather partial to that little bitty thing under your jacket that I suppose you're trying to pass off as a blouse,"

Nick said, and then sighed, realizing that every man here was going to think the same thing.

Lucky grinned. Fluffy had been right. The gold bra was going to be a hit.

"Nope. It's a bra, all right. Shiny isn't it? Do you think it's too much?"

Nick grinned and threw up his hands. "Hell no, it's not too much. If anything, there's not enough. But we won't quibble about inches when there's a party to be had. Come with me, lady. Introductions are in order."

Lucky bit her lip and pasted a wide, charming smile on her face, just as Fluffy had taught her to do. It was the only defense she had against the memories that suddenly seized her . . . of dressing in hand-me-down clothes, of going to sleep hungry and cold, of the laughter and taunts that had followed her all of her life.

If it was the last thing she did, she would forget every memory she had of being a no-count gambler's daughter.

In two hours, Lucky had met, greeted, and smiled at more people than she had in a day at Club 52. But it had all gone perfectly. No one had frowned, or pointed, or snickered behind her back. No one knew her past, and it seemed patently clear that her future lay in Nick Chenault's arms.

"Drink, miss?"

Lucky turned around to find a waiter competently balancing a tray filled with glasses of white wine. It looked refreshing, but Lucky knew from experience that wine would make her sleepy.

"No, but thank you," she said.

"If you would like, I can get you something else. Maybe a spritzer? A mineral water?"

Because he was so insistent, Lucky looked past the brimming glasses to the man behind them all. It was to her credit that she did not gasp, or in any way reveal the shock she felt at the sight of his face.

The skin on his face and perfectly shaped bald head was brown as a berry, in stark contrast to the white collar of his waiter's uniform. In any other setting he could have passed as a distinguished-looking gentleman.

If it hadn't been for the matching set of scars that angled across his face.

From temple to chin. Deep, puckered, and ragged. They should have dominated his face. Instead, they only added to the darkness of his demeanor.

"No," Lucky said quietly. "But thank you. Thank you very much."

He smiled. A slow, generic smile. Until she looked in his eyes. They were startlingly blue, and there seemed to be no emotion whatsoever within them. Lucky swallowed and tried not to shudder. Self-preservation made her turn and walk away. She tried to tell herself she did not hear him laugh beneath his breath, that she'd imagined it all. And then she turned back around, expecting to catch him in the act of watching her. He was nowhere to be seen.

"Good grief," she muttered, and wrapped her arms around herself. "Where do the caterers come up with guys like these?"

"Baby, are you all right?"

Nick's voice in her ear made her relax. "I am now," she

said, and tucked her hand in the crook of his arm. "Have you seen your father or Fluffy lately? I seated them close together hours ago, and haven't seen them since. I hope she hasn't talked him into going off somewhere. . . . I wouldn't put it past her."

Nick grinned. "Dad should be so lucky. Come on, I'll help you look for them. And in the meantime, let's get you something to drink. In spite of the fact that it started out cool, the sun is coming on strong."

Lucky shuddered. "Thanks, Nick, but I don't think I could drink a thing. At least not now. Maybe later."

He didn't pursue the issue. Later he would wonder, if he had, would it have made a difference?

Dieter was riding on a high that no drug could ever have achieved. It had been forty years since he'd set foot on North American soil—the United States of America . . . land of the free . . . home of the brave. And it felt like only yesterday.

But it wasn't. It was a lifetime ago when he'd been broke, frightened, and alone and running for his life. And now he was back, and no one was any wiser. His anonymity rested on the fact that he looked nothing like the young man who'd made a narrow escape across the border into Mexico and points south. The simple horror of his appearance was a better disguise than any Hollywood makeup artist could have contrived.

He inhaled slowly, reveling in the feeling of success, and knew that he could not fail. It was his destiny to survive. It was what he did best.

With studied grace in every movement of his trim, fit

body, he laid his empty tray upon the bar and calmly picked up another with fresh glasses brimming, ready to be savored and shared with the man of the hour. Paul Chenault was having a birthday. It would be his last.

14

Lucky hurried down the hall from her room where, moments earlier, she'd gone to freshen her makeup and her hair. A swift breeze had crashed the party, coming down off the mountains in flurry of dust and leaves, ruffling skirt tails and hairdos as was the case with such mavericks of weather. But with a swift squirt of hair spray and a new layer of lip gloss, she was as good as new.

The doorbell caught her in midstep as she came off the stairs. Instinctively, she paused, waiting to see who it was that Shari admitted. The last person she expected to see come to the party was Will Arnold of Las Vegas Metro.

"Welcome, Detective. I didn't expect to see you today," she said.

Will nodded, then grinned. For a second, he forgot why he had come as he tried not to stare at the elegant young woman in white and gold. Finally, man that he was, he gave up in defeat.

"Miss Houston. You look very . . . beautiful . . . if you don't mind me saying so." The word "sexy" was what he'd been thinking, but he knew saying it would be strictly out of line.

She smiled. "No woman minds a compliment, sir. Come have a drink. Paul is somewhere outside. We'll find him together."

It was then that he remembered why he'd come. "No, thanks. I wish I could, but this is official business."

Lucky frowned. "I'm sorry to hear that. If you'll wait, I'll go find Nick."

"Don't disturb him or the party," Arnold said. "Just give him this fax. It came in less than an hour ago. It's the latest description of a wealthy North American living on the outskirts of a small village in Colombia. We have reason to believe that he *could* be Dieter Marx. The time of his appearance in the area, as well as his wealth and age, all fit the man we're looking for."

Lucky's hand shook a little as she took the paper from Arnold's hand. It was daunting to know that she might be holding the key to the danger and threats under which they'd been living.

"Do you mind if I read it?" she asked.

"Go ahead. In fact, you should. This mess involves all of you."

Lucky began to read. She was down to the third paragraph when nausea swamped her. A film of cold sweat broke out on her body as she groaned and staggered against a chair.

"Miss Houston! What on earth? Are you ill? Shall I call a—"

"Dear God! This man is here!"

Arnold grabbed her roughly by the arm. "Are you sure, ma'am? This would be too much of a coincidence to be believed."

"The scar. I saw a man with that scar. Three deep slashes all the way down his face. He spoke to me."

"Jesus Christ! Are you telling me this man has somehow smuggled himself in as Paul Chenault's guest?"

"No! Oh, God, no! He's wearing a uniform . . . a white uniform. He's one of the waiters serving the drinks."

"I've got to call Metro," Arnold said, and started for the phone.

"Wait!" Lucky shouted. "Security is all over the grounds. Nick's bodyguards will know where they're stationed."

"Then come with me," Arnold ordered, and grabbed her by the arm.

Moments later, Lucky flew off the patio steps, her hand held tightly within the detective's grasp as he searched the grounds for the help she said was here.

"There they are," Lucky said, pointing to Martin and Davis near the buffet, who up to this point had been a thorn in her side. In her eyes they had suddenly taken on the heroics of a marine battalion. "They'll be able to help. They know where Nick had all the extra security guards posted."

"Good," Arnold barked. "Come on," he said, tugging once again at her wrist. "At least I can keep one of you safe."

At his words, Lucky suddenly realized the imminent danger that Nick and his father were in. "Oh, my God! Nick and Paul are in danger! We've got to warn them."

Without thought for herself, she tore free from Arnold's grasp and started running through the crowd, searching above the sea of heads, frantic to find Nick before it was too late.

Will Arnold cursed loud and then ran toward the guards. Moments later, the air crackled from the static of radio current as the two-ways came alive with the message. *The killer is here. Find him before he finds his prey.*

They were side by side, the handsome young man and his aging but dignified father. The Chenaults! It was fitting, Dieter thought, as he quickly slipped the poison into the drinks. His upper lip curled just thinking of their name. Destroying the old man would not satisfy. It was like stomping on scorpions. You had to kill them all, or one by one, they would keep coming back. It would not be enough to know that his nemesis, Paul Chenault, was dead. All of his seed must be destroyed. It was the only way.

The sun was warm upon his bare scalp. But he didn't care. He was used to the heat. Where he came from, it was always hot. And wet. And lonely. So lonely.

Dieter's hands were steady as he positioned the two glasses bearing the deadly potion in the center of his tray. An insurance against the danger that someone else would unwittingly grab them before he made it across the lawn to where they were standing.

A surge of adrenaline shot through his body as he moved

across the grounds with the tray in hand. Soon it would be all over. Vengeance would be sweet, and no one would be any wiser as to how it had happened. Everyone would be in a panic over the two men who would lay writhing on the ground in death throes while he slipped out unobserved. Who would notice a humble waiter trying to get out of the way during the ensuing tragedy? It was a perfect plan, as was everything he did.

"No, I don't plan on living forever," Paul said, laughing up at the friends who'd stopped to pay their respects. "I'll be satisfied with just hanging around long enough to hold my first grandchild in my arms."

Nick grinned. That sounded good to him too. And at the thought of children, his mind instantly turned to Lucky. He raised his head and began to slowly scan the crowd, absently wondering where she'd gone. The last thing he remembered was that she'd gone to powder her nose.

"Just look at Fluffy," Paul went on, waving at Lucille LaMont who was working the crowd like a pro. "That lady's a charmer in spite of being eighty-four. I'll bet she was a terror in her youth."

"Was?" Nick's voice was laughter-filled. "What makes you think she's changed?"

"Drink, sir?"

Nick turned at the sound of the voice. The wine was a tempting and sparkling enticement against the onset of the warm breeze riffling through the crowd.

"Dad? How about a glass of wine?"

Paul looked up. The waiter's shoulder was all that was

visible from where he was sitting. He considered how many of the half-filled glasses he'd already had, and decided that one more would be safe. The thought of refreshment suddenly sounded too good to pass up.

"Sounds good to me," Paul said.

"Sir."

Nick reached out, intent on lifting the two nearest glasses from the tray. But the waiter was quicker. "Allow me." Seconds later Nick found himself holding two glasses of wine and nothing but a view of the man's back as he disappeared into the crowd.

He shrugged, then leaned down. "Here you go, Dad."

"Just what the doctor ordered," Paul said.

"I doubt it," Nick said. "But enjoy anyway. It is, after all, your birthday. To your health, Dad . . . and many more birthdays to come."

Glasses clinked as, son to father, the intimate toast was made. Paul lifted the glass. The wine glittered like liquid gold as the sunlight caught and then speared through the glass and liquid. His lips parted in anticipation of the taste to come.

Lucky ran, pushing her way through knots of laughing people, constantly searching the crowd for bald men wearing white jackets. Twice she thought she'd achieved success, only to find upon spinning them around that she was wrong. All she could do was gasp an apology before moving on to the next and the next.

Fear, coupled with the urgency of her search, increased her desperation as she dashed through the partygoers. With each wasted minute that went by, they were a minute closer to Nick's imminent death. Her pulse pounded and every breath that she took was a pain-filled draft against burning lungs.

And when she thought she could run no more, the crowd suddenly parted. Only for a heartbeat. But it was long enough to see the white jacket, the hairless head, and the horrific scar gouged into the side of his face.

"Thank God," Lucky muttered. At least he was still on the premises.

It was reason enough for her to believe that whatever he'd planned, she wasn't too late to stop. She started toward him, aware that the risk was great, but hoping that by the time she got to him, security would have spotted him too.

Then before her eyes, he paused, raked the crowd with a furtive gaze, then pulled something from his pocket. It was impossible to see what it was, but as his hand paused over the tray, she knew that whatever it was, was going into the wine.

"Oh, no!" she groaned. "Nick, dammit, where are you?"

Before Lucky could think, the waiter disappeared in the crowd with the tray in his hands. She didn't have to see him to know that he was finally making his deadly move.

Seconds passed. Long, horrifying seconds in which she stumbled twice in her high heels before kicking them off in desperation as she continued to run. Shocked whispers of the guests she knocked aside were not important. Her wild, undignified behavior brought sneers of disdain she chose to ignore. There was no time to explain. And less reason to care what they thought. If Nick died, she would not survive the loss.

Out of nowhere across the crowd, as if in answer to a prayer, she saw him, standing tall above the rest. His short dark locks of hair were blowing easily against his forehead in deference to the breeze. He lifted an arm to wave at someone across the crowd, and she saw the oatmeal-colored blazer that she'd helped him choose for today's occasion.

She was going to be too late. She saw the waiter handing him the glasses. As the man turned away, she saw his face. To her horror, the scar twisting upon his countenance writhed like a coiling snake, and she knew that he was smiling. Horror overtook her as everything slipped into slow motion. Raising her arm heavenward, she threw herself forward through the mass. With one last burst of energy, she screamed.

"No, Nick, no!"

The scream shattered the moment, startling the crowd milling around the buffet and sending everyone near into a sudden, startled silence.

Nick spun around toward the sound of her voice. When he finally saw her, she was several yards away and running toward him, her arm outstretched. Her eyes were wide and filled with horror as she pushed and shoved her way through the people between them.

"Don't drink it! Don't drink the wine!" Lucky shouted.

Nick's heart stopped. Without questioning her warning, he pivoted and slapped the wineglass out of his father's hand. Then he dropped his own upon the ground as his father watched in shock.

"What on earth?" Paul muttered.

Dieter Marx froze, and then someone jostled his arm

and the tray full of drinks slid from his hands, falling to the ground in a shatter of crystal.

He turned, unable to believe that it was happening again. But the woman's warning screams could not be ignored. She must have seen him preparing the wine. It was the only explanation.

Rage filled him as he watched Nick Chenault knock the drinks to the ground, saturating the grass beneath with the deadly brew. A red haze slid across his vision and his mouth went slack. A small spittle of drool slid from one corner of his lip as he started to shake. It was that woman . . . Chenault's woman . . . who had called out the warning. For this, she would pay.

And then he heard someone utter her name. *Lucky Houston? Her name was Houston?* He stared . . . and remembered . . . and recognized. He laughed softly to himself. It was fitting that she was here. She deserved to die more than she knew.

Thought became deed as the gun appeared in his hand. There was no turning back, nor time to escape. But it did not matter. The Chenaults would still suffer knowing that the woman had died for their sins. He smiled and aimed through the crowd, leading the barrel just enough that the bullet, when fired, would hit her square in the chest.

Several people saw the gun at the same time. Shouts of warning rang out from different directions at once.

"Get down! Get down!" someone screamed.

Nick grabbed his father and rolled, tilting the chair and tipping the old man into his arms, then shielding him with his body as they fell. All around them, the crowd of partygoers dropped to the ground as a barrage of shrieks and frightened wails filled the air.

Lucky froze. Suddenly she was the only one standing. And all she saw was a man with a gun. He was pointing it at her. His smile was the only warning she would get.

Instinct told her to run. But common sense asked her where. There was nowhere left to go but to her maker. She thought of Queenie . . . and of Diamond, then searched the people upon the ground for Nick's location. She wanted to see his face. Just one more time. Before it was too late.

Nick rolled over just in time to see Lucky's terrified gaze. A man stood less than twenty feet from her with a gun aimed straight at her heart. Fear swamped him as he bolted to his feet.

He never made it.

The gun blast rocked the air.

Lucky jerked, then forgot to breathe, expecting at any moment to feel the onset of pain. It didn't come. And then Nick's arms engulfed her, and she felt nothing but his strength and the beat of his heart against her ear as he clasped her tightly within his embrace. He was shaking.

"Lucky! Lucky! My God, baby. I thought I'd be too late."

Lucky turned in his arms to look behind her. The man who'd held the gun was on his knees, staring at her in amazement as blood ran through his fingers from the hole in his chest. Once again, when it seemed he could not fail, she had prevailed.

The two bodyguards who'd shadowed her every

move for the past few months moved past her to the man on the ground. One kicked Dieter's gun aside while the other raked the area for signs of accomplices. There seemed to be no one else standing except Will Arnold, who was coming toward them across the lawn at a lope.

Dieter's vision was blurring. The woman's face kept going in and out of focus like a bad home movie.

"You bitch," he whispered, and then swallowed blood that was rattling at the back of his throat.

Lucky shrank within Nick's arms. Even in death, the man was still cursing her existence.

"All of you betrayed me," Dieter groaned. "You . . . my best friends." His bitter laugh ended on a cough that bubbled blood up and out of his mouth. "Paulie was a cheat. J. J. knew it and didn't stop him. And you . . ." He looked up, his eyes connecting with the shocked expression on Lucky's face. ". . . you cursed spawn of that Houston bastard. Johnny Houston was no friend of mine . . . or of Paulie's. He left us all. Damn him . . . damn all of you to . . ."

The ground came up to meet him. Grass tickled his nose and then slid through the gap in his mouth. He groaned and gasped. If he'd had a final breath, he would have used it to laugh again. He should have known that all things came full circle.

If Nick hadn't been holding her upright, Lucky would have already been on the ground. Her legs went out from under her the moment she heard Dieter cursing Paulie's name and her father's in the same breath. She groaned.

"No," she whispered, covering her face with her hands as she swayed. The implications of what she'd just heard were too horrible to bear.

"It's over, sweetheart," Nick said gently, and turned her away from the sight. "You're safe. I've got you, and I'll never let you go."

"No . . . no . . . no." She pushed herself out of his arms and staggered toward the ground where Paul Chenault still lay.

She stood, wavering on unstable legs, above the old man as he struggled to pull himself to a sitting position.

"You. It was you," she whispered, unaware that guests were scrambling to their feet and hastening toward all exits in desperation to escape what else might be coming.

Nick stepped between them. Lucky's belligerence toward his father had come out of nowhere, shocking him as badly as it seemed to be doing to Paul.

"Lucky, darling, what's wrong?" Nick asked, and tried to take her by the arm.

"Don't touch me," she said, and twisted away. Her eyes glittered with a fierce, cold fire as she pushed Nick aside.

"You! You're the Paulie who ruined my father's life."

Nick jerked as if he'd been shot. After everything that had happened today, this was the last thing he would have expected to hear.

"Lucky, baby, you're imagining things. Dad didn't even know your—"

"Dear God." Paul's voice shook as he leaned back in his chair. "That's it! For months you've reminded me of someone. J. J. was your father, wasn't he?"

Lucky shrank from his touch as if it were filth. Only

with great effort did she resist the urge to run and never look back.

"What have I done? Dear God, what have I done?" she moaned, and started to pace. She'd been living in the house of her father's greatest enemy. Eating his food, sleeping with his son. Falling in love. She started to shake.

"Lucky, stop it," Nick urged, and tried to pull her into an embrace. "Talk to me, baby. Tell me what's wrong. We can fix anything if—"

"Nothing can be fixed!" Lucky cried, and then closed her eyes and took a deep breath. If she started crying she would never stop, and there were things that had to be said.

Nick froze. Something awful, worse than the threat that Dieter Marx had presented, was sucking up the air, and taking sanity with it.

Paul was silent. And from a distance away, Fluffy saw and suddenly understood more than she thought she could bear.

"We called him Johnny," Lucky said, her fury all the more evident by the stillness of her body as she glared down at the man on the ground.

"I can't believe I never saw it. Even your name should have been the clue. It's this stroke," Paul muttered, and hit his forehead with his hand. "It made me forget so much . . . too much."

"Did you forget that you cheated him?" Lucky asked.

Instinctively, Nick moved between Lucky and his father while Cubby helped him into his chair. It was a protective gesture that he hardly understood, though. Whom did he protect, and from what? His father from Lucky's wrath? Or himself from the pain?

"Get away!" Lucky shouted, and pushed him aside. "I have to know. I've lived my entire life hearing Johnny cry in his beer, blaming everyone and everybody except himself. All he ever said was, 'Paulie stole my luck. If I hadn't lost the Houston Luck, I'd be a rich man by now.'" She threw up her hands. "Talk to me, Paul. Is it true? Did you cheat at poker and steal a family heirloom from your best friend?"

Fluffy was near enough to Lucky to see the spasm of muscles in the young woman's cheek as she struggled to overcome hysteria. She wanted so desperately to comfort the child she'd come to love as a daughter, but she didn't budge. Getting old had taught her one valuable lesson, and that was that truth would free a person in a way that love never could. Even if it hurt, it was better than living a lie.

Paul paled and closed his eyes, unable to look at Nick and admit his guilt, then wondered if the errors of his youth were actually going to be the downfall of this family after all.

"Dad! My God. Tell her! Say it isn't so," Nick whispered.

He was nearly doubled over from the pain of the truth. Each of Lucky's words was another thrust against Paul's guilty conscience. But the horror in his own son's voice was what might kill him.

Lucky was close to a shout as she answered Nick for him. "He can't answer without condemning himself." She was almost sobbing as she turned back to the old man.

"You can't, can you, Paulie? You palmed the ace and took the watch, and Johnny ran and never looked back."

Paul slumped forward in his wheelchair, staring at the ground before him, but actually seeing a rerun of the portion of his life he'd tried long and hard to forget. Then he finally found his voice.

"He wouldn't stop gambling. He even lost his business in a poker game. He used to fix cars, did you know that? He was a good mechanic."

Cubby's huge hand gripped the old man's shoulder. "Sir, I don't think you should be—"

Paul pushed him away, needing to get it all said. "Every time he sat down to a game, he lost sight of what mattered. He forgot that it was day. Didn't care if it was night. He lived for a winning hand."

"Dad . . ."

"Let him talk," Lucky snapped, ignoring the fire of Nick's glare.

"I bailed him out of jail. I paid off wise guys to keep him from getting killed. I baby-sat him until I fell asleep and then woke to find him gone. But he always resurfaced, begging for a loan."

Lucky shivered, unwilling to forgive. And because of her childhood, unable to forget.

"It got so bad that he forgot to eat." Paul sighed. "The last time he came begging for a loan, we got into a fight. I told him he was ruining his life. That he was sick and needed help. I told him he should get away from Las Vegas before it ate him alive. He laughed and dangled his watch in front of my face. Oddly enough, it was the only thing he'd never wagered, and for that I was grateful. I knew how devastated he would be when he someday came to his senses and realized that he'd gambled away all he had left of his family name."

"I'm listening," Lucky said.

Paul grimaced. He could tell by the tone of her voice that what he was about to say, she would not like to hear.

"Then hear me well," Paul urged, and lifted his head. His eyes burned as he looked into the face of his old friend's daughter. "He was drunk. He dared me to a game. Said he couldn't be beaten because he had his 'luck' with him. I didn't bother to point out that he'd had that damned watch with him while he lost everything from his health to his reputation, and it had done him no good. When he got like that, there was no talking. I played his damned game. And yes, I cheated. But only to keep him from losing it to someone else. I would have given it back. But the next day he was gone." Paul's shoulders slumped. "I never saw him again."

Lucky took a deep breath, but her words came out in disjointed disbelief all the same.

"Oh, my God . . . it's all true. I've been living with the enemy." Her frantic gaze swept across Nick's face as her chin trembled. "Even sleeping with the enemy." She crossed her arms across her chest, but it was too late to protect her heart. She'd already lost it.

Nick couldn't talk. And he was deathly afraid to move. Every way he looked at it, his father's past had risen like a phoenix and was now destroying all that he held dear. In his eyes, the club was tarnished. A man had died trying to enact revenge for what he considered a betrayal of trust.

And now the woman he loved was looking at him with hate-filled eyes. He wanted to shout, *It isn't my fault!* But he could tell by Lucky's expression that if he bore the name, he shared the blame.

"Don't blame Nick," Fluffy warned. "All of this happened before he was born. Hell, honey. Even before you were born. Don't let your fathers' pasts ruin what you two have."

Lucky turned away. "We have nothing. I feel nothing . . . except an overwhelming urge to bathe."

Nick groaned. "Jesus Christ, baby, don't do this to us."

"That's a bit drastic," Fluffy said, hoping to interject some sense in this terrible unveiling.

"Fluffy, my dear, Johnny had a saying," she said as she looked into the old woman's face. "If you sleep with snakes, you're bound to get bit. Well, I've been bit and am dying as we speak, and it's all my fault. I let prestige and pretty clothes and money and . . . Oh, hell." She glanced back at Nick through tears. "I even let a man's pretty face get in the way of what I am."

"Don't, Lucky. Don't cut me out without a chance." But Nick's plea went unheard.

"I am my father's daughter, after all," she said, and then turned to Paul, who blanched with each accusation that fell from her lips. "I can't explain it. But I know as certainly as I'm standing here that you destroyed my father's faith in himself when you stole that watch. And I can't stay with the man who did that and ignore what it did to our lives."

"You could try to understand," Paul said.

"Not if I ever intend to look at myself in the mirror again, I can't."

"Please! You're his daughter. Take it now," Paul urged. "It's in the library safe. Nicky . . . go get it. Give it back. I never wanted to keep it for myself. I was keeping it to give to him."

"I wasn't the one who wanted it," she said, and this time, in spite of it all, tears overflowed. "It belonged to Johnny. He's the one who suffered the loss." She hiccuped on a sob and then pushed Nick away as he tried to restrain her from leaving. "Get away from me . . . all of you," she cried. "I don't belong here. I never have."

Paul moaned and slumped within his wheelchair. Nick sprang toward his father and caught him before he fell to the ground.

"Cubby! Call 911," he cried, and felt his world slipping further and further out of orbit as Paul's head lolled against his knee.

The bodyguards reacted instantly, but Will Arnold beat them to the scene.

"An ambulance is already on the way," Arnold said as he reached Nick's side. He glanced down at the man who had died in a pool of his own blood. "Dieter Marx can wait. I think your father needs it more."

In spite of Nick's suffering, Lucky didn't have it in her to sympathize. Her father was already dead. In spite of the heat of the day, she felt cold from the inside out.

When she shuddered, then slumped, Fluffy would not restrain herself any longer. She wrapped her arms around Lucky and tried not to cry. It would, after all, serve no purpose except to make her makeup run.

"Don't, darling," Fluffy whispered, and patted her gently as she held her.

"Don't what, Fluffy? Don't die? It's too late for that. I'm already dead."

Lucky's lips twisted and she turned toward the house with tears running down her cheeks. Her life was as good as over. She'd let the glitter of Las Vegas color her perception of what was right and wrong. She'd known better than to give herself so completely to a man . . . and a gambler at that. This was no more than she deserved.

Nick clutched his father's unconscious body as he knelt. He knew he needed to get to Lucky, to make her understand that they could overcome everything that had come between them. But to get to her, he would have to leave his father . . . maybe to die alone.

"Lucky! For God's sake, wait!" he cried as he got to his feet, but she kept walking toward the house without looking back.

"Don't you walk away like nothing ever happened between us!" he shouted, and had the slight satisfaction of seeing her falter. But she didn't turn, and she paused only momentarily before hastening her step.

He groaned, then dropped back to his father's side, staring down at a man he no longer knew through a wall of unshed tears. Seconds turned into minutes as he contemplated the possibility of going after Lucky. But when his father moaned, and then slowly opened his eyes in frightened confusion, Nick's heart shattered. To keep his woman, he would have to lose his father.

He lifted Paul's head into his lap and waited while the sound of sirens in the distance drew nearer. There was nothing more to be said. He'd made his choice.

15

Manny was not prepared for the total devastation so apparent on Lucky's face as she walked into Club 52. He had no idea of what had gone on at the family estate, or that Nick's father was being admitted into a hospital to be put into intensive care. His first thought was that someone had died. His second thought was that for her to be this distraught, it had to have been Nick.

"*Querida!* What has happened?"

Not trusting herself to speak, she simply shook her head and walked into his office. Without question, he followed her inside.

"*Madre de Dios!* Talk to me. What's wrong?"

Lucky sank into a chair. Concentrating on the design in the carpet seemed to have the utmost interest for her. She would not, or could not, meet his gaze.

"I need to ask a favor of you," she finally managed.

"Anything."

"I need a place to stay." Her lips twisted as she fiercely willed herself not to submit to threatening tears.

"But what about Nick's . . . ?"

She looked up. No life burned behind the green gaze. Only an emptiness that went on forever.

"Are you running away?"

Lucky shuddered, then buried her face in her hands. "Yes. No!" She sighed and looked up. "I don't know. I need time. Time to think. Time to get past the shock."

Of what? But Manny never voiced the question. "I take it this place you are in need of should not be in Las Vegas."

She nodded and swallowed several times before answering. "It would probably be better. Just until I'm able to think without crying."

It was all he could do not to hold her. But he could tell it would be a gesture she would not welcome.

"Do you want to work, also, *querida?*"

She nodded. "I must, Manny. I have to stay busy or I will go mad."

"I cannot stand this any longer," Manny said. "I will help you, but you've got to help me understand. What terrible thing has come between you and Nicky?"

"Our fathers . . . their pasts. Either way you say it, it still means the same."

Manny threw up his hands in a gesture of defeat. "This makes no sense . . . but I will help."

A slight smile broke the chill of her features as she slumped with relief.

"Thank you, Manny. I won't ever forget this."

"*De nada.*"

"Manny, there's only one condition. Don't tell Nick."

He grew still, considering what she had just asked. "I will not bring it up, but if he asks, I also will not lie to him," Manny finally said. "That is my condition."

They sat, staring eye-to-eye, assessing the veracity of each other's request. Finally, Lucky sighed. "Whatever," she said. "Just help me. I can't help myself."

"It is done."

Within the hour, and with less in her bag than she'd brought from Cradle Creek, Lucky watched the city limit sign come and then go as they rode west. She didn't ask, and he didn't offer an explanation as to where they were going. Nearly an hour later, Manny pulled the car into the parking lot of a casino.

"I know it is the middle of nowhere," Manny said. "But all you have to do is call and I will come. You can be back in Las Vegas within an hour."

Lucky looked out the window, squinting against the glare of the sun. There, on either side of the highway in the Nevada desert that would eventually lead to the California border, sat two casinos. The Prima Donna was to her left, Whiskey Pete's to her right.

"Good lord," she muttered. "And a Ferris wheel too?"

Manny shrugged. "For the children," he said. "They have to do something while their papas and mamas play the games."

"But I don't have a car. Where will I stay?"

Manny pointed toward a trailer park north of the Prima Donna. "For the employees," he explained. "Some of them never leave . . . until they quit or get fired."

Lucky closed her eyes, counted to ten, and crawled out of the car. "Let's go before I change my mind," she said.

"It's not too late."

But the look on her face told him he was wrong. "No, Manny. The day I arrived in Vegas, it was already too late. I just didn't know it."

Within the space of two hours, Lucky had a job, a place to stay, and was standing beside the sparsely furnished trailer home as the sun began to set, staring blindly at the disappearing taillights of Manny's car. A chilly wind whipped across her cheeks, sending a spray of sand into her eyes. She didn't care, because if anyone saw her crying, it would be explanation enough for the tears running down her face.

She sighed, then went inside to change. As soon as her on-the-job orientation was over, she would be hard at work. But not behind the felt of a blackjack table. In fact, not at anything that had to do with the games. It was her only request. Taking tickets at the noisy merry-go-round on the ground floor of the casino was a far cry from the opulence and elegance of Club 52.

She couldn't have asked for anything better to take her mind off of Nick Chenault.

"Where did she go? Dear God, Fluffy, you've got to tell me. I need to find her. To make her understand."

Lucille LaMont could hardly look at Nick Chenault's face and tell him she didn't know, but it had to be said, because she truly did not.

"I don't know, Nicky. And before you argue with me, I swear I'm telling the truth. All Lucky said was, 'Fluffy take care of my things.' And I got that message yesterday over the phone. I don't know where she was calling from, or who she was with."

"Ah . . ."

It was all Nick could say as he braced himself against the pain. He couldn't look at Fluffy anymore and see the sympathy on her face. She'd been his last and only hope. Three days had passed since Lucky walked out of his house, and as bad as things had been, he'd never expected it to be this final. Every day, he expected her to call and start a fight, or to blame him for what his father had done. He'd hadn't been prepared for her total disappearance.

"She left nearly everything behind, except, of course, my heart, which she stole, and hasn't thought to return," he said, and lightly fingered a scarf of hers that he'd brought to Fluffy, unconsciously lifting it to his nose, inhaling the scent of lingering perfume. Tears shimmered in his eyes, but there was a bitter smile on his face.

"Nicky . . . I'm so sorry."

Nick shrugged, dropped the scarf onto the stack of clothes that he'd returned, and stuffed his hands in the pockets of his slacks. "Not half as sorry as I am. The Chenaults have managed to ruin her life, when all I wanted to do was love her. I guess I should be thankful that my father is recovering, but dammit, I look at him and see a man I no longer know."

Fluffy frowned. "I think she's wrong to blame anyone but her own father for what happened in her life. And I think you're wrong for taking your father's mistakes upon your own shoulders. If she wasn't so torn by the shock of it all, she could see through to the truth. She's a good girl."

"I've got to find her . . . to make her see that, if only

from your perspective. She's proven that she won't listen to me, or to anything I have to say."

"She won't listen to me either. Not now. I think she's hurting too much to hear anything except the ghosts from her past reminding her of her guilt."

Nick frowned. "Did she talk to you much about her past?" he asked. "When we were together, every time I brought it up she changed the subject or blew off my questions by making a joke of it. Maybe if I'd known where she came from I would understand why she hates and blames us so utterly now."

"Then why don't you go see?" Fluffy asked. "When she's ready, I believe she'll come back. My Lucky girl is not the type to run away from trouble. I think she's somewhere licking her wounds and trying to decide what to do. When she does come back, what you know about the situation may make a difference in whether or not you two work things out."

Nick got quiet. It was strange. Although he'd often wondered about her life before Las Vegas, he'd never thought about seeing for himself. Determination settled firmly right next to the hole that Lucky's disappearance had left. It was a long shot. *But what the hell,* Nick thought. *I am, after all, a gambler.*

"Do you know where she lived?" he asked.

"Cradle Creek, Tennessee," Fluffy said.

"I knew the name of the town. I meant the address," he said.

The old lady shrugged, shifting the white feathered boa around her neck to a looser position. "It can't be all that big. When you get there, ask."

* * *

Fluffy had been right.

Nick came to a stop in front of the gas pump, and he tried not to stare at the unbelievable poverty that abounded in the area. In all his life, he'd never known people in America lived like this. The rental car he'd picked up at the airport in Nashville was nowhere near as elegant as his Jaguar, and yet it was as out of place in Cradle Creek as a butterfly on a dung heap. He got out of the car, and then the moment he did, realized he had nowhere to go.

"Hey, there. Wouldn't be needin' any gas now, would ya?" the owner asked, wiping his hands on a rag that was greasier than the belly that showed through the buttonless gap in his shirt and jacket.

Nick nodded, then as the man pumped fuel into the car, tried not to stare at the child who ambled out of the door behind him. No more than two or three, she walked dragging one little leg, leaving a small, narrow trail in the dust with her dirty, bare feet. The first thing Nick thought was that it was nearly November and the child had no shoes.

"Don't pay her no mind," the man said. "She's one of my youngest girl's brats. She ain't quite right in the head."

The child's eyes darted from the keys dangling in Nick's hands to the shine on his shoes. In a pique of sudden interest, she dropped to her hands and knees and crawled through the dirt until she was hovering over the polished leather surface. Nick's breath caught in shock. She wasn't looking at his shoes, but rather the blurry image of her own reflection. And she was dirty. So dirty.

"Hi, baby," Nick said, and squatted down to her level, trying to ignore the dry trail of dust-encrusted drool and the remnants of several meals upon her face and clothing.

The child tumbled backward in sudden fright. When her face crumpled, the last of Nick's resistance gave way. In spite of her dirt, in spite of the slow, vacant stare, he lifted her into his arms. In that moment, for the first time in his life, the word "undernourished" became reality. He could feel her bones through the skin.

When she smiled, Nick's eyes nearly filled with tears. "Hey, pretty baby . . . are you a good girl?"

"Hell no," the man said, and yanked her out of Nick's arms. "Get!" he said, and swatted at her tiny backside in an absent fashion, sending her sprawling in the dirt. She didn't even cry from the insult.

It was all Nick could do not to deck him. "How much do I owe?" he growled.

"Twenty bucks oughta do it."

Nick peeled off the note, then stuffed the rest back in his pocket, trying to remember why he'd come.

"I'm looking for an address," Nick said. "Maybe you can help me."

The man laughed. "Ain't no street signs here. Who you lookin' fer anyways?" Then he eyed afresh Nick's car and his clothes. "What are you? The law?"

"Hardly," Nick said. "I'm looking for Johnny Houston's home. Can you show me how to get there?"

The man stared, then spit. He almost walked away before he remembered the wad of money he'd seen Nick put away.

"How bad do you want to know?" he asked, fingering the twenty Nick had handed him.

Nick's lip curled. He should have expected this. "Not bad enough to give anyone who hits kids a dime," he said. "Forget it. I'll ask someone else."

The man's face turned red in anger. Before he thought, he blurted out most of what Nick had come to find.

"You want that Houston sonofabitch? Then walk up the hill about a hundred yards. 'Bout now I 'spect he's ready for a visitor or two. It's a certain thing ain't no one here gonna flower his grave."

"What was so bad about him?" Nick asked.

The man spit in the dirt again, and when the child would have toddled back out, he yelled, "Git on back in the house now, dammit! I'm busy! Can't you see?"

Nick waited, forcing himself not to watch as the child tottered her way back inside.

"Because he took hard-earned money from poor miners who didn't make enough to even pay me what they owed, that's why. He never worked a day in his life in the town, 'cept polishing the table at Whitelaw's Bar with a deck of cards. Now . . . if you'll 'scuse me, I got me some things to do."

Nick found himself alone. Unable to resist, he started up the hill behind the station to see for himself the grave of the man who'd garnered such disdain.

The air was chilly . . . almost cold. And in all his life, he'd never seen so many trees. He remembered Lucky saying how she used to play in woods so thick she had to turn sideways to get between the trunks, and wondered if she'd ever been as cold and hungry as the child that he had held. From the looks of the houses hanging onto the sides of this mountain, he doubted if there were many here who at one time hadn't gone cold and hungry.

Besides the obvious odor of poverty, another odor he didn't recognize drifted past his nose. He looked down and noticed the odd-colored dust gathering on his shoes and pant legs as he walked through the grass. Puzzled, he bent down and swiped a finger across the toe of one shoe. It came away covered with a black, sooty streak.

Coal dust?

Smoke hazed the sky. Nick inhaled again and decided that it might be diesel from the refinery that he smelled. Although he could see the smoke, the mine was not visible through the trees. It was just as well; he had no desire to see a place where men were forced to bury themselves alive on a daily basis just to make a living.

Soon he broke out of the trees and into the hillside clearing that was the burying place of Cradle Creek.

Small, odd-shaped stones of every size and color dotted the hillside and up into the trees beyond, marking the residents' final resting place. The names and dates on the rocks had been hand-carved. They lacked the professional touch of a stonecutter, but the love with which they'd been set seemed the same. And as Nick absorbed the solemnity of his surroundings, he realized that dying in the red was just as final as dying in the black. Death was the ultimate accountant.

For nearly an hour, he walked the hillside in a stooped position, reading marker after marker, searching for the Houston name. And finally he came to the last plot on the hillside. He straightened up, sighing with frustration and wondering if the cemetery had been added onto some-where else.

That was when he saw it. Far down the hillside where he'd already been, yet off to the side, as if it didn't really belong with the rest. One small, unpretentious, unpainted cross that leaned at an angle to the ground that it had pierced—a lone, lonely monument to someone's passing. And in that instant, he knew.

Quickly he moved toward the spot. And as he did, he wondered why he hadn't noticed it before. Although the mound of earth atop it was as grassy as the rest, it still had not had time to settle, and protruded on the site instead, like a sore on the face of the land.

He knelt at the cross and tried to straighten it. But when he touched it, he realized that it was cracked at the base, as if someone had kicked it while walking past. Re-luctantly, he was forced to let it lean. His lips firmed and his eyes turned dark. Not even in death could this man es-cape a town's disdain.

Using his forefinger as a marker, he slowly traced the characters of the name upon the cross. But it was an un-necessary task. He'd already known before he knelt that it would bear the gambler's name.

John Jacob Houston. Not even a birth or death date to commemorate his passing. Just the mention of his name. Nick frowned as he remembered the man at the station and the way he'd spit before saying it, then thought of Lucky and shuddered.

"Damn, baby, no wonder you hate. No wonder you can't forgive. If I'd grown up here . . . in a town that hated me as much as this, I'd need to blame someone too."

Nick stared long and hard at the cross at his feet. It was moments before he could trust himself to speak.

"We have ties, Johnny Houston. You knew my father. I love your daughter. What the hell are we going to do about it all?"

No answers came drifting through the air to satisfy his soul. Long minutes passed. The sounds of Cradle Creek faded into the distance as Nick lingered at the foot of Johnny Houston's grave. And as he stood, a sort of peace began settling the pain left behind from Lucky's leaving.

Remembering the man and his passions, an odd notion struck. Before Nick thought, he'd pulled a quarter from his pocket.

"Heads . . . I leave and forget I was ever here. Tails . . . I will be back."

As the coin spiraled in the air above, Nick shivered. He could almost hear the laughter of a gambler's glee. Only after it had landed in the grass at the foot of Johnny's grave, did Nick realize he'd been holding his breath. He looked down, then his breath escaped in a slow, relieved hiss.

"So. It seems I will be back . . . but you should know, Johnny Houston, that I will be with your daughter. And maybe together we can fix your baby's broken heart. Be waiting, old man. For once in your life, don't let her down."

It was an odd thing to say in parting to a man in his grave. Yet in an eerie sort of way it made all the sense in the world. A man who was already dead still stood between Nick and his lady. Maybe he was the only way to put it all back.

Nick headed toward his car and pulled away from the station. He made a turn and drove up the hillside, searching the dirt roads between the houses for a sign of Whitelaw's Bar. He had a yearning to meet Lucky's nearest and dearest neighbor, assuring himself that nothing could be worse than what he'd just seen.

But when he found the place, he realized he was wrong. Worse was more than a state of mind. The man standing behind the bar was an unbelievable combination of fat, degradation, and dirt.

"Welcome to Whitelaw's," Morton Whitelaw said, and rubbed at one of the spots on the bar as if clearing the man a place to lean.

Nick nodded, then stared around the small, dingy room at the odd assortment of tables and chairs. It was impossible not to compare this place to Club 52. And as he did, he realized how, simply by the fortune of birth, destiny could impact life. With no choice for the lot of the draw, a baby is either thrust into a world of love and comfort, or a scratch-for-survival existence.

He shuddered, then blinked. A readjustment of his vision had not changed a thing. It still looked as grimy and sordid as it had when he'd entered moments ago.

"How 'bout a drink?" Morton asked.

Nick shook his head. "No, thanks. I need information, not refreshment." Then, remembering the last reaction he'd gotten to his request, he punctuated his statement with a smile.

Morton Whitelaw frowned. He knew when the fancy stranger had entered the door that he wasn't out looking for a good time. Not in here.

"In here, information costs the same as a beer."

Nick tossed a five-dollar bill on the counter.

"So," Whitelaw said, fingering the bill with relish. "Whatcha need ta know?"

"Someone told me that Johnny Houston lived near here. That one of his girls even worked for you at one time."

Whitelaw grinned and rested his elbows on the bar as he leaned forward.

"You're not the first feller to come askin' about them bitches," Whitelaw said. "Are you the law?"

Nick's fists doubled in anger. But he knew that fighting would not get him the answers he needed, so he held his fury in check.

"I'm not the law. Just a friend of Lucky Houston's. A good friend," he added.

Whitelaw flushed beneath his week-old growth of whiskers. "It'll cost more than five bucks afore I'll say their names aloud."

Nick tossed a hundred-dollar bill on the counter, then braced his hands on the edge of the bar and stared intently into Whitelaw's watery eyes.

"Talk, mister, or I'll take the change out of your damned hide," Nick said.

Whitelaw grabbed the bill and rubbed it between his fingers before holding it up to the light. Finally he shrugged. "What the hell do you want to know? They lived next door. I saw that asshole, Houston, every day of his life. He sat at the back table and played cards with whoever he could talk into sittin' down with him. His middle girl, Diamond, waited tables for me. The oldest one . . ."

Whitelaw paused and tossed back a shot of whiskey. The overflow ran in twin rivulets out and then down either corner of his mouth. Nick looked away in disgust, wondering which he was going to lose first. Patience or temper.

"What about the oldest daughter?" Nick asked.

"She was the worst of 'em all. That bitch didn't take no for an answer and hated men with a passion. I coulda had her . . . if I wanted," he bragged, knowing that anyone who would argue the point was absent. "But who wants a headstrong witch like that?"

Any man with a lick of sense . . . or maybe one with a sense of adventure, Nick thought, but kept his thoughts to himself.

"And the youngest one. What do you know about her?" Nick prodded, almost holding his breath for the answers he'd come so far to hear.

Whitelaw shrugged. "When she wadn't in school, she was at that table, sittin' on her daddy's knee. Hell, she could shuffle and deal better'n most men by the time she was ten. It was my personal opinion that she was old Houston's pet. Being the baby an' all," he explained.

Nick's heart sank. In spite of it all, Lucky had found a way to love the man who'd dragged them to the end of the world and then left them to fend for themselves. He'd come a long way to learn what he already knew. Love and loyalty were synonymous in his lady's heart. He'd had her love and, but for the sins of their fathers, might have had her loyalty as well. Now . . .

He started for the door.

"Hey! Don't you want to know how those bitches cheated me out of—"

"Not particularly," Nick drawled. "Whatever they gained will never be enough to make up for what they lost."

"They didn't have nothin'!" Whitelaw shouted. "So they didn't have nothin' to lose."

"Respect. They never even had a chance to earn the respect they had coming because of people like you. From what I've seen and heard, the people in Cradle Creek judged three innocent girls simply by who their father was. And while every last one of you keeps blaming him for being a gambler, in turn, you allowed him to be one by participation."

"You sonofabitch! I didn't allow no sich thing."

"You let him play," Nick said, pointing to the table in the back. "And every mother's son who sat down at that table did so of their own free will." By this time, Nick was shouting. "What is it with you people? Did poverty rob you of your will to think for yourself? Money doesn't buy brains, you fool. And if it did, you'd probably spend it on something else."

Whitelaw was speechless. Finally he muttered, "What the hell is it to you, what we thought about them? About any of them?"

"Lucky Houston is my lady," Nick said. "Remember that the next time someone comes into this town asking questions. I might not like what you say about the woman I'm going to marry."

Whitelaw gawked. When Nick left, he ran to the window and stared at the sports car as it sped away. He fingered the money in his pocket and frowned, wondering how someone as worthless as a Houston could luck into all of that. And then he remembered.

"Hell, maybe ol' Johnny knew what he was doin' after all when he named them girls. Lucky! She'd hafta be lucky to land a dude like him." Then he walked back to the bar and emptied what was left of the whiskey into his glass. "Here's to me."

It didn't matter that there was no one on hand to witness the toast. The hundred-dollar bill in his pocket was all the company he wanted.

"It's going to snow before the night's over."

Lucky shivered at the waitress's warning and hastened her step as she and several other employees ran from the trailer park to the casino to begin their shifts.

Her hours at the children's playground were long and tiring. As if the music from the carousel wasn't enough, the constant computerized mechanical beeps and whistles from the video arcade rang in her ears long after she was in her bed and trying to sleep. And while she was getting a regular wage, it was small compared to what she'd been drawing at Club 52. The only thing tipped on the merry-go-rounds was the food and drink that was tipped onto the floor.

But choosing this job was the saving of her sanity. Returning to the gaming tables would have been a form of torture for Lucky. Everything about it would have reminded her of what and whom she'd lost.

Nick.

Just the thought of his name made her hurt all over—from the inside out—as she remembered what they'd had together. Right after that memory came another, of herself and her sisters and what they had done without. She groaned. How would she reconcile the two and not lose her mind in the process?

"Hey, Lucky. Do you want to hang out after your shift? I know this guy who's been dying to meet you. Say the word and he's all yours."

"No, thanks," Lucky said. "I'm not interested in starting any relationships."

"Hell, honey. Neither is he!" the waitress shrieked, and slapped her leg, laughing uproariously at her own humor.

Lucky frowned. She'd been running from people like that all her life. Once she'd told Nick that she didn't want to be everyone's girl. Just someone's special and only girl. For a while, she'd convinced herself that she'd had it all.

"I've got to go," Lucky said. "Talk to you later."

The women were friendly, but Lucky was on another wavelength and they knew it. They shrugged, then hurried away.

As Lucky started inside the employee entrance of the hotel-casino, something stung her cheek. She turned and looked up at the sky. The first icy flakes of snow were beginning to fall. One fell on the sleeve of her coat. By itself, it was a tiny thing of little import. Coupled with a few billion others that were predicted to fall, it could be a thing of death.

Lucky shivered. That snowflake's life was something

like her own. It had struggled long and hard to become what it was, only to disappear in a flash at the touch of a fingertip.

Loneliness overwhelmed her. She missed her sisters. She missed Fluffy LaMont. And right at that moment, she would have given a year of her life to be standing within the shelter of Nick Chenault's embrace.

"Hey, better get inside before you freeze," someone shouted out the door.

Lucky obeyed. It took less effort to do so than to explain why she'd been staring at a snowflake upon the sleeve of her coat.

The shift had been long, but it was nothing compared to the loneliness of her nights. Lucky lay snug beneath the covers, listening to the wind blow icy shards of sleet and snow against the metal exterior of her temporary home and could not sleep. She kept hearing Dieter Marx curse her name and her father's existence. And she couldn't forget the shock on Nick's face when she accused Paul Chenault of being a liar and a cheat.

"Oh, God," she groaned, and turned onto her side, cuddling her pillow in lieu of the man in her heart. If she could only forget her childhood promise to Johnny, then maybe she could find her way back to Nick.

Tears choked her voice as she whispered into the silence of the trailer, "Damn you, Johnny. Why did that watch matter so much?"

While she now knew where it was, getting it back was another thing altogether. She didn't have it in her to accept another dollar of charity, especially from a Chenault.

She'd given away her pride for the man's love. She didn't have anything left to trade.

She sighed, then closed her eyes, willing herself to go to sleep, knowing that the time to return to work would come before she was ready.

And just at the brink of exhaustion, near the edge between sleep and dreams, the answer came. Without warning. With little fuss. She sat straight up in bed, staring into the darkness with cool deliberation. She knew what must be done. There was a way to resolve her dilemma, but it involved considerable risk. Yet for a gambler's daughter, was there any other way?

16

It was almost Christmas. Nick went through the motions of each day, while people who worked for him searched the streets for the woman who could bring the light back into his world. And although he couldn't bring himself to call off the search, in his heart he believed that it was futile. He believed that when Lucky was ready, she would come back to him on her own. He had to. It was all that kept him going.

Paul's health improved, but his spirits did not. He lived each day with the guilt of knowing that his past had ruined his son's future. And no amount of reassurance from Nick was able to change his mind. In Paul's eyes, the facts were irrefutable. If he hadn't screwed up so badly, none of the horror of the past few months would ever have happened.

And so they waited, each Chenault lost in his own private misery, for fate to deal the final hand.

Meanwhile, unbeknownst to them, Lucky was busy

setting a plan in motion that would bury the ghosts of the past for all time.

"Manny! One of the girls up front said to find you. You have a phone call," Maizie said, as she hurried by with a tray full of empties.

The conversation he'd been having with one of his managers came to an abrupt end as Manny bolted for his office without any explanation.

"She must be pretty special," the manager said, watching Manny as he ran through the crowd.

"How do you know it is a woman who called?"

The manager grinned. "He was running."

She laughed and walked away.

Manny picked up the phone. Before he answered, he knew it would be Lucky, even though it had been weeks since she'd last called. At that time, he'd sensed she was coming to some sort of decision. But today, the deep husky sound of her voice in his ear made him shiver with apprehension. Was today the day?

"Manny, are you well?"

He sighed and dropped into his chair. "I am fine, *querida*, but it has been a while since you called. I was beginning to worry."

"I've been thinking," Lucky began.

He smiled. "For a woman . . . that is a dangerous thing," he teased.

Lucky leaned her forehead against the wall, absorbing the familiar voice and the laughter in his words.

"Is . . . a . . . everything okay at the club?" she asked.

"*Everything* is walking around like a wounded bear,

chica. The least you could do is put him out of his misery."

Lucky smiled through tears. Nick *was* her everything. But he would probably never be her special someone. Not after he learned what she planned to do. When it was over, chances were that he would never speak to her again.

"I need a ride, Manny. When are you free?"

Manny jumped from the chair as joy crept into his voice. "Are you coming back? For good?"

She sighed into the phone, and the sound sliced through his heart like a cold wind cutting across the mountains.

"I'm coming back. I don't know how good it will be, but I'm ready to do what must be done."

"And that is?"

"Just come get me, Manny. You'll know soon enough. All of you will know."

He frowned. It didn't sound good, but at least she was coming back. Maybe when she saw Nicky she would relent. It was all he could hope for.

"When can you leave?" he asked.

"Now. Tomorrow. Next week. Whenever it's convenient for you to drive this far."

"I'm already on my way," Manny said. "Nick will be overjoyed when he learns that—"

"I'm not going back to Nick's house and you don't tell him I called. I'm going to my apartment at Fluffy's. I'll let her know I'm coming. For now, that's as close as I can get."

"For now, *querida*, it is close enough. You pack. I will be there by two o'clock. Our winter brings darkness early. I want to get you back into the city before nightfall."

Lucky hung up, shaking with anxiety now that the decision had been made. But there was a peace inside her heart that had nothing to do with the fear of facing her demons head-on. Tonight, for the first time in months, she would be sleeping in the same city as Nick. Even though they would be miles apart and he would be unaware of her presence, for the first time since she'd left him, she would sleep unafraid, knowing that he was near.

With as little ado as the day she'd arrived, Lucky walked into the manager's office and announced her decision to leave. Preoccupied with the day-to-day problems of the hotel-casino, he wished her well, took down her new address so he could mail her last check to her, and watched her leave. Out here, employees came and went with as much regularity as the patrons that they served.

Within thirty minutes, Lucky was packed and sitting on the edge of her bed, staring out the window to the bleak landscape that still bore signs of a light dusting from last night's snow.

"Two days until Christmas," she whispered, and at the thought, remembered last year and the meager but happy holiday she and her sisters had shared. "My Queenie . . . and Di . . . where are you now?" Her chin quivered as she buried her face in her arms. "Be safe. Be well. This prayer is my gift to you."

A sharp rap on the office door caught Nick's attention. Grateful for the interruption, he pushed back the stack of papers upon his desk.

"Come in," he called.

Manny burst into the room, his dark eyes glittering, his

nostrils flaring as he drew in one long breath after another. It was obvious that he'd run all the way up the stairs.

"What's wrong?"

"I need off."

If Manny had asked for the deed to Club 52, Nick would not have been more surprised. Manny Sosa did not take vacations.

"Anytime," Nick said, thinking that Manny was referring to the upcoming holiday. "Just let me know what days and I'll cover for you myself."

"No! No!" Manny said, and slapped his hand to his chest in a useless effort to calm his racing heart. "I need off today. Now. This minute."

Nick stared at him, but Manny refused to meet his gaze. Something else besides a vacation was behind the request.

"What the hell's going on, Manny? And don't start hedging around the issue. I want the truth."

It was the opening Manny had been waiting for for weeks. Living with the guilt of having helped Lucky Houston elude Nick's grasp had been difficult.

"I always tell the truth . . . when I'm asked," Manny added.

Nick frowned. "So I'm asking. Why do you need off . . . now?"

"A friend just called. This friend needs a ride. I do not let my friends down."

"If this friend needs a ride so bad, why doesn't this friend just call a cab?"

"Because it is a long way from the Prima Donna to Las Vegas. She couldn't afford the fare. Besides . . . I took her out there. The least I can do is bring her back, now that she's ready to return."

Nick's pulse accelerated. *She?* Suddenly the guilt on Manny's face was too obvious to ignore. "You mean Lucky, don't you?"

Manny shrugged.

Nick was stunned. Manny was the last person he would have expected to betray him. "You sonofabitch. You knew all along where she was."

It was not in Manny to let the accusation pass, especially when it was truly unjustified. "Yes, I knew. And I would have told you anytime had you but asked."

"Why would I think to ask you where Lucky had gone? Why would I assume you even knew?"

Once again, Manny shrugged.

Nick glared at him. Latin men had a definite edge on *norteamericanos.* A shrug was much simpler, and covered a whole lot more than a five-minute argument. And then another thought occurred to him. "Why did you take her out to that godforsaken country?"

"Because she asked it of me."

Nick bowed his head. So simple. No wonder he hadn't guessed. His mind had been filled with all kinds of convoluted plots. He should have realized that wouldn't have been Lucky's way. She was as straightforward as they came.

"And now she asked you to bring her back?"

Manny nodded.

"Thank God," Nick said, and buried his face in his hands.

"But not to your house, Nicky. I am to take her back to her old apartment."

"Why? What's she going to do?"

Nick couldn't quit wondering if the decision that she'd made involved leaving Las Vegas altogether. He could hardly bear to face that inevitability.

"I do not know," Manny said. "All she told me was that soon enough we would all know what decision she had made."

"So go get my lady."

Manny grinned. "I thought you would see it that way," he said. "I won't be long. I should be able to—"

"I don't care how long it takes. Just bring her the hell back, Manny. I'm trusting luck to do the rest."

"Spoken like a true gambler," Manny said. *"Adiós."*

Moments later he was gone, leaving Nick with new fears to replace old worries. The optimism that he'd brought back with him from Cradle Creek was long gone. Coupled with the uncertainty of what Lucky was planning, it made him nervous as hell.

He started to pace. "This has to be a good sign," he told himself. "I have to trust her enough to believe that she would not willingly throw away everything we had out of a sense of misplaced loyalty."

Thankful for the fact that he had promised to oversee Manny's duties until he returned, Nick was soon on the floor of Club 52, mingling with the customers, absorbing the frenzy of holiday visitors who'd opted for slot machines rather than shopping, who'd chosen green felt tables as their holiday green instead of needles of pine.

As he watched, he began to feel a bit like they looked. Out of sync with the rest of the world.

Just come home to me, baby, Nick thought. *I'll never ask for another thing as long as I live if you do.*

But Nick's request was too late for Santa Claus, who had already made up a list of his own, and Lady Luck was too involved in the games of chance going on around them to listen. Nick had to trust in his own Lucky Lady to do what was right for them all.

"Oh, darling, thank God you're back."

Lucky smiled through tears as Lucille LaMont's clutch around her tightened.

"I missed you too," she said, and patted the old woman's cheek, feeling, even through the layers of powder and paint, the fragile, paper-thin texture of her skin. "Looks like you've been busy while I was gone. What have you done to the place? And to your hair?"

Fluffy waved her arm. "I had it cleaned. From top to bottom. As for my hair, my hairdresser called it 'witchy.' I think it adds character to my face. What do you think?"

Lucky grinned, eyeing the coal black hair and the platinum white wings above each eyebrow that had been added for effect. It reminded her more of Dracula's bride than a witch.

"You're already full of character, Lucille. As for your hair, what can I say? By the time I get used to it, you'll be ready for something new."

Fluffy laughed and then shooed away the cat that kept weaving its way between her feet with every step that she took. Today she wouldn't be mad at him for nearly making her fall. She was too happy to get her girl back under her wing.

"We'll make a plan. I'll have a dinner party. We'll invite Nick and Paul and patch things up right. I promise I won't cook. We'll have it catered instead."

Lucky turned away, and in that moment, Fluffy realized that there were serious things her girl had yet to resolve.

"Okay," she said. "Change of plans. What do you want me to do? Just don't tell me you want me to help you pack. I don't want you to go. Tell me you're not leaving again." Fluffy's chin crumpled with her last plea.

It was all Lucky could do not to join her in tears. "No, I'm not leaving Las Vegas. At least, not for good. I may have to take a trip soon, but it won't be for long. If I've learned one thing from living in the foothills of these damned desolate mountains, it's that when I saw the skyline of Las Vegas in the distance, my heart sort of kicked. Kind of a reminder that I'd stayed away from home too long."

"Okay," Fluffy said, drying her eyes before the tears had time to fall. "Then first things first. What do you want me to do? How can I help fix what's gone wrong in your life?"

Lucky's smile disappeared. Shadows settled behind the lights in her eyes as she knotted her hands into fists.

"I need to borrow a dress."

Fluffy grinned. "That's easy enough. I have nearly everything I've ever worn that hasn't fallen apart from age. And while you can't tell it now, once we were nearly the same size. What kind of a dress are we talking about?"

"One that will stop clocks . . . and men's hearts."

Fluffy's eyes grew round, and she pursed her lips. "Why don't I feel like this is good?"

"Because it's not. I need something that will display my uh . . . charms . . . and to such a degree that it will be blatantly obvious what I have to offer."

"Why?" The frown on Fluffy's face deepened. "You don't need enticement, my dear. Nick is already smitten and wounded beyond belief. He wants this resolved as badly as do you."

"It's not for enticement, Fluffy. I'm going to make a bet with Nick, and the only collateral I have is me. It's only fair that he see what he's playing for."

"My dear!"

Fluffy had seen a lot of life in her eighty-four years, but the idea of a young woman offering herself up as the ante on the gambling block didn't sit right.

"Are you sure this is what you want to do?"

Lucky's eyes grew teary. "No. But it's the only way I can think of to fix what Paul broke. If I can settle this pain in my heart, if I can close my eyes at night and forget the look Johnny always wore when he cried about that damned watch, then maybe I will be able to put it behind me."

"Then come with me," Fluffy said. "I think I know just the dress . . . if I can find it, that is."

The second floor of the old Victorian home was soon alive with activity. Drawers, bags, and covers went flying as Lucille LaMont sifted through her belongings. More than one ghost was disturbed as dress after dress was unveiled.

When she finally found the one she'd been searching

for, even Lucky sighed with relief, and then staggered in shock when she looked at it more closely.

"Oh, my God," she said, holding it first one way and then the other, watching as the late evening sunlight beamed through the windows and caught the thousands upon thousands of translucent glass bugle beads covering the semisheer, nude-colored fabric. The dress was sleeveless, and nearly strapless save for two thin strips of jeweled fabric, and its neckline plunged dangerously downward. Once on, it would make the wearer appear to be clothed in nothing but glass. The suggestion of the body beneath would be startling and sensuous as hell. It was perfect. And it scared her to death.

"Of course you can't wear anything beneath it, you know," Fluffy said. "Bra and panty lines would ruin the effect."

"Of course," Lucky drawled, tongue in cheek. "God knows we wouldn't want to ruin the effect."

"You'd better borrow this too," Fluffy said, unzipping a long garment bag. "You don't want to get arrested before you get where you're going."

Lucky's eyes widened as a full-length fur coat fell out onto the floor at their feet. The fur was but a few shades lighter than her own hair.

"Is that . . . ?" She couldn't even finish the question.

"Russian sable. A *friend* gave it to me years ago. I have it cared for yearly so it's still in good condition. I've even been known to wear it now and then." Fluffy shrugged. "I forget the occasion, but it was a gift all the same." Then she winked. "I was quite a honey in my day."

Lucky hugged her tight. "You still are, Lucille. You still are."

The plan was in motion. There was only one person Lucky had left to notify. And that was done the next day, in the form of a letter addressed to Nick Chenault at Club 52.

"What's this?" Nick asked, holding up the envelope that he had just found in the middle of his desk.

The pale blue envelope bore only his name. No return address. No stamp.

"A messenger service delivered it this morning before you got here," Manny said. "I signed for it and swore on *mi madre's* grave that I would see that you got it personally."

He fidgeted, hovering in the doorway, waiting for Nick to open it up.

"Want to help?" Nick asked, grinning at Manny's impatience as he ran his finger beneath the flap and ripped it open.

Manny didn't bother to answer. Yesterday, Lucky had been relatively quiet on the way back to Las Vegas, but the few things she had let drop told him that something like this would be forthcoming. Intently, he watched Nick's face for a reaction.

"What the hell does this mean?" Nick growled, and tossed the letter onto his desk. Without waiting for Manny's answer, he stuffed his hands in the pockets of his slacks and stalked toward the window overlooking the Las Vegas strip.

Manny grabbed the piece of pale blue paper. Even he was surprised by the briefness of the message. But there was no mistaking who it was from.

I will be at your office tomorrow at 10:00 P.M. Bring the watch. It was signed, *L.*

"I don't understand," Manny said.

"What else is new?" Nick muttered, rubbing the back of his neck in a weary gesture. "Did she tell you anything? Anything at all?"

"Only that she was glad to be home."

Nick's heart surged. That she considered Las Vegas "home" was something for which to be thankful. Maybe that meant she had no plans of moving elsewhere.

"Well hell. Why try to outguess a woman? Tomorrow night I'll know what she's up to. And believe me, giving back that watch will be the happiest day of my life . . . as well as my dad's. I haven't seen him this depressed since the year after my mother died."

"But he is well?"

"As well as Cubby can keep him," Nick said. "That man hovers like an avenging angel. Sometimes I think he's keeping Dad in good health by sheer will alone."

"It is good to have a friend like that," Manny said.

"That's what I hear," Nick said. Then he walked out of his office, unwilling to reveal his true emotions. Inside he was a mess of nervous anxiety. He'd been terrified that he'd never see her again, and now that the meeting was imminent, was scared to death for it to happen.

"Ah . . . Nicky. You have more friends than you know," Manny said. "Even your own Lady Luck. What more could a gambler ask for?"

The day had gone from simply cold to bitter. It was a fitting accompaniment to Lucky's mood. Inside she felt as cold and dead as it looked outside her windows.

While she believed that what she was doing was right, the fear of seeing Nick again and not being able to throw herself into his arms was tearing her apart. The only way she was going to be able to get through it all was to stay as emotionally removed from the meeting as possible.

"Think of Johnny," she said to herself as she paced her bedroom, going from dresser to mirror and back again. "I can't think of myself. I have to remember Queenie . . . and Di. All of the bad things that might never have been if Johnny had kept faith in himself."

And yet as hard as she struggled to retain her anger, another feeling kept pushing it aside. The memory of Johnny's weak excuses. The money for their food that he often gambled away. The constant threats of social services coming and taking the girls away from him . . . and from one another. Of having to move constantly, until finally there'd been nowhere else to go. Cradle Creek had, literally, been the end of Johnny Houston's road.

Rationally, she knew that the presence of a family heirloom, no matter what it had been, would probably have made little difference in their world. He was what he was—a man with an addiction he couldn't kick.

But it was her heart that remembered the promise to her father that she'd made. Because Johnny Houston's daughters had lived on broken promises, it was beyond any of the three not to keep their word. It being their only possession, once given, they would have died rather than take it back. And so she faced the night with trepidation, praying for a miracle.

Because so much of her body was going to show beneath that dress, she had rubbed lotion into every inch of her skin. She'd swept her hair into a shining crown of intricate loops, then pinned them loosely upon her head. With every motion of her body, the vagrant curls bounced and teased the lights that reflected off of it. Her borrowed shoes, made years ago to match the dress, were the nearest to Cinderella's glass slippers Lucky Houston would ever come.

From the living room, she heard the clock chiming the hour. Nine o'clock. In sixty minutes she would see Nick again.

And although the urge to leave now was overwhelming, she could not be early. Timing was everything. An entrance was paramount to pulling off this stunt. While she had less than thirty minutes to dress, she still dawdled, picking up her room, hanging up laundry, letting her mind resurrect the image of Nick's face, because it was all of him that she had left.

It took little effort to remember those dark, passionate eyes, or the full, sensuous cut of his lips that could pull a cry of delight from her soul as easily as they could smile. Despite everything she remembered, there was one thing she would like to forget: the shock on his face as she'd walked out of his life.

"Oh, Nick, Nick. I wish it hadn't happened. I wish none of it had." But the emptiness inside her heart was a constant and miserable reminder that it had. She shuddered, and then she threw a shoe across the room. "If that's all you can do, Lucky Houston, then it's time to for you to get dressed and finish what you have started."

She began to dress with the ritualistic motions of a

bullfighter about to go into the ring. Each movement of her body was enhanced by the rapid pounding of her heart. And when, a short time later, a car honked on the street below, she looked out to see that her cab had arrived. The waiting was over.

The last thing to go on was the coat. It felt sinful. She'd never experienced anything like it before . . . except maybe the feeling she got when Nick Chenault took her body by storm.

She stepped out onto the third-floor landing and said a prayer as she locked the door behind her, then turned, staring down the long, steep flight of steps stretching far below her like a cold, dark invitation to hell.

The bitter night air bit at her cheeks like an angry lover. Instinctively she wrapped Fluffy's sable tighter around her shivering body. But it didn't help, because she was shivering from fear, not from the cold.

Moments later the cab sped away, carrying her toward her destiny. From a ground-floor window, Fluffy watched as the cab disappeared around the corner.

"Good luck, my darling," she murmured. "I have a feeling that you're going to need it."

The club should have been deserted at ten o'clock on Christmas night, but it wasn't. Christmas was, after all, a Christian holiday, and Las Vegas was a recreation harbor for people of all persuasions, from all over the world.

The long, flowing robes of Arabs dotted the areas around roulette and baccarat tables. People passed . . . dark, slanting eyes slid past the gaze of round blue ones. Every casino in Vegas was like a Tower of Babel. Thousands of people with the same intent, often unable to understand the person standing next to them. They had only the international language of money to get them through.

And so the holiday visitors played, going from table to table, from the quarter slots to the dollar slots, doing a little holiday shopping of their own. The massive fir tree that had been decorated in Christmas fashion graced the mezzanine above the ground floor in added brilliance to the everyday opulence that was Club 52. And yet in spite of its beauty, few took the time to look up and appreciate its presence. The "strike-it-rich" season of Las Vegas was year-round and took precedence over whatever else might interfere.

Only the employees who worked within the frenetic world of the casino had lives of their own. Most of them were the kind of people who went home after their shifts, who loved more than the sound of cards being shuffled and the clinking of chips.

In the thick of it all, Nick paced the floor of his office, trying to outguess the gambler's daughter as to what hand she was going to play. But he might as well have wished for the moon. There were too many variables in a game of chance.

The watch lay on his desk like a fat gold snake, coiled and ready to strike. Its head was the clockworks, its tail the long gilded chain. The ticking from within was the death rattle warning its prey. Nick stared at it from across the room, silently cursing its existence. Had it not been for that watch, his lady would not hate the sound of his name.

He checked the time and tried to ignore his growing

fear. Any minute she would arrive. Then the waiting would be over. Within the hour he would know what it would take to get her back. "Come on, baby . . . don't keep me waiting," Nick said. Impatiently, he walked out of his office.

The constant movement of people and the hum of their voices on the floor below vibrated through the soles of his shoes. He leaned over the railing, gazing intently into the crowd, searching for a woman with a dark head of hair and a slow, easy walk that translated from sauntering to sexy with the sway of her hips.

He looked down and saw Manny looking up, shrugging as if to say "don't ask me," when the crowd at the door seemed to part, making way for an elegant woman to come through. She was covered from neck to ankle in a rich, dark fur. It was her!

Unable to look away, he could only marvel at her regal bearing and remember that this gambler's daughter had come a long, long way from Cradle Creek.

"Welcome back, baby," he whispered beneath his breath, and blinked as a film of tears blocked the rest of her from his view.

Unwilling for the rest of the world to see his misery, he retreated to his office. It was time for Nick Chenault, the ultimate gambler, to pull himself together and prepare for whatever she'd come to say.

The watch was there. Right where he'd left it. He'd never realized it was possible to feel hate for an inanimate object, but it was inside him all the same as he looked at the watch.

"Any minute now, you sonofabitch, you'll be back

where you belong . . . and so, I hope, will my lady. She can have anything she wants, as long as I get her."

His whispered vow went unheeded, and the watch continued to tick.

On the floor below, Lucky paused as Manny waved and hurried toward her.

"*Querida*, you look fantastic."

Her only response was a cool order. "Manny . . . get a new deck of cards, then come to Nick's office."

The shock on Manny's face was his only response before he hurried to do her bidding.

The stairs had never seemed so steep or so long. But Lucky made it, thankful for the mental protection of the fur that she wore. In a way, a little of Lucille LaMont's outrageous spirit seemed to have come along for the ride. Lucky was grateful. She needed more than backbone to get through the ordeal ahead of her.

Seconds later, she was at the door to Nick's office. Without knocking, she pushed it open and walked inside.

His back was to the door, his shoulders braced as he stared out the window, as if waiting for a death blow to fall. It made her sick to know that she'd caused him so much pain.

Remember your promise, she told herself. *Remember your promise.* Her mantra would be the only help she would get to make it through the next step.

If he hadn't heard her swift intake of breath, he would never have known she'd arrived. He spun in place, and then he watched her pause in the doorway and stare at him like a starving woman before a feast.

Lucky could not look away. From his dark hair to the

cut of his black Armani tuxedo, he was just as she'd remembered. Until she looked into his eyes and saw the pain. And the shadows. And the hope. It was this last that drew her further into the room.

Manny bolted in behind her, out of breath, clutching the cards that she'd asked for.

"I have what you requested, *chica.* I will leave them on the—"

"No. Stay. We will need a witness."

Manny complied, shutting the door behind him and the trio inside, away from the chattering crowd below.

Witness? Nick shuddered. He didn't like the cold tone of her voice, nor the fact that not once since she'd entered had she even tried to smile. Speechless, he waited for her to make the first move. She'd called the party. Let her make the play.

A swift prayer went up as she grasped the edges of the sable. She lifted her chin defiantly as the fur slid into a sensuous heap at her feet.

The air came out of Nick's lungs all at once. As if he'd been hit in the belly with a bone-jarring thud. The impact of Lucky unveiled was more than he'd been prepared to face. She was magnificent . . . and she knew it.

Manny stared at the back of the dress and knew that the front must be even that much more spectacular. From the shock on Nicky's face, he decided he'd been right.

And then Lucky saw the watch, lying in the middle of the desk like a taunt, reminding her that but for it, her life would not be in shambles. She looked at it briefly and then back up at Nick.

Carefully measuring each step, she started toward him,

aware that with every motion of her body, the overhead lights in his office caught and threw back a reflection on the beads of her dress. It was as near to being publicly naked as she would ever want to be.

Nick shook. If someone had yelled fire, he would have been unable to run. Every movement of that lithe, sensuous body beneath the go-to-hell dress was as familiar to him as his own. It clung to her figure with every breath that she took, every step that she made.

"Nick . . . it's been a long time."

He shuddered, then blinked, swallowing several times before he trusted himself to talk.

"You have only yourself to thank for that." The moment he said it, he wished he had not. It was, however, too late to take back the anger he hadn't known was there.

Lucky bowed her head in agreement, and then she looked back up. Another few steps brought her within inches of the desk.

"There," Nick said, pointing toward the watch. "Take it . . . with my blessing. It never belonged to us anyway."

Pain shuttered the expression in her eyes. Nick saw her mouth twist in a grimace of defeat. It was then that the fear began.

"I can't," Lucky said.

"What the hell do you mean, 'you can't'? If you aren't going to take it, then why did you want me to bring it?"

"Luck can't be given, Nick. You either have it, or you don't. The watch means nothing, unless it comes back the way it was lost."

Nerves shot warning signals throughout his body as

Nick stared from the woman to the watch and back again. None of this was making much sense.

"Why are you here, baby? Unless you just came to see me bleed. If you did, you're too damned late. I'm already dead, my body just doesn't know it."

Tears shot to her eyes, making green puddles across the surface before sliding down the centers of her cheeks.

"Oh, hell," Nick said, wanting desperately to hold her. "I'm sorry for airing dirty laundry. Get on with it, lady. Finish what you came to say and do."

"I will play you for the watch. One hand. One winner. For all time."

This time Nick literally staggered beneath the impact of her words. "You? The woman who never bets? You're willing to give up a principle like that for that goddamned watch?"

"I made a promise," Lucky said through tears. "I don't break my word."

"Tell it to someone who believes," Nick said. "You told me you loved me. Make me believe that's still true."

Lucky swayed, and the lights caught in the glass beads like pinpoints of fire.

"Will you play?" she asked, and closed her eyes, waiting for his answer.

Nick wanted to shake her. Instead, he heard himself ask, "So we play this game of twenty-one. If you win . . . you get the watch. We both understand that. But what, pretty baby, do I get if you lose?"

Lucky opened her eyes. At that moment, Nick could swear he saw straight into her soul.

"Me. You get me, Nick. For as long as you like. Under any conditions you name."

So great was his anger that she would sell her body for a watch that for a moment he could not speak. He leaned forward, bracing himself against the desk that was between them. Finally, his words came out in an angry rush.

"Manny . . . bring me the cards!"

17

The loudest sounds in the room were the sounds of their breathing and the sharp, distinctive slap of cards being shuffled. And beneath it all, the muted, repetitive tick of the watch.

Nick burned. From the inside out. With rage. With pain. Furious for Lucky, at Lucky. And at the same time, he had never loved or respected her more for the sacrifice she was willing to make in the name of honor.

As hard and as long as he looked at the beautiful woman before him, the memory of Cradle Creek kept superimposing itself over her face.

Unspeakable poverty.

The years of disdain under which they'd lived.

Outcasts within a town of outcasts.

The strength of character it would have taken to overcome such odds was impossible to measure. He felt humble before her, and yet could not reveal what he knew.

Because he'd seen her beginnings, he knew all too well how viciously she would resent any show of charity from him.

Lucky's emotions ran from complete joy at being in Nick's presence to unbelievable heartbreak every time she looked into his eyes. There was so much resentment and anger on his face that she believed it impossible to remove. It told her in a way he could never have voiced that what she was doing was right. At least one good thing would come out of this: Johnny might get back the "Houston Luck." That he had no need of it no longer mattered. In Lucky's eyes, it was the principle that counted.

"*Querida* . . . do you wish to cut?"

Lucky's fingers shook as she lifted some cards from the stack and set them facedown upon the desk.

Manny quickly restacked them and then stood with cards in hand, waiting for a sign.

Nick's mouth was a grim line of defeat. Either way he looked at it, he was going to come out the loser. If he won, it would be like getting Lucky back by default, not by her choice. If he lost, she took the watch and he still lost her. The only thing that could possibly get him out of this dilemma was dropping dead, and that was not an option he was ready to consider.

Lucky looked up only once. The pain in his eyes was too much to bear. She turned away and whispered, "Deal the cards, Manny. Only two to each of us. Let's get this over with."

Even Manny was overwhelmed by the moment at hand. In spite of the winter chill outside, beads of sweat lined themselves across his forehead and above his upper lip, clinging to the dark, thin mustache.

One card to each player was dealt facedown. Slap! Slap! Lucky closed her eyes, trying to imagine what cards lay hidden simply by the sound. It was a fanciful thought that had no foundation.

The second card was dealt to each faceup. Slap! Slap! Lucky opened her eyes and looked. Her heart surged. Once in fear. Once in jubilation. Her card was a queen of diamonds. Nick's card was a king of hearts. They each counted the same. It told her nothing.

Her fingers shook as she slowly lifted the corner of her hole card and then quickly turned it over, revealing a king of clubs. Out of a possible twenty-one, she had twenty! The only thing that would beat it was blackjack.

Nick's pulse was running ragged. He wondered how long a body could take such punishment and still exist. His eyes narrowed as he slowly lifted the edge of his own hole card and looked to see what fate had dealt him.

A low, painful groan slid from between his lips as he let the edge of the card go flat, unrevealed.

"No . . . dammit, no," he muttered, and bowed his head in defeat.

Lucky's eyes filled with tears. She'd never seen a man in so much pain. For the first time since this had all begun, she regretted the notion of winning back the watch with every ounce of her being. Seeing the man she loved in this much distress was more than she was prepared to face.

"Nick . . . ?"

He lifted his head. Tears shimmered across his eyes, but

there was a small smile upon his lips. He lifted the watch from the desk and dropped it into her outstretched hand.

"I guess this was your lucky day, baby. Merry Christmas," he whispered.

Lucky's mouth went slack. "I won?"

The watch felt lighter in her palm than she'd expected. This tiny thing was the cause of so much pain? It didn't seem as plausible as it had moments ago.

"You won. You'll always be a winner, baby. With a name like Lucky, you couldn't lose."

His voice was deep, but his pain seemed deeper. Desperate for her to get out of the room before he lost control, he leaned forward, planting his hands upon the desk. In doing so, he covered the cards that he'd been dealt.

It looked accidental, but to Manny, it was so obvious. Something told him this wasn't over yet. And when he saw the panic in Nick's eyes, he jumped forward to assist her exit.

"*Querida*, your coat." He lifted it from the floor and held it toward her.

She draped it over her arm, so anxious to escape the tension within the room that she didn't consider what an impact her dress might make on the floor below.

"You might want to consider putting it on, baby. If you don't, I'll guarantee that you and that dress will start a riot," Nick said.

Although his expression was solemn, there was a smile in his voice. And because it was there, it made her pain all the greater. There was no humor in her heart this night. She'd won the prize and lost her man.

Lucky shuddered. *Ah, Nick . . . if only you'd had the luck of the draw then the choice would have been out of my hands. I wouldn't have made you cry, and you wouldn't be going home alone.*

Manny held the fur open, and Lucky walked in. One arm, then the other slid against the sleek satin lining. But there was no joy in the richness of the fabric against her skin. She would have traded it all for Nick's embrace.

At the door, she turned and held out her arms as if to say, "see me." She was covered from ankle to neck in sable. Tears ran unheeded down her face as, one last time, she imprinted his face upon her memory.

"Are you satisfied?" she asked, referring to the fact that she was no longer uncovered, then bit her lip to stop its tremble.

"How can I be satisfied with any of this blessed mess?"

Lucky straightened her shoulders and tilted her chin in a defiant gesture.

Nick started toward her across the room, and each time he took a step, Lucky retreated in kind. Aching for her, wishing he knew how to make this better, he had to admit that now was not the time.

"No," she muttered. "No more."

"*Adiós, querida,*" Manny whispered.

A second later, she was gone.

"Jesus Christ."

Nick stuffed his hands in his pockets and stalked to the window overlooking the street below. Only after he saw her getting into a cab did he relax. Only then did he breathe a quiet sigh of relief.

"Nicky! What have you done?"

Nick turned. Manny had discovered his deception. The

hole card he had not revealed now lay faceup beside its mate. The ace of spades. He'd won after all.

"You had twenty-one, Nicky. Blackjack! Why did you lie?"

"Do you think I want her that way? Besides, you forget. I saw Cradle Creek. I know how she grew up. Giving back a woman's pride is a small price to pay for love."

Manny bowed his head and walked away. A few minutes later, Nick was on the phone.

"It's over," he said. "Yes. I saw her get into the cab myself. All I ask is that if she leaves, tell me when."

Then he laughed. But it was bitter. "Oh, hell. I don't need to know where she'll be going. I already know that. All I need to know is when she decides to make her move."

He grimaced at something that was said to him. "I'm going to need more than luck," he said. And then he ended the conversation abruptly. "Thanks, lady. Merry Christmas to you too. You're one of a kind, Lucille LaMont, and that's a fact."

The line went dead. He hung up, and then swiveled his chair so that he could see out the window, up into the dark, moonless sky. Pain etched deep lines of regret at the sides of his mouth. He felt weightless . . . rootless. Without Lucky, he had no anchor.

"Merry Christmas, my Lucky Lady. I hope this settles your ghosts, once and for all."

Within the hour he was on his way home, an empty, lonely man.

Days later, far down in the city, horns were blaring, bells were ringing, and people's shouts echoed in the streets.

But Lucky Houston was as far removed from the revelry of New Year's Eve as she was from Cradle Creek. The last thing she felt like doing was celebrating. In just two days, she would be on a plane back to Tennessee.

"Queenie . . . where are you?" she whispered, and pressed her hands flat against the windows. "I don't know if I can make this trip alone."

But tonight there would be no miracles for Johnny Houston's baby girl. What she had to do, she would do alone. And when it was over, where did she go with the rest of her life?

Working in Club 52 was no longer possible. She could not face a job that put her in constant contact with Nick. She wasn't strong enough to ignore her own emotions for the sake of a paycheck. Yet leaving Vegas seemed impossible. She needed to know that even if Nick was no longer a part of her life, at least she was still a part of his. There were plenty of other casinos who could always use a dealer. When she got back from Tennessee she would do what she must and find work elsewhere.

"Happy New Year, Nick, wherever you are. Even though it no longer matters, know that you are loved."

Her quiet vow burned in her heart. How could she profess to love a man that she'd destroyed? How could she have been so wrong, trying to make things right?

"Ah well," Lucky muttered, and turned away from the window. "What's done is done. First Cradle Creek, then the rest of my life, whatever the hell that may be."

She crawled into her bed alone and tried to rest. But pride was a cold bedfellow, and dawn was breaking on the horizon before her eyes finally closed in sleep.

* * *

"Here," Lucky said, handing Fluffy an envelope. "This is my January rent. I'll be gone at least two, maybe three days. But when I come back, I'm going job hunting again. Maybe this time I'll have better luck."

Her smile never made it to her eyes. Fluffy glared down at the envelope and back up at the girl, thinking of the stupidity of youth.

"I don't want your check," Fluffy said. "Not anymore."

Lucky's stomach turned. The last thing she needed was to lose the friendship of this woman too. Her eyes grew round as she tried to find a way to speak past her shock.

"Before you get yourself all worked up," Fluffy continued, "you should know the reason why I won't take your money. You don't need to pay for something you already own."

Lucky dropped into a chair with an expression on her face that could only be described as stunned.

"What are you saying?"

Lucille LaMont was a bonafide hussy and had taken great pride in that fact for all of her eighty-four years. But right at this moment, she would have given a year of her life for the right to call this child her own. What she'd done was impulsive, but in her opinion, it was right. She'd lived her whole life on the edge and chose to go out the same way.

"I'm saying that it's yours. The whole thing. My worldly possessions. All my worldly goods. The loot." She shrugged and then grinned. "How many ways are there to say that I made you my sole heir?"

"Oh . . . my . . . God."

"Pooh. God had little to do with it," Fluffy said. "In fact, I suspect he frowned on how I came by most of it too. However, while I haven't exactly mended my ways, I have been too old for years now to cause any trouble. I consider that fact my redemption. And, since I can't take it with me, I'm giving it to you."

Lucky was in tears. Fluffy tried desperately not to submit to the same condition, but it was no use. Seconds later they were in each other's arms.

"I never had a child. It is my one true regret," Fluffy said. "You're about the age a grandchild of mine should have been. Since you seem to have lost your family, and I never had one to lose, I think we should join forces . . . don't you?"

Lucky continued to sob. Her cheek was soft against Fluffy's own. The tremors in her shoulders seemed too powerful for the young woman to withstand.

"You've had it tough, haven't you, girl?" Fluffy said.

Lucky nodded.

"So have I, honey. So have I. I think that's why you stole my heart. We're two of a kind. Survivors who are able to thumb their noses at people who don't understand."

Lucky smiled through tears. "I don't understand you, Fluffy LaMont, but I do love you, and that's a fact."

Fluffy grinned, arching her painted eyebrows in a perfect Garbo imitation. "That's enough for me. Unlike Garbo . . . I don't *vant* to be alone. Not anymore. For as long as I'm here, we'll be the best of friends. And when I'm gone, it's all yours."

Lucky wrapped her arms around the old woman's

neck. "Don't talk about leaving me," she whispered. "Everyone I love keeps leaving me."

Fluffy stilled. "Not everyone, my darling. There's one who did not leave you. It was you who pushed him away."

Lucky turned away. "That will be my greatest regret," she said. "If I could do it over, I would try to find some other way to fix things. But it's too late. Now I have to live with what I've done."

Fluffy's heart leaped in her breast. *Thank God*, she thought. At least she knew that what she'd done would not make Lucky angry. And she hoped it would fix this mess entirely.

"Life will show you the way," Fluffy said mysteriously. "Now. You'd best hurry or you're going to miss your plane. Go! Call your cab! Get yourself on the way to Tennessee so you can hurry back. When you get back, I'll cook."

That alone brought a smile to Lucky's face.

With a swift kiss and a hug, the two women parted. A short time later, Fluffy was alone to live with the guilt of knowing that she'd divulged all of Lucky's plans to a gambling man.

"Oh, lord," she said, as she pulled her cat into her lap and started to stroke his thick black fur. "Lucifer, you old twit. Purr for me. Make me believe that I've at least done one thing right today."

The cat arched its back and hissed. Disgusted with his moods, Fluffy swatted him to the floor.

"Get then," she muttered. "See if I care. I'm no longer just an old, used-up woman with a moody cat. I have friends now, too, you know."

The cat skittered sideways and then dashed across the floor at an imaginary foe. Just two old enemies who long ago had agreed to disagree.

Lucky groaned and shifted on the truck seat, trying to find a spot on the bumpy leather that didn't have a spring about to poke through. The old driver grinned and winked, then shifted gears to negotiate the sharp mountain curve. Being crammed three in a seat had made for a a long, miserable ride from Nashville. But Lucky wouldn't have had it any other way.

The driver and his assistant had been well paid for the job. Having a pretty woman along for the ride, despite the fact that she'd been less than talkative, had not bothered them one bit.

"I been workin' for Nashville Monument for twenty-two years, and this is, without doubt, the longest trip I ever made to set a stone."

"Yes, sir," Lucky said, and nodded.

The driver had volunteered that same information when they had headed east out of Nashville. Again as they'd exited north off of Interstate 40 just outside of Cooksville. And now, only minutes out of Cradle Creek, she was hearing it again. The big one-ton's gears ground again as he geared down once more.

"Looks like we're just about here," he offered.

"Yes, sir," Lucky said, and willed down the nausea that bubbled low in her stomach.

Now was not the time to get a case of nerves. Besides, what could these people do to her that they hadn't already done? As soon as Johnny's monument was set in place, she would be on her way out of Cradle Creek, headed back to Nashville to catch the next plane out to Las Vegas.

Her fingers curled a little tighter around the small flat box in her lap as the first signs of the small mountain town came into view.

"Ooh, damn." The assistant had just gotten his first good look at the town. And then he cast a swift glance at Lucky. "Excuse me, miss," he said. "Just took me by surprise, that's all."

She grinned wryly. "It has a way of doing that, all right," she said. "The sooner we get this over with, the better I'll feel."

The truck was loud. The noise from its engine was enough to send people scurrying to the windows to see what stranger passed their way. If they looked quick, they would not miss the sign on the doors of the big white one-ton: NASHVILLE MONUMENT.

Unknown to Lucky, excitement was growing as, one after the other, people looked at the truck, saw the sign on the door and the load on the back. It didn't take a fool to figure out that someone had ordered a headstone for a grave. Surely it wasn't going to be set in Cradle Creek? But when the truck turned up the hillside just past the station, the word went out. It was!

By the time Lucky got out of the truck and stretched her weary bones, a few of the hardier souls were already braving the cold out of curiosity. She looked down the hillside into the trees and saw them coming.

"Oh, no."

It was just as she'd feared. One more time she would be

forced to bear the brunt of Cradle Creek's disdain. Her chin went up. Her lips tightened as she buttoned the last two buttons on her blue wool coat. The wind whipped the coattails against the back of her knees, but it didn't matter. She'd been a lot colder in this town before and survived it all.

"One last time," she muttered, pulling the scarf around her head a little tighter against the wind's chill. She stood aside and watched as the truck was backed into place and then the men began unloading the shiny black stone.

Absorbed in the process of the men at work, she ignored the low-pitched muttering that drifted through the sharp, winter air. She suspected that they hadn't recognized her, or hadn't yet seen the name on the stone.

"Might be slow settin' this one in place," the driver warned. "The ground's a bit froze."

Lucky nodded. "Just do it right," she said. "That's all I ask."

The old man hitched at his pants. "I ain't had one tilt on me yet, miss," he said. "Don't aim to start now."

"Remember," Lucky cautioned. "Before you set the stone, I have something I need to put down under it."

He nodded. Their earlier instructions had been clear.

Unknown to Lucky, another stranger mingled with the locals, standing far back at the edge of the crowd, ducking his head in deference to the wind as well as the hope that he would not be seen . . . at least not yet.

Nick watched her and ached for her loneliness. A tall, slender girl in blue in a town full of hate. He wanted to hold her. He needed to feel the lifeblood pulsing beneath that satin skin and know that it beat for him. But it wasn't time. And so he waited, like the rest of Cradle Creek, to see what would unfold.

The driver's assistant rose from his knees. "Miss . . . ?"

Lost in old memories, Lucky jerked at the sound of his voice.

"The little hole . . . it's ready just like you asked."

She nodded, then went forward and knelt. The ground was cold against her knees, her blue jeans faint protection against the damp wind blowing down from the mountains. But it didn't matter. What she had to do wouldn't take long.

"I did it, Johnny. I found your luck," she whispered, and tried to smile. But she couldn't feel a smile anywhere inside. Only tears that came without invitation.

She laid the little box into the hole. And when the man knelt to cover it up, she pushed his gloved hands aside and pulled the cold hard chunks back in place herself with trembling fingers. Little by little, she covered up the watch that had cost her so much to retrieve.

"Rest easy, my daddy. I won't forget."

Someone helped her to her feet. She didn't know who. And she could not have cared less. She was too blinded by tears to look around and see a tall, dark man who was sharing her grief. Before she could move, he'd disappeared back into the crowd, and she thought little of his assistance. Her entire focus was on the black marble stone being lowered into place.

It was then that a hiss from the people went up in the

air. The name on the stone was, at last, revealed. Polished to a glassy shine, the black stone gleamed like the veins of coal beneath the ground at their feet.

"It's for old Houston! Can you beat that? Why would someone . . . ? Do you suppose . . . ? Maybe it was a . . . ?"

Gossip was something she'd heard all her life, and so she ignored everything and everyone around her save the men who were doing their job.

And then the deed was done.

"We'll wait down the hill a piece," the two men said. It was customary to give the family members some time alone and today was no different for them.

Lucky nodded, and therefore did not see the same tall man step out of the crowd and speak to the drivers, nor note that as the truck pulled away from the hillside, it kept on going instead of waiting for her below as they'd promised.

"John Jacob Houston."

Lucky looked up. An old woman stood nearby, clutching the edges of a threadbare coat. She squinted up at Lucky, then back down at the impressive black stone.

"Cain't rightly say I ever knowed his given name," she said. She nodded once more at the stone. "Fine piece. Says in the Bible to honor thy father. You done real good . . . even if he might not have deserved it."

Lucky tried to smile. But there was too much pain between her and the people of Cradle Creek to forgive this easily. To be accepted this quickly. She looked back down at the stone as the woman walked on.

Below her father's name was the date of his birth and

death, and the single line that she'd requested be engraved. It blurred before her eyes, but she knew what it read all the same.

IN MY FATHER'S HONOR—Exodus 20:12.

The old man's snort was soft. "It's more than he deserved, but it's a fine thing that you went and did," he said. "'At's one of them ten commandments, ain't it?"

Lucky looked once again, this time recognizing one of Johnny's cronies from Whitelaw's Bar, and nodded.

"'At's the one 'bout honorin' yore father and mother, I 'spect. Good girl. Keepin' to the Good Book an' all."

Lucky nodded, and when the old man thumped her once on the shoulder as he passed, she nearly went to her knees. The approval in his voice was more than she'd been prepared to hear.

One by one, the people who'd been watching filed past, paying respects to the stone when they hadn't the man. But Lucky didn't care about their timing. It was the fact that they'd come at all that made her weep.

And then finally they were gone. She was left with nothing but the sound of silence as she stared down in fixation at the spot beneath the stone, knowing that in death he now had what he'd most wanted in life. His luck.

And then something fluttered to the ground at her feet. She blinked, unwilling to trust her vision. But it was there all the same. An ace of spades now lay on the cold, dead grass, an odd but fitting accompaniment for a gambler and the day at hand.

She bent down to pick it up, then saw the shadow behind her. Startled, she spun around, unaware she still held the card clutched tight in her hand. But when the shadow turned to man, she gasped.

The card fell from her fingers, fluttering with the wind back down to the ground near the stone. There were tears in his eyes, and a tremble to his lips. But no sound of judgment would pass his lips this day. She knew this man . . . and his heart. He'd given it once. Would he give it again?

"Nick . . . ?"

He opened his arms. Seconds later she was fast against the rough warmth of his coat, not caring why or how he'd come. Only that he was here. He was the backup that she'd needed all along.

"Baby . . . are you all right?" His voice was as tender as his touch as he stroked the center of her back in a gentle, reassuring touch.

"Oh, Nick. They came. It might have been curiosity that got them here, but they stayed. They didn't turn away from him . . . or from me. Not this time."

"Not ever again," Nick whispered, and lifted her chin, tilting her lips toward his.

Chilled, their cold lips warmed as their kiss deepened. And when Lucky groaned and then sighed, Nick lifted her off of her feet and turned her in a slow, small circle, while he pressed her face against his neck. If it took the rest of his life, he would make sure she never suffered alone like this again.

"Nick?"

He'd been waiting for the question he heard in her voice. He'd answer her, but he wasn't turning her loose. She'd have to forgive . . . or else understand, even if he had to kidnap her. He wouldn't have it any other way.

"What, baby?" he asked, and feathered kisses down the side of her neck.

"Why the ace?"

"It was my hole card, baby. I've come to claim my prize."

She gasped. And then her head came up, and her eyes blazed green with fire.

"You won?"

He nodded and tightened his hold, fearing the worst. "Now, Lucky, you've got to—"

"You cheated!"

He nodded. It was beyond him to deny it now.

"And you lied by letting me believe that I'd won."

He was beginning to worry. And then she started to laugh. The sound rang out among the tombstones and far down into the miserable little town below. If anyone thought it strange that she was standing in the cemetery laughing, they simply shrugged it off. She was, after all, that gambler's daughter. What more could they expect?

"Lucky? Honey?" He was daring to hope.

"Oh, my God," she gasped, and wrapped her arms around his neck. "I've done it. Oh, Johnny, if you could see me now. I did exactly what I swore I'd never do. I fell head over heels for a lying, cheating gambler."

Nick grinned. "Only on occasion," he reminded her.

"What? That you love me only on occasion, or that you lie and cheat only on occasion?"

"You have to ask?" he whispered, and nuzzled the spot

beneath her ear that he knew did things to her better left unsaid.

"No. I don't have anything to ask you. All I'm saying is, I love you, Nick. Thank God I didn't ruin that too."

"Ah, baby. You didn't ruin anything. But I have something to ask you. I've already talked to your father, and strangely enough, he seems to agree."

Lucky looked startled. The brown demons in Nick's eyes looked too good to be true. "My father? But he—"

"I came several weeks ago. We had a good long talk, he and I. I made him a promise then. And like you, I always keep my promises. I told him when I came back that I'd be with you. It's only fair that when a man proposes to the woman he loves, that her family is in on it all."

Lucky started to cry.

"Ah, God, baby, don't do that again," Nick said.

But Lucky could only shake her head and hold on to the man who'd stolen her heart.

"Lucky Houston, will you marry me?" Nick asked, and waited anxiously to hear the words that would make his world right again.

"I probably need my head examined, but yes, you crazy fool, yes!" she sobbed, and threw herself back into his arms.

Long, silent moments passed when nothing was said but the kisses they gave each other to seal the promises that they'd made. Finally, Lucky was the first to break the silence.

"I wish we weren't so far from home," she said.

"It's not that far," Nick said, thinking of the plane that

he'd chartered and had waiting for them back in Nashville.

She sighed. "I want to be held." She slipped her arms around his waist. "I want to be loved. All night. And forever. By you. And it's too darn far for us to get home anytime soon."

He grinned. "Wanna bet?"

Epilogue

"Mrs. Chenault."

Lucky turned and then grinned. The sound was still as sweet four months after the wedding as it had been the first time she heard it. Nick stood in the doorway to their bedroom wearing nothing but a towel and a smile.

"What do you want, Mr. Chenault?"

He pounced. "You. I want you, baby."

Lucky opened her arms and took him with her as they fell backward onto the bed.

"I finished unpacking," she said, as he covered her face with kisses.

"Good. But you might want to keep the suitcases out. Don't let Shari put them in storage just yet."

Lucky stilled. "Why? Please don't tell me you have to go somewhere. We just spent four months on the most wonderful honeymoon a woman could want. But now I've seen Greece. And Italy. I've seen more islands and more beaches than I knew existed. I've eaten stuff in Istanbul that I didn't want identified. And I was sort of looking forward to playing house now."

More things had been going her way than just the honeymoon. Now that Paul knew that she held no more grudges, he was finally beginning to forgive himself. Fluffy was going strong and had decided to go gray, although Lucky doubted that her hair roots would know what to do.

The pout on her lips was too sweet for Nick to ignore. He leaned over and gave her a kiss, then laughed, wrapping his arms around her and rolling until she was beneath him on the bed.

Lucky moaned softly, then sighed. Nick did things to her with his hands that gave her pleasure that was too great to deny. And as always, the fire in his eyes was too warm to ignore. Lucky shivered as he began unbuttoning her blouse and slipping it out of her slacks.

"In a few short weeks, it will be Christmas again. I want to . . ."

His mouth centered upon her breast as his tongue traced the nipple caught gently between his teeth.

"Ooooh. Uh, I want to decorate for . . . Oh, Nick."

The last of her clothes were on the floor as he levered himself between her knees. Obligingly, she made room, and then when he lingered too long at the edge of reason, she lifted her arms and pulled him on in.

"What was it you wanted to do?" Nick asked, and gritted his teeth at the sweet feel of her body tensing around his manhood.

"I don't remember," she groaned, and arched upward, inviting him to respond.

It was all he needed to feel. "I do," he whispered, and started to rock. "You wanted to play. House, I believe. You be the mommy. I'll be the . . ."

This time, it was Nick who was unable to finish what he'd started to say, because he was too busy trying to finish what he'd started.

He had everything he'd ever needed or wanted. The warm, sweet feel of his lady in his arms. The welcome rush of joy that was beginning to gather down low in his soul. The rush of her breath against his cheek. Her hands clutching him, pulling him lower, closer, tighter. The soft, almost nonexistent sounds of her pleasure as she moaned into his ear.

"Nick!" She locked her legs around his waist and closed her eyes as she started to burn.

"I know, baby," he whispered, and gathered her closer. "I'm with you. All the way."

With a sharp cry of release, Lucky arched against him, and for a moment, hung suspended in time by the uncontained fire rushing through her body. A heartbeat later Nick followed.

And when he could think again without seeing stars, he remembered what he'd been going to say.

"Lucky, darling."

"I sure am," she said.

He grinned. "How much luck can you stand?"

She opened her eyes and gazed with love at the dear familiarity of his face.

"I don't need luck. I have you."

He kissed each corner of her mouth. "You know, we were pretty much out of circulation for a while," he said.

She nodded. "I could not have cared less."

"Lots of things happened . . . lots of things changed and we never even knew it."

"So. It didn't change what we have. For me, that's all that matters."

Nick sighed. "Thank you, baby. You matter the world to me too. But . . ."

Lucky smiled, and then teased the sensitive skin on his backside with the flat of her hands. "But? I thought you took all the 'buts' out of my vocabulary in Nassau."

He grinned. "I did give you cause to retract a lot then, didn't I?"

"Retract? It was more like a plea for mercy, my love. So what in the world are you hedging at saying? Just spit it out now and put me out of my misery."

Nick rolled over, grabbed his towel, and headed for the bath.

"Where on earth are you going?" Lucky asked.

"To get my pants," he said.

"Whatever for?" she muttered, appreciatively eyeing his bare behind as he momentarily disappeared into the dressing room. "You look just fine the way you are."

"I heard that," Nick said, as he returned to the room wearing a pair of shorts. "Had to get my surprise," he said. "I left it in my pants."

She wiggled her eyebrows in a naughty manner. "You always keep your surprises in your pants."

He shook his head and tried to glare. "I think you hang out with too many old strippers."

She grinned, caught the small, flat package that he tossed toward her, and then dropped back onto the bed, tearing through the wrappings.

Seconds later she sat straight up again. Her hair was falling down around her face in a disheveled mess. Her bare breasts were taunting Nick to look but not touch. But it was the complete and utter joy on her face that he knew he would always remember.

"Oh, Nick." She kept reading the name and then clasping it back against her chest.

"Honey, you can't hear it that way," he teased, and took it out of her hands. "It goes in a tape deck, not between your breasts."

She was shaking as he slipped the tape into the stereo. "No, Nick. You're wrong. Maybe you couldn't, but I could hear it in my heart."

Seconds later she was out of bed and into his arms as the music began. Moments later, as the sweet sounds of country music filled the air, a voice came calling. A voice Lucky hadn't heard in over a year.

"It's Di! Oh, Nick! You found my sister for me."

He grinned and tugged the rest of her hair down from the mess he'd made of it earlier. "Honey, from the sounds of that tape, the whole world has found your sister. If we hadn't been gone so long, you would have rediscovered her for yourself a lot sooner. I just happened to beat you to it. Rumor has it that she's going to perform in Vegas sometime next year. Right after the holidays."

Lucky sighed. A missing piece of her heart had just slipped back in place. She laid her cheek against Nick's bare chest as he slowly danced her in a circle around the room.

"About those suitcases," he reminded her. "How would you like to spend Christmas in Nashville with her?"

Lucky started to cry.

"Well hell," Nick said, as he lifted her in his arms and carried her back to bed. "Will I ever get used to the fact that you cry when you're mad. You cry when you're sad. And now I find you also cry when you're happy. Damn, woman. Is there anything else I should know?"

Lucky's arms slid around his neck as she pulled him back down to the bed.

"Sometimes I cry from pure joy."

His mouth tilted up at the corners. "Is that a hint . . . or a request?"

"Take it any way you want to, mister. But just take it," Lucky whispered, and encircled him with her hands.

"Oh, God," Nick groaned. "I don't know if I can do this so soon after—"

"Wanna bet?" she asked.

The last thing he remembered was the smile upon her face.

Trees were thick along the roadside. Snow was spitting disobediently against the windshield as Nick fought to stay in the ruts in the snow-packed roads.

"Damn." He whistled through his teeth as he negotiated a particularly slick spot in the road. "Las Vegas was never like this."

"Nick. I'm scared."

He took his eyes from the road long enough to see panic filling those wide green eyes.

"Why, baby? You two love each other. There's nothing to be afraid of. And you've already met Jesse, so it can't be fear of meeting a new brother-in-law."

The car fishtailed, and he had to turn his full attention back to driving just to make sure they arrived in one piece. It was because he looked away that he missed seeing the tears flood her eyes.

"I can't wait to see Di," Lucky said. "That's true. But what if we never know what happened to my Queenie?" Her voice broke, and she bit her lip to keep from sobbing. "She's my sister, and she's also the only mother I ever knew, Nick. It seems almost sacrilegious to be this happy and not know where she is, or if she's safe. If she's even alive."

"Damn, woman. Don't you know not to borrow trouble? Didn't your daddy teach you anything?"

This time, she managed to grin through tears. "Actually, no," she said.

The mood lightened, and a few minutes later when they turned from the country road into a narrow driveway leading up to a two-story log home nestled against the hills in a thick stand of trees, Lucky began to bounce in the seat.

Nick grinned. She turned hot and cold faster than any woman he'd ever known. A minute ago she'd been in tears, and now she was all but clawing the seat to get out of the car.

"We're here!" she shrieked, and planted a swift, excited

kiss on his jaw as he came to a sliding halt near a split-rail fence.

"Barely," Nick muttered, then grinned as she bolted out of the car.

Deciding to leave their luggage until later, Nick started up the path behind her when the front door opened. A tall blonde came out of the door much in the same manner that Lucky had exited the car. On the run.

A very tall, very nervous-looking man was right behind her.

"Diamond! Honey! Don't jump!"

Jesse Eagle's frantic warning to his newly pregnant wife was too late. She'd cleared the porch in one leap just as Lucky flew into her arms.

Nick was dumbstruck. He'd known that Diamond Houston was pretty. He'd seen her picture. Besides, she was Lucky's sister. But he wasn't prepared for the pure, alabaster perfection of her features, or those same green eyes in another woman's face.

He knew he was staring, but he couldn't seem to stop.

"I know," Jesse said, as he walked up and shook Nick's hand. "I haven't forgotten the first time I saw all of them together, either. They looked nothing alike, except for those cheekbones . . . and those cat eyes. But to this day, I've never seen three more beautiful women in my entire life."

Nick could only nod. His gaze was still locked on the joy on Lucky's face, and the laughter spilling out of her mouth.

"Welcome, brother," Jesse said. "We're going to have to stick together just to survive them."

Nick grinned and offered his hand. "Nick Chenault," he said. "I'm the gambler."

Jesse rolled his eyes, then grinned. "Oh, hell, so I've heard. And I'm the no-count singer who nearly ruined Diamond for life. Welcome to the family. Come in out of the cold. We'll get your bags later. The surprises aren't over yet."

Nick frowned as they started inside, wondering what Jesse meant. Lucky went from his arms to her sister's and then back again, each time remembering something she wanted to share with the other. Before they got in the house, Nick felt like he'd been sucked backward through rapids.

"Nick! Isn't this fantastic? We're going to have the best time! And you'll never guess! Di is going to have a baby!"

Lucky threw her arms around Nick's neck, and accepted the hard, swift kiss he planted on her lips.

"What was that for?" she asked.

"In case I don't get another chance before the action starts," Nick said.

"What action?" Lucky asked.

"Beats me," Nick said. "Jesse just said that . . ."

He forgot what he'd been about to say. Another woman had entered the room.

Amazon.

It was the first thought that surfaced.

Absolutely beautiful, came next. Her hair was red. Wild, luxuriant, curly, red. Everywhere a woman curved, she did and more.

But it was the eyes. Those same deep, green eyes looking at him. It was then he knew. He went still as Queen looked deep into his soul . . . judging . . . and finally . . . accepting.

"Lucky . . . baby, turn around."

Nick turned her in his arms while she was still talking. He didn't need an introduction to know that the last of the sisters had just come home. And when he felt Lucky go weak against him, it was his arms that caught and steadied her until she was able to move.

And move she did. On air. With a cry of joy the likes of which he'd never heard.

"Queenie! My Queenie. You came."

Queen Houston Bonner opened her arms. Just as she'd done all her life. Just as she'd done to Cody Bonner and his children and then their own baby. Giving herself and her love because it was all she had to give.

"Jesus." Cody Bonner's shock was just as evident as he stared at Lucky as Nick's had been moments ago.

"Nick Chenault," Nick said, and shook the big man's hand. "Never saw anything like them myself," he added.

Cody was dumbstruck. "I knew Queen was beautiful. To me she's magnificent. I was just getting used to Diamond when this dark beauty comes flying into the room. Did you ever . . . ?"

"Nope," Jesse said, crossing his arms as he leaned against the door. "Can't say as I did."

"Can you beat the way . . . ?" Nick couldn't remember what he'd been going to say.

"And the way they . . ." Cody shook his head, unable to finish his remark.

The gambler's daughters had center stage.

* * *

"Your daughter is beautiful," Lucky said, as she leaned against the door frame, watching Queen put the baby down to sleep.

Queen smiled. Contentment radiated from her person like a light. Lucky hugged herself with joy. She was still pinching herself on a regular basis just to prove she hadn't been dreaming.

Diamond tiptoed into the room.

"She's asleep," Queen said. "Come on. Let's go outside."

"It's cold," Lucky warned.

Queen grinned. "But quiet."

Cody's three sons were arguing loudly in another room about the merits of one video game versus another when they suddenly fell silent.

Diamond cocked an eyebrow and pursed her lips. "If I was a gambler, I'd just bet money that Henley walked into the room."

The sisters grinned at each other and nodded. They'd each gotten a dose of Jesse Eagle's houseman. The ex-marine's gentlemanly demeanor was deceptive. Obviously the boys had just succumbed to some sort of order.

"Come on," Queen said. "While the gettin's good."

They slipped out the front door and into the cold stillness of the Tennessee winter night. Stars twinkled in a clear, moonlit sky. Somewhere off to their left, a horse whinnied, and another nickered softly in response. A dog barked across the hollow behind the house, and far below Jesse's house came the familiar sound of a train engine straining to pull the cars up the grade.

The sisters cuddled one against the other, absorbing the absolute peace of their surroundings and of the night.

When the engineer pulled the whistle as the train came to a crossing, they shivered and leaned closer together. The sound was long, slow, and mournful. Too vivid a reminder of their youth.

As children, their bond had been out of necessity as much as from love. They'd had to care for one another, because there was no one else to do the job. As they'd grown into women, the bonds of birth had loosened just enough to let each sister grow toward the yearnings of her own heart.

"Are you happy?" Queen asked.

"Yes," both sisters answered in unison.

She laughed. The sound carried into the house and stopped the men's card game in mid-deal.

Cody grinned. "That one was mine. Wonder what was so funny?" He sorted, then re-sorted his hand in disgust. There was no way to make a winning hand out of what he'd been dealt.

Jesse's eyebrow arched as he discarded a pair. "Knowing my girl, I don't want to know."

But Nick sat quietly in his chair, the royal flush in his hands forgotten.

"I'm out," he said, and tossed it on the table in front of them as he headed for the door.

"Damn," Cody said, as he sorted through the flush. "He's not much of a gambler. He just quit a winning hand."

Jesse grinned. "Looks like he's just the right kind of gambler. A man who knows when to fold is one in a million."

"Nick!" Lucky slipped from her sisters' embrace and went to meet him. "Honey, come listen to the quiet."

He sighed and buried his face in the thick coil of hair against her neck, then wrapped his arms around her shivering body.

"I love you, baby, and you're going to freeze," he warned.

"Not now," she said, and snuggled deep against his warmth. "Never as long as I have you."

His slow exhale of relief was sweet against her face as she held him close and leaned against his strength.

Behind them, the door opened. The gambler's daughters were no longer alone. Each stood within her husband's embrace and listened. And just as Lucky promised, it was so very, very quiet. Even inside their hearts.

USA Today Bestselling Author
Sharon Sala
(also known as Dinah McCall)

Lucky
0-06-108198-1/$6.99 US/$9.99 Can

Queen
0-06-108197-3/$6.99 US/$9.99 Can

Diamond
0-06-108196-5/$6.99 US/$9.99 Can